CIRCLE of HURT

Also by Jim Ainsworth...

...Memoirs and True Story Collections:

Biscuits Across the Brazos

"Ainsworth has vividly recalled an adventure that will preserve it for generations. That's no small task."...John Graves, author of *Goodbye to a River* and many other classics

A River of Stories

"Don't breeze through these stories. Stop and think about each one."...J. A. Cross, author of *Memories, Musings, and Mischief*

...Novels:

Follow the Rivers Series

In the Rivers Flow
(subsequently **Rivers Flow**)

"A rare and beautifully written book."...Jane Roberts Wood, a fellow of the National Endowment for the Arts and author of many books, including *Dance a Little Longer* and *Grace*

Rivers Crossing

"A literary home run"...Alice Reese, book and movie critic for *Commerce Journal* and *Herald-Banner*

Rivers Ebb
"Jake Rivers is the most lovable character I have ever encountered in fiction."...Suzanne Morris, author of *Aftermath* and many other books

Home Light Burning
"Ainsworth is cut from the stone of Elmer Kelton and J. Frank Dobie."...Dr. Stephen Turner, author of the *Westward Quest* series

Go Down Looking
"A masterpiece and worthy of a movie."...Dr. Loretta Kibler.

Tee Jessup and the Riverby Series
Rails to a River
"A riveting story with unexpected twists of characters and plots."...Christina Carson, author of *Dying to Know* and many other books

Firstborn Son
"A departure from Ainsworth's other novels, but no less compelling."...Dr. William Thompson, author of many academic books as well as *Hogs, Blogs, Leathers and Lattes...*

*For David
all the best —*

CIRCLE of HURT

A Novel

Jim H. Ainsworth 2017

Jim H. Ainsworth

First Edition

This is a work of fiction. All the characters, names, incidents,
organizations, and dialogue in this novel are either the products
of the author's imagination or are used fictionally.

ISBN 978-0-9904628-2-8

Library of Congress Control Number: 2016919480

Cover Photography and Design by
Jan Herman Ainsworth and Vivian Freeman

Interior Design by Vivian Freeman, *Yellow Rose Typesetting*

Printed in the United States of America

Season of Harvest Publications
2403 CR 4208
Campbell, Texas 75422

For the Unprepared, Old Age may be the Winter of Life.
For the Prepared, it's the Season of Harvest.

FOR JERRY (JACE) CARRINGTON...

Loyal friend and mentor who sets an example of dignity, honor, humility, faithfulness, and courage in the face of great challenges.

I cannot remember the books I've read
any more than the meals I have eaten;
even so, they have made me.
—Ralph Waldo Emerson

CIRCLE of HURT

If history were taught in the form of stories,
it would never be forgotten.
                              —Rudyard Kipling

ONE

1975—Ninety Days till Deadline

CLAYTON DUPREE SLOWED BEATING UP ON himself for getting shot, but couldn't seem to come to a complete stop. Whiskey was to blame, but nobody forced it past his lips. On the rare occasions when he went out in public, it was not uncommon for him to be the butt of jokes, the subject of ridicule. It had been that way most of his life. Women told him it was the ringlets of hair that hung too far over his collar, maybe the dingy white t-shirt, wrinkled too-large jeans and rough-out, worn-out, low-topped boots that made his uniform. He wasn't trying to make a fashion statement with the hair or the clothes. But curly hair looked better worn long and going a long time between haircuts saved money. He didn't care too much about paying laundry or dry cleaning bills either, liked to travel light, and liked the soft feel of cotton.

He usually let the insults pass—unless he had a little whiskey under his belt. And he needed the whiskey to get on

1

a small stage and belt out a song or two he had written. But the loudmouth kid in the Proud-Cut Saloon in Fort Worth who jeered during the performance was just too obnoxious for even him to tolerate. Still, it might have been avoided if the little snot-nose had not followed him outside. And Clayton did have that small .22 in his pocket. He seldom went anywhere unarmed.

The only reason the young fool had lived as long as he had was because he was still young and it was against the law to kill him. The punk looked and acted like a spoiled rich kid, a bully who needed killing, a menace to mankind so-to-speak, and Clayton did his damndest to do mankind a service. But because of whiskey, he got shot by his own gun in a drunken tussle with the kid. And the shooter kid added insult to injury. He smashed Clayton's guitar and took the gun with him when he ran off down a West Side street.

The bullet barely grazed Clayton's side, made a clean ditch through a love handle, but he bled like a stuck hog. He almost passed out driving back to the fleabag where he was staying. He paid the hotel clerk highway robbery prices to bring him some bandages and tape, staunched the bleeding, poured on Old Crow he hated to waste. He wrapped the wound and more or less passed out.

The bar fight and shot fired would probably not amount to much as far as the law was concerned, but bringing a loaded gun into a honky-tonk might be frowned on. Might take months of time and hundreds in lawyer fees to work out, so he roused himself early from the sleep he craved and drove the borrowed Pontiac to the bus station. He boarded a Continental Trailways for Dallas and left the worn-out car for her to

2

find. Cops could trace it back to the woman who owned it. He couldn't remember her name and had given her a false one. She had been mad as hell when he walked out and borrowed it, anyway.

He got off the bus in Dallas with his suitcase full of paper, but few clothes. In a phone booth Yellow Pages, he found a car lot within walking distance. The lot had one pickup that appeared to have led an easy life, a '67 yellow Ford with low mileage. A few words with a salesman on the lot told him the dealer financed junkers at Cadillac rates. Clayton turned down the usurious rate, paid cash, and headed the little truck to a music store downtown. He bought a used guitar, one of two life necessities. His ex-wife confiscated his good one and his cheap replacement had been left in pieces in the bar parking lot.

He limped from the music store to a used furniture store, bought a bed frame, box springs and mattress, a table and two chairs, paid two hungry-looking kids hanging around outside to load them in the back of the pickup, and headed to the place he used for mending when life got too complicated for him to handle. As he headed east on I-30 toward Riverby, a tiny town in the northeast corner of Texas by the Red River, he tried to get his mind off the pain by recalling how long since he had been to the picker shack.

He had been only a boy when he spent his first night there. With Daddy killed in the war and Mama dead of consumption before thirty, Clayton traveled with his daddy's brother and his cousins, a family of itinerant farm laborers. They traveled the Texas harvest trail, picked lettuce and fruit down south and cotton, pecans, and corn farther north. They even spent a season mucking stalls in Kentucky. Whatever needed harvesting, picking, planting, pulling, plucking, or shoveling, the Dupree family was ready.

Clayton was kind of partial to the shack as a boy, thought it an improvement over the tents and worker camps where he could find no privacy, even to take care of personal business. And make no mistake, Clayton needed his privacy. Wasn't that he didn't like people, they just made him uncomfortable, drained his energy. And their mannerisms and talk irritated him, made him nervous and self-conscious.

Maybe it was because he couldn't help but watch their every move, record it in his mind, write it down at night when he could find paper and pencil. Writing it was the only way to control the irritation, the anxiety. He was fascinated by the different dialects in southeast and northeast Texas, western Louisiana and southern Oklahoma. They talked differently, didn't dress alike, and Clayton had written about them all since he was a boy, including his aunt, uncle and cousins. Writing and keeping it a secret occupied almost all of the limited time he had as a boy outside of the cotton patches, cornfields, stalls, and orchards.

During the second harvest season in the shack, Clayton disappeared when it came time for his uncle's family to move on. He had developed an attachment to Willard Dunn, the farmer who hired the family and who owned the shack and lived in the house on Hurt Hill a little west and higher up from the shack. The attachment was mutual.

A widower without children, Dunn loved to tell stories, and he found Clayton's rapt attention a balm for his troubled and lonely soul. And he could see the boy was unhappy traveling with his family. Clayton's uncle, aunt and cousins looked for him a few hours, gave up and moved on to the next harvest. Willard assured them he would be found and cared for. And he was.

Six years later, on the day Clayton turned eighteen, Willard Dunn died. He left the house, picker shack, and farm to Clayton in his will. Willard named a Riverby lawyer as executor to look out for Clayton's interests until he turned twenty-one. Clayton had no interest in farming, talked the lawyer into selling the farm a few months later and moved on with cash in his pocket, thinking he would never return. The lawyer held some of the money in escrow in case he did.

But the world kept conquering Clayton, and the old shack seemed to be a good spot to lick his wounds. Besides that, he stored the possessions of most value to him in a bank vault in Riverby. He felt the need to visit those possessions occasionally. Four years of drought and two years of flood had driven the new owner off Hurt Hill and the place was again for sale. Clayton only wanted to hide for a few days, maybe a week. He thought about owning it again, living in the nicer house up the hill, but the picker shack seemed to be what he deserved. He was still squatting in the shack when Joe Henry Leathers, the son of Willard Dunn's executor, bought it. Joe Henry did not run him off. That visit lasted less than a year, but he had been gone more than six this time.

Two

TECUMSEH (BLAZE) BLAISDELL PARKED WHERE they parked that night, wrapped himself in his dead wife's quilt, climbed the rock hill to the trestle, and hid in the shadows where they had hidden. In the dark, he tried to imagine the fear and anguish that must have filled their hearts, but could not. He stepped out of the night shadows and stood on crossties between the rails like they had, the man taking the train's impact first as if his chivalrous but futile gesture might somehow protect the woman.

The visions of what happened that night attached to him like an evil specter, came unbidden at all times of the day and night. As the train's engineer, he could not possibly have heard or felt the impact when it happened, but he felt and heard it with each replay in his mind. He had been coming here for almost a decade to ask God to take away the visions and forgive him. When the visions became less frequent, he believed his prayers had worked. But the bad dreams returned when Tee Jessup and his son Jubal came to live in the old house on the hill above the trestle. They had driven over five hundred miles to come to this hill, to this farmhouse, by this trestle. And they brought Blaze's horror show back with them.

He looked up at the century-old house on Hurt Hill. It was too dark to discern most of its features, but he knew them by heart. There was nothing to distinguish it, no regal beauty, no remarkable craftsmanship, no stone or bricks to preserve it. The ravages of time and weather and generations of various farm families long ago stripped the pine sides of paint, scarred its walls and roof, rusted the nails that held it together. It was a run-of-the-mill board-and-batten house built in the style of those long-ago times, with a porch across the front and a dog-run down the middle. Blaze sat on the trestle boards, looked into the clear sky and asked for forgiveness again. As the time neared for a train to pass, he stood to leave, but hesitated when the porch light came on. Tee Jessup stepped off the porch and walked to the old barn that had been a tabernacle when Blaze was a boy.

Faint light appeared in the barn hall and around the edges of the corn crib door. Blaze took a deep breath and started up the hill. He knew what was coming next. As he drew closer, he heard the needle scratching as the old forty-five rotated on the turntable and Gene Autry's voice drifted through the woods singing *That Silver-Haired Daddy of Mine*.

Tee Jessup leaned against a support pole in the hall of the barn with a glass of buttermilk in one hand and a single-action Colt pistol in the other as Blaze came out of the shadows into the yard. The decade that passed since losing his family had prematurely aged Tee. A small scar on his forehead served as a reminder of the accident that killed his brother. Other than the felt hat he left crown-down on the kitchen table, he was dressed as he had dressed most of his life—in Wrangler jeans and boots with riding heels. His snap western shirt was partially covered with a wool-lined denim jacket.

Moonlight revealed a five-foot cross that stood regally between Tee and Blaze. The cross had been made with two notched bois d'arc posts held together by strips of rawhide. Someone had reinforced the rawhide strips with two rusted square nails. Blaze removed his cap and stepped carefully around the cross and the grave it marked.

Because the dog had not barked, Tee knew the approaching footsteps had to belong to Blaze. It was well past his usual bedtime, and he tried to hide his irritation at the late interruption. Blaze had at least fifty pounds on him, one of those heavyweight men who was deceptively light on his feet; soft in places, but solid where it counted. Blaze's face showed his Indian heritage with high cheekbones and deep pockmarks, black bushy eyebrows that matched his eyes, and bristly black hair. He replaced his striped railroad cap as he drew close enough for Tee to see him.

"Why didn't you tell me it was your mama and daddy I killed?" The blurted question conveyed a mixture of anger and sympathy. He had been screwing up the courage to ask it for months.

Tee looked toward son Jubal's bedroom window to be sure it was closed. He held a finger across his lips, put down his pistol, drained the last swallow of buttermilk. He motioned for Blaze to follow him toward the stolen Airstream parked in his yard. A Coleman lantern hung from the travel trailer's awning frame by a piece of electrical wire. Tee pumped the Coleman, lifted the globe and put a match under the mantle. The light revealed two folded, wooden slatted chairs leaned against the trailer. Blaze recognized them as tabernacle chairs.

Tee unfolded a chair and pointed toward the other. "Sit."

The big man eased into the chair just as Gene stopped singing. Tee waited, but Blaze said nothing. "What are you doing out here this late, Blaze?"

"Joe Henry said he told you I was the engineer that night."

Tee kept silent.

"I need to know why you kept it a secret all this time. And I need to know if Jubal knows I killed his grandpa and grandma." Blaze had taken a shine to Tee's son when they arrived in Riverby two years earlier—even brought him a rat terrier pup named Rivers and a black tuxedo cat called Flo. Tee appreciated the gesture, though he didn't want the pets. On this isolated hilltop surrounded by woods and bottomland filled with wild carnivores, he expected the pair to last just long enough for Jubal to grow fond of them. But the dog and cat proved him wrong. They protected each other and they protected Jubal. It was an unexpected plus when they brought small moments of peace to Tee's troubled soul.

"It's not a subject I like to talk about. Expect you can see why. As for Jubal, no, he doesn't know yet. He's got a way of picking the right time to ask the right questions. When he asks about it, I'll tell him the truth as far as I know it."

"What is the truth?"

Tee looked down the hill. With the leaves off the trees, Panther Crossing and the trestle where it all happened could be seen on a moonlit night. "On a dark night many years ago, my parents chose that trestle down there to step in front of a train you were driving. I was in an Amarillo hospital when they did it, trapped in a coma from another train wreck that killed my brother and our best rope horse."

The big man wrung his hands. "But why? And why did it have to be my train? Why Panther Crossing? They came a long way to do something they could have done out in the Panhandle. They got trains out there."

"Been asking that question to myself and anybody who would listen since it happened. Don't have an answer for you."

Blaze looked forlorn. "I need to know."

Tee pulled a weed to twist. "They say my mother's grandfather was a Choctaw Shaman. My whole life, she seldom mentioned him to me or my brother. After the wreck that killed my brother and put me in a coma, she started seeing her grandfather in her dreams. She told the dreams to a Catholic priest and he told me about the dreams after they did it. Something in those dreams caused them to step in front of your train."

Blaze looked toward the trestle. "You're Catholic?

"No. My mother met the priest in the hospital when I was in the coma."

"But what reason did she give the priest?"

Tee shook his head. "She never told the priest exactly what she planned. He told her the dreams were only stress from losing a son and having another son that might never wake up."

"But did the grandpa give a reason in the dreams?"

Tee laced his fingers together. "Yes, but I don't want this repeated. Don't want folks around here thinkin' I'm crazy."

"I won't repeat it, but I need to know... it's for my sanity."

"Seems the crazy logic of the dream was that since a train put me in a coma and threatened to take my life, they could give their lives to a train and my life would be restored. I'm sure there's some type of mystical language he used, but that seems to be the gist of it."

Blaze's mouth opened, but no words came out.

"Look, my folks were normal people. They just went off the deep end when they lost my brother and the docs told them I might never wake up. Imagine losing both of your children. My daddy blamed himself for the wreck. He wasn't drunk, but he had been drinking."

Blaze's eyes filled. "Greater love hath no man than this; that a man lay down his life for his friends. Or in this case, their son."

"That from the Bible?"

"John fifteen, thirteen."

"I asked Father Bob, that's the priest, if there could be any forgiveness for the mortal sin they committed. He couldn't offer me any comfort. And, I guess that's what bothers me more than anything. If I ever make it to Heaven, they won't be there. Can't seem to forgive 'em for that."

"But why here? Why did they come all this way to step in front of my train?"

"We lived near the headwaters of the Red River out in the Panhandle. Family legend is that the spirits of our ancestors lived in the Red—that they roam the bottoms around here. The priest said her grandfather told her to follow the river here in the dreams."

The chair creaked when Blaze shifted his bulk. "So why

did you have to come here, too? I would have gone off in the other direction as far and fast as I could."

"Can't explain that, either. I lost my brother, my parents and later, my wife. Jubal lost his mother and will never know my parents or my brother. He only has one grandparent alive. We needed to leave all of it behind, maybe get a new start. Guess I was drawn here because I need to understand why they did it as much or more than you do. Hate to admit it, but maybe some part of me believed that story about their spirits being here." He chuckled softly. "I was desperate."

"That trestle down there haunts me. Can't bear to hear the train passing at night. You can't imagine the visions and sounds I get in my head."

Blaze winced when he saw the look in Tee's eyes. "Then again...I guess you're the only one who can. Didn't mean no harm by those words. How long you been playing Gene Autry's song about daddy and Jimmie Rodgers's song about mama?"

"That's Merle Haggard singing, *Mother, the Queen of my Heart*, not Jimmie Rodgers."

"I know that, but Rodgers wrote it and sang it first."

"Surprised that anybody knows the song at all. Harmony O'Hara found those two old records at a record shop in Dallas. Said she thought of me when she saw them. Wouldn't say why she thought of me. Whoever lived here before left behind the old record player."

"Why do you play 'em out in the old tabernacle?"

"I like the sound in the night air. And I don't want to wake Jubal. Seems I need to listen alone."

"Does it help to play 'em over and over?"

"Don't know if it helps or hurts. Guess you could say it

turns my anger into tears. Sounds crazy, I know, but I like to think maybe they're listening."

"Makes sense. Good music can do good things to a man."

Tee threw the twisted weed into the dirt yard. "My daddy always said a man has to face his demons. Maybe that's what I'm trying to do here. Maybe I need to know if anything my great-grandfather said is true." He pulled an ear lobe. "Maybe my ancestors' spirits do live in the Red and come out to roam these woods and bottoms."

Blaze reached into a bib pocket of his overalls for a pack of cigarettes that had always been there during his drinking and fighting days, but wasn't there anymore. "But you're living right here where it happened. How can you? I parked on the other side of the rails because I can't bear to drive over those tracks."

"You were here on the hill the first morning we came, so you know the story. Jubal and I stopped at the bottom of the hill to sleep in the trailer. Didn't know where we were. Joe Henry woke us the next morning; I roped the wild stud for him; he offered us a roof over our heads for a little ranch work. Then he sold me Wes Simpson's business on the cuff. That's about it."

"You mean to say you didn't know this was the trestle where it happened until Joe told you I was a railroad engineer who quit his job because of the wreck?"

"I knew we were close to the area, but not that close. Never could bring myself to come here before I lost my wife."

Tee nodded toward the cross. "When I saw the cross in the yard, I thought I might be in the right place. I knew then I had to take Joe Henry up on his offer of the use of this house. Something told me I had brought Jubal to the right place."

Blaze pointed at the cross with one finger. "You mean...?"

Tee nodded. "You know the story about what happened. Joe told me the legend, about why he calls it Redheart Hill." Tee pointed a stick at the cross. "That grave probably holds my great-grandfather's bones—the man my mother thinks she saw in a vision."

Blaze raised his huge bulk and looked into the starry night. "You don't see anything strange about driving five hundred miles and this is where you stopped and the second person you see is the one who ran over your parents and you move into the house where your ancestor is buried in the yard?" He ran the words together.

"I'll admit it seems like a long string of coincidences."

"I don't believe in coincidences."

"So what would you call it?"

"Whispers, nudges, pokes, maybe winks. God does those first. If we don't pay attention he might prod us. I think God reaches down and says, 'Pay attention, boy. I'm making this happen for your benefit'. And by the way, this is Hurt Hill, not Redheart Hill like Joe claims. He loves that old legend so much he renamed it. But people been around here awhile still call it Hurt Hill after the family who built the house."

"Yeah, I heard several folks in town call it Hurt Hill. Kinda fits."

"Did you tell the priest where you are?"

"I did. He said I was where I needed to be, that maybe I was led here. Wouldn't tell this to just anybody, but I do feel a connection when the trains pass. It's like Mother and Daddy reach out, trying to explain what they did. Maybe if I sit here on this porch long enough, God will explain."

"So you're a believer?"

"Where I grew up, we had to travel forty miles of dirt road to pavement, then another ten to the nearest church. We missed a lot, but Mother took us when she could and made sure I got dunked in the water. Daddy came some. Am I a believer? Short answer is yes. Seems stupid not to believe when you have everything to lose if you don't and everything to gain if you do. But from what little I know, God's probably not too proud of me."

Blaze looked back at the trestle. "How long's it been? You came about a year ago, the wreck about ten before that. I asked God all that time why he's putting me through this."

Tee jerked his thumb down the hill without looking. "I could have handled the first wreck, but my parents taking their own lives…well, that's hard to take. If God was involved, where was He? And why did He leave me behind?"

"Expect He ain't through with you yet."

Blaze looked toward Jubal's closed porch window. "Jubal won't have anything to do with me when he finds out I killed his grandpa and grandma."

"What happened was not your fault, Blaze. No way you could have known. He'll understand. The boy's been through so much he's like an old soul."

"Mind if I ask what happened to his mama?"

Tee's eyes narrowed. "That's a story for another time."

Blaze started back down the hill, then stopped and turned. "You suppose I could see a picture of your mama and daddy?"

The silence was uncomfortable as Tee stared at him. Blaze seemed lost for words. "If it ain't too much to ask."

Tee went into the house and returned with an old scrapbook. Little black cardboard corners held black-and-white photos against black pages inside. Blaze held the scrapbook under the porch light and studied a weatherworn man with skin darkened by the sun dressed in boots and hat beside a dark-skinned, beautiful woman with long, straight, black hair wearing a gingham dress.

Tee looked over his shoulder. "They were going to a dance in town when that was taken."

Blaze studied the photos of John T and Winona Jessup under the lantern light and memorized their faces. The train whistle blew a lonely sound in the distance. Blaze handed the scrapbook to Tee and hurried back to his pickup.

Tee turned off the lantern and sat in one of the porch rockers when Blaze left. He watched the train pass, wondered if Blaze had gotten away in time to beat it. No need to try and sleep now. Blaze's unanswered questions took him back a year, back to the scenes he replayed hundreds of times, back to the Panhandle, to the ranch he loved and hated.

THREE

1973

TEE STOPPED AT THE RAILROAD CROSSING, rolled down the window, tried to connect, to hear his brother's voice, but heard nothing other than the persistent winds of the High Plains. The train wreck at this spot scarred Tee physically and emotionally, but his parents' later deaths shattered his soul. Losing Sarah added anger and thirst for revenge to his troubled mind.

A few miles west of the ranch where he spent his youth, Tee stood with son Jubal at the graves. Tee's parents and his brother had been gone long enough for the dirt to settle on their graves, but the dirt on wife Sarah's was still fresh.

He stopped in Amarillo to say goodbye to Father Bob, the priest who tried to help him understand why he was left alive. And why he had to forgive his parents and Ford Donovan, the man he considered responsible for Sarah's death. East of Fort Worth, he said goodbye to friend Esther and stole an Air-

19

stream travel trailer from his bankrupt employer. He figured
bankruptcy judges and lawyer cronies would steal it if he didn't.

Tee headed east with Jubal, inexplicably drawn to the
location where his parents sacrificed their lives to save his.
Though he saw their deed as senseless, heartless, cruel, and
unforgivable, he needed to assuage the guilt he felt for surviv-
ing while his brother, parents and wife perished, leaving only
his son for him to love and to love him.

For years, he struggled to understand, to find answers, to forgive and move on with his life. Something he could not explain
told him the answers could only be found near the place that
claimed his parents' lives, the land where his mother said the
spirits of her ancestors lived. Tee never understood what Winona meant by that or any of the other Choctaw legends she sometimes quoted. John T, his father, laughed at the legends, and she
laughed with him—until one of the legends took their lives.

He had visited Northeast Texas before, but had never
been to the hill by the railroad trestle where his parents died.
He and son Jubal trespassed the first night; parked the stolen
Airstream in bottomland near the crossing. The next morning, Tee used experience acquired growing up on a ranch to
help the land's owner capture a dangerous stud. Joe Henry
Leathers, lawyer and rancher, showed his gratitude by offering
part-time work on his small ranch and the temporary use of
the old farmhouse on the hill.

Heavy woods surrounded it and the land behind sloped to
bottomland and Moccasin Creek. Tee and Jubal had lived on
the hill only a few months when Esther came bearing good news.

She slept in the Airstream for two nights. Tee stepped out
on the porch an hour before dawn on the third day because

20

Esther had been up before daybreak the day before. He left the kitchen door open so he could hear the percolator perk, leaned back in his rickety cane rocker, and waited for a light to come on in the trailer.

He rose early most mornings, came out on the porch un-shaven with bed hair dressed in yesterday's jeans and a frayed denim shirt with the snaps undone for his first cup of cof-fee. Today, he was bathed, shaved, and dressed in starched Wranglers, shined boots, and a new Panhandle Slim shirt, ex-pecting to have coffee and an intimate breakfast with Esther before going to work. When the percolator stopped, he poured a first cup, leaned back in the rocker and sipped, watched the Airstream, waited for her shadow to cross the thin curtains.

When the fuzzy light appeared, it looked more like a flash-light than the overhead light he had tested in the trailer. Made him wonder if the generator gave up the ghost and left Esther to wander around in the dark. He gave her time to get dressed and take care of personal business before pouring her a cup and a second for him. Smoking coffee cup in each hand, he stumbled on the bottom porch step when unexpected lights behind the trailer illuminated the dead leaves on the big post oak that sheltered the trailer. Headlights from her Ford Fair-lane temporarily blinded him and he sloshed hot coffee over one hand as he watched her drive away. His mouth opened, but he could not make a sound.

Maybe a thief took her car. Or maybe she went into town to pick up breakfast. But when he looked inside the trailer, all of her belongings were gone. She left no note, only her scent. Guess she meant it when she said he was a wounded creature who might never heal.

Awash in self-pity, he almost wished she hadn't come at all. He had grown almost comfortable in this new environment, far away from the troubles that drove him here. Her surprise arrival confused those feelings. Still beautiful with long auburn hair that fell in ringlets across her shoulders, green eyes that expressed kindness and mischief, Esther brought the good news that he passed the tests that took a year of his life, but the life he left behind seemed to trail along behind her.

She had been a good friend when Sarah left him and took Jubal, but he couldn't keep from associating her with darker memories—things he wanted to forget. It wasn't her fault, but the images, the skin-crawling sensations, the remorse and guilt, roared back the day Esther found him again.

And the bad dreams returned the first night Esther returned—dreams of the night he lifted wife Sarah's frozen and emaciated body out of the snow—the agony of carrying her back to the house on the ranch where he had grown up—of two men carrying a stretcher holding the injured-but-still-breathing Ford Donovan, the man responsible for her death, to a chauffeur-driven limousine after Cutt Ledbetter, Sarah's father, hanged him from a tree on the ranch. Tee kept Cutt from killing Donovan, kept his wife's tormentor alive.

The staccato, brilliant flashes of the blood trail in the front yard of the Donovans' stone house at Blind River Ranch haunted his dreams. They defiled the land of his boyhood, tainted the beloved places and memories of his youth. They came without warning, night and day, and they came with a voice that shamed Tee for not avenging his wife's death, for letting Ford Donovan continue to breathe air his wife would never breathe again. He killed Ford Donovan several different ways in the dreams, always slowly and painfully, but Donovan never died. The visions kept him on edge, evoked flashes of temper, quick irritation, and a general feeling of anxiety that seldom left him alone.

Esther had been part of his life then, she knew all the details, and because she comforted him, listened to his pain, the memories attached to her like the shroud zippered over his wife's dead body. And she also reminded him of the man who walked the earth while his wife lay beneath it.

He emptied her cold cup in the dirt yard, blew on his burned hand, and slumped back into his chair. He felt the cold now. Rivers and Flo seemed to sense his sorrow and came out from under the porch. Rivers put his chin on his leg; Flo rubbed herself against the other one and purred. Blaze told him they were strays whose lives had been fraught with hunger and danger. He had seen both take on other dogs, cats, and varmints twice their size. Although he was reluctant to admit it, they also brought badly needed tenderness and serenity into his life when they seemed to love him unconditionally. Both made him stop several times each day to release anxiety and be gentle.

He poured his third cup from the kitchen coffeepot and returned to his rocker with a quilt for cover this time, decided the new-widower part of him was relieved she left. Tee was not ready to take on a new wife and stepmother for his son; he had too many demons to inflict on someone who had her own troubled past. But the sad and lonely and lost part of him wanted her to stay. He knew he might never find another woman like Esther. Son Jubal was the only person left who loved him, and Tee worried this was too big a burden for the boy to carry alone. He had mostly hidden the anger and remorse that roiled inside him, but feared what would happen if it ever came out.

As the sun's rays crossed the bottomland behind the house and crept through the trees awakening the birds, the sounds of morning in the deep woods soothed his pain and confusion. He imagined he could detect the soulful eyes and brown and white striped plumage of a barred owl as it hooted "who cooks for you?" At least that's what Jubal said the owl was saying. After spending most of his life on desolate plains, the raucous calls birds and critters made in the woods of Northeast Texas to announce sunrise were as welcome as the heavy air was unwelcome. The sounds nurtured him. And it was easy to imagine the owl watching over him and son Jubal.

Tee heard the boy stir in his bed and open the porch window. Jubal's voice was sleepy as he looked through the screen. "How come you're already dressed for work? We goin' in early this mornin'?"

"Couldn't sleep. But we do need to get an early start. And you may have to hang around the office a little longer before school and after."

"What about Esther? She goin' with us?"

"Nope. Esther said to tell you goodbye. Had to get an early start and didn't want to wake you." Tee waited for the questions as the boy lay back in his bed and ruminated on this surprise, but none came. Jubal took his disappointments quietly, almost stoically, like an old man who had suffered much. He seldom mentioned his mother's death or having to leave behind the only homes he had ever known and Cutt, his mother's father and only living grandparent. But the boy seemed to like Esther and Tee didn't want him to be hurt any more than he already had been.

FOUR

THE COTTON PICKER SHACK PERCHED ON THE steep east side of Hurt Hill as if it had been there first and the hill built around it. The shack could only be approached from the rear by horseback or afoot and Clayton had to break limbs and move logs to drive his yellow pickup to the front on a trail only he would recognize. The hidden trail gave him some comfort.

Clayton figured the bed and furniture he abandoned at the shack six years earlier would be stolen or ruined, so he was not surprised to see what was left of them in a charred pile out front when he arrived. He wrestled the new mattress inside with minimal damage to his wound, covered the rest of his purchases with a tarp and left them in the pickup until he rested a little.

There was a wood cookstove and a fireplace that might work again if the bricks lying on the hearth didn't indicate bigger problems. The well hand pump wouldn't work and the cistern water looked suspect. But he decided he could use it for everything except drinking and cooking. He would have to buy a small tank and haul water in for that until he could fix the pump.

He had bought an ice chest and some ice at a gas station. Wondered how long he could keep it from melting. He planned to bathe in cistern water. If the smell got too bad, he would go into Paris and stay in a motel for a night. He was not ready to be seen in Riverby yet.

From the porch, he could see and not be seen. As he looked down the hill toward deep bottomland, the bottom of the bottoms, and Moccasin Creek, an almost comfortable feeling settled on him. He loved being alone. Gave him time to figure out why he nursed a bullet wound in a secluded shack rather than doing what he felt called to do.

When he healed enough, he tried his hand at making a twig chair out of dying cedar he found near the shack. He knew he would spend most of his time on the porch and wanted something to sit on. He wanted a rocking chair, but knew that was beyond his skill level. He was a fair sheetrock hanger and painter, but not much carpenter or craftsman.

Clayton sat gently in the twig chair, tested to see whether it would hold. The rough bark and sharp points from the finger-sized limbs he cut with his pocketknife made pinprick impressions on his back. The slight pain reminded him of *Opus Dei*, the Catholic group who practiced self-flagellation, one of the religions Clayton had tried on for a spiritual fit—without success. But the sharp points served as a welcome distraction from the bullet wound in his side. It had stopped bleeding and left no sign of infection. Daily dousing with Old Crow and rubbing alcohol had done the trick, he expected.

After a week, he drove into Riverby and called Joe Henry Leathers from a pay phone to let him know he was in the shack, asked him to keep it a secret. Said he had some thinking to do and wanted to play his guitar and write a few songs without being disturbed. But he had seen the little terrier snooping, knew he would be found out soon if he hadn't been already. He loved fresh eggs, so he bought a rooster and a few chickens when he picked up the water tank. The vociferous rooster woke him with a start every morning. The rooster, the clucking chickens, and the little terrier would expose him soon enough.

Over the years, Clayton's pages of scribbling had grown too voluminous to carry with him on his travels, so he had talked Cooper Newman, President of the Farmers and Merchants Bank of Riverby, into renting him space in the safe deposit vault of the bank. To stay away from prying eyes, he hired a young boy to roll four steel file cabinets with four drawers each into the bank. All sixteen drawers were filled with his categorized scribbling and a few other things precious to him.

A key lock secured all the drawers in each cabinet, but that was not enough for Clayton. He installed a hasp and loop on each file cabinet to hold locks with four different combinations he kept in his head. He also rented six safe deposit drawers for his most important manuscripts and other important papers and valuables. Riverby seemed the logical location to keep them, the only place where he found solace as a boy and the only place he had stayed longer than a couple of years in his life. In the shack, he felt closeness to his millions of words written on paper and stored in the bank, words that still swirled in his brain.

Clayton spent most of his time on the porch, calmed by the sounds of nature. He entertained and soothed his troubled soul and restless mind by distinguishing and cataloging the calls, hoots, tweets, caws, howls and yelps made by creatures that lived in the woods. He imagined they were singing a symphony especially for him. This led to his guitar and a few words to a song or a story or two committed to paper.

FIVE

THE DISTANT SOUND OF A ROOSTER CROWING interrupted Tee's reverie as he sat on the front porch drinking coffee. *Who lives close enough to own chickens?* But the rooster's crow announced sunrise and reminded Tee it would be another can-till-can't day in a long string of such days to come at work, so he had no more time to ruminate or engage in self-pity.

Jubal slipped out of bed, dropped to his knees, and put both elbows on the window ledge. "You hear that rooster?"

"Sure did. Where you reckon he's coming from? No houses close enough around here to have chickens."

"There's the cotton-picker shack."

"Nobody's been in there for years."

Jubal hesitated then blurted, "I think there might be now."

Tee stopped rocking, drained his coffee, and turned. "How so?"

"Me and Sweetness was down there yesterday and I think I saw a man in the yard."

Tee frowned. "I told you not to ride the mare so deep in the woods without me along."

Jubal shrugged. "Sweetness knows the woods and anyway, she just followed Old Rivers. It was like Rivers wanted to show me somebody moved into the old shack."

"Remind me and we'll go check it out."

"Tonight?"

"I imagine it'll be too late tonight when we get in. Now get dressed. We'll stop by and get you a biscuit and sausage at Prigmore's."

Several days passed before Tee made good on his promise to take Jubal down the hill to check out the rooster crowing and the picker shack. By mid-afternoon on a Sunday, Tee and Jubal had almost a cord of wood stacked on the porch for heat and cooking and a large pile of scrap limbs for kindling, bonfires and wiener roasts. It was cold, so neither had worked up a sweat.

Jubal wiped his dry brow as if he were sweating. "Can we check on the shack now?"

Tee saddled Judson, Joe Henry's gelding they renamed after a horse Tee rode as a boy, and Jubal saddled his mare, Sweetness. Jubal mounted first. "Look at Rivers. He's ready to go." The terrier's ears pointed toward the bottoms, impatient to lead the way.

Tee felt a warm glow as he watched his son move Sweetness into the woods and follow Rivers down the hollow behind their house. The boy sat a horse like a ranch cowboy.

Tee followed his son, but felt inadequate being led into the deep woods by a boy. Maybe Blaze pegged Jubal correctly as a woods-boy. Tee could not get used to his son being a child of the woods and bottomland while he was a child of the prairie. In the country of Tee's youth, trees were mostly seen only in yards, so wooded country, especially heavily wooded bottom-land, was still an uncomfortable mystery to him.

He had already heard enough to know the woods surrounding the dark bottoms made ripe fodder for folktales and mystery. Hard to describe to an outsider, bottomland had to be experienced. Filled with critters seldom seen by man, ground seldom seen by the sun, parts flooded at least once during most years, and black gumbo soil stuck to itself and anything else that touched it. When the land dried, great cracks formed like the aftermath of tiny earthquakes.

Old-timers told stories of small children dropping into those cracks and never being seen again, of grown men attacked by wild hogs, and black panthers that made terrifying screams at night like a woman being devoured. Even Joe Henry said there had been panther sightings and there were definitely wildcats and cougars in the area. Tee had never heard a panther scream, but he had heard and seen coyotes and had once seen a bobcat scurry away.

Tee recited those stories and dangers often to Jubal, but instead of being frightened or cautious, the tales made the boy want to return again and again to the bottoms. Along with danger and discomfort, the bottomlands offered solitude and quiet, a place to commune with nature, and it was this quality Jubal seemed to have discovered almost immediately. With Blaze's tutelage, he was becoming a seasoned varmint hunter and trapper.

Blaze believed tales about spirits of the departed said to live in these woods. He imagined Jubal communing with his grandparents when he roamed. Perhaps Winona's and John T's restless spirits were nearby. Blaze wanted to believe it.

Tee touched the stock of the twenty-two rifle in his scabbard. When Jubal went out of sight, Tee called him back. "This man you say you saw could be dangerous. You stick close till we find out."

Tee was almost embarrassed at his own reluctance to explore the land around where he now lived, to approach what might be a trespasser. When the cotton picker shack came into view, Rivers stopped and sat by a tree, pointing his ears at the shack as if to say, *I told you so.*

Jubal stopped Sweetness beside the dog. The mare whispered a nicker and nodded her head as if also familiar with the shack and its occupant. Tee dismounted and looked down at what still looked like an abandoned cabin. Joe Henry said it had been unoccupied since the last hapless farmer tried planting cotton nearby and housed itinerant pickers there during harvest.

Tee had been in the shack only once, found it full of wasp, dirt dauber and bird nests, and rat snakes. "Looks empty to me. Maybe the man you saw was a hobo getting out of the weather for a night. Probably jumped off the train at the trestle and got back on the next trip."

Jubal pointed. "He was reading a book on the porch. See that twig chair?"

Tee saw movement through one of the two remaining windows that still had glass as he mounted. A man walked out to scatter feed on the small dirt yard he had enclosed with chicken wire. Nesting and egg boxes had been nailed to the eaves under the falling-down back porch. A rooster and six hens pecked at the feed.

Tee turned toward Jubal. "Looks like that old rooster we been hearing."

Neither the land nor the house belonged to Tee, but he felt a proprietary interest because he knew Joe Henry and because he lived nearby. He expected the man was trespassing. He rode to the fence and tipped his hat. "Tee Jessup is my name. This is my son Jubal. We live up the hill."

The man's slow gait and slight stoop made Tee think he was old, but the face surrounded by ringlets of dark brown hair that looked wet appeared to be timeless. The man could be forty or sixty. He studied the horses and dog, avoided eye contact with Tee. "Name's Clayton Dupree. Been seeing the boy and his dog up there now and then. Figured on a visit sooner or later." His expression said he was not looking forward to it.

Tee dismounted and shook the man's hand over the chicken wire. "Don't mean to interfere. Didn't know anybody lived in this old house. Joe Henry never mentioned it."

"That would be my fault. Asked him not to say anything till I got settled in. Promised him I would drop by your house and say hello. Just never got around to it, I guess. I pretty much keep to myself."

"You from around here?'

"On and off over the years. At one time, I stayed in the house you live in and this one, too. With my folks, that is. That was a long time ago."

"You know who's buried in the grave in the front yard?"

Tee had told him a shortened version of the story, but Jubal felt he had held something back.

Clayton's body language said he was determined to do something he would rather not. He motioned for them to follow him and went inside the house. The dirt dauber, wasp and bird nests were gone and Tee saw no sign of rats or snakes. Two chairs and a table were the only furniture in the main room. The second room held a bed. A coffee pot sat on the fireplace grates over fading embers. Black on the chimney bricks said it didn't draw well. Tee saw no vehicle or riding horse, wondered how Clayton brought in his supplies and himself.

Clayton offered them strips of beef jerky from a Ball Mason canning jar and two tin cups filled with coffee. "Guess the boy's too young for coffee, but I'm fresh out of tea. Or ice, for that matter. I did get the well pump to work so I can have water."

Jubal took the cup, glanced at Tee, sniffed, sipped, tried not to grimace.

Tee found the coffee strong, but not bitter. He needed it after biting off a chunk of the jerky.

Jubal's eyes watered from the jerky. "So do you know about the grave?"

Clayton looked at Tee as he answered. "The story may not be suitable for a boy your age."

Tee wanted to hear Clayton's version. "He's already overheard a pretty gruesome tale. Joe Henry told me the legend. Jubal is old enough to get the straight of it if you have it."

Clayton stepped into the bedroom and returned with a picture of what appeared to be a family gathering in front of the Hurt Hill house when it was almost new. There was a boy on an old gray horse, a middle-aged couple on the porch, and a couple of dogs. Two older women sat in rockers in the front yard, one dressed in white and the other in black. Bonnets made it impossible to see their facial features.

"The hapless farmer who cleared and tried to farm that sorry piece of dirt down in the bottoms by Moccasin Creek hired my family to pick his crop one year. He showed me this picture and told me his story one night by a campfire out in the yard.

Clayton paused and let them both get a good look at the picture. "Always brought a box of pictures to show us kids and tell us stories."

Clayton put a finger with dirty nails on the woman in black and looked at Tee. "Said she stood right on your front porch and shot a Choctaw who stood over her husband's body. When a second Choctaw took off running, she levered a shell into the chamber and shot him, too."

Clayton inclined his head toward Jubal. "Said her young son about this boy's age stood right beside his mother when she shot both of 'em. Told that to be true."

Tee nodded. "You believe it?"

"I do. Don't suppose Joe Henry ever mentioned Willard Dunn. I grew to love that old man—one of the few people in this world who paid me any mind, who treated me like I had good sense. He died when I was just a boy and left me the pictures and some of his scribbling and the place where you live. He loved his stories and the pictures that went with them, so I kept the box, sold the place."

Tee could tell nothing about the old woman's facial features, but he could see she was diminutive. "This little woman killed two men right in our yard?"

Clayton frowned. "Then she cut out their hearts, burned their bodies, and buried their hearts there in the yard. Indian legend says without their hearts, their souls will wander lost forever."

The story excited Jubal. "But I thought our grandpa was buried there because they couldn't get his body to town."

"That's true, too. But the old woman buried her husband on top of the hearts as a sign of his dominion over his killers, double insurance they could never be united with their souls."

The talk of Indian folklore and myths made Tee want to change the subject. "Not trying to butt in on your business, but how did you get yourself and all this stuff up here?"

"Come outside and I'll show you." On the porch, he pointed toward a grove of blackjack oaks infested with cockleburs, thorny vines, and poison oak.

Tee saw portions of the yellow Ford through the brush and trees. "How did you drive up here without coming by our place?"

"There was an old trail around Moccasin Creek when I was a boy. Had to cut through a few limbs and vines, but managed to make it. You can do it if you ain't particular about your vehicle."

"None of my business, but what do you do?"

Clayton hesitated as he looked at Jubal, then Tee. "I hang a little rock, do a little painting. Fell off a scaffold and hurt myself. Came here to heal."

Tee glanced at an easel and canvas in the corner. "You an artist, too?"

"Not really. Just dabble. I mostly paint houses and barns."

Jubal looked toward the other corner. "That your guitar?"

"Might be. You play?"

Jubal's smile disappeared. "Nope."

After sunset, Tee had new visions to contemplate as he sat on the porch. He couldn't wait to quiz Joe Henry about Clayton Dupree.

Six

JOE HENRY LEATHERS' LAW OFFICE AT THE
Corner of Texas and Oklahoma Streets on the Riverby Square
was everything Tee's was not. The lawyer/rancher made sure
everything inside his office appeared to have been made at least
a hundred years ago. The windows were covered with hinged
pine boards equipped with rifle ports. When he opened them,
the morning light seemed proud to highlight a huge Ranger's
desk made of oak and held together with bois d'arc pegs. The
arms and legs of his desk chair and side chairs were made from
the horns of Longhorn cattle. The rest of the Longhorns, hide
with hair still on it, adorned the seats. The outside walls were
stucco, the inside antique brick and native rocks. Log beams
crisscrossed the ceiling. Tee always dreaded returning to his
own office when he left Joe's.

Joe emerged from his office kitchenette that had been de-
signed like the rear of a chuck wagon carrying two steaming

cups. With his jeans tucked into the tops of his red, tall-topped boots and bowlegs, most folks would never think of him as a lawyer. He set two steaming cups on the desk and sat across from Tee. "To what do I owe the pleasure?"

"You ever wear a suit and tie like a proper lawyer?"

"Figure I can do lawyer work wearing my ranch clothes, but I can't do ranch work wearing lawyer clothes."

Tee consulted the spiral notepad he kept in his shirt pocket to keep from forgetting the questions he wanted to ask.

"Met the fellow holed up in the cotton picker shack the other day. How come you didn't let me know?"

"Maybe you ain't noticed how hard a man you are to talk to lately. Came over to your office several times to tell you, but you were always with a client."

"Bull. I never saw you darken my door. So what's his story? Clayton, is it?"

Joe Henry nodded. "Clayton Dupree. Quite a piece of work."

"So why's he living in that old shack?"

"Calls it his healing house. He lived there on and off as a boy when he traveled with his relatives. Itinerant farm workers. One day, he hid in the woods when it came time for his relatives to leave. Willard Dunn, the old man who used to own the place, took him in. A few years later Willard died and left Clayton the farm, the shack and the house you live in."

"So you bought the farm from him?"

"Not right away. Daddy handled Willard Dunn's estate. When Clayton decided he wanted to sell the place, he went to daddy first. So daddy bought it. When he died, I inherited it and Clayton gave me a limited power of attorney over some of his affairs."

"And you let him come and go as he pleases?"

"Don't see why not. Can't very well turn down a client."

Joe Henry saw the remaining questions in Tee's expression. "Look, Clayton goes out in the world; gets himself wounded; comes here to mend. I don't see any harm in letting him do it in the shack. Think it would fall down without him. This area and the shack may bring back fond memories, but I think it's mostly because he wants to be alone. And there's damn few places as isolated as that shack. "

"You mean wounded physically?"

Joe Henry looked over the brim of his coffee cup. "Mostly mental wounds, but physical wounds wouldn't surprise me. Ever heard of somebody who was just too smart? I don't mean a smartass, I mean really smart. That's Clayton. Daddy said he had a rough life as a kid, and being smart made him an oddball, an object of ridicule even to his own relatives. So he stopped talking and sort of withdrew."

"I thought he talked a lot smarter than he looks. So, how does he make a living?"

Joe Henry smiled. "If I told you that, I'd have to kill you."

"Seriously, how does he live? Said he hung drywall and did some painting."

"To be honest, I know just enough about him to be dangerous. He may be a sheet rock hanger. I think he writes a few songs under an assumed name. With enough whiskey under his belt, he also plays a mean guitar and he's got one of those crying voices that seems to come from a world of hurt."

Tee leaned forward. "So you've heard him play and sing."

"Once. His voice reminds me of Morgan Bell's."

"The sheriff sings?"

41

"You ought to hear him."

Tee stood to leave.

Joe followed him to the door. "And I heard Daddy tell Mother once that he writes novels under a pseudonym."

"Clayton? What's the pseudonym?"

"Beats me. He wouldn't like the publicity if one of his novels hit the big time and damn sure wouldn't want us to know his fake name."

Tee stared at his friend, eyes wide, waiting for more.

"I know it sounds strange, but when he's around people too close for any period of time, he winds himself tight as a fiddle string. Told me their voices seem loud enough to pierce his eardrums, all their mannerisms, gestures, and tics seem exaggerated. Makes him lose control, but I think his too-close examination of people helps him build characters in his novels and words for his songs."

"Can you find out titles to any books he's written?"

"I tried. He clams up." Joe chuckled. "And if I did, I couldn't tell you. Attorney-client privilege, you know." He laughed and slapped Tee hard on his back.

SEVEN

FROM HIS WINDOWED OFFICE IN THE LOBBY of Farmers and Merchants Bank and in full view of all the lobby customers, President Cooper Newman watched Clayton Dupree lean over the receptionist's desk to sign his name documenting his visit to the safe deposit vault. He hadn't seen Clayton in a long time and wondered how a man could go that long without a haircut and wear clothes an iron never touched.

Holding a key ring with six keys in his hand, Clayton followed a bank clerk toward the safe deposit room. Cooper hurried out of his office to intercept them. He stepped in front of the bank clerk, took the bank's matching keys from her hand, and signaled with his head for her to return to her desk. He flashed a handsome, well-dressed, well-groomed smile on Clayton. "Hey, Clayton. Long time no see."

Clayton stared at his own boots with watery eyes. "About the usual time between visits, I suppose."

Cooper Newman was vaguely aware of Clayton's long-term relationship with the bank that began with his inheritance from Willard Dunn. Willard had been a bank director and Clayton was his informally adopted son. From questions asked by bank auditors when confirmations sent to Clayton came back stamped addressee-unknown, Cooper learned Clayton had certain checks from New York banks automatically deposited or wire-transferred into a savings account at infrequent intervals.

He also knew the account came up as inactive on occasional reports and the balance stayed in healthy five figures. Withdrawals in cash happened once every year or two, and the bank drafted annually for the rental of his six safe deposit drawers and the storage fee for his file cabinets. Cooper studied all inactive accounts regularly, hoping the bank might somehow capture funds depositors had abandoned before the state confiscated them. He also sometimes needed the flexibility of inactive accounts to cover his own occasional late loan payments or overdrafts in his farm account.

Most of the inactive accounts could be explained easily. The owners had moved, were ill, dead, or too old to remember they had an account. But Clayton Dupree was a mystery. Cooper couldn't tell his age by looking at him. And he was the only bank customer with six safe deposit drawers—drawers, not boxes, as well as four four-drawer file cabinets with both regular locks and combination locks.

Clayton sometimes visited the bank with a case covered in fake lizard skin that resembled a woman's overnight case in fashion a decade earlier. Today, he carried only his keys. Cooper Newman wanted to know the contents of the drawers and he wanted to know the source of the New York money. He felt justified in his curiosity because of his position as president of the bank. He suspected nefarious activities. Maybe Clayton was a hired assassin, a bank robber or mobster. Cooper Newman owed it to his customers and the community to find out. There could be explosives in those drawers for all he knew.

The tall, handsome, charismatic, and young bank president made small talk and jokes as he inserted and turned the bank's key into the first drawer. He stepped back and waited for Clayton to withdraw the contents, but Clayton inserted his key into the second drawer door. They followed the steps through all six drawers. When the doors opened, Cooper tried to see into the dark drawers without being obvious. "Need any help carrying these over to the table?"

Clayton kept his eyes down but spoke firmly. "I can handle it from here."

Cooper paused at the vault door and turned to see if Clayton would empty at least one drawer. But Clayton stared at the floor until Cooper left.

Clayton lifted a box from the first safe deposit drawer and carried it to a work table high enough to use while standing. He lovingly flipped back the latch to the mini-vault and put one hand on the stack of crumpled sheets of lined paper. The edges were turned up on most of the pages; some were torn; some were wrinkled from being wet; some yellowed with age.

As he flipped through the pages studying his own handwriting as it progressed from a boy's printing to immature cursive to an adult almost-illegibility borne of a mind that moved faster than fingers, he felt safer somehow. He repeated the ritual through five drawers, carefully checking his mental list and the list he carried in his shirt pocket for two published manuscripts, six unpublished, and millions of words on written lines that would never be published, never be seen by eyes other than his own until he died. He finished one drawer at a time, returned it to its proper location and turned the key to lock it before he withdrew another one.

After a short perusal through all the boxes and drawers, Clayton focused on his boots as he passed through the lobby and out the door to his pickup. Cooper watched him leave and walked back to the vault so see if he had dropped something or left a drawer open. He had not. He returned to his office, stared at reports and paperwork he did not understand, anxiously waited for closing time. When everyone went home, he pulled a small bottle of vodka from his bottom desk drawer and took two deep pulls. From a closet shelf inside his office, he pulled down a large tote bag from a Dallas department store filled with folders.

Like many nights, he studied the list of inactive accounts and loans he kept in the folders. He rounded the numbers, but the total withdrawals he made from inactive accounts had grown to over thirty thousand dollars. Although his scheme was ingenious and he would likely never be caught, Cooper intended to repay every cent with earnings from his cattle operations and profits made from flipping real estate the bank foreclosed on and he bought. He knew he was sitting on a gold mine with his ranch and nearby land if the market would just turn around.

Medical expenses for his wife and car repairs incurred when he ran off the road on the way home from the border one night after an evening of celebration forced him into the first transaction. Then came the five-hundred-acre ranch he could not afford to pass up, then the herd of registered cattle he needed to keep up his banker image, the new brick and stone house on the ranch, the rolling feeders, the white pipe fence. The cattle operation would pay for itself soon enough, but he had not figured on a drop in cattle and real estate prices.

He opened an account in a Dallas bank using a dead customer's social security number and name, then authorized wire transfers into the Dallas account from an inactive account at the bank. The wire transfers were always for the exact account balance so the trail could start to grow cold when the account was closed.

The bogus loans started out innocently enough. A desperate bank customer whose property was on the verge of being foreclosed offered Cooper a twenty-percent kickback if he could just loan him enough money to meet his delinquent payments and avoid the foreclosure Cooper had threatened. The man said he had surefire money coming in only two months.

Thankfully, the man told the truth. The customer reduced his loan by a lump sum, stayed current on his payments, and Cooper was eight thousand richer. There had been one instance of a loan made to a fictitious customer—a Fort Worth dentist Cooper claimed to have known since college and who did Cooper and the bank a favor by throwing a little business their way. Cooper found it easy to turn a legitimate credit report for a real person into a fake for the dentist with a little liquid paper and a few runs through a copy machine. With Cooper's ringing endorsement, the twenty-thousand-dollar note sailed through loan committee and right by the auditors.

Directors felt fortunate to have a man of such impressive cre-
dentials and net worth as a customer in their small town.

The total theft bumped a little under sixty thousand. The
charismatic bank president ran a hand through his hair, took
another pull from the bottle of vodka, and wiped away the
tears of desperation before going home to his wife.

EIGHT

THEY CLAIMED TO HAVE NO AGENDA, NO bylaws, no dues...no purpose, really, other than laughter and mutual deprecation. But each knew better. They found in each other something they could not put into words, something they fervently needed. None would admit to any need, however. People who knew them as individuals were confounded by their need to gather as an eclectic group five or six times a week. It made no sense for a group of people who seemed incompatible to gather regularly in the corner of an old store at an old pine board table to talk. Nobody knew how many there were in the beginning and only the members knew how many there were now. The only requirement for membership was to have suffered hurt or caused others to hurt.

Nobody knew for certain how it started or how it got its name, but most agreed the catalyst was a saddle preacher who once lived in the picker shack on Hurt Hill. The Hurts hired the man, his wife, and four children to pick cotton one year. The family had a tent they set up in the back of their old flatbed truck, but the Hurts insisted they stay in the picker shack.

Cotton harvest was nearly over when Herschel Hurt and his wife Florine came across the saddle preacher mid-sermon on the banks of the Red under a willow tree one Saturday night. They were so moved by his words they kneeled before him and asked for his blessing after the sermon. He baptized them in the river that night. Thereafter, the saddle preacher and his family had a home in the picker shack and the family had work with the Hurts. Wife and children stayed there after harvest and the husband returned to his horseback preaching circuit.

A few days after the second cotton harvest, the preacher came home to find his four children hungry, his wife gone. When the Hurts found out, they brought food and as much comfort as they could, but the preacher would not be comforted. He lost his faith, turned to the bottle. But Florine Hurt would not tolerate alcohol on her property. She confiscated and emptied all of it, brought the preacher to Prigmore's store where she had three men waiting at a table in the corner.

One was a widower whose wife died and left him with five kids to raise, one lost a leg in the first big war, and the third was a binge drinker who had not touched a drop in five years. She sat with them the first day, coaxed each to tell a short version of his story to the preacher and the others. She brought the preacher every day except Sunday until he could be trusted to go alone. They began to call it Miz Hurt's Circle. She objected, wanted it to be their gathering, not hers. The men shared their hurts and became close friends. The preacher stopped drinking and went back to harvesting and preaching.

When the last of the original members and both Hurts passed on, Don Prigmore's mother had a brass sign made. She hung it in the corner over the table where the men gathered. The sign simply read *Hurt Circle*. She said Florine had not wanted the group named for her, but the word hurt still fit. The original members had all suffered hurts that seemed irreparable, hurts that could only be understood by others who suffered similarly.

The table in the corner remained empty until Abel Gunter emerged from seclusion to have a hamburger at Prigmore's with attorney Joe Henry Leathers and Sheriff Morgan Bell. They seemed to be the only ones who knew Abel. When your only associates are a lawyer and a sheriff, folks speculate about a possible dark past, one that might have involved legal problems—especially when one who is past middle age arrives in a small community. Don Prigmore invited them to sit at the Hurt Circle table, thinking the hurt requirement long forgotten. But when Prigmore related the legend of the corner with humor, Abel did not laugh.

Abel had purchased a modest farm near the river from a family estate and entered the community without fanfare, coming into town only when necessary. The day after meeting with Joe Henry and the sheriff, he returned to Prigmore's unannounced, sat at the pine table with a book and a cup of coffee, and started reading. Dawson, his mixed breed dog that resembled a border collie, always rode in the back of his pickup and waited patiently outside the door of Prigmore's while Abel enjoyed his coffee and book. Folks said Dawson was a marvel with both sheep and cattle.

Abel raised a few cows and fewer sheep, sold Coastal Ber-

muda sprigs, had no family and no history, at least none anybody seemed to know. He had no telephone for several years,
drove a non-descript used pickup. His farm was hardscrabble
at first, his first house an abandoned shack, but folks talked a
lot about his appearance. Some days, he showed up in a worn
suit and tie, other days in khakis and work shirt or overalls.
His clothes, even his overalls, were always clean and pressed
when he came to town, even on days when he worked cattle
and sheep; his hair always neat. Nobody could put a finger on
exactly why, but Abel seemed to ooze confidence and inspire
trust. Folks said he had a quiet dignity about him. He became
a magnet for those who needed help.

Older widows said he was ruggedly handsome, with eyes
milky blue and sad, shiny as if on the verge of tears. Folks said
those eyes had seen a lot of heartache and trouble. Course
that was pure speculation. Only Joe Henry Leathers and Morgan Bell were thought to know anything about his past. Town
folk were left to speculate as to how he qualified to sit at the
Hurt table.

And Abel was always armed with a book—never the Bible,
but usually a book having to do with theology. He maintained
that Bible reading should be done in private, not in public. He
believed words were valuable and used them sparingly. When
he spoke, people listened.

The Hurt Circle experienced a new genesis when a discussion some called an argument about Scripture begun one Sunday at church spilled over to Monday and presented itself at
Prigmore's. When customers who believed neither religion nor
politics should be discussed in public gradually moved out of
hearing, Sheriff Morgan Bell, Toke Albright, Blaze Blaisdell,

Harmony O'Hara, Reverend Enoch Essary, and Abel Gunter were left at the Hurt table. That's when they began to discover they all had something in common.

The discussions were about which passages in the Old Testament accurately prophesied the coming of Jesus; why Moses was kept from entering the Promised Land because he hit the rock with his staff instead of just telling the rock to yield its water; why God let Satan punish Job mercilessly; why He hardened Pharaoh's heart against His chosen people several times instead of making him let them go when Moses asked the first time; why the Levite Uzzah was struck dead for trying to keep the Ark of the Covenant from tipping over; why or how could Jacob, a mere mortal, really wrestle with God? The list seemed to expand every week.

At first, Reverend Enoch Essary was taken aback when the men argued with a Bible expert like himself, but soon recognized he could learn a few things about theology from the group, especially Abel Gunter.

A former railroad engineer, Blaze Blaisdell toiled on Joe Henry Leather's ranch, baled a little hay, mowed a few lawns, used his old tractor and worn-out shredder to shred pastures, and worked the occasional funeral for the funeral home. But mostly Blaze liked to make original works or restore old things using metal or wood. He also led the singing at Enoch Essary's gatherings every Sunday. Many of Enoch's followers avowed they came to hear Blaze sing rather than the sermon. The reverend's voice had been compared to the sound of fingernails on a blackboard, and Blaze's was smooth, deep and mellow.

But it was more than that. Blaze was, well, a force. His huge, gentle, bulky presence exuded something people wanted to see and feel in church even when he merely recited the list of sick and infirm who needed special prayer mentions or reported the day's offerings and attendance. Blaze's wife had died giving birth to a son who died hours later. When a well-meaning friend had suggested their deaths were God's will, Blaze had come close to killing him. He took up the drink to drown his sorrows.

When Enoch Essary convinced him to come to his church and sing, Blaze soon gave up alcohol and anger. His wife and son had left him with a bubbling cauldron of love he needed to pour on needy souls. He washed best friends Toke Albright and his family and Morgan Bell and his family in the cauldron of his love regularly. The deaths also left him feeling helpless—helpless to protect his wife and son. That helplessness fueled a desire to protect others, especially women and children. Blaze simply loved people. His exuberance, especially with children, shined through. Congregants looked forward to the times when Enoch's raspy voice failed him and Blaze delivered the sermon.

Everyone knew why Blaze qualified for membership in the Hurt Circle. Losing a wife and newborn son would have been enough, but he was driving the train the night a husband and wife died on the tracks at Panther Crossing. They knew he sacrificed a lucrative leadership position and years of seniority with the railroad because of a tragedy not his fault. But the deaths and the accident changed him from a hell-raising drinker and fighter to a soft, gentle man.

Toke Albright, a former deputy sheriff under Morgan Bell, was led reluctantly into church on Sundays by his devout wife Lydia. Known for his skills with dozers and maintainers,

Toke had been persuaded to give up law enforcement for a better-paying job running heavy dirt-moving equipment. But he had not given up on his dream of becoming sheriff. Folks assumed he would take the sheriff's job when Morgan Bell retired. Some said he was half-serious when he occasionally checked Sheriff Bell's pulse during a meeting of the Circle or during a poker game. His membership qualifications for the group were not readily apparent.

Sheriff Morgan Bell, the only elected official in the group, was second to Abel in least words spoken. Highly thought of in the county, he had been sheriff for almost three decades. He knew when to arrest a delinquent and when to escort him home to his parents; when to draw his weapon and when to keep it holstered. His voting numbers were so high he had not drawn an opponent in the last four elections. But he was in his mid-sixties now and retirement was often discussed. He promised to endorse Toke when that time arrived.

On rare occasions, Bell could be coerced into a little music. Though he had one of those crying, trembling voices that seemed to come from a life of suffering, he never sang without his fiddle in hand. Even if he didn't play it, he needed it to shield himself from curious eyes. Morgan never sang anything that had not stood the test of time and was especially fond of old country, folk songs, and mountain ballads. He was a fan of Jimmie Rodgers and could do a passable imitation of the singing brakeman in *Blue Yodel No. 9*, *In the Jailhouse Now*, and *T for Texas*. He knew the history of Hurt Circle and felt qualified for membership, but did not readily reveal why. No outsider questioned him about it.

Harmony O'Hara, the woman in the group, always intro-

duced herself as Harmony, then laughed as she told folks her real name was Maureen. Said she had changed it after growing tired of being confused with the famous actress. Of course, the only thing Harmony had in common with Maureen O'Hara was the fire in her belly and in her eyes. And Harmony was a much better name for a woman who made most of her living as a barroom singer and player of pianos and guitars.

She joined the group without invitation, saying she had not survived dozens of barroom brawls and taunts from drunks by being timid. Her ready smile and raucous outbursts of laughter seemed contradictory to the group, but she promised to reveal her qualifications when the time was right. She said her love for cattle, horses, and cowboys had been a bane and blessing all her life, especially her love for cowboys. Behind her back, folks said Harmony had been down the street and around the block. Harmony would not deny that. She looked older than her chronological mid-forties, but the miles of her life were not shown by lines in her face, but by the pain, sadness, and challenge in her eyes.

Most days, Harmony's coal-black hair fell across her shoulders in two braided pigtails secured with turquoise-studded leather bands to match the turquoise rings she wore on two fingers of each hand. She had dark skin and referred to herself as "The Singing Squaw" when she performed.

She had a few brushes with fame when she was bright and new. One song made it to the top forty on the country list. That led to singing in major venues in the Dallas-Fort Worth area, but Harmony admitted she let the sudden fame and riches go to her head. She wasted or gave away most of the new money to a host of cowboys and needy friends. And the fame was fleeting. Most things about her shouted irreverence, but she kept her deep and broad intelligence hidden. Like Abel, she brought a book to the meetings, was a prolific reader, painter, and aspiring writer.

Joe Henry Leathers sat in with the group once or twice most weeks, but he considered himself more of a listener than a participant. The others agreed. Not enough hurt in his past, they said. He occasionally brought Tee Jessup with him as a guest. The group fascinated Tee, but he mostly listened.

NINE

WHEN TEE FIRST SHOOK HANDS WITH ABEL Gunter, the older man's probing but sad eyes seemed to hold him more firmly than his hand. They stood together awkwardly outside the door to Tee's office. "Blaze does a few jobs around my place, but says you're a better hand with livestock. Would you be interested in helping me out occasionally?"

"If it's something I can do as well or better than the next man, I sure would." Tee hoped the work did not involve sheep, because he knew next to nothing about them except they ranked near the bottom on the livestock intelligence scale.

With each visit to Abel Gunter's Crimson River Ranch, Tee understood better why folks likened Abel to a prophet who lived high atop a mountain where people made the path to seek his counsel wide and deep. Abel did not live atop a mountain, of course. Just the opposite. He had lived in a one room shack while he built a small cabin with logs cut from local trees. The cabin and its roof were the same color as the trees and leaves that surrounded it.

On his first visit to the ranch, Tee figured he was lost when he came to what appeared to be a dead-end. As he looked for room to turn his pickup and trailer around, the log house seemed to beckon him as it peered out of the deep woods. The house sat scarcely high enough to keep it above the flood plain of the Red River.

Abel had once grown Bermuda grass all the way to the riverbed to sell as sod, but when the grass became too labor intensive, he discontinued it to concentrate on his cattle and sheep. The livestock were his family and they all had names. Tee was pleased to discover the number of sheep barely qualified as a flock.

Abel quickly measured Tee's abilities with cattle and left him alone when it was time for castration, dehorning, or branding. Abel found those things difficult to watch. He stayed inside when Tee hauled cattle to the sale, saying he dreamed about them for days after they went away.

The sheep were a different story. Abel preferred to tend to them himself. Sheepherder had been a derogatory term where Tee grew up. But Jubal was anxious to learn about sheep and cattle, and enjoyed working with Dawson the dog as they herded the sheep, separated the lambs from the ewes and guided them into pens where Abel treated them for flies, pests and diseases common to sheep. He called his treatment "anointing them with oil" and always quoted the 23rd Psalm to Jubal as he smeared his mysterious oil on their noses and heads. He coaxed Jubal into memorizing the psalm and explained what each line meant.

Tee laughed on the way home after a day's work on the ranch. "Never expected I would have a sheepherder for a son."

Jubal smiled. "I'm a cowboy who likes sheep." The boy grew silent after that.

Tee reached across the seat and poked his arm. "Whatcha thinkin' about?"

"Why does Abel sing those songs all the time?"

Tee laughed. "He told me they're his favorite hymns. Says singing *Amazing Grace* and *Farther Along* is like praying loud enough for God to hear. Says it helps him stay in constant touch with the Holy Spirit."

"I don't understand much about the Holy Spirit."

Tee kept his eyes on the road. "I don't understand much either, but we're both gonna learn."

"Do you know the words to those songs?"

Tee was a little embarrassed. "I know some, but not all. I like the chorus of *Farther Along* where it says, *Cheer up my brother; live in the sunshine, we'll understand it all by and by.* I thought *By and By* was the name of the hymn for a long time."

"Understand what?"

"The gist of the song, I think, is that there are things we humans will never understand until we're in heaven and Jesus explains them."

"What about *Amazing Grace*?"

Tee tried to sing, "I once was lost, but now am found; was blind, but now I see. That's about all I remember. Are you impressed?"

Jubal laughed. "I guess, but I can recite the 23rd Psalm and know what it means when he says that about anointing his head with oil. Do you?"

TEN

WHEELER PARKER SAT IN THE PASSENGER SEAT of the enclosed van in the hall of his thoroughbred barn and stables just inside the Texas side of the Oklahoma border. The smell of onions and fried grease mixed with stale human fear-sweat, urine and feces, was enough to make a fastidious man like Wheeler nauseous. The source of the smell, thirty illegal workers from Mexico and Central America, had unloaded into the barn hall and into various horse stalls a few minutes earlier.

It had rained on and off for several days and Wheeler worried he might have to house and feed this group longer than he wanted because their services would not be in demand until it dried enough to work in the fields. He could spread them out to the small hovels he constructed in the woods below the barn, but keeping them longer than a few days was dangerous.

After that, he would have to turn them over to another coyote for transport to other states. That meant his slice of the pie got a little thinner.

Thunder rolled and mixed with the strong pattering of rain and marble-size hail on the metal roof of the barn. Wheeler turned to the driver, whose name he did not know and did not want to know. "From the smell in here, I guess you fed this bunch."

The driver barely acknowledged the question. "Nope. They ate what they brought."

"And a lot of them didn't bring a bite. How the hell do you stand that smell all the way from the border? Why don't we take care of this in my office?"

The dark-skinned driver kept his eyes straight ahead. Wheeler wondered how an American got into the business of driving truckloads of wetbacks for thousands of miles. "It's worse because of the humidity. Besides, you never allowed me in your office before. Why start now?" The low spots and chug holes in the gravel parking lot filled with water and overflowed, making it look more like a lake.

It was true. Parker never allowed the coyote inside his office. But the smell tonight was worse. Wheeler tried not to think about the previous occupant of the seat he sat in. "Let's do this thing and get it over with before I puke."

The driver handed him an envelope and Wheeler satisfied himself it contained the money due for accepting thirty wetbacks. He started to open the door.

The nameless driver kept his eyes straight ahead. "You know Antonio Salinas?"

"Know the name. Never met the man. I understand he

provides safe passage across the Mexican border for coyotes like yourself."

"He owns a truck farm on the Mexican side. Transports produce all over Mexico, Central America and into the states. Big *hombre* in Mexico."

"So?"

"He has a bastard son he needs your help with."

"A son? Why me? I'm not in the babysitting business."

"Wants you to put him to work or find a place for him to work."

"No thanks. I don't hire many people here without papers. Calls attention to me and I obviously don't need attention. I keep a couple of stable hands who are wetbacks, but that's about it."

"He's legal. Born in Texas. The old man knocked up a *bracero* on his farm, brought her across the border to have the kid so it would be an anchor baby. Antonio let the boy use his name, gave him money, but never really claimed him, so his mama raised him."

"Neither here nor there to me. Can't do it."

The driver pointed at the envelope. "You might want to reconsider if you aim to keep that kind of payoff coming. Antonio can stop it. Besides, he's a big player with Rio Grande Construction. He's the reason you get a paycheck for doing basically nothing on the job site over by Riverby. Put the boy to work there."

Wheeler squirmed in his seat. He didn't like to be threatened. "What's in it for me?"

The driver chuckled. "A continued flow of easy money and the big *jefe's* everlasting gratitude."

"So why is he trying to get rid of the kid?"

"The boy is wild, gives the old man a hard time, brags about being the son of the *patrón*. Embarrasses Antonio in front of his wife and other kids. I understand he comes right out and demands his rightful share of the old man's money. Antonio says he's an ungrateful bastard."

"My guess is there's something you're not telling me. This kid's real trouble, ain't he?"

The driver almost nodded, but not quite. "The boy's had a few scrapes with the law. Needs a little breather. Thinks this will be a short stop on his way to Nashville. Fancies himself a country singer and ladies' man. He's a pretty boy."

"Sounds like trouble I don't need."

"I figured you might say that, so here's the straight deal. The boy is said to be an efficient and experienced coyote and drug mule. Antonio said if you help him he will increase your supply routes. Some of these illegals want to go deeper into the states. He's working on a route all the way to New York and up and down the eastern seaboard. Should quadruple what goes in your pocket."

"Quadruple? Are we talking drugs or workers? The drugs scare me more than the wetbacks."

"Think about it. Smuggling thirty smelly wetbacks takes a huge van that calls attention to you. The grass and powder you can fit into one fenderwell or spare tire will net you more than the thirty that rode here in this van."

"Jail time is in direct proportion to the payoff, too."

"It's mostly harmless grass. Expect it'll soon be legal, anyway. We'll be rich by then. Besides, how come you got cold feet all of a sudden? You already got a man who can keep you in different cars and a man who knows how to launder money."

"Our numbers man died. That's why I backed off."

"Find another one. You don't even have to tell him what you're doing. The other one didn't catch on, did he? The kid that's coming may be a little off, but he knows how to run drugs and keep the law off his tail. And he ain't afraid of anything or anybody."

"Say I agree. When will the boy show up and what's his name?"

"Angelino Salinas. Likes to be called Angel. Thinks it impresses the ladies. He's on his way now, I expect. He's coming whether you help or not. He'll be in a fancy fast car. Not sure what kind. You'll know him when you see him."

As the van pulled away and headed south, Wheeler Parker thumbed through his Rolodex mind and made a mental list of the people who owed him favors or money.

ELEVEN

THE DISTINCTIVE ARTISTRY OF TECUMSEH (Blaze) Blaisdell was evident in the ornate letters, *Tee Jessup, CPA,* carved into a rustic pine board that hung outside Tee's office at 200 Texas Street on the Riverby Square. News traveled fast last year when Esther brought the exam results, and Blaze carved it, stained it, and hung it as soon as he heard Tee passed the exam. For good luck, Tee tiptoed to tap the sign as he and Jubal arrived. He was embarrassed when he noticed a woman watching him. She sat on the iron bench between Joe Henry's law office and his, cradling a large purse as if it were a child.

The woman's voice was raspy, like she had been crying. "Mr. Jessup, I'm Wilda Waters. I used to work for Wesley Simpson. I know office hours don't start for a little bit, but I need to talk to you."

Tee recognized her name. He extended a hand and Jubal did the same. "Tee Jessup. This is my son Jubal."

Wilda's handshake was limp. Jubal's look said hungry and Tee sent him to Prigmore's for breakfast.

Wilda looked toward the locked door. "If I could maybe steal a minute of your time."

"Sure." Tee opened the door and motioned her in.

Wilda looked around the room as if arriving home from a long and weary trip. Tee tried to imagine what she thought about the changes he had made. When he purchased Wes Simpson's accounting business from Joe Henry, the office was abandoned and reeked of dust, rat urine and mildewed paper. Perfumed customers and the odor of perms from Verda's Four Forces Beauty Shop in the back occasionally overpowered the other smells. File folders and scraps of paper littered the tops of all surfaces, dust bunnies skittered about the pine floor partially covered with worn linoleum.

Now, the smells were gone, and the office, though still filled with paper and folders, had a semblance of order. The cheap metal desk and mismatched side chairs were still in use; the ten-key adding machine with the numbers worn off sat beside a desk-size electronic calculator; the plastic curtains that seemed better suited to a bathroom than an office now hung in the bathroom at Hurt Hill. File cabinets with some broken drawers remained, but Tee had added a new one.

The peeling wallpaper had been torn off the walls and most of the yellowed and water-stained sheetrock removed to expose antique brick and pine boards. Eighteen feet above, white paint still peeled from the stamped tin squares that covered the ceiling. The worn linoleum on the floor had been peeled away and the pine boards underneath varnished. Blaze installed temporary partitions to allow Tee and his clients a semblance of privacy for tax interviews. Blaze itched to make the whole thing over and Tee was trying to accumulate the money to buy the building from Joe Henry so he could turn Blaze's creative skills loose.

Wilda's eyes seemed to take in all the changes. "I like what you've done with this old office."

"Thanks. Mostly Blaze's work. Don't have coffee made yet. Can I offer you a cup or are you in a hurry?"

She turned and walked back to the little side room that served as file room and kitchenette. "I'll make it."

Before Tee could protest, the woman started spooning grounds. As the percolator perked, she used the time to walk around, scanning the room from floor to ceiling with wide eyes as they made small talk.

Tee smiled as she handed him a cup of coffee. He guessed her to be mid-fifties. Many clients had mentioned her. "Guess you know your way around here."

She stroked the wooden counter top as if it were a kitten. "Ought to. Worked here for nearly thirty years. Guess you're wondering why I came. I know I don't have an appointment, but I thought I might catch you before the real start of tax season. I need help with my taxes. My husband died last year and I'm not sure how to handle that."

Tee pointed to a chair in front of his desk. "Sure. Have a seat."

Wilda withdrew a folder from her large purse and laid it on his desk. Hers was a simple return and Tee completed it in a few minutes, grateful to start the day with an easy one. "Keep your seat and I'll make you a copy and type out an invoice."

"I can do that."

Tee laughed. "How much are you going to charge?"

Her face colored. "I meant copying the return, not preparing an invoice, but I can do that, too if you'll tell me the amount."

Within minutes, she paid in cash and stuffed her copy of the tax return and the IRS copy into her big purse. She stood in the middle of the room until the silence became awkward. "I wonder if you could come out to my car and help me with some boxes."

Tee hesitated a second. "Sure."

She opened the back door of a rusted Plymouth sedan and handed him a box filled with ledgers and folders. Three more sat on the seat.

Tee made three more trips before all the files were stacked on his work table. Wilda seemed at a loss for words as she ran her fingers over the tops of the post ledgers and journals as if caressing them. She started to cry.

Tee was confused and embarrassed. "So, tell me about the files."

"They're account ledgers for clients from back when Wes owned this business. General ledgers, cash disbursement and cash receipts journals. All of them are posted and in balance, by the way."

She clicked off titles as if running a ten-key adding machine as she laid a fingernail on the folders. "There are FUTA, SUTA, 941's, 943's, W-2's, and 1099's, and sales tax reports here. You know, all the quarterly and annual reports you have to file. About thirty small businesses. All the annual reports are done as well as the reports for the last quarter."

Tee wanted to look at the cheat sheet he kept in his lap

drawer to help him remember report acronyms. "So, why are you bringing them to me?"

"They're Wesley's old clients. I took them out of here when he died and you can go ahead and have me arrested for theft. I didn't think about anybody buying the business when I did it. I was out of a job and thought these people needed my help, but it was wrong and I know it. These clients rightfully belonged to Joe Henry after he bought out Wes and now to you."

"But you've been keeping their books and doing quarterly reports at your home since Wesley died?"

She nodded. "I owe you for all the fees I collected."

Tee tried to keep his inward smile from showing. "Shoot, I think I owe you a debt. By the time I got settled in here, those reports would have been late. I figured the write-up clients just left when Wes died." He knew better, but had not pressed the issue before and did not intend to now.

She stopped her handwringing and leaned forward. "You mean that?"

"Sure do. If you turn over these files to me, what do you aim to do then?"

"I got a job offer at the five-and-ten next door. Not what I want to do, but I have to support myself with my husband gone."

"Would you like to work here?"

"You'd hire somebody who tried to steal from you?"

"To tell the truth, I'm still new at this public accounting thing and I'll need a hand to get through tax season and the first quarter reports. What kinda money did Wes pay you and when can you start?"

Wilda laughed. "Is now too soon?"

They worked out the details of Wilda's pay and hours and she sat in the corner at the small desk she used for more than a quarter century, spinning like a small girl. "I have my own cushion. Can I bring it from home?"

"Don't see why not. I hope you type."

"Hundred words a minute without errors in high school."

"You'll do."

TWELVE

TEE OPENED THE DOOR TO HIS OFFICE AT TEN till eight, later than he intended. He barely made it to the coffee pot before Jack Prince walked in with a tentative smile on his face. Last year's experience with Prince had left Tee baffled. The man had visited his office two or three times a week during tax season with no clear purpose other than to talk and was repeating this year. Tee urged him to make an appointment to get his tax return done, but Jack didn't like making appointments.

Tee groaned inwardly as he extended his full cup toward Jack. "How about a cup? Wilda makes good coffee."

Prince shook his head. "I know she does. I've had many a cup in here with Wes."

"What can I do for you this morning?" As he eyed Prince's ever-present briefcase, Tee knew the true answer was nothing. Jack seemed to like hanging around an office where tax returns were prepared. Oh, he would always come up with a question or two to find a way to delve into the complexity of his personal finances. But Tee had heard the stories about Jack's business empire and his service as a bank director enough times to recite them from memory.

But Jack seemed to forget or maybe not realize Tee knew about his business failings, too. About how business had been off at the auto dealership for the last two years and cash flow was always a problem. Tee did not have the time or patience for the boasting today, but he could not take the chance of offending one of the most influential and wealthy citizens of Riverby.

He sighed as Jack opened the briefcase and asked him to look over a 1099 he received for oil royalties. "Will I have to pay taxes on that whole thing?"

Tee looked it over. A few bucks under three thousand. "You'll have to report it all on Schedule E, but it's not enough to cause you big problems."

"I don't think they sent me that much money. Will I get any deductions from it?"

Tee sighed but smiled wearily. "Same as last year. Depletion allowance. I think it's still twenty-two percent."

Prince sat in front of Tee's desk and started thumbing through the contents of his briefcase. "There was some other paperwork I was going to show you, but I can't seem to put my hands on it."

"Uh, huh."

Jack closed his briefcase, watched as Wilda came in and walked back to the beauty shop bathroom. "Listen, Tee. Have you or Wilda found any files around here on my business dealings? Wes used to do some consulting work for me in addition to my taxes."

"What kind of consulting?"

"Oh, various stuff. It was confidential. That's why I'm asking. Just wanted to make sure my privacy was protected."

"Haven't found a thing other than the normal stuff and you've seen all of that. Anything I see or Wilda sees is always kept completely private. I pride myself on confidentiality."

"Good to know."

"So, are you about ready to set an appointment to get your taxes done?"

"Not quite yet. You of all people know how complicated that is. Takes at least two boxes and two briefcases to get it all organized for you to go over."

It was true Jack brought in that much data last year, but most of his information could easily have been summarized in two or three folders. Jack wanted Tee to have to search through the boxes for what he needed. He was under the mistaken impression Tee would spread the word around Riverby about how complicated Jack's financial matters were. But Tee didn't.

On his way out, Jack pointed at the small calendar Wilda had fashioned for the front window ledge. She had converted a big tent-type desk calendar by pasting colored construction paper over the normal calendar sheets and numbered each page from one to seventy-five. She flipped the calendar each day before she put down her purse. Today's number was sixty.

"Sixty days till the deadline. We got plenty of time."

THIRTEEN

THE LUXURIOUS BLACK LEATHER DESK CHAIR dwarfed Jack Prince's small, delicate frame and contrasted sharply with his pale, sweating skin. The massive desk piled high with paperwork brought to mind a vision of Scrooge's clerk, Bob Cratchit. Unlike most people, Jack secretly relished the task of gathering information for filing his tax return. Perusing the records of the past year allowed him to revel in his accomplishments, to see the risks he took and how they paid off. Even the failures gave him chills as he saw how close he came to the edge of the cliff without falling off. Every success made him richer in money, every failure richer in wisdom. Though he never filed his return until he used at least one extension, he began gathering the data in early January because he found it so stimulating.

He kept his most important files in a two room shanty a block off the square. His tiny office building sat like an island on a large lot formerly occupied by cotton bales. The little building had served as an office for the abandoned gin across the street. It still looked like a cotton gin office from the outside, but the inside featured windowpane paneling, the best luxurious wall-to-wall shag carpet, central air and heat. Jack worked out of several offices: one for his real estate holdings, one for his automobile dealership, one for his hardware store. But the tiny shanty was his and his alone—no secretary, no employees. Nobody got to see his personal records, not even his wife.

It was an hour past most normal people's quitting time when he finished, but Jack Prince was not normal people. He never craved the security and comfort most people seemed to enjoy at home. He wanted excitement. He needed to be in the game, not a spectator. No couch and television for him.

He left the office and drove around the square in Riverby, slowing at each building he owned. Jack Prince liked to think of his rental income in annual figures. Monthly sums seemed paltry. Barbecue Shack—twenty-one hundred—check. Glamour Girl Beauty Salon—twenty-four hundred—check. Butane/propane store—three thousand—check. His completed journey around the square and the two blocks off the square clicked off almost fifteen thousand in annual income. But he stopped at the behemoth he created by purchasing four adjoining buildings that became vacant.

Carpenters on his payroll for more than nine months wearily packed their tools to call it a day. The sight so depressed him he didn't stop to get a progress report. It also soured him on the usual pleasure of driving out in the country to see the land he planned to develop or the farms he leased to others.

Preparing for his tax return and managing his other investments had kept him from his GM dealership for more than a week, so he decided to stop before going home and surrendering to his wife's intrusive questions. Of course, a visit to the dealership was no longer necessary since son Kyle assumed a managerial role there. He took a year to carefully train his son, felt confident in his able management, and had humbled himself, sacrificed his earned rewards by stepping aside to keep from intimidating the boy. He was glad to see everyone had left for the day when he parked next to a lineup of new cars and trucks.

It was hard to repress the glee he felt when he saw the mound of paperwork wanting his attention and approval in his desk in-tray and overflowing beside it. Son Kyle might be filled with youthful vigor, but Jack was gratified to see some things still needed the old man's personal touch. But the pink telephone slips marked urgent disturbed him, especially when he saw they were from Pinky Hartwell, his representative for General Motors Acceptance Corporation, the financing arm of General Motors. Prince Chevrolet's entire new car inventory was on a floor plan with GMAC, meaning Jack didn't own a single new car. When one sold, the floor plan balance had to be reduced accordingly.

He thumbed through four messages over the last four days from Pinky, but knew it was too late to return the calls today. Unlike himself, Pinky was a slave to the clock and left promptly at five. The calls would have to wait until tomorrow. He waded through the other paperwork before going home to Roxie. He dreaded laying his soft body next to his lithe, athletic wife, fresh from tennis, softball, volleyball or her daily three-mile sprint.

He slipped quietly out of bed the next morning after a sleepless night. Roxie's early morning vigor made him tired, so he showered in the guest bathroom, skipped his usual coffee, and closed the door softly behind him. He was the first arrival at Prince Chevrolet. He locked his office door, shuffled papers and stared at the walls until regular office hours began at GMAC.

Pinky's friendly, cheerful voice relaxed him. "How are things, old buddy?"

"Fine, mighty fine. Just returning your calls from the last four days. Sorry I wasn't here when you called and I got in too late last night to call you back. What's up?"

"Well, we did our usual audit this month and I was a little worried about four units on your lot that were sold and applications for titles made without payment to us."

Jack leaned forward in his swivel desk chair, ran a hand through his hair. "What four units?"

"All compacts." Pinky rattled off the VIN numbers.

"I've been out a few days, Pinky. I'll take care of this right away. How much money are we talking here?"

"A little over twelve grand. You should have the paperwork. You haven't seen it?"

Jack was waiting when son Kyle arrived around ten. Jack stood and handed him the list of VIN's. "Why are you getting here so late and why did you not send in floor plan payments on four cars?"

Kyle stood eye level with his father, a younger duplicate of the older man with more hair. "We ran a little short on cash last month. Sales were down, and we had some maintenance expenses in the shop. There were some travel expenses, too."

Jack shook his head. "You mean like that useless convention in Vegas? How much did you lose?"

Kyle did not answer.

"So what's our bank balance?"

"I don't know. Have to check."

Jack chewed on the end of a ballpoint pen until Kyle returned. "Bank says we got about eleven hundred."

Jack shook his head. "What's the reconciled balance?"

"What's reconciled mean? Figured we got just what the bank says we got."

"This won't do. Close the door behind you when you leave and don't go far. We need to talk about this later."

He drove back to the gin lot office, pulled a phone from a wooden box beside his desk, and dialed a private number he knew by heart. Wheeler Parker answered on the first ring. When silence greeted him, he knew who was calling. "Jack. How much you need this time?"

Jack breathed deeply. "Fifteen thousand." He had to have twelve, but a little extra would clear up a few other niggling matters.

"Whoa. That's a right smart above the usual. You know how much you'll have to wash to net that?"

Jack was insulted. "I got enough sense to figure that. I can do it if I have a couple of weeks to get it done."

"How soon you gotta have it?"

"Today, tomorrow at the latest."

"You can't keep doing this, Jack. I told you at least a dozen times I need at least forty-eight hours."

Silence.

"You still got the car we left last time?"

"Still here."

"Still got a clean title?"

Jack hesitated a few seconds. "Yes."

"I better not find out you hocked that car."

"The title's still clean, but I still don't understand the car swaps. And I don't like them."

"It's simply a precaution. Makes the trail go cold in case anybody picks up a license plate number at a bad time. Our boy will drive up at about eight tomorrow night in a black Barracuda. He'll leave you the black car and you give him the keys to yours. Title, registration in the car pockets exactly like before. You sell it cheap as soon as you can and deposit the money like always. Goods will be in the trunk."

Jack's free hand shook. "Goods? I told you I can't have anything to do with drugs. Don't wanna see 'em, don't wanna touch 'em."

"Who said anything about drugs? Don't say that word to me, especially over the phone. The money, Jack—the money. You take your share and launder the rest. You know the drill. No huge deposits, no round numbers, spread them out by days and do it in at least three accounts. I'll send you bills like before and you make up some of your own and then pay with business checks."

Jack's hands shook as he hung up the phone. *Like before? Wes Simpson always handled those details. Can I handle it again without him? What if I leave a trail?*

FOURTEEN

AFTER DOING FIFTY RETURNS IN TWO WEEKS without her, Tee looked forward to his first tax appointment after hiring Wilda. She brought an air of professionalism missing during his first tax season. Answering the phone, making appointments, and filing and retrieving files by himself interrupted tax sessions and irritated some clients. And his next client was not a man to irritate. Tee was honored when Wheeler Parker called for an appointment. He had never officially met the man he had heard much about.

Parker owned the Wheelhouse, a night club less than a mile across the Red River in Oklahoma, as well as a nearby liquor store that thrived on business from the dry towns on the Texas side. He also owned a horse stable and training facility Tee had not seen. Harmony O'Hara worked in his club and helped occasionally with his horses. Wheeler was rumored to gamble, bootleg, and book a few bets on both sides of the state line. Folks joked his mother had known he would be a wheeler-dealer when she named him. He had not disappointed.

Tee stood to greet him when he walked in, but Wheeler laid a Hartmann alligator briefcase on the table and went directly to Wilda. Gave her a warm hug. Tee stared at the briefcase and speculated about its cost. At least two hundred, maybe more, he figured. Parker was not what Tee imagined. Dark complexion, average height, wide across the shoulders, he wore spectacles suitable for an accountant and an expensive suit and tie.

He was gregarious and seemed genuinely interested in every word Wilda uttered. Parker was near her age, and Wilda seemed infatuated with the handsome man. Her solicitousness toward Parker wore a little thin as Tee was forced to stand idle during their small talk.

Tee liked to guide first-time clients through their interviews, but Wheeler clearly liked to be in charge. He removed seven folders from his briefcase and laid them on Tee's desk. He picked up the top folder. "My return is in this one. Had a fellow over in Bonham prepare it for the last two years, but there's something about it I don't think is right. Hope you can put your finger on it."

Before Tee could respond, Parker picked up the other six folders. "These are returns for some of my employees, mostly Mexicans. First returns to file in the USA for them." Wheeler stood and turned to leave.

Tee leaned back. "You got a sec to let me look over these in case I have questions?"

Parker's demeanor changed from friendly to impatient and he remained standing. "The Mexicans' paperwork is simple.

Just W-2's. They should give you names, addresses and social security numbers. Easy stuff. Names of dependents are written on slips of paper. They all got a passel of kids."

Tee flipped through them. "They all have the same address."

"Yeah. That's one of my rent properties."

"Six families, all with a passel of kids. They all live in one house?"

"It's an apartment building."

"No separate numbers on the apartments?"

Parker glanced at the door. "You ask a lot of questions."

Tee allowed a second or two to digest what seemed to be an attitude turned condescending. He felt the embers in his gut start to glow and tried to cool them. "That's what I do when I prepare tax returns. Can't expect to do one without asking questions. So, how about child care? That might save taxes."

"No child care. Wives stay with the kids or kids go to work with the whole family."

There was tense silence while Tee opened the other folder. "I see your return for this year has already been prepared."

"Weren't you listening when I told you a fellow over in Bonham did it?"

Tee's repressed anger came to the surface. "You said he prepared the last two years. Didn't say he prepared this one. And the preparer's line has been blacked out."

"Well, yes I did, but have it your way."

Tee figured Wilda sensed the rising tension when their voices rose, knew he was overreacting, but could not seem to stop himself. "My point is, I'll have to charge you to look over the return and it's unlikely I'll find anything. Probably a waste of money."

"My money to waste. Trust me, there's something wrong with that return. No way I can owe that much."

"Has it already been filed?"

"Hell, no. Why would I file it and then get you to look at it?"

"Ever hear of a 1040X? You can amend a return already filed."

Tee picked up the other six folders again. "And the Mexicans all having the same address might throw up a flag at the IRS."

"Let me worry about that."

"I'll need five prior years of returns."

"You didn't find those in Wes Simpson's files?"

Tee scratched his head. "I looked. Didn't find a folder for you."

"Why do you need that far back?"

Tee took a deep breath. "All kinds of reasons. You might qualify for income averaging, might have a net operating loss carryover, unused investment credit. Might even find something this year I can use to recapture taxes you paid in prior years."

Tee stood, feeling good about rattling off a list of reasons. They stared at each other a few seconds until Parker stepped out of the mini-office and looked toward Wilda as if he needed her help. "Be a lot of trouble, but I will either bring 'em by one day next week or send somebody with 'em. I got a busy week."

Tee glanced at the deadline calendar. Fifty-four.

FIFTEEN

A YOUNG MEXICAN WAITED AT TEE'S OFFICE door the next morning, holding the alligator briefcase. Tee nodded toward it and smiled. "Bet I know who sent you."

The young Mexican did not return the smile. "Nobody sends me anywhere. I go where I please."

Tee studied the man. Could be twenty or could be as old as himself. He considered the attitude and how to respond, knew waiting gave him an advantage. "Then what are you doing standing in front of my office door?"

"You Yessup?"

It was too early in the morning for the tone. "Who wants to know?"

The man's long hair was anointed with a liberal dose of oil and combed back into a ponytail that hung to his waist, giving him the look of a Comanche warrior. His surly face had strong, chiseled features and he stared at Tee with black, probing, angry eyes. Had it not been for the oily hair and surly attitude, one could have seen him as unusually handsome. But Tee found the hostility and arrogance repulsive. Plus, a cloying smell clinging to the man triggered Tee's gag reflex—maybe a mixture of women's cologne and overripe fruit of some kind. It also brought forth an unpleasant memory Tee could not identify.

"Name's Angel Salinas."

"Angel? Really?"

His eyes narrowed. "*Si*, Angelino." He spoke the name as if Tee should pay homage, tapped the briefcase with his free hand as if it contained gold. "Old Man Parker said to give what's inside only to Yessup, so I ask again...you Yessup?"

Tee looked around to see if anyone was watching. He was embarrassed for himself, and worried that the anger he felt inside showed. He had already taken Jubal to school and was pleased he wasn't there. He took a deep breath to try to repress his overreaction, but could not bring himself to submit to such surly behavior. "Look, I need to get to work. Move aside."

Salinas tapped the briefcase again. "I'll ask you once more. You Yessup or not?"

"No, I'm not Yessup. My name is Jessup."

Angel jerked as if he might strike Tee. "How do I know that?"

"Why do I need to prove it? How do I know your name is Angel?"

The man's face darkened. "When I go back and tell Old Man Parker you wouldn't let me deliver what I came to deliver, you will have much regret."

Tee opened and closed his right fist. He tried to think of Jubal. The boy had seen his rage come out before and he didn't want to lose control again. He produced a key and held it in Angel's face, stared and waited.

The Mexican smirked. "You gonna open the door or not?"

"Not as long as you're standing in the way. For all I know, you got a gun inside that fancy briefcase and came here to rob us."

"You think all of us are robbers, don't you?"

"You need to go on back and tell Wheeler Parker to send somebody with manners next time. Or maybe come himself."

Salinas clinched his teeth as his free hand hovered over his back pocket. Tee braced himself. He had seen the outline of a switchblade there. He knew he had let it go on too long, but just couldn't seem to stop himself. "So, you gonna pull that blade I saw in your pocket or you just gonna stand there and drool?"

Salinas looked toward the square and saw people starting to mill. Wilda parked and walked toward them. He seemed disappointed when she approached. He dropped the briefcase on the ground, clicked it open and handed Tee the files, all completely enclosed in a tote bag covered with tape.

"You're lucky this time, *gringo*. Next time, I'll gut you like a catfish." He closed the case and walked away.

Wilda stared at Tee's face with alarm. "What happened? Who was that?"

"Your hero's errand boy."

"Your face is red. And what's that smell? Smells like spoiled pumpkins."

Tee dropped the taped folders on his desk and saw Wheeler Parker's note. *If this tape has been disturbed, call me at once.*

A week later, Jubal snoozed on the vinyl couch Tee bought at a garage sale. Tee looked forward to some sack time, but knew if he stopped in the middle of preparing one of the most complicated tax returns he had ever done, he would lose much of what he accomplished during a day's worth of research and preparation. He made a silent vow to finish before going home.

The return was Wheeler Parker's, and Tee felt he was onto something with it, something big. When he finished, he leaned back in his chair and put his hands behind his head. He had to check it over again, but if he was right, Wheeler Parker would be pleased. But even without checking, Tee was about as sure as sure could be. He stood, raised both fists in the air and silently mouthed a big Yes. The big man would eat his words. He wrote a note on Wilda's desk asking her to make an appointment for Parker to come in as soon as possible. The deadline calendar said forty-six.

SIXTEEN

JACK PRINCE WATCHED FROM THE DARK showroom as a black Barracuda pulled into the parking lot, around the building and into the open service bay. Jack hurried to the shop and pressed the button to close the bay door. Angelino Salinas jumped out of the car. "Why you close the door?"

The face was new to Jack. "You're new. I always close the door. Where's the old man who usually comes?"

"He ain't the man anymore. Too slow."

Jack pointed toward a red Camaro parked on the lift racks. "Keys are in it. You need to get in it and go right now."

Angelino studied the red car. "The car, she's red. You no gotta black one?"

"What's wrong with red?"

"She'll get attention."

"And you think that black one doesn't? I took a tan Caprice in trade today. You'd be smarter to take it."

Angelino curled his lip. "Too slow. Need something that can move. You know what I mean, man?"

Jack sneered and pointed toward the Camaro. When Angelino got behind the wheel, Jack opened the service bay door. Satisfied with what he saw, Angelino got out of the Camaro, walked to the Barracuda, opened the trunk, and tossed the Barracuda keys to Jack.

Jack gasped and clutched his neck when he saw white powder and small leavings of what could have been tobacco, but was likely marijuana, scattered around the outside of six ice chests. The black satchel he expected sat beside the chests. "What the hell do you think you're doing?"

Angelino picked up two chests and carried them to the Camaro. He started back for two more before answering. "Whatchu think, man? That I'm gonna leave this cargo with you?"

Jack rushed to close the bay door. "You are not ever, and I mean ever, supposed to bring any of that poison in here. I don't want anything to do with it, and I don't want to see it. Did Mr. Parker not tell you that?"

Angelino shrugged. "What difference does it make, homie? Hold your horses for a few more seconds and I'll take it off your hands." He removed the last chest, and closed the trunk.

Jack brushed his hands as if ridding himself of a deadly toxin. He made a pushing motion with both hands toward the door. "Get it out of here. Now."

"Okay, man. Take it easy." He put the last chest in the Camaro's trunk and closed it. "Open the door."

Angelino made the tires squeal as he backed out and left

a trail of rubber on the parking lot outside. Jack almost faint-
ed with anger and fear that people had heard and would ask
him about it. He closed the door. He could see no trail left by
the chests, but swept anyway. He vacuumed the Barracuda's
trunk, removed the satchel, and walked to his office.

In his locked dealership office, he counted the stacks of
various denominations. Though he considered his worth to
be ten times greater than the seventy-five thousand he was
looking at, it always gave him a thrill to see that much cash,
but sad he could only keep a small portion.

He trembled when he thought about what he had to do in
the next few days to earn it. Wes Simpson had typed articles
of incorporation and obtained employer identification numbers for corporations with no assets other than the cash that
flowed through them, no real purpose other than as washing machines for illicit money. Wes also showed him how to
deposit cash and write checks out of accounts to launder it
and make it appear legitimate. But now Wes was dead, and it
seemed to Jack they needed new corporations, new numbers,
so the old trails could grow cold.

With trembling hands, Jack completed six deposit slips
for six accounts in three banks for varying amounts totaling
twenty-two thousand, placed three thousand in his pocket to
hide in the gin office safe. He wrote six checks out of each account totaling twenty thousand to the dealership. Tomorrow,
he would deposit the first cash in two accounts at Farmers and
Merchants Bank, travel to Bonham to make cash deposits in
two more accounts at a second bank, then return to make
the final deposits in the Red River State Bank in Riverby. He
would then deposit the checks on separate deposit slips to the

dealership account and write a check to GMAC. He would call Pinky and tell him the check to pay for the cars sold out of trust was on its way.

In a week or so, invoices would arrive from various locations from various companies for unspecified materials and services that would complete the washing of the total amount. Jack would pay some from the dealership and some from the other shell corporations where the money was deposited based on the descriptions on the invoices, then transfer funds to bring his account back into the black. Then he had to find out from his son what happened that made all this necessary. It all made him nauseous. He went to his gin lot office to lie down.

SEVENTEEN

COOPER NEWMAN WATCHED WITH SOME satisfaction as Jack Prince walked to the teller window. Here was a man more nervous than himself. If he had not known him, Prince's suspicious behavior would have alarmed Cooper enough to call the sheriff on suspicion of a bank robbery. But he did know Jack Prince, and he thought he had figured out what he had been doing. On at least three prior occasions Cooper had tracked, Prince deposited large amounts of cash, but slightly under the amount that would trigger a report to the IRS.

Cooper considered himself to be a master of subterfuge and thus took pride in his ability to detect it in others. He wondered why an automobile dealership would deal in large quantities of cash. And most of the cash went into other accounts, not Jack's three dealership accounts. When he investigated, he found little activity in the accounts receiving

97

the funds. Cash in—then a few days later, checks written to take it out. The accounts had no physical addresses, only post office box numbers. He didn't recognize the payee names on the checks or the signatories on the accounts. And the signatures on the checks were illegible.

Jack Prince was next at the teller window when he felt the bank president's breath on his neck and a hand on his shoulder. Cooper Newman was almost a foot taller. "Why don't you come on back to my office, Jack? We can do your transactions in a little more private environment."

Jack moved the zipper to the bank bag back and forth and wished he had locked it. "Appreciate it, Cooper, but all I have is the daily deposit for the dealership. This young lady has done it so often she knows what to do without me saying a word." Jack was grateful he had the foresight to bring his daily legitimate deposit. But Cooper put his huge arm across Jack's sparse shoulders and guided him to his office.

Cooper's office walls were glass, but he had recently installed blinds and pulled them closed after ushering Jack to a chair across from his big desk. Jack squirmed. "I hate to take up your time with a simple deposit, Cooper. Besides, I got a man coming to look at a rent property in a few minutes and another one to look at a car right after. What did you want to talk about?"

Cooper sat in his black leather executive chair the bank bought at the same time as the venetian blinds. "You know that crazy fellow who lives out on the old Willard Dunn place? Stays in the old picker shack. Name's Clayton Dupree."

"Heard about him. Don't know him. Why?"

"Well, I can't reveal confidential information about bank

customers, but I've been running checks on suspicious cash transactions lately. If we have irregularities, I'd rather catch 'em instead of the bank auditors. Bank examiners questioned a few things last time they were here. Asked me to be on the lookout."

Jack felt a little bead of sweat run down the middle of his back. "So what do you watch for? And what did this fellow you're talking about do exactly?"

"Made some bank transactions to accounts that look like they might be bogus. Fake, you know."

"Why would he do that?"

"Who knows? Maybe he's hiding money from the IRS. Maybe it's ill-gotten gains."

Cooper leaned forward, put on his best conspiratorial expression, looked around the room as if he expected to find somebody watching. "You can't say anything, but the man has more safe deposit boxes than the law allows and even locked file cabinets back in our vault."

Jack momentarily forgot his own troubles with this revelation, began thinking about how he could meet this man who lived alone in a shack, possibly entice him into buying a piece of real estate or a new car. "You reckon they're full of cash?"

Cooper slid a copy of a deposit slip for $9,238.29 across his desk. "Speaking of cash, I understand you made this deposit. Am I right?"

Jack glanced at the deposit slip as if it were a coiled snake. "Who can remember things that happened that long ago? Look, Cooper. As you probably don't know, I do business with a lot of used car dealers, renters and contractors. I don't recognize that one."

Cooper opened his middle desk drawer and withdrew two more deposit slips, waved them in the air. He slid them across the desk. "How about these?"

Jack Prince stood. "What is this, some type of interrogation? What are you getting at?"

Cooper smiled and pressed both hands, palms up, against the air. "Calm down, Jack. We can work this out."

Jack's voice quivered. "Work what out? I don't know what you're talking about."

"They taught us in banking school about laundering money. You know what that is?"

Jack sat back in his chair as if he had been struck. "I have no idea."

"It's washing dirty money, usually cash, to make it clean. You know, taking it through several washing machines, various businesses and bank accounts, and then using it to pay legitimate bills. That makes it clean…and legal to spend on legitimate things. And does away with the trail, supposedly."

"You're not suggesting…"

"Keep calm, Jack. Of course I'm not suggesting anything of the sort. But if someone launders money, they usually take a hefty percentage for the job. Say a quarter. I'd be willing to settle for five percent in order to remove any suspicion this money might be illegal."

Silence. Jack was too shocked to speak.

Cooper knew he had hit home. "A banker can be very helpful in these situations. In fact, he's almost essential over the long term. And five percent is a pittance."

"Say I knew what you were talking about. How would that work exactly?"

Cooper pointed at the bank bag. "Say for example, if you had ten thousand cash in that bag, you would just hold out five one-hundred-dollar bills in a separate bank bag. Bring both bags in to me. I'll make the deposits after lobby hours and keep the bag with the five percent. Take a load off of you, wouldn't it? And I can get you plenty of bank bags, complete with locks. I even have some inactive accounts we can use."

Jack Prince's voice quivered. "Have you ever heard of a consortium, Cooper?"

EIGHTEEN

TEE ROCKED ON THE PORCH, LISTENED TO Jubal's self-talk through his bedroom window, his humming and singing, tossing and turning, and questions whispered through the screen until he heard the boy's breathing become rhythmic, blending with the call of whippoorwills and the chirping of tree frogs.

Tee crept off the porch and walked to the '57 Chevy pickup that had belonged to his father and refurbished by Father Bob. He carefully lifted the wooden box out of the bed. The pine box was made to look primitive-but-sturdy with wrought iron hinges, hasps and rope handles, the kind one might have found in a prospector's cabin or slung across his mule a hundred years earlier. *Jack Daniel's* was printed on the front with *Old No. 7* in a circle logo underneath.

He wanted the box for the way it looked, and also for what

it represented—a client's respect and gratitude. The box was a gift from Wheeler Parker. Tee had been reluctant to examine his already-prepared federal tax return and his Oklahoma state return, figuring he would have to charge for time that yielded no benefit. But Tee got lucky. He found only one missed deduction, and that didn't amount to much. But a review of his prior years' returns led Tee to ask Wheeler a few questions that turned a three-thousand-dollar liability into a four-thousand-dollar refund because of a net operating loss carry-forward and investment credit not taken in a prior year. The seven-thousand-dollar turnaround was a princely sum to Tee, but Wheeler was more excited about having his suspicions confirmed. A man who relied heavily on instinct, he did not know what was wrong, but knew something had to be.

The day after their meeting to discuss the results, Wheeler Parker arrived with the gift—a case of aged Old No. 7 whiskey in this vintage collector box. He also peeled off seven hundreds—ten percent of what Tee saved him. He stuffed them into an envelope he took from Tee's desk. Tee reluctantly refused both, stating he had been well-paid. Besides, he was unclear whether professional ethics rules for CPAs allowed him to receive the box and was almost certain he could not accept a gift of cash based on a percentage of a client's refund. It seemed like a silly rule, but it was still a rule.

His still-new CPA certificate had been hard to come by, and he couldn't risk losing it. Wheeler left with the box and the envelope filled with hundreds, but Tee found the box in the seat of his pickup later that night. Wheeler was already across the state line, so he decided to wait until tax season ended to deal with the problem. Tee liked the box, plus he didn't want to get on the wrong side of Wheeler Parker by refusing it twice. Not yet, anyway.

He opened the hasp and found a note on parchment explaining the box was a replica of a Tennessee Volunteer Chest.

> Tennessee men who responded to General Zachary (Rough and Ready) Taylor in the Mexican War of 1846 used boxes like these to carry their beans and bacon, their powder-and-ball paper cartridges, their stores, supplies, and personal effects. Slung from pack saddles, the boxes saw duty in the Civil War, Spanish-American War, and both World Wars as munitions carriers.

Stuffed between the bottles, Tee found the envelope with the seven hundreds.

He was afraid not to return the hundreds, but decided he wanted the box. His great-great-grandfather fought in that Mexican War and his great-grandfather and three uncles in the Civil War. He saw the box as a symbol of his growing credibility as a man who knew or was at least learning his way around tax laws and regulations. He needed the money and had no ethical or moral scruples against taking it, but couldn't take the risk. And his instincts told him not to trust Wheeler Parker.

He pulled one bottle out of the Volunteer Chest and left the box sitting on the kitchen table. On the porch, he turned a nail keg upside down and set the unopened bottle of Jack Daniel's and two glasses on it.

He smiled when he looked at the bottle and two glasses, wondered why he brought two. Esther was long gone, and there was nobody else to drink with him. He put his hand on the cap of the bottle, but couldn't bring himself to turn it. The smell of whiskey had made him nauseous since the day he found the bottle of Jim Beam near where his brother and his horse died and he was almost killed.

Tee had sat on the old porch or in the tabernacle hall almost every night for more than a year, waiting for head-lights to come down that lonesome road and up Hurt Hill. He wasn't exactly lonely, just more or less hungry for a messenger, human or spirit, to come to Hurt Hill and bring a change to his life. It seemed to Tee he was due something better. He added to his record collection when he could, always selecting sad songs. He worried that too many of them made him cry, especially the songs about lost loves, brothers, and mamas and daddies. He knew the words to one of John Denver's songs by heart. Denver seemed to have gone into his brain and pulled out his thoughts.

> I'm sorry things ain't what they used to be
> But more than anything else
> I'm sorry for myself
> 'Cause you're not here with me . . .
> But they all know I'm crying
> And I can't sleep at night
> They all know I'm dying down deep inside

He knew he wasn't supposed to cry over the words to a song, but, more and more, he found tears running down his cheeks when it and others played. Losing all his family except Jubal left him feeling cheated, sorry for himself. But crying over sad songs was better than the anxiety that came with visions of himself with a baseball bat and Ford Donovan on his knees in front of him.

But tonight was different. With his first tax season under his belt and a good start to his second, a satisfying feeling of accomplishment washed over him. He allowed himself to reflect on what he accomplished in a little over a year in his new home. He still couldn't believe people addressed as "doctor" asked him for advice and actually listened when he gave it. Local medical doctors as well as professors with PhDs from nearby Red River College found their way to his quaint office in downtown Riverby.

And it was a good thing the second tax season was here. He had enough money in the bank to last a few months, but wondered how he and Jubal would have survived without cowboy day work. He was about to go inside when he saw what looked like a flashlight by Moccasin Creek Bridge. Tee watched the light flicker through the first leaves of spring until he could see it was a car or pickup, not a flashlight.

He waited with curiosity, expecting the car to cross the rails and head across Panther Crossing, away from his hill. The car lights bathed the old trestle as the familiar clatter of an approaching train and its whistle seemed to be a cry for forgiveness and to announce the arrival of whoever was coming up the hill.

When the lights did not turn to cross the tracks, Tee straightened in anticipation of a visitor, turned the nail keg over and put the bottle and glasses inside. Before he recognized Cooper Newman's new '75 Chevrolet pickup, the banker stepped out and stood on the grave in Tee's yard.

Dressed in full cowboy regalia, complete with a new hat

and boots, all in the latest style, Cooper stumbled and waved like a clown might wave to a circus audience. The hat was creased properly and looked like at least a 10X to Tee. He closed Jubal's window, hoped he was sound asleep. Cooper Newman was a large man with what Tee saw as an entitled look about him—entitled to respect because he was tall, dark, handsome, and charismatic. But through clients, Tee learned that Cooper, first in line when God handed out good looks, was way back when He handed out superior intelligence and business instincts.

Through tax interviews with clients and in helping them with bank loan applications and financial statements, Tee learned Cooper was a bank president who had little notion of how banking worked. Looks and charisma had sabotaged him into a job that depressed him because he didn't know how to do it. Clerks, tellers, and one junior loan officer handled the technical details at Farmers and Merchants Bank while Cooper hobnobbed, the only real skill he seemed to possess. And rumors were circulating the bank was in trouble and Cooper had a drinking problem. Tee hoped that was not true. Cooper had sent him many referrals and he wanted him as a friend. Cooper even invited him to a big barbecue to celebrate his new ranch. Tee was impressed with the ranch, especially with the rolling hay and grain feeders adorned with the name of the ranch.

His pickup had a double gun rack behind the front seat that always held two expensive-looking rifles. And the rifles in the racks varied from week to week. Cooper pulled one from its rack as he stepped out. He held the rifle over one shoulder and stopped at the first porch step. He put a flat hand over his eyes as if shielding them from the sun that had set hours earlier. "Permission to enter the porch, sir." His speech was slightly slurred.

"Permission granted. Unless you're aimin' to shoot me, that is." Tee returned the salute and pointed toward a second rickety cane rocker, wondered if it would hold Newman's large frame.

"Never know when a coyote or skunk might run across the yard while we're visiting." Cooper tested the rocker by dropping instead of sitting. "Thought I would run out and see if you're still working night and day till deadline day again this year. Hardly saw you last year from January to May."

Tee laughed. "I think I may be a recluse at heart. I've done hard labor and long hours on a ranch most of my life, but it never taxed my brain or my butt like running this little business has."

"From what I hear, it's paid off. I've heard several people brag on you. They like to talk about that slogan of yours. What was it again?"

Tee shook his head. "Not sure what you mean."

"You know, something you say when a question stumps you."

Tee chuckled. "That happens a lot. You probably mean, I don't know the answer now, but I will by tomorrow morning."

"That's it. People were impressed with that. The honesty. Want you to know I sent as many customers your way as I could."

"I know that and I appreciate it. Need all the help I can get."

"You need any money to expand, you know where to come."

"Might take you up on that."

Cooper gestured toward the house and its surroundings. "When you get ready to get out of this dump, I might could find you a house in town and loan you the money to buy it. Man in your position has got to keep up appearances."

"Never can tell." Tee ignored the disparagement of the place he had grown comfortable with, wondered how Joe Henry would respond to his house being called a dump.

"Say, Tee, don't suppose you got any good bourbon around here."

Tee smelled liquor from the minute Cooper stepped out of his pickup and the smell followed him all the way to the porch. "Sorry, no. Can't afford good bourbon and it doesn't agree with me, anyway." He decided not to mention the Jack Daniel's. He wondered if Wheeler Parker bragged about giving the whiskey and the wooden chest to Tee. Probably spread it all over town.

"How about a Dr Pepper? I got some of those sugarcane ones from Dublin."

"Sounds good."

Tee went into the kitchen and returned with two of the hard-to-come-by Dr Peppers. They rocked and sipped while Cooper seemed to struggle with why he had come so far out so late at night. Finally, he stopped his nervous rocking and turned toward Tee.

"Listen, Tee. I know Blaze is your client."

Tee's antenna went up and he didn't answer. He was new at this, and likely had an exaggerated notion of client confidentiality. Blaze was a good man with his hands who might be called a creative genius, but he was terrible with money. He hoped he wasn't in trouble with the bank.

Cooper pressed. "I know because he told me. Said you helped him with paperwork he needed to renew a loan with my bank. That paperwork saved his ass and mine."

Tee was relieved. "Yeah, I've helped him with loan paperwork and his taxes."

"Well, listen, I don't want to bore you with the details, but me and a couple of other old boys are putting together this little consortium, see?" He paused and stared into Tee's eyes for emphasis. "And I mean these guys are the real thing—movers and shakers."

"And what's this consortium gonna do?"

"Well, it's already formed, but you're being invited in. We aim to keep our options open, and feel like we can make this little town really take off. First thing is to buy some real estate we have our eye on."

"Where?"

"One of our guys has a few contacts in Washington, and word is there's gonna be some federal money spent around here, that we're gonna get ourselves a big government lake. We aim to buy that little motel out on the edge of town. It's rundown and about to go under. Then there's a couple of restaurants we think might be bought cheap before folks find out what's coming. Maybe even build us some apartments or cabins and some storage buildings for lake tourists sure to come. Plus, I'm usually the first one to know when a property or business is facing disclosure. We figure we can swoop in and save the day."

Tee had heard the rumors about the federal money, the lake, and the troubles at the motel. He was still surprised at the things clients had to share in order to get their tax returns prepared. But he figured if he knew, several others did, too. "Really? Heard a few things about the lake, but no details."

Cooper took another swig from his Dr Pepper. "Well, now, if I was to tell you what our connected guy told me, I'd have to kill you. He's on a first name basis with our congressman and both senators. And we need to keep this hush-hush. Word gets out; the real estate we're talking about will skyrocket before we can get our hands on it."

"So what's this got to do with Blaze ... or me?"

"We want both of you in the group. We all know you're pretty new in town, but we've seen enough to know you're all right."

"Appreciate that. What's the buy-in?"

"Ten thousand apiece."

Tee saw no reason to be coy about his fragile financial condition. Cooper probably knew his bank balance, certainly knew he rented an old shack. "Well, I'm flattered you boys would consider me, but that's a little rich for my blood. I've got the business to pay for and I need to get on my feet before I could consider something like that."

"No problem. I'll loan you the money."

Tee wondered if Cooper meant a personal loan or a bank loan. "Thanks, but I don't see taking on any more debt till I get this business paid for."

"I understand you being conservative and all, but there won't be any risk. I'll loan you the money on liberal terms. By the time you have to make a payment, your share of the group ought to be worth four times what you paid in. We'll either cash out or somebody will buy your share. No money invested, 400% return. I think you bean counters call that leverage."

"That would be leverage, all right. I'll think about it. What about Blaze?"

"We want him in the group cause of his standing in the community. And we need his skills to inspect property and do repairs and remodels."

"And what did he say?'

"Said he wouldn't even think about it until he talked to you. Said he never does anything without consulting you first."

Tee laughed. "Well, he may consult me, but I have never given him a single piece of advice he followed. If you want him in, I may need to tell him to stay out."

Cooper laughed, but didn't seem to get the joke. He appeared to be sobering up. "Well, we don't need him for his money smarts, we need his skills. We need him and we need you. Not just for your money, but for your tax and bookkeeping know-how."

"I'm flattered. Who are the other members?"

"You're gonna be surprised when I tell you. Jack Prince and Wheeler Parker are in along with me. Talk about your movers and shakers."

Tee smiled. "Like I said, I'll think about it."

Tee was truly flattered as he watched Cooper's taillights travel the gully that passed for a road. The visit had lifted his spirits. Who would have thought he might be considered for membership in such a group after only a year in this little community. He wondered if Wheeler Parker recommended him.

NINETEEN

TEE HAD BEEN IN THE BANK MANY TIMES, but never in the boardroom. He arrived early and Cooper Newman took his elbow and led him inside. The physical contact and shepherding made Tee a little uncomfortable, especially when he detected a mint or mouthwash trying to overpower the smell of alcohol. Cooper indicated a seat, told him to help himself to coffee, and went back to the lobby to wait for Parker and Prince. Tee was filling his cup when the unlikely pair came in together.

Parker's attitude changed from confrontational to syrupy friendship after Tee saved him thousands in taxes, but their original meeting still played itself in Tee's head as Wheeler shook his hand in a death grip as if daring him to flinch. Tee returned Parker's smile and squeezed back. Prince's limp, soft handshake was almost welcome.

Blaze entered, wide-eyed and nervous, seconds after Newman sat at the head of the table. Cooper pointed at the coffee, but Blaze shook it off and shot Tee a questioning stare that seemed to ask *what am I doing here?* Tee tried to make his nod and shrug reassuring. The shared experience of John T and Winona's deaths had changed from a wedge between Tee and Blaze to a bond. He helped Blaze get out of a few financial predicaments, but Blaze refused to let Tee get ahead in the seesaw of favors that seemed to never stay still. Because his skills were so varied and Tee's so narrow, Tee had trouble keeping the seesaw balanced.

Cooper opened the meeting by repeating most of the things he had already told Tee—the boost to the local economy coming from a government lake and possible parks, the real estate investments, storage buildings. Jack Prince mentioned a few struggling businesses he would like the group to acquire. Tee kept his eyes on Wheeler Parker, who seemed bored, but kept smiling.

Cooper Newman rattled on, unperturbed by Parker's lack of input. As he trailed off into a litany of his own power and accomplishments, Tee gave up on waiting for a pause or a conclusion and interrupted. "Listen, I appreciate being invited to this meeting, but I thought it was to discuss whether or not I would join your group. I'll keep everything I heard a secret, of course, but seems like it's a little premature to tell me about your plans until I put up my money. I assume Blaze feels the same way."

Blaze seemed embarrassed by Tee's interruption.

Cooper's face showed mild irritation as he looked toward Wheeler, but spoke to Tee. "Well, we figure that's just a formality. I already told you I would loan you the money at a very competitive rate. No payments for at least a year, two if you need it. We should have made enough by then for you to pay off all or most of the note. If not, well, we can renew it for another year. The same goes for Blaze." Blaze sent a hopeful look toward Tee, but he ignored it.

"I appreciate all that, but you'll recall I said I was not in a position to take on more debt right now. Your ideas sound good, but we both know there are no guarantees." Tee blinked as the faces of Prince, Parker, and Newman took on the familiar faces of conmen and swindlers from his days in the corporate world—men who had bankrupted companies and put people out of work.

Wheeler Parker put both elbows on the table and fixed the smile that Wilda found charming on Tee. "Look, Tee, we need your expertise and assistance in doing accounting and tax work more than we need your money. This could get complicated because we intend to protect ourselves and keep the risks minimal with corporate veils and some deft maneuvering. Most of what we do will be kept confidential to avoid the appearance of conflicts of interest." He looked at Cooper Newman, then Jack Prince, for affirmation he knew was assured. They nodded vigorously.

Tee put his elbows on the table, too. "Again, I appreciate your confidence in my abilities. I want to work with you on anything I can help with. But for now, I like a straight-up professional relationship, rather than a partnership. I do work, you pay me. That way, we keep things neutral and normal and I can be more objective."

Wheeler looked toward Cooper and spoke to Tee. "Your way will put a lot less money in your pocket." He turned to

Blaze. "Mr. Blaisdell, this could get a little complicated. I know you have business to tend to. We need your construction expertise and skill in this deal and we can discuss that at a later time. Why don't we set up a meeting at one of the buildings we intend to buy and you can look it over. Cooper will give you a call."

Blaze got the idea he was being dismissed, but wasn't sure. "Okay, Cooper. You let me know when and where."

"Sure will, Blaze. Thanks."

Parker turned back to Tee when Blaze closed the door. "Look, Mr. Jessup, what would you say if we gave you ten percent of this deal with no risk on your part, no investment?"

"How would that work?"

Parker folded one hand over the other and looked at Prince and Newman. "Wes Simpson did a lot of work for us before he died. He accepted our offer of partnership and we made him a rich man as a result."

Tee raised his eyebrows. "That so?"

Wheeler turned toward Cooper. "Did you bring the files?"

Cooper produced copies of six bank statements for Wes Simpson. He pointed to the six figure balance and various large deposits he had underlined. "These all came from this group."

Tee tried to keep away thoughts of what he could do with sums like those. "Guess I'll take your word for that. What did he do to earn those big numbers?"

"Same as you will. Prepare tax returns for the various entities, do accounting work for these businesses like producing invoices for services and products. Then you bill 'em at four or more times your going rate. Simple as that."

Tee looked at the numbers, felt his resistance weakening. "Well, I'll be happy to consider it and I sure don't mind charging high fees, but I'd need to understand more about why."

Jack and Cooper looked at Wheeler for an answer. "It's merely a matter of taking maximum advantage of tax deductions and getting good documentation for those deductions. You should understand that."

Tee stood. "I do. I always tell my clients I will go right up to the jailhouse door with 'em, but I ain't going in. I got a kid to raise. I'll look at what you need on a case by case basis if that suits. Now... until you have more specifics, I've got a client waiting at the office."

Wheeler stood. That smile again. "You know, it's sort of sad, but Wes got into some trouble there at the end. Seems he kept a lot of cash he couldn't explain and he did some returns for illegal Mexicans with fake social security numbers who got big refunds they didn't have coming. Seems he took a little money under the table. Worrying about that is what killed him."

Tee thought of the six returns he prepared for Wheeler Parker without meeting any of the people involved. "Didn't know that, either." Tee felt a cold chill as he walked out of the boardroom.

TWENTY

BLAZE JUMPED FROM THE BENCH OUTSIDE
Tee's office and followed him inside.

Tee's pent-up anger released as he confronted Wilda. "You
know anything about Wes doing bogus tax returns?"

"What do you mean?"

"I mean doing tax returns claiming refundable credits
people were not legally entitled to."

"I don't understand."

"Was there any trouble at all when he died? Like did anybody come around and discover a stash of cash?"

Wilda slumped in her chair and seemed bewildered.

Tee softened his tone. "Sorry, but you seem to know more
than you're letting on. Were he and Wheeler Parker involved
in something?"

"As God is my witness, I did not know what was going on.
All I know is Mr. Parker came around when Wes died asking

me if I had enough cash to get by on until I could find another job. He was kind enough to give me ten one-hundred-dollar bills. It was a lifesaver for me and my husband."

"What did you have to do for the money?"

Wilda looked as if she had been struck. "Nothing. Really. Well, he did say Wes died owing him money. Wes told him he had the cash to repay him in this office. I promised to let Mr. Parker know if I found it."

"Did you?"

"Did I what?"

"Find it?"

"No, but I think I may know where it might be."

Tee glanced at Blaze, who watched the tense exchange with wide eyes. They followed her to the tiny broom closet beside the beauty shop wall. She pointed to the floor. "I think there may be something under there. I accidentally caught Wes down on his knees here one night after business hours." She felt the need to clarify. "I came back for my purse and he seemed startled when I did."

Blaze found a safe under the floorboards in a matter of minutes after Tee gave his permission to tear out some boards. "I can open this thing, but it may take a day or two."

"Never figured you for a safecracker."

"Never opened a safe, but I have picked many a lock and figured out combination locks for folks. It's just a matter of listening for the tumblers when they fall into place."

Wilda walked to her desk and returned with a slip of paper. She handed it to Blaze. "That won't be necessary."

"This the combination?"

Wilda nodded. "Wes trusted me with it the night I caught

him putting documents inside. Said if anything ever happened to him, to grab the safe, take it home to Bill and he would know what to do."

Tee didn't know whether to feel betrayed or pleased. "So, why didn't you?"

"I didn't want that safe at home, putting myself and Bill in danger. And what would I say if Wheeler came in and asked me about it? I was never a good liar."

"So, did Bill tell you what was inside and what he was supposed to do if you brought it home?"

"Bill and Wes were best friends. Drinking buddies, you know? He would never tell me a secret like that and I would never ask."

She held up both hands in a defensive posture. "I didn't eavesdrop, but you know it's hard not to overhear a few things. I was under the impression Wes was afraid of Wheeler Parker."

Tee shrugged. "So?"

"So that made me afraid. When I first learned about the safe, I started watching and Wes's trips to the safe seemed to coincide with visits from Wheeler. Wes made copies for almost an hour sometimes. I usually made all the copies, but Wes made these himself. Then he would take them back to this little broom closet and put them on a shelf. I guess he put them in the safe later. He told me once those copies were his insurance policy in case anybody ever asked him the wrong questions."

Blaze turned the dial back and forth and opened the safe. It was brimming over with paper. He removed two armloads and passed them off to Tee. When he returned for the rest, he whistled. "Tee, take a look at this."

Tee whistled, too. Wilda gasped when she saw the stacks of hundreds. "How much is there?"

Tee took it to a table and counted. "Looks like a little over fourteen thousand."

Wilda put both hands over her mouth. "Put it back. You have to put it back."

Blaze reached out a tentative hand to calm her. "Why?"

"Because all our lives will be in danger if we keep it."

Tee thumbed through the documents. "Why do you think our lives are in danger?"

"I'm not sure. I just think it could be a really bad thing."

"Maybe Wes just liked to keep a safety stash of cash for emergencies. Some people do that."

"No, I don't think it belonged to Wes. Wheeler Parker used to bring his fancy briefcase in here a lot and I saw some cash in it once. I wasn't snooping, I just happened to see it."

"So you think it's Parker's?"

"Yes."

"And you think he's willing to kill to get it back? I thought you admired the man."

"He gave me the thousand when I needed it. But I always felt it might be hush money in case I might know something."

Blaze looked over Tee's shoulder. "What's the other paperwork?"

Tee sifted through the stack. "There's cancelled checks, purchase orders, receipts, and invoices from various businesses I don't recognize and some invoices from Wes Simpson." Tee handed her four of the invoices. "Did you prepare those?"

She examined them. "I don't recognize them. Look at how big those numbers are. I think I would remember it if I had seen them."

"Any one of these would be about equivalent to two years

accounting work for most businesses around here. I'm beginning to see what Parker, Prince, and Newman were asking me to do."

He smiled when he picked up several more folders. "Bet these are the bogus tax returns." He showed one of the handwritten worksheets with names and social security numbers to Wilda. "This Wheeler's handwriting?"

"Yes."

Tee paced. "I need to talk to Joe Henry, but he won't be back till the end of the week. He may know about the safe or the money. The building is his, after all." He was thinking aloud and made his statement sound like a question. Blaze and Wilda shrugged.

Tee rubbed his forehead. "Guess we better turn it all over to the sheriff."

Tee called the sheriff and the dispatcher told him the sheriff was unavailable and would not be back until tomorrow. No details.

Blaze seemed to come out of his state of shock. "How about we put everything back and close it till Sheriff Bell gets back."

Tee tossed and turned all night. He was tired of being broke, couldn't get his mind off the consortium possibilities or the money in the safe. Were both opportunities to improve his and Jubal's life or were both traps? He was ashamed when he kept imagining finding the safe alone. Would he have kept the money? Should he just do the simple tasks outlined by Wheeler Parker to earn more money in an hour's work than he stood to make in a normal year? He visualized the things he and Jubal could buy, the security the money could bring.

He knew both were wrong, but could he resist? After hours of staring at the dark ceiling, he decided he could resist both, but his resistance was fueled by fear rather than conscience. He was ashamed as he walked to the window and looked out on a starless and moonless night and wondered what kind of person he really was.

TWENTY-ONE

SHE WALKED INTO TEE'S OFFICE WITHOUT AN
appointment, dropped an armload of folders on a table already
stacked with folders, placed her hands on her hips like a man,
and scanned the room. When she found the coffee pot, she
took one of the hanging cups and poured it full. Tee, the client he was working with, and Wilda silently watched, not sure
what to say.

Harmony was decked out in plenty of turquoise, a white
western shirt obviously handmade with red snaps, an ornate
yolk with red piping that ran all the way to the red belt in the
loops of her Wrangler jeans. She had on white eel boots with
riding heels and red tops that matched her belt. She waved
the cup in Tee's direction. "Don't let me bother you. I'll go
back and visit with the girls till you finish." She looked at
Wilda. "Come get me when he's finished, will you, honey?"
She walked back to Verda's beauty shop.

Tee knew Harmony was brash and he liked her boldness, but he was looking at a full day of back-to-back appointments. And he couldn't get his mind off the stack of folders she brought. They distracted him from the tax return he was preparing. Wilda appeared at the opening to his cubicle-office, looked at Tee with a question in her eyes. Harmony made Wilda nervous. She had that effect on a lot of folks, especially women. Tee shrugged and got back to the task at hand. He could hear Harmony's robust laughter coming from the beauty shop accompanied by a chorus of giggles from Verda and her two customers.

As Wilda made copies of the return he just prepared, Tee made a mental note to remind Blaze to completely enclose his cubicle so he and his clients could converse in private. The client was a friend of Wilda's, so she escorted her outside, giving Tee a quizzical look as she tapped her watch and held up ten fingers to indicate how much time they had before the next appointment. He walked back to the beauty shop and waved Harmony in. She sat in front of his desk, holding her empty coffee cup.

Tee picked up one of the folders. "So, what's in these?"

"Blaze told me you liked to look at tax returns from the beginning of time, so I brought in a decade's worth. When I dug into those old musty boxes last night, I sort of began to understand what they say about you."

Tee rocked back in his swivel chair. "And what do they say?"

"That you can read those old returns like a trashy novel. Well, I can tell you, you'll find plenty of dirt on me in those dusty papers. Never thought about how much information we have to hand over to the tax people. There's enough in those folders to write a six-hundred-page tragedy."

Tee laughed. "Anything that might send either of us to jail?"

"Is there such a thing as a crime, romance, trashy, and tragic novel all mixed up into one?"

"Yeah, I think I may have read one or two."

"You read it; I lived it."

Tee glanced at the folders. "So, how many years did you bring me?"

"Ten was all I could manage to carry. I got more if you need 'em."

"Ten should be more than enough. When will you be ready to do this year's return?"

"How long do you need to go over my life story?"

Tee turned to Wilda as she returned to her desk. "When's the next open spot?"

Wilda consulted her desk calendar. "Cancellation tomorrow at four."

Tee looked at Harmony. "That work for you?"

She laughed. "Kinda sad you think you can learn my life story in a day, but I can make that time."

Tee spent his reading time that evening going over those prior year tax returns, the novel of Harmony O'Hara's life. He found she had not exaggerated much. He intended to only look at the last three years, but found the trail so intriguing he scanned all ten. There was a divorce, three husbands, three casualty losses (two fires and a flood), a soaring royalty statement and bank account fueled by record sales followed by what looked like a possible bankruptcy, all tangled with two honky-tonk bars.

She came in the next day dressed pretty much like the

day before, just in different colors. Her dark hair streaked with gray was again in pigtails. One could see why they called her the singing squaw. She lugged a framed painting almost as tall as she was to the table beside Tee's desk. She set it on the table and leaned it against the wall. Inside the rustic, weathered-wood frame, a lone young cowboy stood beside a saddled horse on an open prairie. The colors were so perfect, the details so accurate, Tee thought she must have somehow stolen them from his mind. The horse was a close replica of Concho and the cowboy was definitely his brother Jubal, the prairie was High Plains. The clothes, the hat, the chaps, even the saddle were accurate. Tee felt his eyes begin to tear and a catch in his throat. It took him several seconds to find his voice and it came out in a whisper.

"Who painted this?"

She pointed to the lower right corner.

Tee read. "H. O'Hara. You painted this?"

"Sure did. Look familiar at all?"

Tee could not form the question for a few seconds. "How did you know?"

Harmony smiled. "I knew you were carrying a heavy load, so I pressured Blaze and Joe Henry to tell me part of your story. The rest I learned at the library in Bonham from newspaper articles on microfilm. This picture was with one of the articles. Couldn't find a color shot of this good-looking cowboy, so I hope I got close on the colors."

"I'm overwhelmed. I never saw this before. Never knew it was in the paper."

"As I understand it, you were about two months away from waking up from your long sleep when that picture was in the paper. When the accident happened, they printed this snapshot, but I never found one of your parents. "

"The picture was taken at a rodeo a few hours before he died. He had just won the tie-down roping."

Wilda couldn't stay away any longer. She looked over his shoulder at the painting. "Beautiful. Who is that?"

"My brother Jubal and our horse Concho." Saying the words made his voice more ragged, his eyes more full.

Wilda knew she was missing some information Harmony and Tee shared, so she fumbled, hoping to be brought into the story. "Well, isn't he handsome. The whole scene looks like something out of a movie. Where is he now?"

Tee stepped back to absorb the painting. "My brother and the horse died a few hours later. Happened over a decade ago. Train wreck."

Wilda's fingers covered her lips as if to shame herself for saying the wrong thing. "I'm so sorry. I knew you lost your parents, but I didn't know you lost a brother."

Tee also was at a loss for words. "One day, we'll sit down and I'll tell you the whole story of my brother and my parents." He took a deep breath as the awkwardness of the situation hit him.

He looked at Harmony, then at his watch. "Wilda, it's almost quitting time. I need you to come in a half hour early tomorrow if you can, so why don't you head on home early tonight."

TWENTY-TWO

WILDA GATHERED HER PURSE AND THE Tupperware containers that had contained the chicken salad she had for lunch, turned off lights not needed. She paused at the coffee pot. "Do you want me to make y'all some more coffee?"

Harmony shook her head. Tee answered. "No, thanks."

He waited until Wilda left. "Got Cokes in the icebox." The refrigerator was on loan from Wilda.

"Got any beer?"

"No, but Joe Henry left part of a bottle of bourbon over here the other day, I think. What about that?"

"Put a dribble in a glass with one of those Cokes, and you talked me into it."

Tee turned his back so she could not see as he mixed the drinks, poured a full jigger for her and enough to color the ice for himself before he poured in the Cokes. He handed her hers. "Bourbon and Coke. Coming right up."

They clinked glasses and sipped. He studied the painting a few minutes. "I'll just come right out and say it. I'd like to buy that painting if it's for sale."

She laughed softly. "It's not for sale, but you might talk me into swapping it for a couple of years of tax returns. Heck, I might give it to you if you let me hang it around a few places before you take it."

"A few places?"

"Yep. I think it's one of the best paintings I've ever done. Most of my other stuff looks like the amateur I am. But the whole time I was painting this one, I felt God guiding my hand. Can't explain it any better than that."

"I don't know anything about painting, but I can say I feel myself just out of the picture, like I'm watching Jubal and Concho back there behind the setting sun. Of course, I was only a few feet away. They don't take pictures of the guy who comes in second."

"About as fine a compliment as I have ever had on a painting of mine."

"You said you wanted to hang it around. Around where?"

"Mostly in businesses around Riverby. Might want to take it over to The Wheelhouse when I'm performing."

"But why?"

"I make part of my living by painting. People see this work I might get a few requests to paint specific scenes or portraits for folks. Probably not much market for paintings in Riverby, but who knows?"

"I'm flattered, I guess, you would take the time to find out about my past and paint this, but I'm curious as to why. Earlier, you said you could see I was carrying a heavy load. What did you mean?"

"I know pain when I see it. I've sure experienced plenty of it my life." She pointed at the stack of folders. "You know that if you looked in those. As for you, I can see it in those tiny lines around your eyes that shouldn't be there at your age. Having trouble sleeping?"

"I missed a few nights."

"How many?"

"About ten years' worth. I slept better after Jubal was born, but then it got worse after his mother left me. When she died, it got worse still."

"I can see you're still holding in a lot of anger. If you don't mind my saying."

"Looks like you've had your share of hard times, but I couldn't have told it for sure without reading those forms. How did you read me? Am I that obvious?"

"Don't know if I can explain except to say I have a lot of experience with cowboys who carry around a lot of guilt, anger or pain. You seem to have all three. Knowing what I know, I understand the guilt and pain, but who are you mad at?"

Tee thought about Sarah's frozen body and Ford Donovan's attacks on her and her mother. "If I told you, I'd have to kill you. Besides, the story is so long we would never get your tax return finished."

Harmony kept up a steady stream of conversation as Tee sifted through stacks of receipts, checks, and lists. He discovered Harmony's real name was Betty Johnson, not Harmony O'Hara.

She smiled when he mentioned it. "I may be the only person you'll ever meet who's named for a honky-tonk. When I opened my first nightclub in Fort Worth, I needed a catchy name. Harmony O'Hara had a ring to it. I had already start-ed using it as a stage name when I performed. It's the name I used for my first record and the one that sold a few copies, so I knew it would draw some patrons who like to drink and dance a little, maybe listen to me sing. Who wants to hear Betty Johnson sing?"

"I see three casualty losses in your history. Looks like two fires and a flood."

Harmony laughed. "When I was flying high with a record deal and selling lots of records, I bought a big house in a ritzy part of town. It burned a year later. I used the insurance money to buy a house down on the Blanco River. Don't ask me why I went way off down there, but you can guess it had to do with a cowboy. Anyway, the river flooded and ruined my house."

"The second fire looks like your nightclub." Tee framed it as a question.

Harmony cleared her throat, told the stories matter-of-factly. "That's right. A drunk fell asleep in the bathroom and we didn't know it when we locked up. He helped himself to the bar, fell asleep smoking and started a fire. You can imagine a fire fueled by all that whiskey. I got there in time to see the bar explode right before my eyes."

Tee didn't know how to react to those stories, so he moved on. "None of my business, but what happened to the hus-bands?"

"I think you may have heard me say more than once at the Circle that cowboys have been the bane and blessing of my life. I have always loved everything about cattle, horses, ranches and the cowboys who work 'em. I love saddles, bridles, blankets, spurs, the whole shootin' match."

Tee chuckled. "I get the feeling cowboys don't do too well in the husband department. So tell me about the bane part. Try not to hurt my feelings."

She lifted her empty glass and clicked a long fingernail against it. "My first love fell in love with this. Loved it better than he did me or our little girl. We rode the trails together when we were kids. I worked cattle and horses right alongside him, went with him to compete in rodeos. It wasn't enough."

She looked toward the painting. "The second cowboy wasn't really a cowboy, but boy, did he look the part when I met him in Killeen when I performed in a small bar down there. Didn't know till he popped the question that his real uniform was Army, not cowboy. He took me with him to Germany. We were there less than a year when he disappeared. Just left one night and didn't come back."

"So what happened to him?"

"Army said they didn't know. Guessed he might have been shanghaied into East Germany somehow. I never believed that. We found our old wrecked car a week later, but no husband. I was pregnant with our son and had a hell of a time getting through the red tape to get back home."

"So, he never saw your son?"

"Nope, but the boy turned out to be as handsome as his daddy."

"So what about husband number three?"

"Another cowboy, of course. A good man. Broke his neck when a horse he'd been riding for several years got spooked by a rattler and threw him. Rattler bit him. Died before anybody found him. And...like most cowboys, he died broke. Gave me another girl, though."

137

"Guess you know I was a third-generation cowboy once. Grew up on a ranch." He held up both hands in a defensive posture. "But, as you can see, I'm a numbers-cruncher now."

She laughed. "Once a cowboy, always a cowboy. When I came to Riverby, I needed a lawyer. Found Joe Henry Leathers, a cowboy lawyer if I ever saw one. Then you come along, a CPA. What's that stand for, Cowboy Plus Accountant? Wherever I go, cowboys turn up."

"So what brought you to Riverby?"

"The college. Always wanted my degree. Went at it sporadically for about ten years."

"I understand you got it. What was your major?"

"Literature." She slapped her knee. "Who would think an old worn-out cowgirl like me would want to get herself a useless degree like that."

"I'll bet you had your reasons."

"Always wanted to be literate. And I would like to write."

"Like write books?"

She nodded. "Always loved reading and thought it would be wonderful to write something that other people might enjoy. I kept it a secret from my cowboys."

She wrung her hands and looked around the room. "When I lost my daughter, I needed a change of place and pace. So I came here where there was a college."

"What happened to her?"

Harmony's eyes filled. "She just disappeared one night. A beautiful thing with a beautiful voice. We had recorded our version of Neil Diamond's song, *Play Me* a few hours before she left. You know it?"

"Don't know all the words, but I remember it."

Harmony played an air guitar and sang softly, "You are the sun, I am the moon. You are the words, I am the tune...play me." She paused and pulled a red bandanna from her jeans and dabbed at her eyes. "Course Annie could sing it better than me."

Tee's eyes widened. "Wow. That was beautiful."

"Anyway, we had a fight. I suspected she had been dabbling in drugs. Couldn't tolerate that. We fought about it and her latest boyfriend. I hate the last words passed between us were harsh."

"You still don't know what happened to her?"

"Joe Henry has some connections to a private eye who's looking, but I can't afford to launch a real search with paid detectives. Police tried, but they think she chose to go and that's all there was to it. Several people in the recording studio heard us arguing before she left."

"Not knowing has got to be terrible."

"To tell the truth, that's another reason I came here. We had a clue she'd been seen over in the Wheelhouse Bar across the line. That's why I started working for that sorry Wheeler Parker, hoping she might show up there."

"No luck?"

"Not yet. On the bright side, that little story is what got me in the Hurt Circle. I bet your story would get you in."

Tee tried to keep filling out forms and flipping through files. "Assume the other two kids are okay?"

"Don't get me started on how wonderful they are. I'll keep you here all night."

Tee leaned back in his chair. The return was almost complete, but would need serious proofing before he turned it loose. Listening to the novel that was Harmony's life kept his attention away from the lines he was filling in. "Damn, Harmony. You have, indeed, seen some hard times."

He leaned forward with his arms stretched on the desk. "Yet, you seem to have come through it all with a cheerful outlook on life. I'd like to know how you do that."

He looked up and saw Jubal back from ball practice, peering in the window. Tee motioned for him to come in and Jubal groped for the key he kept in the watch pocket of his jeans. "Harmony, have you met my son?"

Harmony turned and smiled. "No, but I heard about him. Jubal, is it?"

"Jubal, this is Miss Harmony O'Hara."

Jubal walked over and extended his hand. "Pleased to meet you, ma'am."

Harmony's smile said she appreciated good manners. "Well, Jubal, you must have to beat the girls off with a stick."

"No, ma'am." Embarrassed, he turned to study the painting.

Harmony placed her hand over her heart. "Oh, my, he's the spittin' image of his uncle, ain't he?"

TWENTY-THREE

ON HIS WAY TO WORK, TEE FELT GUILTY ABOUT dreading his afternoon appointment with Enoch Essary. He always feared saying something unintentionally that might offend the preacher. And he never knew whether to call him Enoch, Brother Essary or Reverend Essary. And Enoch's aggressive behavior in saving souls made Tee imagine the pastor might have discovered what transgressions he had committed to deserve the misfortunes his family experienced, might know about the times he shook his fist at God.

Enoch Essary came to Riverby in a new automobile with a portable microphone and two heavy speakers in the car's trunk. He claimed to be an ordained minister dissatisfied with his denomination. He kept quiet about which one that was. He purchased a rundown, abandoned church. Said he could see in his mind the church's former splendor with its stately oak trees, a tabernacle, and accoutrements reminiscent of the Deep South before the Civil War. But the church building had been neglected for more than two decades and seemed ready to be torn down.

Enoch announced to anyone who would listen that the church's doors would be open to all religious persuasions. It would be called By the River Church. But Enoch could not wait for the restoration. With his microphone and speakers, he began to evangelize on Sunday mornings from the gazebo on the square. When people complained, the sheriff denied him permission to preach from the square on Sundays, so he preached on Saturday nights.

Tired of hearing stultifying sermons about a vengeful God and a terrifying hell delivered in hot sanctuaries, people seemed to bathe in the open, welcoming atmosphere as they stood around the gazebo or sat in chairs brought from home. And they were pleased to exchange their usual suffocating suits, ties, hats and bonnets for casual clothes. Starlit skies seemed to wash them in religious fervor. Many claimed to see the Face of God looking down on them and blessing their gathering to hear His Word. They waved their arms to heaven in the open atmosphere.

Many said if Enoch Essary had the voice of Billy Graham, he would be traveling around the world saving souls. So instead of complaining about his thin, raspy, tinny voice, they saw the voice as a blessing that kept him in their small town.

It wasn't that Enoch spoke with captivating fervor. Harmony O'Hara originally judged the preacher a pontificating braggart and blowhard who seemed more concerned about his own fame than saving souls. But she changed her mind when she joined him in a prayer vigil at the bedside of a woman who lost a child in the womb.

His sermons differed from most preachers. Enoch found a way to envelop them not in the hellfire-and-brimstone-versus-future-rewards-in-heaven congregants were used to, but in the love here now and the prosperity coming in this life rather than just the afterlife. Within a month, he attracted about twenty followers. In six months, he had almost a hundred and was second only to the First Baptist in regular attendance. When some Baptists started attending his sermons on Saturday night before attending their regular church on Sunday, his became the largest congregation in Riverby.

Attendees were astonished when Enoch failed to pass around a collection plate. Instead, he drove a nail into a telephone pole a few yards away and hung an old tow sack for folks to drop their contributions. He knew from past experience it would work. Money didn't exactly flow in, but it was enough to live on.

When his congregants ran from a rainstorm and left paper, napkins and other refuse on the square one Saturday night, the mayor and town council asked Enoch to move his church indoors. Since work on By the River was going to be extensive and had not even begun, the Commissioners' Court offered temporary use of an abandoned building off the square that had been used for public auctions of antiques and junk. The property was mired in back taxes and other debts. Volunteers had it ready for church within a week. And Enoch still had his microphone and two speakers.

When a strong smell of leaking propane in the old building signaled possible danger, Enoch talked the bank into letting

JIM H. AINSWORTH

him use an eleven-acre parcel complete with mobile home, a pond, and a large hay barn they had repossessed. He assured everyone services would be held under the hay barn and the mobile home would double as a church office, construction headquarters, and parsonage. Congregants were impressed when a man of Enoch's standing in the community moved into a rundown trailer house.

He made building a perimeter of wood fires around the hay barn during cold Sundays seem exciting and adventurous. When smoke engulfed the congregation during a wind change, he quoted Psalm 104: *He makes his messengers winds, his ministers a flaming fire.*

When Enoch asked Blaze's advice on the dilapidated church, the old building became a fertile field for Blaze's creative mind. He had been waiting to be asked. Enoch encouraged his enthusiasm, speaking in sonorous tones about the history of the church grounds. Blaze, not satisfied to repair it, determined to restore it to its former stately presence. He poured not only his heart and soul into the project, but most of his assets. He even added what Tee considered a dangerous level of debt.

Enoch stuck his head in Tee's office door in late afternoon. Tee waved him in. Enoch glanced at the deadline calendar that said *thirty-two days* before sitting in front of Tee's desk. "Tee, I want to begin by telling you I get down on my knees every night to thank God for bringing you to Riverby and for getting me out of that terrible mess with the Internal Revenue Service. Those people are like hounds from hell."

In the previous year, Tee managed to pull Enoch's chestnuts out of an IRS fire that had plagued Enoch for two years.

He had opted out of paying social security taxes on his income as a minister for several years, but the IRS claimed he had not filed the proper form to claim this exclusion. Enoch said he had, but lost his copy. Tee went to Dallas without Enoch and negotiated a settlement that kept the preacher from paying a huge penalty, and with a sworn affidavit from Enoch, got the exclusion backdated.

"Glad I could be of help. That's what I do these days. Seems like I work for the IRS on some days. Others, I spend my time fighting 'em. Keeps me conflicted."

"You know if you ever need help with conflict in your life, I remain your humble servant."

Enoch plopped five years of prior returns on Tee's desk. "You asked for these last year and I couldn't find them."

Surprised, Tee reluctantly thumbed through the returns to see if he could find anything relevant to the current year. "I see you were married with a child five years ago. I didn't know that."

Enoch's expression seemed to indicate he had been waiting for Tee to make that discovery. Enoch was known for being intense, but the tension normally present in his face and body seemed to flow out of him. "Yes, Eileen and Tess died in a terrible accident."

Tee could not hide his shock. "I'm so sorry to hear that. Can I ask what kind of accident?"

"Car accident down south, close to Houston."

Tee couldn't find words to ask a question or express a sentiment, but Enoch broke the uncomfortable silence. "Tee, I know something about your history because of Blaze's connection to your parents' terrible death. You've been through a similar tragedy and I desperately need someone to confide in."

"Well, if I can help in any way, I'm willing to listen."

"Do CPAs have such a thing as attorney-client privilege? I know you kept my secret about the Social Security taxes."

"We don't have exactly the same thing, but we are bound to keep your personal data confidential. They call it work-product, I think. Either way, I never divulge anything told to me in confidence."

"I'm sorry to burden you with my problems, but I sometimes feel I'm drowning in other people's problems to the point I become dangerously depressed."

"Guess you do hear a lot of sad stories."

"My sad story is my family was leaving me when the accident occurred. My wife was running away with a member of my congregation—a deacon in my church."

Tee's groan was not followed with any comforting words.

Enoch's eyes filled. "Days later, we found more than three thousand in church funds missing."

"Your wife stole from the church?"

Enoch shook his head. "Her paramour was the treasurer. Whatever Eileen was, she was not a thief. I resigned my position and wandered like a vagabond until I came to Riverby. The Hurt Circle welcomed me as a brother and through them, I began to heal."

"I guess that helps me understand and appreciate the group more. Nobody understands what it's like to be hurt that much other than a person who has had his own suffering."

"Tee, I appreciate your listening and keeping my secret. I know I can come off as overzealous when I'm behind the pulpit or even in normal conversations. But my daddy was a minister and that's the only kind of preaching I knew. The Circle is showing me how to be more empathetic and less preachy. I want to help you, for example, if you will let me."

"Well, I appreciate that."

They were shaking hands after the simple return was done when Jubal came in from school. Enoch tousled Jubal's hair. The boy hated it when people did that. "Hello, Jubal. How was school? I hear you're a good student and a fine athlete."

Jubal looked toward Tee. "School was fine."

"I know several boys your age who come to our church. Think you could get your dad to bring you next Sunday? It will be our first full service at By the River."

Tee looked at Jubal. "Blaze has been telling me we need to come. We just might do that."

TWENTY-FOUR

THEY WENT THE BACK WAY, DRIVING DOWN the same dirt roads he and Jubal traveled horseback a few times. By the River Church buildings and grounds reminded folks of the way churches used to be. It sat way back in the woods, surrounded by giant oaks, as if God put it there in the secluded area, surrounded it with His creations, and waited for worshippers.

Tee had driven past the small church a few times and he and Jubal had watered their horses there occasionally, but as he drove the winding dirt road on a cool early spring Sunday morning, the path to the church seemed bathed in holy light. Blaze's restoration was almost complete and that was part of it. He had not changed the basic structure of the century-old building, but had added a few touches of his own. A giant wooden cross made from cypress adorned the east side of the building to catch the first rays of sun. Small metal crosses

149

Blaze made in his forge adorned the step railings going up to the porch. The old tabernacle still waited for Blaze's tender touch, but even it seemed to have risen from the dead.

Nothing, of course, impressed like the giant Post Oaks and Red Oaks that formed a protective canopy over the church. The parking lot still had watering troughs, hitching rails and posts for horses and buggies. When Tee saw the sun's rays filter through the trees and settle on the cross, he understood what Blaze had been so excited about.

Blaze waited for them on the porch. Tee tried to indicate the church building and its environs with a sweep of his arm. "My hat's off to you, Blaze. What you've done out here is impressive."

The bell in the tower rang and Blaze grinned. He had fixed the bell, too.

Tee and Jubal were the last to enter, so they sat on the last row, though there were two empty pews in front of them. Enoch's voice seemed to scratch their eardrums when he raised it several octaves in the small sanctuary. The weather was warm enough to keep the windows open and Jubal heard the sound of a bobwhite quail. He turned to whisper. "Is that Bob White? Think he followed us here?"

Tee shook his head and put his index finger over his lips. He found it hard to focus on Brother Essary's sermon, but he was moved by Blaze's voice as he led the singing. The sermon was mercifully short because Enoch had a funeral to preside over in the afternoon. Tee glanced at Jubal as they walked down the church steps and shook hands with Enoch, Blaze and most of the other congregants. Blaze walked beside them to their pickup. He leaned down to Jubal's level. "Lydia Albright and I alternate teaching Sunday School, so I teach it next Sunday, and I especially want my woods-boy to come."

Jubal looked up at Tee, who shrugged. "If you want to come, it's fine with me." Tee talked more with Blaze as he watched Jubal and a few of his friends in the churchyard, hanging on every word spoken by Freddy Albright, Toke and Lydia's son. Freddy was known for being the best all-around athlete in the school and one of the best students.

Tee was surprised to see Abel Gunter walking toward them. He had not seen him inside the church. "Hey, Abel."

Abel spoke to Tee. "Any chance I could get you out to my little ranch next Saturday? I need a few things done before you start working seven days a week."

"Sure. See you there."

On the way home, Tee asked Jubal if he would like to return next Sunday. The boy seemed to glow as he nodded enthusiastically. Tee wondered if he was also glowing or if it was the lifting of the burden of guilt he carried for all the things his son had endured during his short life. Maybe God's house would be where he could find forgiveness for his part in that. Maybe he could find some peace and release from guilt there. They made a pact to return and shook on it.

TWENTY-FIVE

ABEL'S LOW-LYING CRIMSON RIVER RANCH was not the High Plains, but the work still reminded Tee of his boyhood home. He and Jubal helped separate calves from their mommas, turned bulls into steers, moved herds into different pastures, gave shots, punched in fly tags, dehorned and doctored. The work helped put a little food on the Jessup table, kept their horses from getting fat and stale, and Tee from becoming soft in his sedentary job. Jubal's skills with horse and rope also grew. And the boy loved watching Dawson work both cattle and sheep.

Abel suggested to Tee that they meet for breakfasts on alternate Saturdays, even on days when they did not work on the ranch. Tee felt honored enough to take time away from a busy tax season. Abel cooked bacon, eggs, and biscuits with the same precision he applied to everything else.

His prayers before breakfast inspired Jubal and he asked

Tee if they could make them a ritual before their own meals. Abel never volunteered personal information, including his age, but once likened his life to the leaning bois d'arc tree in his yard. "It seems to lean a little more each year, leaf out a little later, lose at least one limb and add another pod of mistletoe. When that old tree is gone, so will I be."

But it wasn't Abel's age that stoked Tee's curiosity; it was his mind and his past. The more he observed and listened to Abel, the more fascinated he became. Despite the rumors, Tee could not imagine a man with such a kind, gentle nature having a criminal past. But he did want to know what deep hurt qualified Abel for membership in the Hurt Circle. Blaze claimed not to know, but said a man who had been hurt could look into Abel's eyes and see the hurt there. "It oozes out of his pores," Blaze said. He was right. An observant person, especially one who had suffered much, could see the pain in Abel's eyes. And Tee could see it.

Abel knew his cattle and sheep, but was impressed when he saw Tee treat illnesses and injuries and manage cattle behavior using remedies born of tradition and experience. He knew such methods would not likely be in books, so Abel always invited Tee into the house to ask questions and write Tee's answers. These note-taking sessions always happened over coffee for the men and iced tea for Jubal in Abel's dimly lit living room that looked more like a library. Filled bookshelves lined all the walls.

When a sudden downpour came as they finished one Saturday's work, Tee and Jubal rode their horses into the hall of Abel's barn. Abel shook the rain from his hat as he and Dawson stepped in after them. "You heading out?"

"Yep. I had a couple of things left, but this rain looks like it's gonna be around awhile. I'll finish it next trip. Nothing that can't wait."

A bolt of lightning followed by a sudden clap of thunder made Jubal's eyes widen. Abel put his hand on the boy's back. "Radio says this could get bad. Come inside and wait. The road going out of here can be treacherous in a downpour."

Tee seemed tentative, so Abel kept his eyes on Jubal. "Got beans on the stove."

Another thunderclap convinced Tee. They put the horses in two milk-stalls and left them hay and water. Abel always refused his help in the kitchen, so Tee went into the living room. He had noticed the lack of any family portraits or anything that might indicate something about Abel's past. Of course, a stranger would find little of Tee's own past hanging on the walls or sitting on tables at Hurt Hill.

Tee perused the bookshelves at every opportunity, trying to find some clue to Abel's past. He found few, but did become familiar with Abel's library. The old man offered the loan of any book on the shelves, but Tee declined. He had heard Abel say at a meeting of the Hurt Circle, "When it comes to books, neither a borrower nor lender be, because people seldom return borrowed books."

Absorbed in reading titles and authors, Tee was surprised to find Abel standing beside him, holding two plates of red beans, cornbread, and fried potatoes. Abel indicated the shelves with a nod. "A man's life is a reflection of the books he has read."

Tee accepted a plate but kept his gaze on the books. "Have you read all those?" Tee knew there were hundreds, maybe more than a thousand, on the shelves in the dark room.

155

"Ralph Waldo Emerson answered a similar question some-thing like this—*I can no more remember all the books I have read than the meals I have consumed, but they are what made me.* But yes, I have read everything up there except these."

He pointed to about a dozen books stacked horizontally to distinguish them from the others. "Those are my latest acqui-sitions and as yet unread."

"Am I mistaken, or do you have them arranged by type of book and by author in alphabetical order?"

"You're observant. It may seem obsessive, but I often refer to a book I read years before to solve some problem in my life or to recall a memorable quote, and it's satisfying to be able to find them."

He laughed at Tee's astonished expression. "A man who is organized has more power. He walks with a sure sense of purpose. "

Tee held his plate in one hand and pointed to various shelves filled with textbooks, theology, biographies and auto-biographies, history, literature, farming and ranching, self-help motivational books, and novels. "I didn't figure you for a man who reads so much fiction."

"I read occasionally for escape or pure pleasure, of course, but don't make the mistake of discounting fiction. Stories are how we learn. G. K. Chesterton said, *It's not enough to be told about something that happened; we want to know what it felt like to the people involved. Historians cannot do that, so fiction can be truer than fact.* I have found history is about events, and fiction is often about the meaning of those events."

Another clap of thunder and bolt of lightning interrupted. When their meals were finished and Abel had allowed them

to wash and dry their own dishes, the storm seemed to inten‐
sify as Jubal looked out the window. "You think Rivers and
Flo are okay?"

Tee pulled him close. "Blaze knows where we are. He'll
likely check on them. If not, they'll get under the porch like
they usually do."

Two hours later, Jubal fell asleep on the floor while Tee
and Abel talked. Abel smiled. "This storm isn't showing any
signs of letting up. Best not go out until daylight. I've got two
single beds in the guest bedroom."

Tee was hesitant. "Hate to impose on you. We can bed
down in the barn."

Abel seemed insulted. "Nonsense. I can stand the compa‐
ny. We'll have a good breakfast in the morning and you can
go on your way."

"Well, I hate to put you out, but don't guess we got much
choice."

With Jubal fast asleep in the bedroom after a cup of hot
chocolate, the two men sat at the kitchen table over glasses
of milk. "I could fix some coffee if you like, but it keeps me
awake."

Tee smiled. "Nope. Like a cup in the morning, but almost
never at night."

The talk was awkward at first, but Abel broke the barrier
by asking about Tee's family. "It's hard to keep a secret in a
town this size. Blaze's railroad incident caused Harmony to do
some research. She shared it with me. It may not be a subject
you'd care to discuss."

Tee surprised himself by relating the story of both railroad
wrecks.

Abel's sad eyes seemed to grow sadder. "The things I might have to say about what happened would make me angry if said to me in your situation, so I'm at a loss for words until I learn more about how you feel now."

"Believe me, I've heard it all. Father Bob, the priest I told you about, made me very angry before he showed me how to get past it."

"Suppose he told you it was God's will and you rejected that."

"I did, but he finally persuaded me to trust him enough to accept some of what he said."

Abel smiled. "Him with a capital H, or him the priest?"

"Both, I think. Though I still don't understand how God could cause such a thing to happen or what possible good could come of it."

"My personal belief is God doesn't usually cause such things to happen, but when they do, one must have faith He will use it for good."

"I guess my faith is not strong enough."

"Faith, like most things in life, takes practice and patience. You have to keep trying it on for size. One day, you'll discover it fits."

"How did you get your faith?"

"I considered all the alternatives and didn't like any of them. If here and now is all there is, then that's not enough."

Tee smiled. "I like that. Makes sense."

"A man needs something to believe in. It's the sustenance of life. And the story of Christianity is the most amazing one ever recorded. Think about it. A man who lived only a little more than thirty-three years and delivered his message for just over three sent a few disciples indwelt with the Holy Spirit out into the world to spread His message. That message had a greater effect on the world than all of the great scholars, leaders and conquerors who ever lived. Seems to me a reasonable man can draw only one conclusion from that. He simply had to be who He said He was."

Abel chuckled softly. "Of course, I was a fool for many years."

Tee leaned back in his chair and smiled. "So now that my life has been laid bare, how about you? Any family?"

Abel's gentle smile disappeared. "What about Jubal's mother?"

Confessing his past to Abel seemed cathartic and somehow right, so he told him the story of wife Sarah and Ford Donovan's sexual abuse of Sarah and her mother that led to their deaths. Abel sat with rapt attention as Tee told of the deadly night on Blind River Ranch. Tee's fists clenched and unclenched during the telling. "The man is responsible for the death of my wife and tainted all my memories of the place where I grew up."

Tee inclined his head toward the bedroom where Jubal slept. "Ford Donovan also laid claim to my son. Tried to kidnap him and take him to another country."

Abel noticed the fists. "During your interviews with clients, do they tell you secrets about themselves unrelated to their taxes or the business at hand?"

Tee managed a smile. "I've heard it said folks will tell their CPA things they won't tell their shrink. Guess that's because we already know so much after doing their taxes."

"It's more than that, I expect. I sense a vulnerability and

empathy about you because of what you've been through. I expect others sense that without knowing your past, so they reveal more of themselves."

"Maybe, but I never saw it that way."

"I expect that's one of the good things that came out of your tribulations. You have an opportunity not afforded to many. My advice is to take advantage of it."

"How do you mean?"

"Your clients will be a treasure trove of information about human nature. Observe how they make decisions about important things. They will teach you what works and what doesn't."

Tee contemplated advice he had never considered before, wondered if it could be true. "So I might get as much from them as they do from me?"

"Probably more."

Tee was emboldened with the discussion and his own unburdening. "So you never answered my question."

"I supposed you surmised from my shelf of textbooks I might have been a teacher at one time. I studied psychology at first, but switched to literature and language and taught courses in junior college. But I soon became bored and got a job selling sucker rods to oil drilling outfits. Then I sold office furniture, then cars."

Tee laughed. "Cars? You were a car salesman?"

Abel smiled. "Don't underestimate car salesmen—or salesmen of any stripe, for that matter. Nothing happens in business until a sale is made. I made four times the money I made teaching. In my last year in the business, I was one of the top ten car salesmen in the country. I even taught courses on how to sell and eventually graduated to doing motivational seminars."

"How did you get so good at selling? You seem so quiet and reserved."

Abel walked to the shelves. "I read books like this." He pulled down a copy of Napoleon Hill's *Think and Grow Rich*. "Those books were my silent mentors. I read them until the pages dog-eared. Then I read Norman Vincent Peale, who some would say started this whole self-help and positive thinking movement. That's when I began to realize Peale's message had somehow been swallowed by the new-age gurus and changed slightly to make it secular and palatable to guys like me."

"Guys like you?"

"People who pretended to believe but were really skeptics. Abel laid a Bible on the table and put his hand on it. "One night, after I made a presentation to a large group, a preacher wrote verses from this book beside each of the statements in my handout materials."

"When I talked to him about the verses, he quoted Ralph Waldo Emerson who said, *All my best ideas were stolen by the ancients.* I laughed at the irony and knew he was right."

Tee reflected on that for a few seconds. "Did you start using Scripture more in your presentations after that?"

A deep sadness came across Abel's face that shocked Tee. "No. There was a pause in my life shortly after and I left behind motivational speaking."

"What pause?"

Abel stared at Tee until the silence became uncomfortable. "I want you to know I didn't read those books so I can quote from them or brag about reading them; I read them because I needed them, needed to learn. Now it's past midnight. I'll share the rest of my story with you when you're ready." Abel went to bed.

TWENTY-SIX

AS DEADLINE DAY LOOMED FOR HIS SECOND tax season, Tee realized he had learned more in less than two years of running a small town accounting firm than he had learned working ten years for big and small corporations. Though he never gave up the dream of owning his own ranch, he began to accept that his small business was the best route to that goal. He began to understand it wasn't so much what he taught clients about taxes and other financial issues, but what they were teaching him about life—how to live it and how not to live it. And watching how successful clients ran their businesses taught him how to run his.

He also learned that it wasn't solely about how much he knew, but about how much he cared; that clients who were also friends would forgive his occasional mistakes; that clients wanted to talk about their personal lives to someone who could keep secrets. Tee was surprised at how much he did care about most of his clients. Oh, there were some hard cases he dreaded seeing, but he looked forward to most.

When Toke Albright requested a before-opening-time appointment, Tee did his review of prior year returns the night before. He knew Toke had been a deputy sheriff under Morgan Bell, had learned to operate heavy equipment from his father. Other clients told Tee that Toke was a great law officer, but left his law enforcement job to work in the bottoms, building levees for flood control.

Unlike most men who lived in the country, Toke had no cows, no horses, and no crops of his own. He allowed Blaze to bale the weed-infested meadow behind his house. Wife Lydia, a devout Christian who strongly believed her place was in the home, took care of her husband and son Freddy, a sophomore and Jubal's hero. Tee was grateful Freddy had taken him under his wing at school.

Tee sent Jubal to Prigmore's for his breakfast a few minutes before seven. He could walk to school from there. He had the lights on and was pouring water into the percolator when Toke walked in. Tee looked over his shoulder. "Have a seat. Coffee will be up in a few."

Toke sat at the round table where Tee had started doing some of his interviews when no other clients were present and when the cubicle's walls closed in. Tee handed him a cup of coffee and they exchanged small talk. But Toke seemed to be in no mood, so Tee took the small folder Toke brought in and began filling out his 1040. Lydia had everything organized. He asked him some questions about safety clothing and tools he needed in the dirt-moving job before moving on to the farm schedule.

"Don't see any hay sales this year."

"Nope. Blaze got his hay baler re-popped. Nobody else was interested in baling it."

"Yeah. He told me he had to choose between repairing it or making payments on it, so he repaired it. Lot of good that did."

"Now the dealer owns a hay baler in good condition and Blaze is out money with nothing to show for it. Looks to me like they could have cut him a little slack."

Tee spoke without looking up from last year's schedule F. "Does seem a little unfair. Did you lease the land out for grazing or get any income from it at all?"

"Not this year. Maybe we don't need to fill out a farm schedule."

"I hate to just quit it. We've been depreciating your little tractor and the shredder."

"Won't they disallow it?"

"You're supposed to show a profit on your farm every so often. Guidelines say you can get by with losses for up to seven years. "Let's keep it this year and see what happens next year. We'll show expenses and no income."

Tee completed the farm schedule and carried it to the 1040. When he finished, he turned the return around for Toke to look. Toke pointed to the total tax line. "They sure gonna get their share, ain't they? Make a little extra, pay a little extra."

"Yep. Their hand is always out. They got their part of the extra money you made on the new job. How's that working out?"

Toke's expression turned cold. "You ever hear anything about me being forced out of my deputy job?"

"Not a word."

"Nothing about the pistol whipping I gave Frank Blount? Lots of folks think I was forced out because of that."

Tee shook his head. "Never heard anything about any pistol whipping."

"He made an unkind remark about my wife. Got what he deserved."

"So folks think you were fired for taking a gun barrel to a fellow who insulted your wife?"

"I was off duty, so technically, I wasn't even supposed to be carrying my service revolver, much less use the barrel to protect my wife's honor. So there was talk, a complaint or two."

"So did the sheriff fire you?"

"Morgan Bell was not just my boss, but my best friend. I left partly to take the heat off of him, but partly because I needed more money. We got a boy may want to go to college in a year or two."

"Yeah, Freddy sure seems like college material. I appreciate how he took Jubal under his wing when we first came here."

"Freddy's always been like that. Age difference never seems to bother him. He's a good boy. And Lydia and I both think a lot of Jubal. We like having him around."

"So do you regret whipping Blount?"

Toke looked behind him to the awakening square with a law officer's eyes. "Would do it all over again. Man's got to stand up for his woman." Toke tugged at an earlobe. "Course, I had been drinking. Used to have a little problem with the bottle."

"Hadn't heard anything about that either." Tee figured problems with alcohol might be what qualified him for the

Circle of Hurt. He picked up the return and stood. "Help yourself to another cup of coffee. You know where it is. Wilda's not in yet, so I'll go back and make copies of this."

When he returned with the copies, Toke was standing by the front window with his coffee.

Tee handed him two copies. "You know the drill. One for you and one for the IRS." The client copy file had an invoice clipped to it.

Toke walked back to the table and removed his checkbook from a shirt pocket. When he handed the check to Tee, he seemed reluctant to leave. Tee walked him to the door, where Toke hesitated again. "Joe Henry told me you hated being a tax man. That true?"

"It used to be. I was raised on a ranch and that's all I ever wanted to do. Just doesn't feel right sitting in an office pushing a pencil. Guess I had a low opinion of people who sit on their butts all day."

Toke waved the tax return copies. "So you're miserable doing this?"

"I was at first, but now I can see I might be doing something worthwhile. Helping folks out. Anyway, it puts food on the table. Why?"

Toke dropped his head. "Guess misery loves company."

"You really miss the law, don't you?"

"It's in my blood. But it's not just that. You know Wheeler Parker?"

"A little. Why?"

"He's my boss on this levee project, you know."

"So I heard. Thought he had his hands full with that bar over the state line."

"The Wheelhouse. That's the bar. Guess I don't want to know what all he does through it and what else he does."

Tee noted the sarcasm. "Hard to work for?"

"You might say that. Guess a man's gotta do what a man's gotta do. See you."

Tee followed him onto the sidewalk. "I know this is not the time, but someday, I'd like to talk some things over with you. Just so you know, I've been through something like what you went through with Frank Blount. Plus, we're both in jobs we don't particularly like. Maybe we can help each other."

Toke smiled. "Sure. Sounds good." He took a few steps toward his pickup and turned. "Truth be told, I had more than a little problem with the bottle."

TWENTY-SEVEN

TOKE ALBRIGHT AND LEONARD TOON SAT IN the shade provided by a bulldozer Leonard had been operating all morning. Toke finished the bacon sandwich and boiled egg wife Lydia made for him and washed it down with iced tea from his thermos. Leonard ate his last handful of Fritos and jerked the pull-tab on a Coors.

Toke's eyebrows arched. "Where'd you get that?"

"Where you think? Cooler in my truck. It's still rodeo-cool. Want one?"

"You know how Wheeler feels about drinkin' on the job."

Leonard's eyes scanned the piles of pushed over trees and mounds of dirt surrounding them. "Don't see any sign of Wheeler Parker anywhere around here. You know as well as I do, he never shows up till payday. Even then, he usually sends out a flunky."

"He might surprise us one day. He sees you drinking a beer and operating heavy equipment, your ass is grass."

"I'll take my chances. My back hurts today and beer's about the only thing that helps. Drove all the way to Oklahoma to get it and I ain't lettin' it go to waste."

"Guess that explains the trips I've seen you take to your pickup this morning. More than one, as I recall."

"Toke, you're my boss and friend, not my mama."

Leonard was halfway through a long pull on the Coors when Toke rose to his feet in a hurry and pointed west. "Better hide that beer. That's Wheeler Parker's Oldsmobile." The Olds stopped in the grass and weeds a few feet short of the area where the ground had been scraped bare.

Leonard hid the beer can behind the dozer tracks. "Guess he don't want any dust on his new Olds."

The Olds seemed to be still rolling when Parker stepped out and walked toward them at a fast pace. Wheeler was always in a hurry. When he had covered half the distance, a young dark-skinned man caught him.

Leonard stood beside Toke to greet their boss. "Where'd the other feller come from? Didn't see him in the car."

Toke shook his head and waited. He didn't care too much for Wheeler Parker, a high-roller who seemed to have his hands in too many pots. But enough extra pay to cover two months of expenses was hard to turn down. Rio Grande Construction from South Texas had hired Wheeler to manage the flood control project Toke and Leonard were working on. Toke did not understand why and was only mildly interested in the specifics. The checks he received every payday cashed just fine.

Toke gave his boss a two finger salute. "Afternoon, Wheeler."

"Taking a lunch break, boys?"

Toke nodded. "Just about to go back to it."

Wheeler pointed to the young Mexican beside him. "Boys, this is Angelino Salinas. Rio Grande sent him to help out with maintenance. I expect him to get here earlier than you do in the mornings or stay later after work to keep everything fueled, greased and maintained."

Toke looked at Angelino. The lean, muscular, handsome young man was dressed better than any wetback he had ever seen and was almost pretty, but the ponytail made him look like more trouble than he was worth. "Sounds good, Wheeler. What will he do the rest of the day?"

"He can run that little Farmall with the box blade over there, cut up felled trees and keep the brush burned." Wheeler paused to wait for Toke's argument. None came. "Or whatever you damn well tell him to do around here."

Toke turned to Angelino. "You ever work on dirt moving projects like this before?"

"*Si*. Plenty."

"I don't see any way for you to get to and from work and you'll need it if you get here early and stay late."

Angelino pointed toward a high ridge just off Hurt Hill. "Left my wheels in the shade of those thorn trees over there."

Wheeler frowned. "You let me worry about those details, Toke." He pointed toward the small tractor and looked at Angelino. "Go ahead over there and get started."

When he was out of earshot, Wheeler spoke. "We use this boy for a few other odd jobs, so there may be times when he ain't here or works only part of a day. Just keep track of his time and turn it in. Don't need to question his comings and goings. I'll be paying him in cash."

Toke watched the Mexican try to figure how to crank the tractor. "Whatever you say."

Wheeler caught the hint of sarcasm in Toke's voice and spoke to Leonard. "Go on over there and show him how to crank it."

He turned to Toke when Leonard was far enough away. "I know this sounds a little strange and I can't explain it except to say this boy has some money behind him. Seems some of his relatives buy a lot of heavy equipment here and somehow get it into Mexico for resale and vice versa. Means big money for the construction company. So I been told to cut him a lot of slack."

Toke climbed on his dozer. "He'll need a chainsaw."

"I'll send one with him tomorrow."

Clayton was shocked when the first sound from what had to be a large engine assaulted his senses. He stepped off the porch and walked a few feet down a steep incline before he saw the source of the intrusion. The offending dozer had hardly begun destroying beloved trees and upsetting the delicate balance of nature when smoke billowed from a second. A smaller tractor with a box blade attached was also working, but could not be heard above the din of the dozers.

He watched helplessly as they desecrated the final resting place of King, the blue tick coonhound Willard Dunn had given him for his fourteenth birthday. He could not see them, but he imagined the dozers uprooting his bones. He spoke softly, "That sweet old boy treed many a coon for me." A conversation with himself seemed like daylight, conversations with others like dark.

Clayton watched in horror for most of the morning, slowly realizing these gargantuan machines would be part of his life in the shack for the indefinite future. Though he was barely settled in, he decided he had to leave his haven at the earliest possible time, but could not decide where to go. As the days passed, he found himself appreciating the night quiet even more because of the insults to his senses during the day.

But he also acquired an unwanted curiosity that bordered on voyeurism about the three men working in the bottomland below his shack. The men so interested him he drove to Bonham to buy a set of binoculars. As he leaned against a tree on the incline, he began scribbling about what he imagined their lives were like based on their mannerisms and gestures. He could see them talking and gesturing to each other, but could not hear their words. He bought a bow saw and lopping shears at Prigmore's on the Riverby square, cut limbs in three trees in order to give him a less obstructed view of the men and their machines from his chair on the porch. He could see through the holes he cut without being seen. The men became characters in his head, with names, distinguishing features, families, histories. Writing about what he saw began occupying most of his days; singing and playing the guitar took his nights.

He found it easy, perhaps compelling, to categorize the men as he had the birds and animals, to rank them, catalogue their innermost desires, fears and anger. It was easy to rank them, too. The lean fortyish one with a well-creased straw hat was clearly the boss. His clothes were ironed, his shirt tucked, and he walked with a sense of authority, his gestures smooth, almost choreographed, his demeanor serious. The other one wore a greasy cap and wrinkled clothes, his movements somewhat disjointed, almost clumsy, and his gestures wild and erratic. His personality seemed happy-go-lucky. On what Clayton assumed was the day after payday, he made several trips to his pickup for cans of what he assumed was cold beer. He never saw the older one drink. Although the men were all of average height and build, he decided the boss became tall in his character description, the one with the greasy cap wide and soft, and the young one more muscular.

Clayton found the youngest one to be the most interesting character. Before the others arrived in the morning and after they left in the afternoon, his behavior was erratic, his gestures violent. To the sound of loud Mexican music from his car radio, he took swings at an imaginary adversary, stabbed an unseen opponent with the two switchblades he carried in his boot and back pocket, even challenged an invisible enemy with a pistol. Sometimes, he took target practice at anything that crawled, moved, or made a noise in the woods. He drank from a bottle wrapped in a paper sack early in the morning, at noon, and at quitting time. When either of his coworkers' back was turned, he exhibited a litany of obscene and violent gestures, including drawing two fingers across his throat. Clayton began to look forward to the men's arrival each morning and regret their departure each night. The curiosity he considered somewhat stimulating turned to morbid after he had written a hundred pages of notes on the three men.

TWENTY-EIGHT

JUBAL BEGGED HIS FATHER FOR WEEKS TO move the Airstream down to Panther Crossing near the trestle so the two of them could sleep there and hunt varmints on the weekends. After they cleaned the accumulated leaves and tree droppings off the trailer on a Sunday afternoon, he renewed his request, but Tee was losing patience. "Jubal, I already told you we can't just move the trailer down there. We don't own that land."

"But I asked Zeke if we could and he said yes."

"You actually asked him?"

"Yes."

Tee was alarmed. "How did you get past the dogs?"

"I didn't. Saw him down by the trestle one day. He took a liking to Rivers."

The next Sunday afternoon, Blaze helped them move the Airstream to Panther Crossing. When they finished, Blaze and Tee sat under the tabernacle and watched Jubal wander in and out of the woods around the crossing.

Tee smiled as he watched his son play alone. "Why do you reckon he likes to spend so much time down there?"

Blaze shrugged. "Same reason I did, I imagine. He feels a sense of peace there. Didn't you tell me once he mentioned seeing your parents in the woods around here? Makes sense he sees their spirits where they died."

"You really believe that?"

"He may not see 'em, but maybe he senses their presence. He knows what happened. And yes, I believe in guardian angels. They're in the Bible. Who says Jubal can't have two of his own? Anybody deserves an angel or two, it's him."

"Seems he likes being alone a little too much for a boy his age."

"You weren't like that as boy?"

Tee thought about his brother and how much he had enriched his boyhood. He had always felt guilty that Jubal had no siblings. "My brother kept me from being alone much, but I used to ride my horse down to the Canadian once in a while by myself. I enjoyed those times."

"See?"

"All the same, I worry a little he's spending too much time with Clayton Dupree, a recluse if I ever saw one."

"He still teaching him to play guitar?"

"Ah, he says he is, but I have my doubts. Jubal doesn't have a guitar and hasn't asked for one."

"Like I said before, Jubal is a woods nymph."

"What if I don't want my son to be a woods nymph?"

Blaze looked at his friend. "Sorry. Didn't mean any harm."

After school the next day, Jubal opened the Airstream and went inside for some chips and cookies he stored in the cabinet. He looked out the windows to check the view, imagined himself and Tee, sheltered from cold and rain, watching critters roam at night. But the day was pretty, so Jubal left the trailer and returned to the area beneath the trestle where he could sit and be almost unnoticed by wildlife, could watch the occasional snake or turtle in Moccasin Creek. He found squirrels, rabbits, and birds often approached within a few feet of his lair if he kept still.

After church the next Sunday, Blaze met Tee and Jubal at the trestle. Both were mounted and Tee held the reins to a saddled horse for Blaze. Joe Henry's stock trailer was parked in Ezekiel Mulroney's native meadow. One of Joe Henry's heifers walked over a downed fence to have her first calf in the privacy of Mulroney's woods. As they rode closer to Ezekiel's house, they were greeted with the expected barking of what appeared to be at least thirty dogs, mostly curs. Some were missing parts of ears, blood dripped from many of their mouths, and others had blood on their fur. Some of the mutts were inside the cyclone fence that surrounded the front yard of Mulroney's shack. A few were always in the road.

Tee carried John T's bullwhip in case one of the dogs attacked the horses' legs. "Why do you suppose Zeke keeps some locked up and turns others loose?"

Blaze chuckled. "Says the ones outside are trained not to run off, the others are in training."

"Never been by here when there wasn't at least one fight going on. I think he half-starves 'em to make 'em mean."

"I know he does. Makes no bones about it."

"How many you think are killed in fights?"

"Why you think they call this road Ghost Dog Run? It's in memory of the ghosts of dead dogs folks say roam around here at night."

Zeke's compound stood like a gaping wound on the otherwise pristine Blackland Prairie. The land around it remained in its natural state, unscarred by plow, machine, or human desecration of any kind. The woodlands behind it also remained primitive, marred only by many signs warning trespassers away. Ezekiel Mulroney maintained the area had never been hunted and was teeming with wildlife including cougars and panthers. He considered them all to be his personal property to be harvested when the time was right to sell hides or meat. He just never found the time to be right.

A dozen abandoned cars and trucks lined the road beside Mulroney's shack, standing in perfect formation. With their yellow, green, black, and bright blue tarps, passersby were known to say they reminded them of a chorus line in various stages of undress. Tarps blindfolded some of the wrecks and others covered missing doors, side and back windows. Two stood tarp-free and appeared ready for use. A '57 Cameo pickup was backed into the shelter. Ezekiel drove it in parades and on other special occasions. A battered '49 Ford sedan sat beside the house to meet his other travel needs.

Jubal shifted in his saddle and pointed. A black baldy walked out of the woods and grazed the sparse grass of the prairie while her calf nursed. "Well, looky there. Thought they might be long gone."

Tee was relieved to see them in the open. Only a good cow dog could have found them and brought them out of the deep woods. A man horseback would have almost no chance in the thicket. "Question is can we get 'em back home before dark."

Blaze recognized this was an area where Tee's side of the seesaw was heavier than his. "We could easy if Zeke's dogs or Zeke don't turn on us and cause that little momma to turn back for shelter. You got a plan to keep that from happening?"

"Rivers can keep her out of the woods. If she does get back in, he'll bring her out. We sure can't ride in there. Only problem is Zeke's mutts. They could come over and try to kill him if we turn him loose."

"No they won't." Ezekiel Mulroney seemed to appear from nowhere, a twelve-gauge shotgun on his shoulder. "That heifer's been in here for nigh onto a week. I went down to Joe Henry's and told his secretary."

Blaze shrugged. "Sorry about being so long, Zeke. I just found out yesterday."

"Next time, I'll just come to your house and tell you direct. Damn lawyer don't need to be ranching, anyway."

Tee watched the heifer. "Can you hold your dogs back? Don't want the boy's dog cut up."

Zeke caressed the stock of the shotgun. "I can't, but this can."

Tee could tell by the look on Jubal's face he wanted to let Rivers show his cow sense. They had no need for his services at Crimson River because of Dawson, but Rivers did a lot of cow work on Joe Henry's Two Hearts Ranch. Tee looked at the eager terrier, who had not taken his eye off the cow and her calf. "Okay, boy, show 'em what you got."

Rivers worked his way along the perimeter of the pasture

next to the railroad, slowly crept between the pair and the woods, squatted, and waited for further instructions."

Zeke took the gun from his shoulder. "I'll be damned."

Tee's chest swelled visibly as he stole a glance at a grinning Jubal. "Good boy, Rivers."

Blaze stayed put in case the heifer decided to run in his direction while Tee and Jubal rode opposite sides of the pasture toward the pair. They headed the young cow and her calf toward the open trailer. Rivers walked behind in a crouch uttering occasional low growls to let the heifer know what was good for her if she tried to run. Zeke's dogs watched quietly from the corner of his yard. Blaze penned the calf against the trailer wheel, picked it up, and put it inside the trailer. Tee slipped a rope around the heifer's neck and she went into the trailer to be next to her calf.

When the trailer gate was closed, Zeke reached down to pet Rivers. "That's a mighty fine piece of cow work if I ever saw one. No runnin', no barkin', no yellin', no throwin'. You got yourself a first-rate dog there."

The comment took Tee by surprise. "He'll do. How did you keep your dogs quiet?"

Zeke spoke over his shoulder as he turned and started back to his house. "Cause I told 'em to."

Blaze smiled when he saw the look on Jubal's face as Zeke walked home. "Ain't many like Zeke. Don't like the way he does his dogs, but he's a man to depend on in a pinch."

TWENTY-NINE

TEE ARRIVED LATE, A RARE OCCURRENCE, and found an impatient Harmony O'Hara waiting with what looked like fire in her eyes. A short woman with a complexion like biscuit dough sat beside her. He knew the hour he had set aside for routine tasks like paying bills was about to be stolen. Harmony had a full cup of coffee. "Get yourself one. You might want to add a drop or two of Joe Henry's tonic in it. You're gonna need it, I think."

Wilda shrugged when Tee glanced at her. He sat at his desk and looked at the stranger. "Don't believe I've had the pleasure."

The woman seemed to jerk when she realized he was speaking to her. "My name is Dimple Dalton."

Harmony took over. "Dimple is my aunt, Tee. She just paid off the house she has lived in for thirty years and the bank won't turn over her title."

"Why not?"

"Well, Mr. High-and-Mighty president Cooper Newman told her she still owes property taxes and the county has filed a lien. Says he didn't know about the lien till she came in to claim her title. He even claims there's back premiums due on her insurance."

Tee looked at Dimple, who seemed to be shrinking with every word. "Guess I'm confused. Are the taxes and insurance paid up?"

Harmony leaned forward. "They're included in the payment she makes every month to the bank. Bank didn't trust her to pay them herself."

"They're supposed to keep the insurance and tax payments you make in an escrow account and pay them when they're due. So, you're saying the bank didn't?"

Harmony slapped down a folder. "She kept meticulous records of every payment. There's a schedule in there and she marked when she made every payment with the check number."

Tee flipped through the tiny amortization book. "This just shows principal and interest. How much was your total payment including taxes and insurance?"

Dimple handed him a copy of her last cancelled check. Tee leaned back. "Whoa. Almost double your P and I. How come so high?"

Dimple shrugged. "They told me about five years ago my payment had to go up because taxes and insurance had gone up a few years back and I had to catch up. Said my payments should've been increased years ago."

Harmony pointed a finger at Tee. "I checked at the tax office and with her insurance agent. She owes three years of back taxes and her insurance was cancelled about five years ago."

"But how did you not know this? You would have received delinquent notices from the tax assessor and a cancellation notice from the insurance company."

Dimple looked to Harmony to explain. "She stopped receiving anything from either one about the time the payments doubled."

"You never questioned that?"

Dimple's voice broke. "I never complained. Getting bills from the government always upset me. Bank said they would have both copies sent to them. Seemed simpler."

"So what does Cooper say?"

Harmony's face darkened. "He fed her a line of bull about the payments being too low during the early years of the mortgage. Said Aunt Dimple just never caught up."

"So what do you want me to do?"

"Come up with an amount she got cheated so we'll know how much to sue for."

"If you're gonna sue, you might talk to Joe Henry about this instead of me."

"I asked Joe Henry. He said he had a conflict because he does legal work for the bank. He sent us to you."

"I have a client coming in just a few. Harmony, you go back to her insurance agent and to the tax office. I'll need copies of bills and statements for as far back as you can get 'em. Leave the paperwork with me and I'll see what I can do."

Harmony returned at four with two folders. Tee was with a client, so she waved them at him and handed them to Wilda.

Tee's curiosity was aroused as he went through the paperwork that night. By midnight, he determined Dimple's escrow account should have at least an extra two thousand in it and all taxes and insurance should be current.

He called Harmony the next morning and told her to make an appointment with Cooper Newman. "Tell him it's to discuss a loan. That will be true. Don't mention Dimple or me."

Two days later, Harmony went inside the bank just before closing time. Tee waited until she was inside Cooper's office before following. Dimple was afraid to come. A look of irritation and concern crossed Cooper's face when Tee walked in. "Good to see you, Tee. But Harmony and I were about to discuss a transaction."

Tee took a seat. "Harmony asked me to sit in."

He placed a thirteen-column pad on Cooper's desk and laid out Dimple's case, pointing to the numbers as he went. He waited for the facts to soak in. "Looks like the bank owes Dimple two thousand and change plus all back taxes need to be paid."

Harmony could hold back no longer. "And you owe her a clean title."

Tee waited for Cooper to react. When he did not, Tee continued. "Then there's the matter of leaving the house uninsured for almost five years. The local agent says he thought Dimple switched companies when she didn't renew with him."

Cooper showed his most charming smile. "Well, before I came, there was a lot of trouble with escrow accounting around here. Some things weren't taken care of like they should've been. You know, we have hundreds of clients with mortgages and escrow money is consolidated in a few accounts. We'll sure get this taken care of."

Tee smiled. "I assume somebody reconciles those consolidated accounts."

"Well, they're supposed to, but you know how hard it is to get good people."

Harmony drummed long nails on his desk. "When will you get this taken care of? And what about all those years of not having any insurance? What if her house had burned? And what about her credit rating for not paying her bills? Aunt Dimple always took great pride in paying her bills. Worked as a seamstress and at a lunch counter all those years to pay off her home."

Cooper seemed afraid of Harmony as he looked at Tee. "What seems fair to get this settled?"

Tee looked at Harmony, got her approval, then at Cooper. "Three thousand and a clear title would go a long way to making Dimple right with the world."

"When?"

Harmony chimed in. "This is Wednesday. You should be able to get it done by Friday at noon."

Cooper stood and extended a hand to each of them. "Done. And be sure to tell Dimple how sorry I am this happened."

THIRTY

COOPER CLOSED THE BLINDS AND TOOK A long pull from the bottle of vodka he kept in his desk drawer as he peeked between the blinds to watch Tee and Harmony walk down the street. He thought he saw Harmony's shoulders shake with laughter. *Bitch. And what about Jessup? After all I did for him—referring clients, inviting him into the consortium.*

He had underestimated Dimple, not known she was Harmony O'Hara's aunt. He could easily cover the three thousand and get the back taxes paid, but what if Tee or Harmony decided to dig deeper? He had robbed at least six other escrow accounts, mostly widows and widowers approaching senility or already in nursing homes. That could add up to the high five figures and a possible felony charge. He could not let that happen. After a few more swallows of liquid courage, he decided to determine if his membership in the consortium had any real value.

Jack Prince was not pleased to receive his call. "You're only supposed to call this number in the event of a dire emergency. Even my wife doesn't have this number."

"This is an emergency. I made a mistake on an escrow account here and I need to make up the shortfall."

"You call that an emergency? And you sound drunk."

Cooper breathed deeply to ease his panic and to keep his words from slurring. "Look, I'll be honest. I have at least one teller down here seems to have caught on to what you and Wheeler Parker been doing. I may have to buy her off."

"If she knows, you must have screwed up. No way we left a trail she could follow."

"Jack, if I go down, I ain't going alone. Be a shame to waste what we got going with the group. I think ten thousand will get us out of this mess."

It was Jack Prince's turn to panic. "I'm a rich man, but I don't keep that kind of money lying around, Cooper. I work at a car dealership; you work at a bank. Which one has a lot of money?"

"What about Wheeler? That's pocket change for him."

"It may be, but you don't know Wheeler Parker. Trust me, you don't want him to see you as somebody who panics and starts drinking. All kinds of bad things can come down on you. Believe me, I know."

Cooper was surprised when he heard his own voice break. "Then what the hell am I supposed to do?" The line went silent. "You still there?"

"You told me once about that crazy hermit and his file cabinets full of money. Surely you got a man who can get in one of those. You could probably make a withdrawal from his stash and he would never even know."

Cooper called a locksmith who specialized in opening safe

deposit boxes. He had recently drilled one for the bank when an old man died without leaving any instructions or family behind. He quickly fabricated the paperwork necessary to drill a box or drawer, though the specialist seldom looked at such forms. For a small bonus, the locksmith agreed to come just after closing time.

He made sure he was in the safe deposit vault at closing time, told his assistant he wanted to go over some of the paperwork inside his own box and would secure everything before he left for the evening. The locksmith arrived an hour after closing time as instructed, gave a cursory glance to the paperwork offered by Cooper, and began drilling Clayton Dupree's safe deposit drawers. After completing the drawers, he opened all the combination locks on the file cabinets and the locks on the cabinet drawers. Cooper escorted the specialist outside and watched him drive away. It was dark and there was no traffic on the square when Cooper Newman parked his truck in the alley behind the bank and brought in several large trash bags. He emptied the contents of everything into the bags. He wanted to scan the contents as they emptied, but was too frightened to take the time.

Jack Prince was waiting at his gin lot office when Cooper arrived. Neither could wait to see what was in those bags. Jack emptied the first one in the middle of the floor when Cooper went back for the second. Cooper was not happy to see him rummaging through the contents when he returned. "Hold your horses, Jack. You wait till I get in here with all the bags before you start picking through this stuff."

Jack feigned surprise. "Just thought I'd get started. This could take hours."

Cooper sneered. "Wouldn't take long to stick a wad of bills in your pocket. You help me carry the rest in."

By the time they emptied the third sack, they began to panic. Jack Prince's rug was covered in dead spiders, piles of old photos, dozens of hand-written journals and notebooks, thousands of pages of typed and hand-written words, a pile of cheap jewelry, scrapbooks, guitar picks, cans full of keys, a few child toys that looked to be antiques, ten fruit jars full of coins and a few bank envelopes with small bills inside.

Cooper tossed two hands full of paper in the air and almost screamed. "This is all pure junk. What kind of nut would keep this stuff in a safe deposit vault?"

"Can't believe you just dropped the file cabinet stuff in with the safe deposit drawer stuff. Stands to reason if he had anything valuable, he would have kept it in the drawers."

"Excuse the hell out of me. I was a little short on time and garbage sacks."

"Bingo!" Jack held up a small locked bank bag and a small metal lockbox.

Cooper rubbed his hands together. "You got a straight razor around here or a pocket knife to open that bank bag?"

Jack thought of the floor safe where he kept a hunting knife and a small pistol. "I don't keep that kind of thing here."

"Got one in my truck."

When Cooper left to get his knife, Jack pulled the spring loaded chain on the key ring attached to his belt, selected the key that fit his own bank bag, and placed it in the small lock. He smiled when it clicked open. He had time to pull three envelopes from the bag, but decided to leave the fourth. He relocked it and put the three envelopes in his desk drawer before Cooper walked back in.

Cooper sliced open the bag and removed the remaining

envelope. "This looks interesting." He removed five wrapped bundles of hundreds. "Looks like five grand here. At least that makes it worth the time and risk."

He used a screwdriver and hammer to break open the lock on the small lockbox. "More damn paper. Why would he keep it in a locked metal box?"

Jack wondered if the envelopes in his desk contained five thousand each. "Look at the mess on my shag carpet. Better take this stuff back where you got it."

Cooper stuffed the five thousand in hundreds in his back pocket and put the paper and other junk back in the garbage bags. He had no idea which drawer or file cabinet they belonged in and didn't care. "I can't get back in the bank tonight. Have to wait till tomorrow night. Even then, it will be hard to do without looking suspicious."

"How often does this crazy come in to check his stuff?"

"Hardly ever. I've known him to go years without coming in the bank. He usually brings in more junk when he does."

"So, you're just gonna take it home with you tonight? What's your wife gonna say if you bring this stuff in the house?"

"I won't be taking it in the house."

"Okay, what if she sees it in your pickup?"

"She won't see it because I'm not staying at home right now."

"I see. She kick you out for the drinking? Where are you staying?"

"You know Jory Shelton's farm south of town? It borders my ranch."

"That place has been abandoned since Jory died. House roof has fallen in."

"House is no good, but the barn's not too bad. The loft is pretty cozy."

"You're kidding. You're staying in a barn? What about running water?"

"Been there a few days till the wife cools off. There's a pool and an outhouse."

"You're bathing in a pool where cattle drink and do all sorts of other disgusting things?"

Cooper was tiring of the questions. "Folks don't take kindly to a bank president having marriage problems. Hard to keep it quiet if I rent a motel room or a house around here. Not to mention the expense. I'll make the barn work till I get back on my feet. Plus, she visits her invalid grandmother in Paris almost every night. I sneak over to my house and clean up while she's gone."

Cooper put a finger in Jack's chest and pushed hard. "Keep this under your hat."

Prince pointed at the bills Cooper had stuffed in his back pocket. "Just remember, I got nothing out of this little venture. I never saw this stuff. So you keep my secrets and I'll keep yours."

THIRTY-ONE

CLAYTON DUPREE CLUTCHED WHAT LOOKED like a woman's overnight bag under his arm as he knocked on the door to Tee's office at dusk. Wilda saw what she assumed was a vagrant when she opened the door a crack. She looked him up and down. "We're closed. Can I help you?"

Clayton kept his eyes on his rough-out boots with worn heels that made his legs look bowed. "Looking for Tee Jessup."

Tee heard his name and walked out of the coffee room with a Coke in one hand and a hamburger fresh from Miss Shiflett's in the other. "Hello, Clayton. Come on in. What brings you down here so late?"

Clayton handed him an envelope with an IRS return address. Tee read it and motioned him to his cubicle. His appointments had been back to back for weeks, and he and Wilda were staying late for the onslaught sure to come the last day of tax season. Clayton seemed reluctant to sit, but Tee persuaded him. Between bites of his hamburger, Tee read the letter again. "They say you haven't been filing returns. How many years since you filed?"

"Been at least five. Had a drinking buddy who used to work for the IRS. Said he would take care of me. Guess he didn't."

Tee had already come to the conclusion Clayton Dupree hid his brilliance behind a façade, but he continued to be amazed at how otherwise bright people could be so naïve about things like the necessity of filing a tax return. But having seen the workings of tax law and the absurdity and corruption of the system, he could empathize with someone like Clayton, who chose not to participate.

Tee dropped the letter on his desk. "Looks like they found you. What do you want to do?"

"Just get 'em off my back and out of my life."

"Could be you didn't have to file if your income was below the filing requirement. If it was, I can write a letter saying so or just file a return with no tax due."

Clayton reluctantly handed him a 1099 from a publishing house in New York. "Been in my post office box since January, I guess. Never bothered to open it till a few days ago."

Tee's eyes widened when he saw the income on the form was more than he made the past two years combined. "Looks like you have to file at least for this year. Are there more of these 1099's in years before?"

"Two. But my ex-IRS friend said they were below the filing requirement."

"Is this your only income? How about painting or carpenter work?"

Clayton kept his head bowed. "That's it."

Tee smiled. "Any expenses associated with this income?"

Clayton shook his head. "Nothing worth fooling with."

"It will look strange if you have no expenses at all. Plus it will cost you taxes. Got a typewriter?"

"It's an old one that belonged to Willard Dunn."

Tee's half-eaten burger was going begging, so he took another bite and drained his Coke. "You want a Coke or anything?"

Clayton shook his head. "Where's Jubal?"

"He's out there playing with some boys on the square. At least he better be."

"I saw a boy out there. Just didn't recognize him. Jubal's coming along on his lessons."

That was one of the longest string of words Tee had heard Clayton volunteer. "He doesn't talk much about it to me. Won't play a lick for me, but I sure appreciate your helping him out."

"Think he wants to surprise you one day by playing a song all the way through."

Tee laughed. "Look forward to that day."

Tee read the 1099 again. "I see these are publishing royalties for book sales, but the book titles have been blacked out. Mind if I ask what kind of books?"

Clayton raised his head and met Tee's questioning stare. "Just books. Nothing you would care for. Like to keep that sort of thing private."

"I understand, but if you change your mind, I'd definitely be interested in reading anything you wrote."

Clayton stared at the top of Tee's desk and said nothing.

Tee talked him into estimating the cost of paper, pens and pencils, postage and a few other minor expenses, but he still showed a hefty profit. When Tee pointed to the taxes due line on the return, Clayton sucked in a breath. "Big Brother gets his take, even for people like me who want to be left alone. Don't take nothing from them, they shouldn't take from me."

"I agree, but they do. A good bit of what you owe is self-employment tax."

"Self-employment tax?"

"Yeah. That's social security taxes for people who work for themselves. It's double what employees pay."

Clayton was quiet for a few seconds until Tee asked, "You okay with paying this? I completed an extension to file for this year in case you need time, but there is no extension for paying. You'll still be penalized if you extend without a check."

"I have enough cash to pay what I owe."

"I wouldn't try to send cash. How about a check? Do you have a bank account?"

"I do. Will they take a counter check?"

"A personalized one would be better, but they will accept a counter. Just be sure to write your name and social security number on it in case it gets separated from your return. If you're okay with this, I'll get Wilda to make copies."

"How much do I owe you?"

"Wilda will figure it out and give you an invoice." He handed Wilda a time slip with the completed return and she left to make copies and prepare an invoice.

Tee tried to fill the awkward silence broken only by the sound of the copy machine and Wilda's typewriter. "None of my business, but can I buy one of your books from you?"

Clayton stood. "Nothing you would read. Guess I better pay up and get out of your hair."

Blaze stuck his head in the door as Clayton walked back to Wilda's desk. "Saw the lights. Are you closed?"

Tee rolled his eyes. "Come on in."

Blaze took one step inside. He could not see Wilda or Clayton from where he stood. "Guess you know what I want. But I can come back tomorrow. Just thought I would get it out of the way."

Tee leaned back with his arms behind his head. "Shoot, what's the hurry?" He pointed to the deadline calendar Wilda had flipped to one. "You got nearly a whole day left." Tee handed him an extension form with numbers filled in based on his return last year. "Do I need to remind you this is a wild guess? I used last year's tax due. Attach a check and get it postmarked by tomorrow. You know the drill. I kept a copy."

Blaze took the form, sat at a table and wrote a check for the estimated amount due. Tee looked over his shoulder. "Be sure to write your social number on it and the form number 4868 as a notation on the check."

Blaze signed, folded the form and put it and the check in the envelope Wilda had addressed for him. "Coming to the singing tomorrow night?"

"What singing?"

"You ain't heard? A rare performance by Morgan Bell and other members of the Circle of Hurt right out there on the square. At least that's what Harmony O'Hara has been telling folks."

"Did you say Morgan Bell? I heard he could sing, but wouldn't do it in public."

Blaze smiled. "Plays the fiddle and has a classic singing voice you won't believe."

"What time is all this happening?"

"Who knows? My guess is about sundown."

"Are you singing?"

"Sure. You and Jubal be sure to come."

Wilda returned from the copy machine closet with Clayton's copies and an invoice. Clayton peeled a hundred from a roll in his front pocket and started to the door. Tee caught him in time to give him his change.

THIRTY-TWO

Deadline Day

TEE WAS AN HOUR EARLY TO WORK THE
next morning, but Morgan Bell already waited on the bench
outside his door. He looked impatient to Tee. The sheriff stood
and extended a hand. "Sorry to be early for my appointment,
but got up early and came on down. I like to see the sunrise
on the square."

Tee had been a little intimidated when the sheriff came in to
get his tax return completed the previous year. His name rolled
easily off the tongues of most folks in Riverby. What surprised
Tee the most was the complete absence of negative comments
about the sheriff in the community. Sheriffs made enemies;
stepping on toes was a necessary part of the job. But after three
decades of law enforcement, Bell's reputation seemed impecca-
ble. If he had enemies, Tee figured they lived somewhere else.

And Morgan was not a typical Texas sheriff. He did own
a triple X Resistol hat with a cattlemen's crease, but he pre-

ferred gimme caps most days. Said he was advertising for local merchants who gave him the caps. There was a uniform, but it spent most of its life in Bell's closet. To keep from filling his khaki or blue denim shirts with holes, he wore his badge pinned to a belt loop on Wrangler jeans or khaki pants most days.

It also seemed to Tee that most lawmen were big men who had to hold their own in fistfights or wrestling matches with lawbreakers. Bell was five-nine in his boots and stretched to tip the scales at one-fifty. It was said he could hold his own with most men, though nobody had specifics. He was in his early sixties, and it was starting to show.

It also seemed to Tee that people who ran for office of any kind, especially the office of sheriff, tended to be outgoing and talkative, even overbearing. Not so with Bell. His demeanor was quiet, modest, non-confrontational, and shy. Tee wanted to emulate his qualities, to seek his counsel.

Morgan's tax return reflected his lifestyle; simple and straightforward, no dependents because his only child, a daughter, was grown and gone. The only complications were the few expenses he incurred unique to being a sheriff. Wife Peggy always had their data organized in two folders, one for income and one for expenses. Tee thumbed through the items he recognized from the previous year, entered the totals on the correct lines. But the last stack of receipts surprised him. "Looks like you had a lot of legal and maybe medical expenses last year, Sheriff."

Bell leaned forward and smiled. "Told you before to call me Morgan, especially when I'm in here at your mercy, telling you all my secrets." He leaned forward and picked up the stack of receipts.

A rare, shamed look appeared when he leafed through

them. "I know she put these in there by mistake. Let me take 'em back."

Tee handed him the stack and went on with the rest of the return. When he finished, he made small talk with Morgan while Wilda made copies. He handed the original and copy to Bell when she returned. "You know the drill. Take that original home and get Peggy to sign it. Need to mail it today."

The sheriff nodded. "Guess you saw who those expenses were for."

Tee had noticed Melvin Cobb, Bell's deputy, listed as a defendant on the invoices for legal services. There were also medical expenses. "Sorry, Morgan. I was just trying to be sure to include everything I needed to. Like everything else you tell me, it stays here."

"Well, you know everything else about my life, may as well tell you this. Melvin Cobb is my son and he's been a thief. Caught him in the middle of a burglary. Said he was just looking for food. From the starved look he had, I believed him. But he did write a few hot checks, did at least one burglary. He's also abused alcohol in times past."

Tee's eyes widened. "I had no idea." But the information did explain a lot of things. People wondered why Bell had hired such a young man with no experience in law enforcement.

Morgan walked to the coffee pot and refilled his cup—atypical for him. While Wilda was busy typing, he sat and spoke softly. "I ain't proud of it, but I got involved with a woman right after I was elected sheriff. She fawned over me when I was checking out The Wheelhouse one night, looking for a felon. Guess I let the gun and badge go to my head. One thing led to another."

"No need to tell me anything you don't want to."

But Morgan Bell seemed to want to unload. "I never knew I had a son till he was almost sixteen and I caught him pulling that burglary. I told him to call his parents. Imagine my surprise when his mama walked in and said I was his daddy. He was a mess, and I guess, and maybe still is. What I'm most ashamed of is putting the boy on the county payroll. Justified it in my mind by telling myself I needed to keep an eye on him to keep him from taking up stealing again. Thought I could turn him into a man. Still do."

Tee thought about commiserating, sharing some of his own woes, but refrained. "Did Peggy forgive you?"

"Peggy's more than I deserve. She was hurt, of course, but she's the one who insisted we get him some help and pay for it. I told him he would have to give up the drink before I would hire him."

"I hate to ask, but are you sure he's your son?"

"No way to know for sure. All I know is that his birth certificate is dated almost exactly nine months after I got involved with his mother. I know who I was looking for in The Wheelhouse that night and I looked back at case files and made sure of the date. Sad thing is…my daughter was born two weeks after he was. I hope she never finds out what a pig her daddy is."

"We all make our share of mistakes. Don't beat yourself up too much."

Morgan walked to the window and looked out on the square. "Speak of the devil; he's coming across the square now."

Tee walked over and watched as Melvin Cobb came across

the square. Unlike his father, he wore a full deputy uniform, a silver belly hat and a .45 on his hip. The young man coming across the square moved with athletic grace. Tee was surprised he had never noticed that Melvin looked like a younger version of Morgan Bell.

Morgan frowned as he watched. "He's coming for me. Might as well get you paid and get out of your hair."

"I hate to bring it up, but I still have that safe back there. Joe Henry said he told you about it."

"He did. If it has the stuff he said it did, the district attorney will want to take a look before we move it. Joe Henry is trying to find out if Simpson has any living relatives. I'll need some paperwork to allow me to take possession of it. Can you keep it here till then? Won't be much longer."

"Whatever you say. Sorta like having a rattlesnake in the closet, though."

Tee dropped Morgan's check on Wilda's desk and walked outside with the sheriff. He was curious as to Melvin's mission. Out of breath, Melvin shook hands with Tee. The handshake was firm, the smile charming. "Morning, Tee. Keeping the IRS off the sheriff's back?"

"Trying my best."

Melvin turned toward Morgan. "Sheriff, got a report of a mad dog over on Dallas Street."

As the sheriff and his deputy scurried across the square, Tee wondered if handling a rabid dog was about as exciting as law enforcement got in this peaceful little town. He also wished he had asked Morgan Bell if Melvin knew he was his father. But he had little time to wonder. It was the last day of tax season.

THIRTY-THREE

MORGAN BELL HAD JUST LEFT WHEN TEE saw Jack Prince headed his way, carrying two briefcases. He had no appointment, but was expected. He had spent deadline day in his office last year, no reason to think he wouldn't do it again. Tee knew Prince would happily keep him there past midnight to have another story to tell, so he quickly and courteously told Jack that going over his data on this last day for filing was not going to happen this year. Jack mildly protested that he only wanted to ask a few questions, so Tee told him to take a seat and wait. *Fool me once, shame on you. Fool me twice, shame on me.* Tee was determined not to fall into Prince's trap again.

He had already taken a wild guess at Jack's possible tax liability and completed an extension form for him, but Jack seemed to enjoy the spectacle of bringing in all his data on the day he called Armageddon. He wanted as many people as possible to see how complex and bulky his business affairs were and tried to strike up conversations about the complexities of his many business holdings and the heavy boot of government with everyone who came into Tee's office. But the people who streamed through the office on deadline day were too focused on their own returns to listen to Jack.

Tee felt uncomfortable having him sit in the front of his office as a steady stream of procrastinating clients with appointments anxiously picked up their returns to get them postmarked before the deadline, but could see no way to stop him.

When all the completed returns were picked up and the last client left at closing time, Tee tried to persuade Jack to leave his records behind so he could start going over them next week. But Jack held onto the records like they were natural appendages. He wanted to explain each transaction, receipt, check, deposit slip, and contract of his complex business life to his taxman.

He also wanted to discuss the consortium. "It's been a few weeks now, Jessup. How can you turn down such a good opportunity?"

Tee shook his head. "Too busy to talk about that today, Jack."

He ushered a reluctant Jack out and waved goodbye, recognized he would not file his return until a day before his extension expired. He would arrive without appointment and they would repeat the game Jack liked to play. He thrived on the drama and living close to the edge; filing on time would bore him. He wanted everyone on the street and at the post office to see him mail his bulky tax return at the eleventh hour on the day when his final extension expired.

Tee locked the door and turned toward Jubal, asleep on

a side table, his head on a chair cushion, tired from baseball practice. He knew his son had not had supper and felt guilty.

Tee planned on taking his first weekday off in more than two months the next day and didn't want to return to a cluttered office, so he tidied up and moved all files away from prying eyes before he roused Jubal. "How about I buy you a late burger and fries?"

Jubal looked out at the Riverby Square gone dark. "Prigmore's kitchen is closed. Thought Blaze was gonna sing."

Tee had forgotten. He looked out on the dark square. "Guess they're not gonna sing after all. How about a burger from Miss Shiflett's? She's always open." Tee felt a little guilty calling so late, but it was true she was almost always open. Miss Shiflett sold hamburgers through her kitchen window a block off the square, only closed when she went to bed, and it was an hour before her bedtime. She also had a soft spot for Jubal and his daddy. She had been his first client when he bought the firm. He called her and ordered.

When she handed Tee the burgers and fries through her kitchen window, she waved at Jubal. "So, are you boys going to the singing tonight?"

"Nobody was down there when we left."

"You best go back. I'm leaving right now."

Tee was tired, unsure he wanted to go back, but he knew Jubal did. They carried their burgers to the bench outside his office, got two Cokes from inside, and watched as kids from high school placed lanterns around the perimeter of the square gazebo and opened folding chairs on the brick pavement in front. When Tee and Jubal went around the corner to throw away their empty sacks, they heard the sounds of instruments being tuned, laughter. Harmony O'Hara, Sheriff Morgan Bell, and Blaze were tuning up.

Tee and Jubal walked over and sat on the gazebo steps as the few available seats began to fill. Blaze came over when he saw Jubal. "How's my woods-boy?"

Jubal put balled fists on his hips, a pose the soon-to-be teen copied from Freddy Albright. "Pretty good."

Tee nodded toward the sheriff. "Didn't recognize Sheriff Bell at first."

Blazed chuckled. "Just remember, the sheriff loves to play and sing, but don't seem to want anybody to hear him. Too bashful. And you probably won't hear any songs you ever heard before."

The sheriff was dressed in overalls, brogan shoes, and a floppy hat that reminded Tee of old family photos of his father's family. The bones in his face seemed more prominent and he looked leaner in the outfit, like a Depression-Era farmer who had missed a lot of meals. He even appeared slightly stooped, something Tee had not noticed before, as if carrying a heavy load across his shoulders. Tee had heard the sheriff described as "skin and bone", soft-spoken and shy. People who didn't know him wondered how he ever captured criminals. Of course, there weren't many criminals in Riverby.

"I like old songs. Just surprised he goes to all that trouble."

Blaze smiled. "Yep. Seems to think people won't recognize him in that getup. Feels singing in public is beneath the dignity of the sheriff's office. And he won't sing anything published after 1950 and prefers 'em even older. Likes original country, folk, gospel and mountain music."

"I didn't know the three of you performed together."

"First time in public. This is Harmony's idea. If a crowd gathers, the sheriff is likely to clam up."

Tee looked around the square. People sat in their cars with the windows down and others brought chairs to sit on the brick street.

Morgan Bell tuned his fiddle and Harmony her guitar. Blaze tested his ukulele and harmonica. Harmony took charge. "Let's start with one we all know. You boys okay with *I'll Fly Away?*"

Blaze let Harmony sing most of it solo before joining in on the chorus. Morgan played his fiddle, ignoring the crowd. She followed it with *You Are My Sunshine* and then coaxed Blaze to sing *Down in the Valley* solo. An hour of songs passed before Morgan lent his voice. They sang *Down to the River to Pray* together. Blaze made a pleading motion with his hands. "How about a little of the Singing Brakeman, Sheriff?"

Morgan reluctantly sawed his fiddle to get up his nerve, then sang a Jimmie Rodgers classic, *Daddy and Home*. Tee's father had introduced him to the music John T had loved as a boy and Tee had found some old 33 rpm and 78 rpm records in a garage sale. The sheriff's voice was eerily similar to Rodgers'.

Joe Henry sat beside Tee as Morgan finished. "That wouldn't be a tear I see in your eye, would it?"

Tee was not ashamed. "Reminds me of my daddy in more ways than one. The words, of course, but Daddy loved Jimmie Rodgers voice. Never heard it done better. Morgan's a real talent. The voice and the yodel sound just like Jimmie Rodgers. The sheriff even looks like him in that getup."

"Yep. He's got the blue yodel down. Too bad he keeps his talent hidden under his own personal bucket."

"If I could sing like that, you couldn't get me to shut up."

The trio interrupted them with Blaze and Morgan singing "From this valley they say you are leaving" Harmony joined in for the rest of *Red River Valley*. When it was finished, the sheriff consulted his pocket watch and stood. "About time to call it a night."

Morgan's wife, Peggy stepped forward from the shadows. "Sing one more Jimmie Rodgers railroad song."

Morgan smiled at her, glanced at Blaze and sang *Train Whistle Blues*. It was Blaze's turn to tear up.

People in cars got out and people sitting stood. All clapped. Tee walked up the gazebo steps and shook all the performers' hands. "Really appreciate y'all letting us listen in. Brought back a lot of memories. Good ones."

Joe Henry walked back across the square with Tee and Jubal. Tee shook his head in wonder. "Is this a Hurt Circle normal event they've been keeping secret?"

Joe looked over his shoulder as they put up their instruments. "Nope. I expect it was Harmony's idea. I heard they've been singing awhile, but only for themselves. You can feel privileged."

Under a broken streetlamp a half-block off the square, a '67 yellow Ford pickup sat in the dark. A few doors down from the bank, its owner bent on one knee inside a dark alcove said to be the former home of a long abandoned livery stable. The old barn was falling in and some considered it a public hazard. But others kept talking about a historical marker that would likely never come about. When the singing was over and the crowd dispersed, he walked toward his truck. He had come to town to get a counter check for paying the IRS, but found the bank too crowded to conduct personal business. The post office was also too crowded. He hated obeying instructions from Big Brother, anyway. One day's violation of their arbitrary deadline would not matter. And it felt good to defy them. When he saw the musicians start to gather, he knew tomorrow was soon enough.

THIRTY-FOUR

Deadline Day Plus One

TOKE ALBRIGHT POKED LEONARD TOON'S shoulder as Leonard unwrapped a sandwich. "What did you do to make the Mexican mad?"

Leonard looked toward the red Camaro parked in the shade of a giant pile of uprooted trees. Angelino Salinas sat on the ground leaned against one of the car's stolen spoke wheels chewing on what looked like a tamale. "Don't let him hear you call him Mexican. Says he's Spanish; that Cortez, the famous explorer, is his granddaddy a few generations back. Says Cortez is his middle name."

Toke frowned. "His attitude was real good when he got here, but it sure has turned sour. Figured you said something to piss him off."

"I been as nice as I can be." Leonard removed his sweat-stained and greasy cap, wiped his forehead with a sleeve. "Seriously, you haven't noticed anything strange about him?"

"Like what?"

Leonard made a circling motion with his index finger and pointed to his forehead. "I think he may be screwed up in the head. Don't tell me you ain't noticed he acts strange."

"Well, he does turn the charm on and off pretty easy. Might have a chip on his shoulder."

Leonard shook his head. "It's more'n that. I'm here to tell you this guy is screwed up. He lies when telling the truth is easier. Makes him mad as hell he has to service the equipment we operate. At least three times this week, he swears up and down he's used the grease gun and filled the tanks up with diesel when I know damn well he didn't. I ran out of diesel in the heart of the day more than once. Ain't you?"

Toke had noticed, but remembered what Wheeler Parker had told him about cutting Salinas a lot of slack. "You never mentioned that to me."

"What do you think I'm doing now? Figured I'd make sure first. I'm sure now. I watched from behind the levee this morning. He got here about fifteen minutes early, not the hour early he's supposed to. Sat in the front seat of his fancy car playing Mexican music and drinking instead of servicing the equipment."

"Well, he's Wheeler Parker's man. He brought him down here. I'll speak to him. If he don't straighten up, I'll ask Wheeler if I can fire him."

"Be careful what you say to him before then. If you ask me, he'd cut both our throats for a peanut butter sandwich. You seen that big blade he carries? Showed me a pistol he keeps under the seat of his car the other day, too."

"Seems like I know somebody else keeps a pistol and a hunting knife in their pickup."

"Sure do and a rifle and shotgun on my gun rack." Leonard pointed to his head again. "But I ain't got a screw loose. All I'm saying is watch your step. Mark my words. Something bad wrong with this ol' boy."

Leonard leaned in closer and looked Toke in the eyes. "I'm serious. We're talking pure evil. I can see Lucifer himself in his eyes and hear him in his voice. If his name really is Angel, he's a dark angel, for sure."

Toke stood and smiled. "Evil, huh?"

"Did you sleep during Brother Essary's sermon last Sunday? His sermon on the forces of darkness perfectly described a demon like we got on our hands. Just ask Lydia."

Two hours later, Leonard climbed back aboard his dozer after his eighth trip to the ice chest in his pickup, got his feet tangled between the joy stick and brakes, started the dozer forward, fell on the track and got carried to the blade. Cut, dazed, bleeding, and seconds away from being crushed, he pulled himself over the blade and stumbled out of the way just in time. The dozer kept going. Toke turned in time to see Leonard jump over the blade and roll out of the path. He stopped his dozer and ran over to stop Leonard's.

On the way to the clinic in Riverby for stitches, Leonard admitted "about six" trips to the beer cooler in the back of his pickup. Toke waited until his friend was bandaged and in good hands before going back to work. They were now behind schedule. The long day got a little longer as Toke stopped near a trash pile on the county road by the bridge over Moccasin Creek when he thought he heard the sounds of a dozer running. The sound made him climb over the creek embankment instead of driving around it. It was shorter and quicker and he could see without being seen.

Angelino was on Leonard's dozer making a mess of two days' work. Toke ran toward him, waving and making halt motions with his hands and arms, but could not get his attention until he walked in front of the dozer. Angelino stopped inches from Toke's boots and revved the engine as if he might run over him. Toke recalled Leonard's warnings as he looked into the Mexican's eyes. Angelino smiled and let the engine idle.

Toke waited for him to climb down. "What the hell are you doing?"

Angelino shrugged. "Helping out till you got back from the hospital. How is the old drunk?"

"You ever run a dozer before?"

"No, but I been watching the two of you. Pretty easy. Look what I got done while you were gone."

"I'm looking at it, all right. Do you have any idea what we're trying to accomplish here by moving all this dirt and building these levees?"

"Just doing what I saw the drunk doing before he fell off."

"What you're doing will cause water to run where we don't want it to go. Take me the rest of the day to fix the damage you did."

Salinas's quick and hot temper flared as he thought of the switchblade in his boot. He could gut Albright in a heartbeat. "What did you want me to do while you were gone, sit on my ass?"

"You could've been doing what you were supposed to do early this morning. Or you might have used the chainsaw or the box blade on the little tractor the way I showed you. I didn't exactly have time to stop and give you instructions while Leonard was bleeding, now did I?"

"It's his own damn fault."

That was too much. Toke stuck a finger in Salinas's chest. "Where you comin' from with this attitude?"

Salinas's eyes flashed. He stepped back as if struck. "I never liked this shit job anyway. Never liked working with that old drunk. Or you."

"That old drunk you're talkin' about is worth a dozen of the likes of you."

Angelino held out an open palm. "Before I have to gut your fish belly, pay me and I'll be on my way."

"If I didn't know better, I'd take that as a threat." Toke spat into the open palm.

Toke stared until Angelino stepped aside, then climbed aboard the dozer and yelled from the seat. "Wheeler Parker will bring out payday money on Friday, like he does every week. This is Wednesday. But you can go ahead and haul your ass on down the road right now. Maybe, just maybe, I'll tell the boss to pay you for the two and a half days you got coming, less the damage you did the last few hours."

Toke pulled away and began to reverse the damage. Salinas's Camaro cut a circle in the loose dirt and pulled away with wheels spinning, clods flying.

At quitting time, Toke killed his engine, but could still hear a dozer running. He looked behind him in time to see the other dozer turn over Leonard's pickup and crush it into an embankment. Angelino backed up, pointed the dozer toward Moccasin Creek, and bailed off. A big oak stopped the dozer before it dropped into the deepest part of the creek. Toke gave chase, but he knew the Mexican was long gone. He had likely parked his car by the railroad tracks and sneaked in through the thick woods. When Toke climbed aboard the dozer to back it off the incline, he saw the small tractor on its side in the creek.

+≥—≤+

Clayton's brow furrowed as the happy fellow stumbled and fell off the dozer after too many beer runs to his pickup cooler. When he went out of sight in front of the blade, Clayton thought he had lost a character in his novel, wondered if he would write his death as a murder or an accident.

When the boss returned, Clayton watched him walk in front of the dozer being driven by the angry one, held his breath to see if the young man would stop. After a confrontation with his boss, the young Mexican drove his red car over the railroad tracks and out of sight. Clayton furiously scribbled. The men already had names in his work of fiction and this was a major event.

Clayton was about to finish recording the scene when he saw the Camaro reappear on a levee below his cabin. The Mexican opened the car door and leaned against a fender. While the boss operated his dozer, Clayton slipped through the trees and down the levee to the idle dozer.

Observing the carnage kept Clayton from going to the bank for a counter check and mailing his tax return. Now he would be two days late. But he liked to be in a more relaxed frame of mind when visiting the safe deposit vault. Visiting what he had left there always soothed his troubled mind. He figured one more day wouldn't matter much to Big Brother.

THIRTY-FIVE

TOKE LEFT IN A HURRY FOR THE SHERIFF'S office. Deputy Melvin Cobb sat in Morgan Bell's chair. "What can I do for you, Toke?" Melvin felt insecure around Toke, the man who had been deputy before him.

"Where's Morgan?"

"Sheriff Bell is off duty."

"Where is he?"

"Guess he wanted to be left alone, so he didn't say where he'd be tonight. Be back in the morning."

Toke turned to walk away, then came back. "Can you get him on the radio?"

"I tried to reach him a few minutes ago, but he's not answering. Sometimes, he just likes to get away from it all."

"Look, this is an emergency."

Melvin nervously placed his hands on Morgan Bell's desk. "Why don't you tell me what the emergency is? Maybe I can help."

Toke told him what Angelino Salinas had done.

"I'll get right on this."

"We need to find Morgan. This guy is dangerous and he's probably on his way to Mexico. We don't have long to stop him."

"I'll put out an APB and have law enforcement all over the state looking for him in a matter of minutes. Give me a description of him and his car."

Toke had never missed law enforcement more than he did as he stood helplessly on the courthouse steps. He wanted to be the one to catch the scumbag who called himself Angel, but felt helpless. He thought about going to the clinic to tell Leonard about his truck, but worried it might cause him to have a heart attack and die. He still owed money on that old truck. Another heart flare-up might be one too many. Tomorrow was soon enough.

As he walked to his pickup, Toke remembered Wednesday night was "choir practice" night, and the sheriff often went into radio silence for an hour or so prior. He called it his ruminating time. Toke had an hour to kill before choir practice so he went home to check on Lydia and Freddy.

Melvin Cobb headed for his patrol car. He intended to catch this man called Angel. Then maybe the sheriff would respect him.

At the supper table, Toke pushed around his food and listened to wife Lydia's usual Wednesday night pleadings about the value of church, home, and family, and the evils of gambling. The woman was a saint, and everybody in Riverby knew it. Toke knew he didn't deserve her. Everybody seemed to agree with him on that. He didn't want to frighten her, so he didn't tell her what had happened in the bottoms.

He took a sip of iced tea. "Going to prayer meeting, I guess."

She put a hand to her forehead. "You know, I feel a little faint tonight and Blaze said the meeting would be cut short. Think I may stay home."

Toke's attempts at living a pure life were intermittent, trailing behind Lydia to By the River Church on Sunday where he listened to Blaze lead the singing and the good Reverend Enoch Essary drone on with a voice that scratched bad enough to make the wind bleed. But Wednesday night prayer meetings were one step too far for Toke. He played poker on Wednesday nights. He didn't tell Lydia that his poker buddies called their meetings choir practice. He liked to dress up for his one night out during the week, dressing like he did in his lawman days sans the badge and gun.

Toke pushed the end of his Ranger belt through the silver keeper and glanced at Lydia. She was a lovely, gentle woman who wore no makeup and styled her long hair like a Pentecostal. He gently put his large hands around her small arms and pulled her close. Her voice was pleading as she put her hands on his chest. "Freddy needs help with his math homework tonight and you know I'm no good at math."

He knew it was an excuse. Lydia thought playing poker was a sin, any winnings ill-gotten, and losses took food off the family table or the offering plate at church. Toke glanced at his son and his homework at the kitchen table. The boy was the spitting image of his father and Toke's pride and joy—a star athlete in three sports who made above average grades.

He walked over to his son. "Write down any questions you have on problems and leave them out on the kitchen table. I'll look 'em over when I get home. We'll get up a few minutes early in the morning and solve the problems together." He looked to Lydia for approval.

She stepped in front of him before he pushed open the screen door. "Now Toke, you know what we can afford to lose on such foolishness as poker, and it ain't much."

He smiled. "I know, honey. Hope you get to feeling better."

He understood her concern, but Toke kept meticulous records of his gambling and was, in fact, several hundred dollars ahead for the two years he had played at Prigmore's hay barn. He dared not let Lydia know, but his winnings had recently been used to pay for much needed dental work for the whole family. He told her it was overtime pay for dozer work. Lydia would have given up a tooth rather than use poker winnings to pay for a filling. Toke was so confident of his gambling skills that he planned to take his winnings to Louisiana for some real gambling.

In the meantime, he went to Don Prigmore's barn for a weekly game with men who mostly played in overalls or greasy jeans and shirts with holes in them. Prigmore, owner of the store on the Riverby square that was considered headquarters for everything from dry goods to groceries to firearms, hosted the game in the alley of his hay barn.

Sometimes, but not often, the most powerful men in Riverby dropped by dressed in their best starched Levis or gray wool pants and tie. When Jack Prince, owner of the local GM dealership and major landlord, graced the group with his presence, he always arrived in a custom made shirt and shoes that cost more than Toke's best boots.

Wednesdays were quarter ante, three bump limit, but every other Friday night was high-roller night with table stakes. On rare occasions, a pot might reach a thousand dollars. Toke had waited two years to be invited to a Friday game, likely only in the event Don Prigmore could not pull together five players without him.

More important to Toke, Sheriff Morgan Bell was just a kibitzer at Friday games, but almost always showed for a few hands at Wednesday games. The games were technically illegal, so the sheriff's presence legitimized them in Morgan's mind and in the minds of the players. Toke counted on him showing up tonight.

On the way to the game, Toke tried, but could not chase away his dream of returning to the law not as a deputy, but as sheriff. Toke planned to run for Bell's job when he decided to step down. It was a secret everyone guessed but nobody talked about. But the primary election was only days away and it was too late for Toke once again. His only hope now was for the sheriff to change his mind before the general election and support Toke as a write-in candidate. The old man could pretty much choose his successor.

THIRTY-SIX

THE MAN CALLED ANGEL FIGURED HE HADN'T gotten along in this world by being stupid. Crushing a pickup and turning over a tractor didn't seem like serious crimes, but he knew Texans took great pride in their pickups and tractors. They probably hadn't noticed the shotgun and rifle he stole from the gun rack and the pistol he took from under the seat of Leonard's truck, but they likely would soon. Either way, the law was already looking for him and they would expect him to head straight to Mexico. He decided to stay hidden in the bottomland woods and think, at least until dark. He had nine thousand dollars coming from Wheeler Parker tomorrow at noon and he couldn't leave without collecting.

The law would be watching the major highways and the border for the red Camaro. He could easily find other ways to cross the border, but he didn't want to leave his car behind. And he had dodged the law many times by doing what they least expected. He decided to head to Oklahoma and find Wheeler Parker to collect what was due him instead of waiting until tomorrow to meet him. There was just one problem. He was nearly out of gas and both stations in Riverby closed at dark.

He eased along secluded dirt roads until he passed a house with lights on. A '53 Chevy was parked in front. He found an isolated spot under some trees and watched the small woman roam from one window to the other. No sign of a man. He decided she was not a threat, even if she did catch him. He removed the siphon hose and can he always carried and crept to the car in her yard.

Lydia Albright was a woman of routine. After washing and drying the supper dishes, she put Freddy back to his homework, walked through the house rearranging doilies and dusting furniture. She sat in her reading chair by the window and began her nightly reading of Scripture. She was a few verses in when she sensed a presence in the yard. She peeked into Freddy's bedroom to be sure he had not walked outside, found him already asleep. She peeked through the curtains and caught a glimpse of movement. What she suspected to be a big dog or coyote became a man as he drew closer—a man carrying a gas can and siphon hose headed toward her old Chevy. She couldn't make out his face in the dark, but he appeared to be Mexican. *Probably a poor migrant worker, broke and trying to get enough gas to get to town and buy groceries for his family.*

She walked silently into the kitchen, opened a Ball canning jar and pulled five ones from her stash. As consolation for attending poker every Wednesday instead of church, Toke put three ones in the jar each week if he lost, five if he won. She would not use the ill-gotten money for her own purposes, but found ways to use it to benefit others. She walked out on the porch with the cash in her hand.

Angelino cursed when the Chevy's tank only yielded four gallons, but it was enough to get him to Paris and maybe into Oklahoma. He was putting the cap back on the can when he heard a rustling of leaves and light footsteps. He turned enough to see a moonlit shadow approaching him with one hand in the air.

Lydia never saw the pistol until it was pressed against her forehead. She froze, kept the hand full of dollar bills high in the air. She had never had a gun pointed at her before, much less felt the cold steel of a gun barrel pressed against her head. There was enough moonlight to see the eyes that stared at her and the evil behind them. Leonard Toon had told her about those eyes and she knew she was looking at the man Leonard and Toke worked with—the man called Angel. And Leonard was right. The eyes, the face, were pure evil. She looked up and said a silent prayer.

Her voice trembled. "I came out to ask you not to take all of our gasoline. That old car is hard to start again after it runs out of gas and I'm here with my son alone. We probably won't need it until my husband comes back, but we might in case of emergency."

Angelino stared at the woman as if she were mad. Lydia extended the bills toward him. "I will be happy to give you money for gas."

Who did she think she was talking to? A beggar? He turned the revolver in his hand, pulled back his arm, and hit her beside her left eye with the grip. She dropped to the ground as if she had been shot.

✦⸺⸻✦

Wind blew through Angel's hair and the Camaro kicked up a dust cloud as he left Toke Albright's house with enough gas to reach Wheeler Parker and collect the money due him. He was doing eighty on the dirt road and feeling good until he passed the black-and-white. He saw it turn and the red light in his rearview mirror. *What kind of hick law dog patrols dirt roads at night?* He sped up, thinking he could outrun the cop, but thought better of it. He could outrun the patrol car, but not the law's radio. The cop had caught him speeding on a dirt road. He probably had no idea about what he had done with the dozer.

To be safe, he put his gun in his jacket pocket before he pulled over. He tried to appear meek and apologetic as Sheriff Bell wrote out the ticket for speeding. Irritated at the Mexican for delaying his arrival at poker, the old man ripped it out of his ticket pad and stared at the man with a pony tail driving an expensive car that might be stolen.

Morgan Bell had been writing tickets and enforcing the law longer than the young Mexican had lived. He looked hard into his eyes, trying to detect things he could have easily seen a few years before. "Do I smell liquor on your breath, boy?"

Angel kept both hands in the pockets of his jacket. "I had one beer before I left the house. That's all." Technically true, but he also had four strong pulls from a bottle of white lightning before he crushed Leonard's pickup.

Bell's memory search distracted him from making the Mexican show both his hands. "You got papers to be in these United States of America?"

Angel resented the question he had been asked since he first got a Texas license to drive, but he sucked it back. "*Sí.*

Born here. *Familia* live in Texas for two generations." Truth was a stranger to Angel Salinas, so he felt no remorse for the lie. And part of it was true. He had been born in Texas. Salinas's father, a wealthy Mexican landowner, had impregnated his mother, a *bracero* who worked on his farm. His father sneaked her across the border and stuck her in a little hovel in a long row of such shacks housing women in similar condition who wanted to be close to a Texas hospital. Angel was delivered in the emergency room of that hospital. Angel and his mother stayed in America long enough for him to be granted a birth certificate, no longer.

"You got a job?"

"*Si*. On the levees down by Moccasin Creek driving dozers."

"Who's your foreman out there?"

Salinas's face took on an even darker hue. He knew the old bastard lawman was trying to catch him in a lie. "Toke Albright."

Morgan studied him a few minutes longer. Angel figured the lawman was enjoying watching him squirm. Bell handed him the ticket, and Angel accepted it with one hand. "Where you from originally? You look familiar."

Angel sucked in. "Laredo. *Mi papi* is a truck farmer." Antonio Salinas was a truck farmer, but on the Mexico side of the border. Antonio allowed him to use his name, but never acknowledged him as his progeny. Angel and his mother lived little better than the other *braceros*.

"So how come you're so far north? Don't see many Mexicans around here out of season."

Out of season? The old bastard was treating him like he was some sort of fruit or vegetable instead of a human. Angel forced a malevolent grin. "Got tied up with a *senorita* didn't like truck farming. Thinks I can be a singer."

The wheels of Morgan Bell's experienced mind turned as he looked away from the handsome young Mexican to focus his thoughts. He made a circling, receiving motion with his hand as a way of telling him to go on as Morgan looked through the Camaro's window. A rifle, shotgun and pistol lay in the back floorboard. The long guns looked familiar.

"Sure carrying a lot of weapons around. Expecting trouble?"

Angel was getting nervous. "I buy and sell old guns some."

The sheriff was close to figuring out where he had seen the face before. He couldn't remember what the man had done, but his face was definitely on some paperwork in his office. He needed a few more minutes. "So where did you buy these and how much you want for 'em?"

Salinas's face grew darker. This fish belly law dog was making fun of him. "A flea market down in the valley."

The words brought the old song to mind, and Morgan knew that those words usually jogged his memory when he needed it most. He whistled the tune and managed a couple of verses in a half-hearted low tone as he walked around the Camaro. "Down in the valley, valley so low. Hang your head over, hear the wind blow."

When he caught a glimpse of the ponytail tucked under the man's coat collar, he knew. The guns belonged to Leonard Toon, and Morgan did have a poster on this guy. Vehicular manslaughter. Wire services said the fugitive ran over a young man, a high school kid, and crippled him, then backed over his girlfriend when she came to help. The boy was now a paraplegic. The girl was dead. The killer drove a black Barracuda, but there were no plates identified. This fellow was driving a red Camaro, but that didn't exclude him.

This was a big fish Morgan Bell possibly had on the line and he didn't want to scare him until he set the hook. He turned to face Salinas. "Need to see both your hands."

A crow cawed as Angel stepped back one step. He fingered the .38 in the pocket of his blue jean jacket, the same gun he used to get away from a mule-headed father down in Zapata who thought his daughter was too young and too white to be in the car with him alone. The little wench led him on. Wasn't his fault she fought him and tore half her clothes off in the process. The father would have killed him if he hadn't pulled the pistol. He had no choice.

The sheriff's experienced eyes watched the dead look come into Angel's eyes. Morgan slowly put one hand on his pistol grip as he reached for his cuffs with the other. "I need you to place your hands on top of your car. I got a few more questions to ask down at the courthouse. Won't take long."

Angel knew he could not do that. Knew they might tie him to the girl and boy in Bastrop County. The Barracuda he had been driving might still be on Jack Prince's dealership lot. He stepped back another step. "You're just after me cause I'm Mexican. I ain't done nothing wrong."

Morgan Bell stepped forward as his years of experience were outweighed by his advanced age. Angelino Cortez Salinas fired the .38 from his jacket pocket. The bullet tore a hole in the jacket and a matching one in the sheriff's shirt. Morgan managed to get off an errant shot as he fell. The bullet found its way to the Camaro's radiator.

Bird wings rustled leaves as birds left their roosts, protesting with hoots, calls, and caws. *Roses love sunshine, violets love dew, angels in heaven, know I love you.* Morgan Bell would never hum or sing his favorite songs again.

THIRTY-SEVEN

THE RADIO IN BELL'S CAR SQUAWKED AS ANGEL stood over the sheriff's body, slapping at his ears to stop the ringing. "Come in sheriff, this is Deputy Cobb. Be on the lookout for a red Camaro. Toke Albright reported major damage by Moccasin Creek earlier." Then silence. "Sheriff?"

Adrenaline pumped. This was big trouble. Salinas needed to get the black-and-white off the road into the trees and the sheriff's body and his car out of sight. He was about to drag the sheriff to the trunk of the patrol car when he heard a tractor coming down the road. No time for hiding now. He ran for his car.

The tractor came over a hill just in time for the driver to get a good moonlight view of the scene and the man running from it. Freddy Albright had not heard the shot over the noise of the tractor, but he locked eyes with Angelino Salinas for a split second.

When the boy stopped the tractor and ran toward the murder scene, the Camaro left two trails of smoke and dust as it spun away. Watching the scene from his rearview mirror, Salinas cut his lights and stopped.

Freddy had been on his way to the Prigmore barn to find his father. His mother had come into his bedroom with her head bleeding and passed out as she reached his bed. When he could not revive her, he carried her to the car but it ran out of gas before he got out of the driveway. He left her in the seat and climbed on their tractor.

When Freddy kneeled over the sheriff's body and saw the open eyes of a dead man for the first time in his life, he panicked. He had to get away and get help for his mother quickly. Sheriff Bell was dead and that was awful, but he needed his patrol car. He had just opened the door to the black-and-white when he heard squealing tires and turned to see the Camaro smoking like it was on fire, backing toward him. The Camaro's rear bumper caught him in the shins and the sheriff's car door crushed his chest.

Angel was a mile away when he realized the boy and the woman had seen his face. Someone would come looking for that sheriff and find the boy. Every cop in Texas and surrounding states would be looking for his Camaro. The car's temperature gauge was already registering hot and it couldn't be on the road, anyway. Going to Oklahoma in this car would be too dangerous. Deep in a pit of anxiety, he came to a sliding stop to keep from colliding with a train at Panther Crossing. He considered the secluded area under the trestle while the train passed, wondered if he could drive the car down there without getting stuck. From there, he could walk to Moccasin Creek Bottom in the morning for his meeting with Wheeler Parker.

Parker would pay him his money and arrange to get him out of the country. He moved slowly across the track after the train passed. That's when he saw the Airstream.

Toke parked his beige Ford pickup in front of Prigmore's barn right on time, looked for the sheriff's black-and-white with a red spotlight on the driver's side, but didn't see it. As he sat at the poker table with the regulars, Jack Prince arrived in gray wool slacks and shiny Florsheims.

Don Prigmore wasted no time in dealing the first hand of five card draw. Toke pitched two quarters in the pot and spoke to Prigmore over his cards. "Heard anything from Morgan?"

"Told me this morning he would be here. Expect him any minute."

Blaze, always late due to real choir practice and prayer meeting, walked in a little earlier than usual because the prayer meeting had been cut short. As was his custom on choir practice nights, he swapped his usual railroad cap for his daddy's worn-out Stetson. Blaze didn't enjoy poker and wanted to be sure all the chairs were occupied before he arrived. He preferred to kibitz.

But Morgan Bell's chair was empty. Don Prigmore motioned toward it. "You can sit in till the sheriff gets here if you want." Blaze reluctantly sat in the chair, figuring Morgan Bell would save him by the time the hand was over.

Jack Prince called the bet and nudged Toke with an elbow. "What you need the sheriff for? You aimin' to turn us in for illegal gambling?" Jack looked around the table to see if his remark drew any laughs, but was disappointed.

Bets done on the first round, Toke placed two discards on the table and said, without looking up, "I'll take two."

Don dealt two, and Toke spread the cards in his hand. "Had a little incident in the bottoms today. Leonard got himself hurt. When I took him to the clinic, the Mexican working with us went nuts and wrecked his truck and a tractor. Tried to drive a dozer into Moccasin Creek."

Prince leaned back in his chair. "Really? How come?"

"The man calls himself Angel if you can believe that. Says his real name is Angelino Cortez Salinas. Least that's what he says. Who knows what it really is. Leonard tried to warn me about him, but I wouldn't listen. Now Leonard's in the hospital and his truck's wrecked."

Blaze shook his head. "Leonard told me about him. Said the man was like the devil's own demon. Said he even smelled like evil might smell."

Jack seemed to forget about his cards. "How bad is Leonard hurt?"

"Cuts and bruises, but I worry about his heart when I tell him about his truck. Imagine how much damage a dozer can do to a pickup in a few minutes. All the tires are blown and it's crushed against an embankment. Leonard still owes money on that truck."

Prince rubbed his eyes with his thumb and index finger. "What's the price tag?"

"Hard to tell. The truck's totaled and the tractor is on its side in the creek."

"Did he get away?"

"He got away from me, but I know what he's driving. Tried to tell Morgan, but he was off duty and Melvin Cobb said he couldn't be reached. Cobb was gonna put out an APB."

"APB?"

"All points bulletin. Goes out to law enforcement agencies all over so they can watch for him."

Don Prigmore laid his cards face down on the table and bounced the deck. "Cobb really said Morgan couldn't be reached? He's probably on his way here. He meanders through the back roads sometimes. Says it's his time to ponder on the meaning of life."

Blaze stood. "Do we even know if this Angel demon has left? Any chance he might be hiding right under our noses?"

Toke stood, beginning to realize he made a mistake by leaving his family alone. "I need to go check on Lydia and Freddy just in case."

Blaze frowned. "Don, what back roads does Morgan take?"

"Different ones, but comes across Panther Crossing and across Moccasin Creek Bridge most of the time. Not too far from Toke's house, come to think of it."

Toke ran out the door. Blaze followed. "You check on the family and I'll see if I can locate the sheriff."

THIRTY-EIGHT

TOKE BERATED HIMSELF AS HE LEFT THE POKER game. Salinas was likely halfway to Mexico, but that was not an excuse for leaving his family alone. He pushed the old Ford pickup pretty hard and almost ran into his own Allis Chalmers tractor as he topped a hill. His headlights revealed the bloody scene.

He stumbled out of the truck and had to step across Morgan Bell's dead body on the way to his son.

Toke sat on the bloody dirt and cradled Freddy's head in his lap. "How bad are you hurt, son?"

"Mama's sick. Needs a doctor."

"What happened? Why are you on the tractor instead of in the car?"

The words came at a painful cost. "She passed out. Her head's bleeding." Tears rolled down his cheeks.

Toke wiped at his nose and eyes with a shirt sleeve, knew he had to be brave for his son. "Can you move?"

When blood ran from his nose and mouth and Freddy's breathing hurt like being stabbed with a knife, the fright left the boy's eyes. He seemed to calm himself. "No, go get Mama first."

Toke managed to pull open the damaged door of the sheriff's patrol car. He found the keys in the ignition just as Blaze arrived. Blaze fell at Morgan Bell's feet as he rushed toward Toke and Freddy. He pushed himself up and stumbled to Toke's side. "What do you want to do first?"

"He says Lydia is hurt, too. Help me put Freddy in the patrol car and then go check on her. I'll take him to the clinic. You bring her."

Toke feared he would faint as they tried to gently lift Freddy into the back seat. Freddy's scream ricocheted through the trees, down the bottoms, to the creek. Coyotes heard it as a death wail and answered with their yips and howls.

Toke held the damaged door with one hand and eased the patrol car toward town. He glanced at the dead sheriff as they passed.

"Who did this thing, son?"

Freddy grimaced. "Red Camaro...Mexican driving it." His eyes rolled back and Toke thought his son was dead.

Blaze found Lydia lying in the seat of their old car, blood running into the cracks of the vinyl seat covers. He carried her to his truck and headed to town.

Jack Prince gave Toke and Blaze time to get out of sight before leaving the game. He decided to head to the Shelton farm before going to his office. Pieces of Jory Shelton's abandoned house were scattered in the yard and on the drive that led to it.

Otherwise, the place looked pretty much like it had when Shelton lived there. Jory shot himself while crossing a barbed-wire fence with a shotgun in his hand. Because he had used guns all his life and was an experienced hunter, everyone assumed he was drinking or committed suicide. Jory left no living relatives, at least none anybody could find. The bank repossessed his property. It bordered Cooper Newman's cattle ranch.

Jack honked his horn outside the barn. Newman pushed open the barn door and walked out. Jack put one foot out the car door and stood. "Get in. We got a major problem that's going to take all of us."

The smell of alcohol came into the car with Newman, but he seemed to be listening as Jack told him what Angel had done at the construction site. Newman's headache showed in his eyes as he turned to Jack. "So, what does this have to do with me?"

"You still don't get what's going on, do you? This Angel character is a mule for Wheeler. He knows me as well as Wheeler."

"He doesn't know me, does he?"

Jack shook his head. "How much have you had to drink? He may not know you, but he knows what the consortium does, or at least his old man does. One of us goes down, we all go down."

"I never signed up for this kinda crap."

"Hell, you think any of us did? You asked to come into this. Can't believe you're still living in that old barn."

"Me and the wife are still having a few problems."

"Ever think of cutting back on the booze?"

In his gin lot office, Prince used his special phone and called Wheeler Parker.

Wheeler barged through the door less than an hour later. "What the hell is the emergency? This is a big night at the Wheelhouse."

Jack pointed a skinny finger at him. "I'll tell you what the emergency is. That young greaser you brought in is about to get us all thrown in jail. I knew he was trouble the first time I laid eyes on him." He told him what Toke said at the poker game.

The news rattled the normally composed Wheeler Parker. "Toke Albright give you any idea where the bastard was?"

"Said he figured he was on his way to Mexico. Toke's on his way to find the sheriff."

Wheeler ran his fingers through his thinning hair. "We need to get to him before the sheriff does. He knows too much."

Jack's voice was reedy. "And how are we gonna do that?"

"I think I may know. He's got a good deal of money coming from me. We were supposed to meet around noon tomorrow. Don't think he'll leave the country without collecting. He'll need the cash, especially now. He'll either come to me at the horse farm or wait for me where we usually meet."

Cooper slumped into Prince's leather couch. "So what are we gonna do with him if we find him?" He winced as if he did not want to hear the answer.

Wheeler looked at both men. "Depends on him."

THIRTY-NINE

THE CAMARO WAS OUT OF WATER AND smoking, so Angel pointed it under the trestle at Panther Crossing. The car's front wheels entered the water and stopped. He covered it with as many leaves and limbs as he could find and climbed back to the road to be sure it couldn't be seen from there. He easily broke into the Airstream and found a jar of peanut butter, some crackers, a bag of stale potato chips, and two Hostess chocolate cupcakes, enough to sustain him till his meeting with Parker the next morning.

He tried to relax at the small table inside the Airstream, but could not. Waiting on Wheeler Parker now seemed a mistake. By morning, everyone in Riverby would know what he had done and Parker would keep his distance. He needed to meet him now. He needed wheels and a telephone. From the Airstream window he saw a light coming from the window of a shack a few yards north.

Using the flashlight he found by the crackers, he walked

toward the house. The flashlight revealed more than a dozen yelping, fighting dogs inside a pen made for two and a larger pack in a fenced yard filled with junk. More dogs patrolled the fence perimeter. The dogs were a problem, but the shack seemed his only choice.

A small shop or barn was surrounded by what appeared to be junk cars. All were covered by tarps except two. Signs on the fence read *If You Can Read This, You Are in Range* and *Security Provided by Smith & Wesson*. Under the signs, *Trespassers* was scribbled on a wooden sign shaped like a headstone. Angelino sneered as he fingered the .38 in his pocket. *White trash.*

He felt the coolness of a gun barrel against his neck as the dogs quieted. "Help you?"

Angel expected a long beard and filthy clothes as he turned, but the man with the shotgun smelled of soap, was dressed in clean overalls and a tattered denim shirt. He was tall, thin, and stooped, his fingers so gnarled with arthritis that pulling the trigger on the shotgun would not be easy.

Angel's voice was unsteady. "Car broke down back there. Hoping I could use your phone."

"No phone."

Angelino looked at the uncovered cars, a '57 Chevy Cameo pickup and a '49 Ford. He pointed toward the Ford. "I got money. Any chance I could pay you to take me to town so I can use a phone?"

Zeke looked at the hole with burn marks around it in Angelino's coat. "Wouldn't do any good. Ain't nobody to tow you this late at night in Riverby. How far away is your car?"

"About a mile down the road on the other side of the tracks. I can call an *amigo* to come get me if I had a phone."

"You ain't gonna freeze or starve till morning. Go on back to your car and I'll see what I can do for you after sunup." Zeke eased the shotgun barrel back an inch.

Angel turned and headed back toward the trestle. Even if he killed the old man, he didn't have enough bullets to kill the dogs. And he was probably telling the truth about no phone. He had to wait. The travel trailer was as good a place as any.

Blaze paid little attention to the dogs as he passed through Ghost Dog Run and drove over the trestle at Panther Crossing a few yards away from where Salinas hid. He couldn't bear to look toward the trestle, not on this terrible day. His mind wandered, trying to absorb what had happened.

Bellies full of hamburgers and beans, Tee and Jubal were still in a celebratory mood as they sat on their porch—Tee because he made it through a second tax season, and Jubal because Tee promised a campout and varmint hunt tomorrow. Jubal pointed toward the trestle. "Looks like Blaze's pickup comin' up the road."

Blaze parked his truck in the yard and closed the door softly. He walked toward them like a man with an oxbow on his back pulling a plow. Tee could see he was the bearer of bad news. Blaze smiled at Jubal, dropped to a knee to look the boy in the eyes. "I need to talk to your daddy. Think you could give us a minute or two?"

Jubal glanced at Tee. When Tee nodded, he ran into the house and into his bedroom to watch though the porch window. He cracked the window in time to hear his father moan and to see him put both hands behind his head and pull as if trying to keep from falling backward. Jubal tried but could not make out their whispers.

"I can't get my head around this. Lydia and Freddy in the hospital and Sheriff Bell dead. This just can't be, Blaze. Not in Riverby."

"I know. We don't know how these things are related, but Toke found Freddy lying beside Morgan's dead body. Morgan shot and Freddy hit by a car. I found Lydia in their old Chevy bleeding from her head. Toke says he knows who crippled Freddy. Stands to reason the same man killed Morgan."

"Who?"

"A young Mexican kid who was working in the bottom down there with Toke and Leonard. Said they got crossways this afternoon over some damage the kid did. Toke is blaming himself for the whole thing. It's bad."

"They catch the Mexican?"

Blaze shook his head. "Expect he's halfway to Mexico by now."

"What's he driving?"

"Toke says a red Camaro. Melvin put out an all points bulletin. Might catch him before he gets to the border."

"Why would he do this? What set him off?"

"Leonard Toon says he's pure evil. A demon from hell. I know one thing. A man that would do such things deserves a special place in hell."

"What do we need to do?"

"Don't know yet. We're without a sheriff and Toke is too broken up to think. I think I'll put together a search party in the morning if nobody else takes charge. Melvin will need all the help he can get."

"Search party? I thought he was gone to Mexico."

Blaze shrugged. "Probably. But what if he's not?"

"Let me know what I can do when you decide."

"Sure will try. Me or somebody else will call or come out. You gonna tell the boy?"

"I'll have to sooner or later, but not tonight. Let him get a good night's sleep. He'll be really upset. He loves Lydia and Freddy, even the sheriff. We got a horseback hunting trip and campout planned tomorrow. That's ruined, but I may wait till then to tell him."

FORTY

WHENEVER TOKE FELT SLEEP OVERTAKING HIM
during the night, he walked between Freddy's room and Lydia's. As dawn broke, he was with Lydia. Freddy was expected
to be unconscious for a few more hours. Doc Pierce said there
had been some blood around Lydia's brain, some swelling and
blurry vision. During a few coherent moments, Lydia prayed
herself out of the deep hole the man called Angel had dropped
her in.

Doc Pierce said it was either go home or go to a hospital in
Paris or Dallas where more extensive tests could be done. The
clinic was at the limit of its medical technology in her case and
could do little more for her, so he reluctantly agreed with Lydia's
decision to go home to her prayer room and turn her healing
over to God. And she said she needed to be home to be with
Freddy. One side of her face was still purple and one eye wandered aimlessly as a nurse and Toke helped her into a wheelchair.

249

She told the Lord she would manage with one eye if He would let her keep enough of her vision to read her Bible. The part she kept was still blurry, but Doc Pierce said it might clear up.

Seated in the wheelchair, she looked at Toke. "Why is Freddy not with you? You make him go to school?"

Doc Pierce advised that Freddy's injuries should be kept secret from his mother until she was out of danger. Toke took a deep breath, drew a chair next to her wheelchair, and patted her hand. "Lydia, Freddy was hurt, too. He's going to be all right, but you need to know what happened before you see him."

Lydia's hand went to her mouth. "Hurt how? He was in bed asleep when I went outside."

"Guess you don't remember, but you managed to get all the way to his room. Passed out on his bed and he carried you to the car. He was taking you to the hospital, but ran out of gas before he got to the road. Came back to get the tractor and came looking for me, but he got hit by a car."

"How bad?"

"Doc Pierce says he'll recover."

Lydia read Toke's face, knew he was holding something back. "Where was he hurt? Where is he now?"

Toke sighed deeply. "Broke both his legs and two ribs. There was some internal bleeding at first, but they stopped it in time. We're lucky one of the ribs didn't puncture a lung. Doctors said his days as an athlete may be over, but he'll live a normal life otherwise."

"I'm ready to see him."

"He's here in the hospital. You can see him as soon as you wipe away those tears so you can show him a smile."

Lydia's eyes showed stark fear as she clasped her hands,

looked up, and uttered a silent prayer as Toke wheeled her out of the room. She turned her head to face Toke. "Did the same evil person who hit me hit him?"

"Looks that way."

Lydia had never encountered evil before. She had seen sin, but had led a sheltered life away from evil. This made the world seem no longer safe. "Was it the man Leonard told me about at church, the evil one?"

Toke hung his head. "We don't know yet, but it looks like it. Freddy said he was driving a car like the one the Mexican drives."

They found Freddy asleep. She patted the bed beside his hand and whispered, "My boy."

Toke gently pulled back the sheet. Lydia gasped at the casts and bandages covering his upper body and both legs. He whispered to Lydia. "He'll be on crutches awhile. Best not to wake him yet."

Lydia hid her maternal pain. "God is good. With His help, we'll all get through this."

She took Toke's hand in hers. "How long has it been since you slept?"

Toke managed a crooked smile for the first time since it started. It was so like his wife to think of others before herself. He told her about Morgan Bell as he wheeled her to the door.

<hr />

The county judge and all the commissioners were waiting outside the clinic when Toke rolled Lydia out. The judge spoke to Lydia and then handed Toke a sheriff's badge. "It's not Morgan's, but it will have to do for now. Hope we can talk you into accepting it. We'll place ads in the papers and do a campaign to see that your name is written in for the primary. As you know, there's no opposition in the fall election."

Toke stared at the badge as if it were a black widow spider. "Never wanted the sheriff's job this way. It's not right."

One of the commissioners stepped forward and patted Lydia's shoulder. "Forget right or wrong, Toke. That's all out the window for now and you have to know it. You're the man we need to find who did this to your wife and son and to Morgan Bell. You're our best...no, our only hope."

Toke looked at Lydia. "I would need to talk to Peggy Bell first."

The judge nodded. "Understood. But she's already given her blessing. She wants you to find the man who left her a widow."

Lydia's look gave her assent. She could not speak.

Toke hugged her before turning to the commissioners' court members. "I'll take the job on one condition. I get to hire a deputy of my choosing."

The county judge produced a Bible and administered the oath of office. There was no joy in Toke as he raised his right hand and accepted the badge. The position he sought for years no longer held any allure. But the badge gave him the authority and resources to pursue the other mission that now burned in his heart. He wanted to come face to face with Angelino Salinas one more time.

The judge helped Toke pick up Lydia and get her into the seat of their pickup. Toke gently questioned her about details of exactly what happened on the way home. The theft of gasoline explained a lot of things and eased his guilt that their car had not had enough gasoline to get her to the hospital.

Enoch Essary and Harmony O'Hara waited on the porch when Toke and Lydia arrived. They tenderly hugged Lydia and Harmony forcefully hugged Toke. "We'll take care of her. You got a killer to stop before he kills anyone else."

After they helped Lydia into her knitting and reading chair, Toke found a uniform shirt he wore when he was a deputy, pinned on the badge, and left for the courthouse. The county clerk and her employees stared at him as he walked past the empty jail toward the office occupied by Morgan Bell for more than three decades. He closed the door behind him, but had neither the time nor the inclination to savor the reality he dreamed of for at least ten years. When he sat in the chair, the enormity of what happened the night before settled like an anvil on his shoulders and he could not think clearly enough to take a first step toward finding the killer who had maimed his wife and son. Almost in a panic, he rifled through the drawers in Morgan's desk as if Morgan had left a clue to finding his killer there.

He found a bottle of bourbon in the back of a bottom drawer, slowly pulled it out and set it on the desk at the moment Melvin Cobb walked in. There was an awkward moment of silence as Melvin studied the bottle, then Toke. "You're wearing Sheriff Bell's badge and now you're gonna drink his whiskey? That bottle's stayed half empty for more than a year."

"I know. Expect I enjoyed the last drink taken from it. Did you find out any information about Salinas?"

"Are you saying this fellow who smashed Leonard's pickup is the same one who shot the sheriff?"

"That's exactly what I'm saying."

Melvin picked up the top sheet from a pile on the corner of the desk and handed it to Toke. "That him?"

Toke stood. "Where did you find this?"

"Walked over to see Leonard after you left last night and got a description. Sheriff Bell told me to always study any incoming wanted posters. I remembered the ponytail."

"That's him, all right. My bet is Morgan knew he had a wanted man when he stopped him. Looks like this cold-blooded killer murdered a young girl and maimed a young man in Smithville, Bastrop County."

"Yep. Looks like you and Leonard worked right alongside a killer for weeks."

Toke held up the poster. "This is good police work, Melvin."

"Thanks. I'll make copies."

Cobb's elbow grazed the bars to the county jail when he bumped into Blaze in the hall. Toke was staring at the bottle again when Blaze walked in. "What's Melvin in such a big hurry about?"

"He found a wanted poster on our killer. Gone to make copies."

"That's a big break, I guess." Blaze pretended not to notice the bottle as he sat innocently across from Toke, the ancient chair groaning with his bulk. "Seems strange to see somebody sitting in Sheriff Bell's chair. I dropped by to see Lydia and they said you already took her home."

"She wanted to go, and Doc Pierce said they had done all they could for now. Said to keep an eye on her and bring her back in a couple of days."

"Probably good advice. Doc Pierce is a practical man of medicine. Went in to see Freddy, but he was still out."

"They've about got his whole body in a cast. May be a few

days before he comes home. May come away with a permanent limp."

"Freddy's a tough kid. He'll be fine. How long since you
slept?"

The Sheriff's chair squeaked as Toke squeezed the bridge
of his nose. "I got an opening for a deputy."

Blaze shrugged. "You fire Melvin?"

"Nope, but he's just a kid. I need a man with experience."

Toke tried to answer the unasked question on Blaze's face.
"Morgan's been short a deputy for months. I think he held off
on hiring so Melvin could get more experience. Want you to
take the job. We can use Melvin, too."

"Me?" Blaze shook his head. "Tell me again how long
since you slept? You're not thinking right. I don't know a thing
about being a lawman."

"I can teach you. I'd eventually want you to go to school
and get certified, but I need a deputy right now."

"Why me?"

"Cause I trust you. And you're a kind-hearted and God-
fearing man."

"I ain't fired a pistol in years. Don't even own one."

"We'll go down by the levees and practice. Anyway, you'll
probably never have to fire one on the job."

Blaze sat wide-eyed, incredulous. "What would I tell Joe
Henry? He gave me a job when I needed it bad. And I got
those lawns and pastures to mow and there's the funeral home
and I'm still not finished with the church."

Toke walked over to the window. "You know as well as I
do Joe Henry can find somebody to do what you do on the
ranch. Tee Jessup's done with all his tax work, so I imagine

he can do your share till Joe can find somebody. And lawn mowers and casket carriers ain't hard to find. I'll give you time off to finish the church after we catch this killer."

"People won't accept me. They know me as a carpenter and train engineer."

Toke stood and paced, faced away from his friend, hands behind his back. "Look, Blaze, I'm gonna level with you. I never much wanted to go to church with Lydia before. Concentrated on staying awake rather than on what you and Enoch tried to get into my hard head. But, when this happened, I remembered what Leonard Toon said about evil. He saw it and I didn't. If I had, my wife might still have both eyes and my son two good legs... and Morgan Bell might be alive."

Blaze's face colored a little. "You're bein' too hard on yourself. Nobody saw this comin'."

"Just the same, I been watching you in church, even listening to Enoch a little closer. You're both men to be admired. I see what church has done for you. I aim to follow Lydia's lead and yours from here on out."

The huge man put his hands on his knees and looked at the scarred wooden floor. "Those are mighty fine sentiments, Toke. I knew you'd come around sooner or later. Always been a good man."

Toke smiled. "I figure you to be the voice of reason when I get ready to haul off and shoot somebody before I get my head back on straight. You might save somebody's life."

"I know you have to be about as mad as a man can get, but you won't shoot anybody."

Toke stared. "If I find Salinas by myself, I'm likely to kill him and ask questions later."

Blaze removed his railroad cap and ran his fingers through his black frizzy hair. "And you think I wouldn't send the man to perdition myself?"

"No, I don't think you have it in you to kill a man, no matter how evil."

"I already killed two people."

"You know that's bull."

"I never figured on having to wear a uniform and carry a gun all day."

"You and Morgan Bell are the best friends I ever had. I aim to find this killer and that may mean I have to do some traveling. Maybe to Mexico. You'll be in charge if I have to leave."

"What are you aimin' to do if you find him down in Mexico?"

Toke's red eyes looked at his friend as if he had asked a silly question. "Let's hope we find him together."

"If you do find him down there, you best bring him back home and let the folks here take care of him."

Blaze jerked his thumb toward the jail outside the office door. "Otherwise, you could wind up on the wrong side of those bars out there or in a Mexican jail."

Toke spoke as if he hadn't heard. "There might be all kinds of problems in the courts if it turns out he's a citizen of Mexico. Might get deported and then come right back to kill again."

Blaze stood. "If you got a badge, I'll take the job, at least till we can find this devil that calls himself Angel."

Toke found a badge and administered what he could remember from an oath of office. "To tell the truth, Blaze, I'm so rattled I don't know where to start."

"I think you should find Wheeler Parker and get as much information as you can on Angel. If he was on his payroll, he should have an address and other information on him. Meantime, I know the country where it happened like the back of my hand. I was out there last night talking to Tee and had sort of an eerie feeling like maybe there was evil still lurking around."

"You think there's a chance he might not have hightailed it?"

"You said he stole a little gas, but not much. And Morgan's pistol had been fired once. Could be he's hit."

Toke nodded as he headed toward the door. "You may have undersold yourself as a lawman. Let's go."

Melvin handed Toke the wanted poster copies as they headed out. Toke handed some to Blaze and kept some. "You head on out there, warn Harmony and Enoch to stay with Lydia. Get my guns out and give one to each. Harmony knows how to shoot. Better warn Zeke and Tee, too. They're the only other ones close by. Give them all a poster."

"Will do. Then I'll try to find some tracks. I used to be a fairly good hunter."

FORTY-ONE

TOKE WAS ASHAMED HE HAD NOT BEEN thinking clearly enough to see the obvious. He rubbed his eyes as he headed to the hospital to check on Freddy before leaving to find Wheeler Parker. Doc Pierce greeted him outside Freddy's door. "He's awake. Been asking for you and Lydia. Still needs a few days bed rest and a few weeks of recovery, but Freddy's a tough kid."

"Thanks, Doc."

Freddy greeted him with a smile full of pain. "They tell me Mama's gone home. How is she?"

"You're both gonna be just fine. She's a little woozy yet, but you know how tough she is."

Freddy pointed to the posters in Toke's hand. "What's that?"

Toke showed him one and Freddy's face gave Toke his answer before he spoke. "That's him. Wanted for vehicular manslaughter. Guess he's done this before. Bastrop. Where's that?"

"Several hundred miles southwest of here. Lost Pines country."

"I see you're wearing the sheriff's badge." Freddy looked out the window. "I want you to catch the man who hit Mama."

"I'm gonna do everything I can to do that, son. But he may be long gone across the border."

Freddy studied the poster again. "He ran north last time he hurt somebody, not south."

"Never thought of it that way, Freddy. Maybe he's as unwelcome in Mexico as he is here. I hate to run, but I'm burnin' daylight. You gonna be okay till I get back?"

"Go catch him, Daddy."

Toke didn't call Wheeler Parker in advance because he didn't want him to know he was coming, hoped he would find him at either the bar or his stables. He stopped at Parker's horse farm just inside the Texas border and entered a long barn hall where Wheeler stabled his thoroughbreds. He spoke to an older Mexican mucking an empty stall. "Looking for Wheeler Parker."

The Mexican focused on Toke's badge and pointed to a door at the end of the barn hall.

Toke walked in the room without knocking and laid the poster on Parker's desk. "You know about this?"

Wheeler glanced at the wanted poster but stared at Toke's badge. "Shouldn't you be out working on levees?"

"Do you even know what this bastard did last night?"

Wheeler leaned back in his chair. "Haven't heard."

"He killed Morgan Bell, crippled my wife and son. May have put her eye out. I need to know everything you know about him. Where does he live? Is he legal? Most of all, did you know he was wanted?"

Wheeler picked up the poster and pretended to study it. "Can't believe this kid went so far off the reservation. He seemed normal, maybe a little high-strung. Didn't you see him that way?"

"No, I didn't, so how about answering my questions."

"Far as I know, he's legal, but these wetbacks have their ways of making up fake paperwork. He used to live in one of those hovels out by the Wheelhouse with a whore. But the whore told me...day before yesterday, I think...he got rough with her and she threw him out."

"You got an employee file on him? Address? Anything?"

"Now, Toke, you know how it is with these people. They come and go. Here in the states one minute, gone the next. It's called cheap labor for a reason."

"He do anything for you before you brought him out to work for us?"

"Just an errand boy. A flunky. Washed dishes in the bar. Mucked stalls here. Did what I told him. I told you why I hired him. Supposed to have big connections down in Mexico. If he did what you said, he's called in all his chips and gone back across the border."

Toke slammed the door on his way out, frustrated with Parker's indifference. Parker picked up the phone.

The Mexican who mucked stalls hailed Toke from the other side of the barn. He leaned down behind the stall door as he spoke. "You looking for Angelino Salinas?"

"Who's asking and why?"

"*Jefe*, look away from me when you speak. Don't want the *patrón* to see you talking to me. You want information or no?"

Toke kept his eyes straight ahead. "Yes."

"Why do you look for him?"

"He pistol-whipped my wife and crippled my son. Plus, he shot and killed the sheriff." Toke was a little ashamed that the loss of his old friend had become secondary to avenging what happened to his family.

The man nodded as if in sympathy. "Angel is a bad *hombre*. His old man used him as a drug mule and coyote. His *papá* owns truck farms on both side of the border. *Senoritas* love him, especially the ones too young to see evil, but Angelino is mixed up in the head."

"Why are you telling me this?"

The man removed his cap, squeezed the bill, and answered without turning. "The girl he killed in Bastrop County spent many nights with my granddaughter at my house. Salinas sneaked into my house one night and touched my grandson. The boy is nine. I want to send Salinas straight to hell." The accent was heavy again.

"You mean Salinas likes little boys?"

Abraham did not turn. "He is a man from *el Diablo*. I want to send him back."

"Any idea where I might start looking for him?"

"He was thrown off his papa's farm and won't be welcome back there."

"So you think there's a chance he's still in the area?"

"My cousins say he can't be a coyote anymore with the family connections, so I think he's a drug mule. Brags about Parker coming to Riverby to bring him money."

"Any special days they meet?"

"Thursdays."

"Places?"

"He never said."

"Today is Thursday." Toke took a note pad from his pocket, wrote the telephone number for the sheriff's office, handed it to him and pointed to the barn hall. "If you see Parker leave, use that phone over there and call me."

Toke waited for the man to nod. "What's your name?"

"Call me Abraham. I am from Bastrop County."

Forty-Two

TEE TOSSED AND TURNED ALL NIGHT THINKING of the Albright and Bell families. He knew first hand some of what they were experiencing, but he also knew he didn't have the words to comfort them. On his porch at pre-dawn, he sipped coffee and tried to calm his nerves. Rivers and Flo lay in their usual positions beside his chair, but their presence did not have its normal calming effect. He could not release the anxiety that returned with this new tragedy. For the first time in years, he had begun to find relief from the recurring nightmares and anger. Hurt Hill had become a sanctuary of sorts. Now, it had been invaded.

He probably heard the shot that killed Morgan Bell, but thought nothing of it, because gunfire from hunters was common at night in the bottoms. Tee's first inclination had been to cancel their hunting and camping trip after he heard the terrible news, but that would leave them with nothing to do but mourn and stress about what happened. He decided to camp by the trestle as planned and tell Jubal what happened over a peaceful campfire. As if anticipating the trip or sensing Tee's tension, Rivers jumped up from his half-sleep, growled, barked twice, jumped off the porch and disappeared down the dirt road toward Panther Crossing. Flo stretched and followed at a slower pace.

They had stored cooking and eating gear in the Airstream, but had to carry perishables because there was no electricity at Panther Crossing. The generator was hard to crank and too loud. Jubal liked to pretend they were leaving on a long cattle drive, so they packed their saddle bags as if they were. They pulled together more than would be needed and saddled the horses.

Jubal was the first to mount. "You about ready?"

Tee closed the last buckle on his saddlebags and looked over Judson's hip at his son. "I would've been ready a long time ago if I had more help with packing."

Jubal grinned. "Did you get the eggs? I'm starving."

Tee shook his head. "Nope, forgot the eggs. I'll be right back."

As the door closed behind Tee, Rivers returned, breathing hard, his barks so urgent to Jubal that his front paws came off the ground with each one. He turned toward the trestle, made a circle—a ritual Jubal recognized. Rivers wanted him to follow. He hollered at his father, poked Sweetness with his heels, and followed his dog in a run. Tee's head was in the refrigerator retrieving the eggs. He went back for a jar of preserves and was balancing the eggs and preserves when he heard a gunshot down by Panther Crossing.

Blaze found the keys to the deputy's patrol car and drove to Peggy Bell's house. He was embarrassed when she opened the door in her housecoat. Her eyes were swollen; her hair needed shampoo and a good brushing. She spoke to him through the screen door, did not invite him in. "Blaze. I heard you were a deputy now."

Blaze took off his cap and looked past her to the easy chair where Morgan Bell always rested after a hard day enforcing the law. "Sorry to bother you, Peggy. Toke asked me to look in on you and see if there's anything we can do."

Peggy's red eyes were almost expressionless. "Everybody asks that. It's like a broken record. Anything we can do? Well, unless you can bring my husband back to life or kill the cowardly piece of human garbage who shot him, I guess not."

Blaze had never seen her angry. Her rage was palpable. He could feel the heat of it through the screen door. He felt his face turn red from it. "Toke's on his trail and I hope I am."

"Come back and see me when the monster is dead."

Blaze returned to his patrol car and headed to Toke's house. He felt he needed to hear Lydia describe what happened and see exactly where it happened. Maybe he could find some tire tracks or footprints to follow. At her small kitchen table, he watched Lydia feel her way around the percolator and spill grounds on the wooden counter top as she made him a cup of coffee. "I sent Harmony and Enoch on home. Appreciated their help, but I needed to be alone with the Lord to pray for my Freddy."

Her one good eye wandered until she found his hand on the table and patted it. Blaze sipped and tasted some of the stray grounds. She drummed her long fingers with worn nails on the tabletop. "Lord, I do wonder how my boy is going to deal with not playing sports. He seemed to live for ballgames."

Blaze looked out toward the yard and envisioned the gun striking Lydia's face. Wondered how many times she had played that back in her mind—and her just wanting to give the thug a few dollars. "A mighty fine athlete."

He imagined the car ramming into Freddy's legs and chest. Something rose up inside him he had never felt before. Blaze slowly spun the cup in his saucer and rose. "Well, Miss Lydia, best be on my way. Wish you hadn't sent Harmony home. You still got your weapons handy?"

"She and Brother Enoch will be back shortly. Insisted on it."

"Mind if I explore out in the yard where this awful thing happened?"

She hesitated, seemed unable to speak, but nodded her assent.

Blaze stood in the spot where Lydia had been struck. There were blood droplets all the way to the house. He looked up and saw a huge bolt of lightning over the tree tops. Strange. He didn't hear any thunder and the clouds in the southeast didn't look like storm clouds. It was too cool for heat lightning. For a few seconds, he was almost spellbound and couldn't seem to move, as if some evil force had wrapped him in a foul embrace. He walked to the other side of his car and dropped to his knees. "Lord, if it be thy will, help me to find the evil one that did these terrible things before he hurts somebody else. Thank you."

Blaze drove to the spot where Morgan Bell had been shot and Freddy injured. He stood in the shadows, felt and smelled the same evil presence. Maybe God was using his sense of smell to help him. Morgan Bell and Angelino Salinas were the only ones who knew exactly what happened that night, but Blaze played the scene in his head as if he had been there. Toke shared Freddy's account with him, so he played that scene too.

With Sheriff Bell dead, nobody had examined the scene closely for clues, and Blaze didn't know how to go about it. Besides, everybody knew what happened and who did it. What was the point? There were still some dark tracks in the road where the Camaro spun down to where the dirt was hard enough to burn rubber. *Where was the killer headed and why? And why did Salinas stick around and harm three more people instead of running away as soon as he finished his carnage at the levees?* Blaze spoke aloud to the trees and wind. "Where is he, Lord?"

He followed what he hoped were the right tracks to Panther Crossing. Like always, he paused and said a little prayer of forgiveness for Tee's parents and for himself. He forced himself to look over at the trestle where he and Toke played as boys and reminisced aloud. "Many a catfish been fried down there under that old bridge."

The weeds were so high he couldn't see well, but it looked like limbs and brush had accumulated under the trestle from that last little flood. He made a note to talk to the commissioner about that. The trestle ditch needed to be cleared, else water might back up and flood cropland along the creek. Tee's Airstream seemed to be intact, but he made a mental note to check it after he talked to Zeke. His dogs might have alerted him to something.

He crossed the trestle and kept north, wondered if he was following the same path Salinas had. He knew Ezekiel Mulroney's shack was ahead, dreaded seeing the half-starved and mangled curs trying to kill each other. Zeke said a hungry dog was a tougher dog. Now that he had a badge, Blaze vowed to make Zeke take better care of his animals. He honked his horn and Zeke came out carrying his shotgun.

Blaze pointed toward the gun. "You won't need that. It's just me."

"What are you doing in a patrol car?"

Blaze gave him a short history of what happened the night before and handed him one of the wanted posters. "We think this is the man who did the killing and maiming. He was driving a red Camaro. Don't guess you saw anything unusual last night."

Zeke studied the photo. "This man was by here last night. I *thought* he was up to no good. Said his car stalled on the other side of the railroad tracks. Never saw the car."

Blaze sat up straighter in the seat. "You sure it was him? What time was that?"

"Sure it was him, can't be sure of the time. But I'd say between eight and nine. Not too long after sundown."

"See anything out of the ordinary this morning?"

"I heard a few shots fired, but that's normal. Dogs acted up a little more than usual."

Blaze turned his car around and stopped a few yards south of Zeke's to survey the area, get his head straight. As he looked toward the trestle, the area where he spent his boyhood and the place that changed his life, a whirlwind blew up in the open field between Ezekiel's house and the crossing. Always fascinated by what his mama called dust devils, he watched it travel across the Blackland Prairie and hover over the trestle. Inside the whirlwind, he saw two faces he had committed to memory. When he rubbed his eyes, they disappeared.

He eased the patrol car along, watched the trestle area and surrounding woods for movement. A few feet short of the rails, he pulled up. He needed to think this through, maybe contact Toke on the radio, if he could figure out how to use it. He fiddled with the knobs, got loud static, and turned it off. Something said he needed to be quiet. He felt the same chill as he felt at the crime sites, smelled the same smell.

He got out and walked to the banks of Moccasin Creek under Panther Crossing. Under the trestle, he saw a glint of red, and pulled away a few limbs to reveal the red Camaro. A second dust devil kicked up leaves and twigs as it traveled up the trail to Hurt Hill.

FORTY-THREE

TEE DROPPED HIS EGGS WHEN HE HEARD THE gunshot, mounted and spurred Judson down the hill toward Panther Crossing. Halfway down the hill, he met Jubal and Sweetness in a run, dragging a man who held onto Jubal's stirrup with one hand and a pistol with the other. He lost his grip on the stirrup just before Tee arrived. Jubal shouted, "Daddy, he shot Rivers."

When Angel Salinas stood, Judson's chest hit him at full gallop. The collision sent the pistol flying and Angel to the ground. Tee turned and rode the horse over him again. He dismounted, put the gun in his belt, untied his rope from his saddle, put a loop around Angel's feet, remounted, and dragged him back up the hill at a lope. Jubal and Sweetness followed.

Tee dragged Angel Salinas into the hall of the old tabernacle, dismounted and stood over him with the gun in his hand. He wanted to shoot him, to rid himself and the com-

273

munity of this evil, but he held back because he didn't want Jubal to see him kill a man, even this man.

"Jubal, you go see if Rivers and Flo might be back under the porch."

Salinas lay in the middle of a large dark, wavy circle caused by the blood of many hogs. The Hurt family and Willard Dunn hung hogs there to scrape their hides and drain their blood during hog-killing season. With no sunlight, the stain had lightened only a little over the years. Tee cringed as he put his fingers in Angel's oily hair and pulled his ponytail back to look into his eyes.

Angel grunted. "Yessup. Your damn horse nearly killed me."

Tee's suppressed demons churned. "Wish he had. Left me to finish the job."

Both ends of an old well rope hung from a pulley above Tee's head, the long end fastened to a double-pronged hook screwed to a barn pole. He fashioned a loop in the short end and pulled it tightly across the man's wrists, loosened the long end from its hook and pulled Salinas to a standing position. When only the stainless steel tips that adorned the toe-boxes of the Mexican's pointed-toe boots touched the ground, Tee refastened the rope to the hook. Angel's jacket showed wear from the dragging, but had not worn through. Tee started to pull it away from his back, but decided against it. He didn't want Jubal to see blood.

Salinas groaned with every pull, trying to ease the pain from whatever was broken inside him, cursing Tee with each stab of hurt. As if in a trance, Tee removed John T's short bullwhip from its nail, slung it back and made it crack as he and his brother had when they were boys. It was a satisfying sound, sending chills down Tee's spine. He lashed it across Angel's back, enjoyed his scream of pain.

He got close to the Mexican's face, felt his breath on his cheeks. His putrid odor, mixed with the smell of blood, sweat and dirt—had turned malefic. "That hurt? Think it hurt when you shot Morgan Bell? How about when you hit a defenseless woman or smashed a young boy's body with your damn car? Think they hurt?"

The reply came out as a gurgle. "They were in Angel's way. Don't get in Angel's way."

Tee hit him with the whip again. The Mexican screamed as the lash cut across his back and legs. When Jubal returned, he heard his father use words he had never heard him use before as Tee circled the man, taunting and chastising him. As he cracked the whip again and drew back for another stroke, Tee felt a weight on his arm and turned to see his son hanging on it. "Daddy, you're gonna kill him!"

Wild-eyed, Tee looked at Jubal as if he had forgotten he was there. He became aware of his own labored breathing, smelled his nervous sweat. He looked around as if seeing the tabernacle on Hurt Hill for the first time. Tee slowly realized he had been back at Blind River, and the man hanging from the rafter had been Ford Donovan. As he recovered his composure, he approached Salinas. The smell almost made him retch, but he stood eye to eye to him. "Ought to cut you open and spill your blood and guts on the floor of this barn like the swine you are." He poked him with the whip handle.

Jubal stood behind his father, fists balled tight. "He shot Rivers. I heard him yelp."

Tee seemed not to hear. "You hit a helpless woman with a gun barrel who was trying to help you. She may lose an eye because of you. Then you crippled a young boy who was on his way to being a great athlete. You don't deserve to breathe the same air as those fine people. And then you go after my own son."

Jubal's eyes spilled over. "What boy?"

Tee took a deep breath, seemed unable to focus, to figure his next step. He pulled the gun from his belt, contemplated shooting his captive with his own gun or hanging him by the neck until he was dead, or by his feet until all the blood drained from him. But he could do neither in front of his son. He kneeled and hugged Jubal close. "He hurt Freddy and his mother, but they're both gonna be all right."

"You want me to go in and call Sheriff Bell?"

The question made Tee realize the dilemma he was in with the sheriff dead. He needed time to think. "He killed Sheriff Bell, too, Jubal."

Jubal seemed ready to shatter and collapse on the blood-stained dirt at his feet. Tee hugged him again and walked him a few feet away, never taking his eyes off Salinas. He began to feel weak and nauseous.

"Do something for me. Go see if any of those eggs I dropped can be saved. I need time to think and you said you were starved. We can both think better on a full stomach."

Tee tied the Mexican's ankles with bailing wire and gave him enough slack to put weight back on his feet. He kept an eye on him as he and Jubal built a fire outside the hall of the tabernacle. The boy managed to get sausage and eggs going, but his movements seemed awkward and nervous as he stole glances at his father and the Mexican. Tee spooned coffee grounds into a pan, filled it with water and set it on the grill Jubal had placed on burning embers. Tee kept one eye on his captive as he and

Jubal ate out of the same cast iron skillet. Jubal seemed to relax as he poured them both a cup of cowboy coffee.

Jubal spit out a few grounds. "What are you aiming to do with him?"

Tee grimaced and shook his head. "Not sure yet. I need to tell you more about what he did." He kept his eyes on Salinas, spoke loud enough for him to hear as he told Jubal what he had done in Bastrop County, and details about what he had done to Lydia, Freddy, and Morgan.

"Will Freddy be able to play ball again?"

"We don't know yet. Looks like his mother might lose sight in one eye, too." He pointed at the man tied to a well rope. "You think a man who did all those things deserves to live?"

Jubal looked confused. He stared at Tee as if he were a stranger. "Dunno. I don't guess."

Tee looked at his boots. "That was an unfair question for a boy...or a man for that matter. I'm sorry." Tee drew a circle in the dirt with his finger. "It's just that I've been in a situation like this before, and I have always thought I might've done the wrong thing back then."

Tee put his finger to his lips as he heard a car approach. "Get in the corn crib and don't come out till I call you."

Jubal went into the crib and watched from a crack in the door as his father pulled the gun from his belt, pointed it toward the hall opening and pulled back the hammer. Jubal studied his father's expression, wondered what had happened to him. When Blaze appeared in the hall entrance, he sighed deeply.

Tee released the hammer and pointed the gun at the roof. "Well, you're a sight for sore eyes. Might've shot you."

Blaze walked over and stared at the man called Angel. "Looks like you got our man. How'd you find him?"

Jubal came out of the corn crib and walked close to Blaze, carefully avoiding eye contact with the man who shot his dog. "Rivers found him. He led me to the trailer. When I got there, Rivers had a good hold on his leg. Then he shot my dog and took out after me. I was still on Sweetness, but he hung on to my stirrup. Daddy and Judson knocked him down and stomped him pretty good."

Blaze looked into Tee's wild eyes; saw the sweat on his face and soaked shirt. He winked at Jubal and showed them both his badge. "Better let me take it from here."

Blaze looked at the gun in Tee's hand still pointing at the roof and put his big mitt over it. "That his gun?"

Tee seemed uncertain, but finally released the gun. "That badge on your shirt is a relief. Thought I was gonna have to take the law into my own hands."

Blaze put the gun in his gun belt. "We'll be needing this for evidence, I imagine."

Jubal looked up at his friend. "He shot Rivers, Blaze."

"I know, son."

Blaze looked at Tee. "Get Jubal and go look for Rivers. Expect Flo will be with him."

He pointed toward the Mexican. "Let me handle the killer."

Tee hung the bullwhip back on its nail. "How did you know he was here?"

Blaze stared at the dirt, crumbled horse manure, and hay at his feet. "Couple of angels in a dust devil told me. I'll explain later."

FORTY-FOUR

WHEELER PARKER QUICKLY CONSIDERED HIS
options after Toke Albright left his office. He imagined his
hands around Angelino's throat as life left his body. The
pretty boy bastard would ruin everything unless he could be
stopped before the law got to him. Jack Prince didn't answer
the private phone at his gin lot office and wasn't at the dealership, so he reluctantly called Cooper Newman at the bank.

Newman paced as Wheeler fed him the news. "I still don't
see what this has to do with me. I don't even know this wetback, and now you're telling me he may have killed the sheriff."

"You wanted to be part of the consortium. Hell, you
pushed your way in. Well, Salinas was a drug mule and a coyote for the consortium. Thought Jack told you that."

"Nobody said anything to me about drugs or smuggling
wetbacks."

"Why the hell did you think we needed to launder money?"

"I know you think I'm stupid, but I know illegal money can come from lots of places. I thought you were just dodging taxes or something like that."

"I can just hear your lawyer making that defense in court."

"So what do you want me to do?"

"I'm supposed to meet the Mexican at Moccasin Creek at noon today, but I can't leave after Toke was here. I could tell he was suspicious. He may be waiting somewhere now for me to leave so he can tail me. I might lead him right to Salinas."

"The wetback ain't gonna meet you after what he did. He's long gone."

"Maybe, but we owe him nine grand for mule work. I was supposed to bring it today."

Cooper Newman heaved the heaviest sigh of his life as he felt his world crumbling. "So you want me to meet him and hide him somewhere or what?"

"You need to get him and bring him to me. I can get him out of state, at least."

"Even if he's still around, he doesn't know me from Adam. He won't come out from his hole when he sees me."

"Jack Prince has one of those customized vans on his parking lot. I use it every time I meet with Salinas to pay him. When he sees that van, he's supposed to open the side door and roll inside. Wear some sunglasses and a cap. You show him the money when he sees you're not me and tell him I have a plan to get him to Tennessee."

"What if he refuses?"

"You're always bragging about how good you are with pistols and rifles. You'll need to go armed. Hold a gun on him and make him drive here."

"Where am I gonna get nine grand?"

"You're the president of a bank. Write a hot check. You can redeposit it before closing time if things work out."

Cooper groaned. "Where do I meet him exactly?"

"By Moccasin Creek Bridge. Be sure you're out of sight on the north side of the work site. He waits in that little hollow spot by the bridge where people dump their trash."

"You know if he's got good sense, he's already in Mexico, so we may be okay as long as he stays gone."

"Yes, but he ain't got good sense. Salinas is crazy. I intended to get rid of him today after the payoff and he probably suspected it. That may be what set him off on this killing spree."

"So you're asking me to go out there and invite a crazy killer to jump in the van with me and travel to Oklahoma to visit someone who plans to get rid of him. I may be stupid, but I'm not that stupid."

Wheeler took an exasperated breath. "Look, you're probably right. He's not likely to show today, but he's almost certain to come someday to get his money and he will come with a vengeance. Worse, he may send his old man's henchmen."

"He won't be coming after me."

"His old man knows who the members of the consortium are. Trust me; we all need this nutcase out of our lives for good."

"I still don't see how I can get a trigger-happy nut case to get in the van with a stranger without getting killed. And I need to know what you intend to do with him if I deliver him. I have to know what I'm getting into this time."

Wheeler let several seconds pass. "Newman, you're in big

trouble with the bank. You know it, Jack knows it, and I know it. You're gonna have to come up with at least a hundred grand to keep your job and maybe stay out of prison. You get this done for me, the consortium will get you out of the mess you're in."

The confrontation left Cooper's voice. "Level with me. The only way you're gonna be free of Salinas is if he's dead. Who's gonna do that?"

"You let me worry about that. Just know that if we don't get rid of him, the problems you have at the bank will be minor compared to the hell he can bring down on us."

"What's he driving?"

"A red Camaro."

Abraham listened for the click of Wheeler hanging up the phone. He hung up the extension in the barn hall and trotted toward his Dodge pickup.

Cooper made a quick trip to his own safe deposit box and withdrew all the cash inside. It wouldn't be enough to pay the Mexican what he was owed, but enough to flash in case he had to show a roll of cash.

He was grateful his arsenal and his hunting clothes were in his pickup and the barn and not at home. He went to the Shelton barn, dressed in camouflage from head to toe, and made sure the 30.30, the twelve-gauge, and his nickel-plated Colt revolver were all loaded and ready before heading to Moccasin Creek.

Clayton Dupree entered the bank a few minutes after Cooper Newman left. An envelope stuffed with his tax return and addressed to the IRS protruded from the back pocket of his baggy jeans. He politely requested a counter check and was given one. The teller gave him unrequested details of what had happened last night.

He walked over to a counter in the middle of the lobby, filled out the check, stuffed it into the envelope and sealed it.

Maud, the older lady who helped him with his visits to the safe deposit vault returned from a restroom visit as he headed out the door to the post office. When he saw her, he went to his pickup, retrieved his safe deposit keys from their hiding place inside the headliner of the truck, and walked back into the bank. The post office could wait a few more minutes.

He displayed his keys to Maud as he had always done, signed the register and followed her to the vault. His key would not work in the first box. He looked at Maud. She took the key and tried it herself. "Well, that's a first. Let's try another one."

They went through three before Clayton started to panic. He was so upset he struggled to recall the combinations to his locks on the file cabinets. When he opened the first one, he found the drawers in the first empty...and the second...and the third. He turned to Maud, his anger and fear overcoming his shyness. "What have you done?"

Maud put both hands over her mouth. "Mr. Dupree, I assure you there is some mistake which the bank will correct."

Clayton's eyes were red, his face dark. "How's the bank going to correct losing my most valuable possessions?"

"Come with me."

They marched into Cooper Newman's office and found it empty. She turned nervously to Clayton. "Don't worry, Mr.

Dupree. This bank has never lost a thing out of a single safe deposit."

Clayton was not comforted. "Who's been in there recently?"

"Mr. Newman has been the only visitor to the vault in several days and that was earlier this morning to visit his own box. But my goodness, there's no way anyone could carry out all your belongings without being seen."

"Obviously they did. Have you had any boxes drilled lately?"

She nodded. "I did see an invoice from our specialist today, but I'm sure there was no reason to drill your boxes. Why don't you wait here until Mr. Newman returns? I'm sure he will have a good explanation."

"Who has to approve the drilling of a box?"

"Why, the bank president, of course . . . a lawyer, maybe, or a family member who has power of attorney usually requests it."

"And where is the bank president now?"

"Why, I'm not sure. He didn't say where he was going, but I'm sure he'll return soon."

Clayton sat in his truck a few minutes until the crowd around the square began to close in, then headed back home.

FORTY-FIVE

COOPER FOUND A SPOT BESIDE THE TRASH
pile by the Moccasin Creek Bridge and parked the van where
it could be seen by Salinas. He kept the roll of hundreds inside
his shirt in case he needed them to show the crazy Mexican.
A few minutes after noon, he decided the man called Angel
was not coming. He never thought he would.

He got out and walked down in the depression by the
creek and around the brush pile. No sign of footprints. The
ground was wet from a light shower overnight, so there would
have been some if the man had ever been here. He climbed
back into the van and took a long pull from the bottle of vodka he brought to ease the tension. It didn't work. Now he was
desperate. He might even have to leave his job and be a fugitive if the law got to this killer before him or Wheeler Parker.

In case he had to run, he needed money and the eight
grand he had with him was not nearly enough. As he took

a second pull, he saw Clayton Dupree's yellow Ford truck in the van's rear view mirror. He spilled vodka on the seat and himself when he ducked down in the seat.

Clayton slowed, but kept going. Cooper watched as he headed the old Ford through the trees, up a trail that was almost invisible from the county road. *Maybe the safe deposit drawers and file cabinets were a ruse. Maybe the old hermit's real money is stashed somewhere up that road. It probably leads to his shack on Hurt Hill.*

Newman decided to make one last effort to find the Mexican while he gave Clayton time to settle in his shack before he paid him a visit. There was a slight chance Salinas might be waiting at the turnoff beside Panther Creek that led to the bottoms. If the Mexican wasn't there, the trestle would be the right place to approach Clayton's shack.

He saw a black-and-white coming down Hurt Hill as he neared Panther Crossing and the trestle. He pulled the van in the ditch to avoid being seen, rolled out the sliding back door, and hid in the tall weeds by the creek. He waited, confident his camouflage outfit would conceal him. When the patrol car stopped short of Panther Crossing and turned down the trail toward the bottoms, he saw a Mexican with his head on his chest in the back seat of the car. He took a chance and stood on the trestle side rails to get a better look. That's when he saw the red Camaro halfway into the creek. The Mexican he wanted had not left.

Desperate now, he poured vodka on the steering wheel and all the surfaces he thought he had touched and wiped it off with his handkerchief. The futile gesture made him feel better, but pouring the last of the bottle down his throat was better yet. He pulled his long gun from the back of the van, pulled his camouflage cap just right, tightened the laces on his hiking boots, and sneaked up Hurt Hill toward Clayton's shack.

＋═══＋

Finding directions to Moccasin Creek had been easy for Abraham. He parked near the brush pile and followed Cooper Newman up Hurt Hill.

＋═══＋

Clayton Dupree's shack was visible only during the months of deep winter when the trees shed their leaves. In April, part of it could be seen if one was looking for it. Clayton paced the porch, bemoaning the loss of almost everything he valued in his life before slumping into his twig chair to figure out a way to recover his possessions. When he saw the patrol car in the bottoms, he left the chair and skulked from tree trunk to tree trunk to get a closer look. He tried to forget about snakes and dropped to his belly to watch as a dark cloud roiled over him and he heard another rumble of thunder.

He was still too far away to distinguish faces, but he could see forms and thought he recognized one. He watched as the driver pulled his passenger from the back seat. The passenger's hands were cuffed behind his back. The driver led him to a small mud hole in front of a bulldozer and forced him to his knees. The man in cuffs struggled and shouted words Clayton could not hear.

The driver calmly watched him struggle until the cuffed man appeared to give up and changed from a defiant posture to a compliant one as if begging for his life. When the driver placed a burlap sack over the man's head, Clayton eased closer to try and hear. The driver kneeled beside the man on his knees in the small pit; put his cheek against the rough sack, his lips close to the beggar's ear. Clayton still could not make out all the words, but he heard enough to fill in the blanks. He wrote the words to the scene he was witnessing in his memory to be transcribed later.

The lawman felt the dried mud from the tow sack against the day's stubble on his own cheek; smelled the fear-sweat; heard the echo of his captive's pleadings progress from panicked screams to vile curses to whimpering. The voice against the captive's ear was so deep it seemed more godly than human. It seemed to be pleading as well as commanding. "Lucifer sent you out of the bowels of hell to this earth to kill and maim innocents. God sent me to send you back to perdition."

Only whimpering answered. The driver stood. "I didn't ask for this duty, but you killed and maimed and destroyed families. You showed no remorse, kept right on, snuffing out the brightest parts of people's lives."

The covered head drooped but still said nothing. The bottom woods became quiet. The man in the sack stopped begging; birds stopped singing; squirrels stopped barking. A gun appeared in the lawman's hand as he affected a regal stance, pointed the barrel toward the tow sack. Thunder clapped as a shot rang out and the man with the sack over his head shot backward, jerked once and lay still. The woods' sounds returned as the gunman looked up the hill. The lawman seemed to listen as the life whispered out

*of the man and the disturbed creatures of the woods
whimpered down. He studied Hurt Hill again, removed
the cuffs and placed the gun on the dead man's chest.*

*He nudged the man's body to be sure he was
dead, lifted his eyes to the rolling clouds. "Lucifer,
behold your messenger, your son. Hell is back to its
quota of demons now and Earth is less one. Whether
it was the Hand of the Almighty or my own hand
that slew this vile creature, justice has been done."*

*He dropped to one knee, ignoring the mud. "Lord,
if it was not Your Voice who told me to slay this demon,
to silence this messenger from Satan, if it was not
Your Hand that killed him, I beg Your forgiveness."*

Smoke belched from the dozer's exhaust and the tracks began to move. The blade pushed enough dirt to cover the body, made a few passes over the dirt. The driver killed the dozer, put his hands together and dropped his head as if in prayer.

Clayton used the sound of the dozer to cover his movements from tree trunk to tree trunk, trying to get close enough to see and hear better. He was sure he could hear the words of an old folk song coming from the man as if pulled from deep inside him by some invisible force. The words echoed along Moccasin Creek and through the bottoms as he walked toward his car. *Write me a letter. Send it by mail. Send it in care of... the Birmingham Jail.*

Clayton stayed still until he was sure the man was gone. He wanted to go to the grave, but thought better of it. He returned to the porch, picked up his ever-present pencil and tablet, threw them in the pickup and headed down the hill.

FORTY-SIX

TOKE DROVE MORGAN BELL'S PATROL CAR down Ghost Dog Run, maneuvered to keep from hitting the dogs that tried to bite his tires. He stopped in front of Zeke's house and honked. When Zeke did not emerge, he pressed the horn and did not let up until Zeke showed himself.

"Turn that damn thing off, Toke."

Toke motioned for him to get in. "Looking for Blaze. Said he was coming out this way. Have you seen him?"

"Yep. He was here about mid-morning. Showed me a wanted poster. I told him I saw the feller on it last night. The wetback told me his car broke down on the other side of the tracks. Blaze got all excited when I told him. He took off that-a-way." He pointed toward the trestle.

Toke crossed the rails at Panther Crossing and headed up the washout they called a road to Hurt Hill. He saw Tee and

Jubal walking down the hill toward him. Both carried long guns. He pulled alongside. "Looking for Blaze. You seen him?"

Tee told him the whole story. "Thought you might be coming to arrest me for whipping the Mexican. The boy and I been looking for our dog. Rivers found the wetback down by our trailer and took a bite out of him. He may have shot him."

Tee pointed down the road. "Shot him right about there." He put his hand on Jubal's shoulder and winked at Toke. "Figure the dog's somewhere licking his wounds. Expect to find him."

Toke removed his hat and ran his hand though his hair. "You say Blaze took Salinas into custody?"

"Yep. Cuffed him and put him in the back seat. Made him mad as hell when the Mexican sat on a bunch of Morgan's new gimme caps."

"How long ago?"

"An hour, maybe more."

Toke shook his head. "I been looking for him the better part of an hour. He's had time to get back to the jail with his prisoner. Dispatcher was supposed to radio me if he came back. Just checked again and he hasn't shown up. Not answering his radio."

Tee stuck his head in the window out of Jubal's hearing. "Toke, I figure it's nothing, but I heard a gunshot a little bit ago. Figured it was Clayton shooting varmints. Happens a lot, so I didn't think anything about it. There's no way the Mexican could have gotten away. Do you think?"

"Hope not. Any way to get to Dupree's shack without walking down from your place?"

"There's a trail Clayton cut out on the other side, but get ready for a little mud and a few scratches from limbs."

"Where is it?"

"Starts at that trash pile in the corner by Moccasin Creek Bridge."

"I been by there a hundred times. Never noticed a trail."

"You have to be looking for it. Tree limbs make it look impassable. Clayton's the only one who uses it and he tries to keep it concealed. Anything I can do to help?"

"You might approach the picker shack from your end on foot." Toke looked around the area as if he saw something move in the woods. "On second thought, I saw an old Dodge pickup parked there I didn't recognize. Might belong to one of the killer's friends. There's a chance Salinas could have got away. You need to stay with the boy. Maybe get inside and keep your weapons handy."

Tee looked at Jubal. "We best get home. Rivers may have already come back. Might be under the porch in his usual safe spot. If he's not, we'll split up and do some real hunting as soon as we find Blaze."

They didn't find Rivers at home. Tee tried to calm his son, but both were restless. Tee snapped his fingers. "Let's take our guns and go check on Clayton. Rivers visits him pretty often. He may have gone there when all the commotion started around here. We would have found him right where you saw him shot if he had been hurt bad, right?"

Toke parked his scratched and muddy patrol car in front of Clayton's house. There was no sign of Clayton's pickup, but he knew that meant nothing. Clayton was said to have hiding places for everything. He walked on the porch and knocked. The door was open, so he let himself in and hollered for Clayton, saw nothing to indicate trouble. He sat in the twig chair on the porch and looked toward the bottoms, surprised at the view Clayton had from his porch perch. He had probably seen everything that happened on the day Salinas pushed Leonard Toon's pickup into the creek. He started back to his car and noticed fresh dirt in front of the dozer.

Tee and Jubal arrived as Toke started walking down the hill. They followed. At the dozer, Toke pointed to tire tracks. "Ten will get you twenty one set of those tracks belong to Blaze's patrol car."

Tee looked around. "So why would he come down here?" They all looked at the fresh dirt in front of the dozer, wondered if things had gone awfully wrong and Blaze might be under that dirt. But nobody spoke their fears.

Toke kneeled and put a finger on the tire tracks. "Tracks go in and out. You can see where he turned around and headed back. Maybe Blaze took the west route to town and had car trouble. I came in on the east side. I'm gonna get my car and go back to the main road. See if I can connect the dots and see which way he headed when he got to the county road."

"What about the other tracks?"

"That Dodge pickup I saw parked over there had slick tires. Could be it."

"Mind if we tag along?"

Toke shrugged. "On the slight chance Blaze lost his prisoner, Salinas might be roaming these woods. My car will be safer than wandering around, I guess."

They followed the tracks to the west side of Tee's Airstream, where Blaze's patrol car was parked out of view of the road. Blaze sat in his usual spot on the trestle, only a few yards away.

FORTY-SEVEN

CLAYTON HID BEHIND THE TRASH PILE WHILE the van passed. He had seen Cooper Newman sitting in the van when he passed him earlier, even though Cooper tried to duck. He followed the van to Jory Shelton's barn, watched Cooper stumble out in his fancy hunter's getup. He vomited in the yard, wiped his mouth, and went inside. Clayton parked near what was left of the old house, left his pickup in plain sight. He didn't care if Cooper saw it when he came out or when he looked out from the loft. In fact, he wanted him to see it. He intended to be the man's worst nightmare. A .22 pistol bought to replace the one he lost in Fort Worth lay beside him on the seat. He fingered the gun, picked up his pen and paper, and wrote more about what he had seen.

When he figured Newman had enough time to lay down his rifle and maybe pass out, he walked into the barn, holding the gun ready. Shooting the man who stole his life would be easy.

Cooper lay passed out in a pile of hay. It looked as if he tried the stairs to the loft and fell. Clayton climbed the stairs and found stacks of garbage bags. One look inside a bag told him what he needed to know. He carried them downstairs, filled the front seat with some, put the rest in the bed close to the cab and tied them down. He would have to drive slowly on the way home.

He was turning the pickup around when he saw Cooper Newman stumble outside and walk toward a nearby pond. Cooper kneeled on the bank, stared at his reflection for a few minutes, and then fell face down into the water. Clayton waited for him to come up, but he did not. He rushed over and pulled him out face down by his boots, watched him cough up the water he swallowed. When he began to breathe normally, Clayton retrieved his pen and pad, sat beside Cooper's prone body, and wrote these words. He knew the legend by heart, knew where they would fit in his novel.

Narcissus was a youth who knelt daily beside a lake to contemplate his own beauty. He was so fascinated by his own beauty, that one day, he fell into the lake and drowned. At the spot where he fell, a flower was born, which was called the narcissus. When Narcissus died, the goddesses of the forest appeared and found the lake, which had been fresh water, turned into a lake of salty tears. The goddesses asked the lake, "Why do you weep?"

The lake replied, "I weep for Narcissus."

The goddesses replied, "Though we always pursued him in the forest, you alone could contemplate his beauty close at hand."

"But, was Narcissus beautiful? the lake asked.

"Who better than you to know that? After
all, it was by your banks that he knelt each day to
contemplate himself."
    After a long silence, the lake replied, "I weep for
him, but I never noticed that he was beautiful. I weep
because, each time he knelt beside my banks, I could
see, in the depths of his eyes, my own beauty reflected."

Clayton thought that was a fitting story for Cooper Newman. He waited for Cooper to revive enough to be sure he was
going to live before leaving with his retrieved treasures.

Toke approached his deputy at a trot. "What the hell are you
doing and where is your prisoner?"

Blaze looked toward Jubal, pointed to his lap and smiled.
Rivers was cradled there. Flo lay a few feet away. "Found both
of 'em under the travel trailer."

Tee and Jubal stroked the cat and dog as they breathed
sighs of relief. Jubal was confused. "That was the first place
we looked."

Blaze chuckled. "I imagine they hid in the woods till
things settled down. Flo was licking Rivers' wound, just like I
figured. That'll help him heal quicker. He can walk, but he's
afraid because he can't run."

He reached over and stroked the top of Flo's head. "Looked
like she brought him a rat and a bird, but he didn't eat either
one."

Jubal, ecstatic, dropped down and took Rivers into his lap.
"How bad is he hurt?"

Blaze pointed to the red streak down his side. "Bullet

grazed him enough to bring blood, but I don't think he'll have to have stitches. Figure it was a ricochet. He'll need some time to heal, but I expect he'll be good as new."

Toke paced the crossties. "So answer my question. How did I miss you when I passed here not long ago? And where is that murdering Mexican?"

Blaze smiled. "Maybe you're losing your touch or maybe I know how to hide pretty good. Remember how we used to hide under this trestle as boys?"

Toke was not interested in old memories. "Where's our killer?"

Blaze pointed toward the bottoms. "He's down there. Restin' easy."

Tee kneeled and patted Rivers and Flo. "Jubal, let's put 'em inside the trailer and feed 'em. They may need to stay inside till we can bring the truck and carry 'em home or to the vet."

Tee took Rivers and Jubal carried Flo to the trailer.

Toke waited until the trailer door closed. "You have to shoot him?"

"I intended to, but I'm just not sure, Toke."

Toke was relieved that Salinas wasn't running loose, but felt cheated out of his chance to face him personally. "Please stop with the nonsense and explain yourself. This could be really bad. I hired you to keep me from shooting him, now you took it on yourself."

Tee returned and sat beside Blaze, whose smile seemed sad. "Tee knows this is where I come regularly to ask forgiveness. I was doing that when you walked up."

Toke waved his arms in exasperation. "Forgiveness for what?"

"Look, I fully intended to take this devil down there and execute him, so I'm guilty no matter what. I watched Tee almost kill him and I figured he wouldn't last a night in our jail until you strung him up, so I figured I would do everybody and mankind a favor. Maybe keep you two out of jail."

"So you just shot him?"

Blaze looked toward the bottoms. "I sent up a pretty strong prayer before I turned toward the bottoms instead of heading to the jail. Asked the Lord to guide my hand. I forced the killer to his knees and pointed the gun, but for the life of me, I don't recall pulling the trigger. Thunder clapped, and I just don't know. I know it sounds crazy, but I was in sort of a trance. Guess I did, because he's sure got a hole in him."

Toke continued to pace the crossties. "Hand me your gun."

Toke rolled the cylinder, found a spent shell, smelled the muzzle. "Damn, it's sure enough been fired. Hell's bells, Blaze. We're in a fix. You can't just go executing a prisoner, no matter how bad he is."

Blaze hung his head. "I know that." He pointed to the trailer where Jubal was feeding his pets. "But this devil tried to harm our woods-boy, killed or maimed two down south, killed Morgan, hit one of the nicest women on Earth, who happens to be your wife, and crippled your son. He had to be stopped."

"You think I don't know that?"

"And he tried to kill Rivers. The man didn't deserve to live."

Tee pitched a rock into the creek. "This have anything to do with us saying they might just deport him so he could come back and kill again?"

Blaze looked at Tee, then at Toke. "You both said we

would have to try him here, pay for his lawyer and court costs. This county can't afford it, but that wasn't my reason."

Toke watched the storm that kept threatening but not happening. "Suppose we could keep quiet about the whole thing. Say he got away. They'll likely never find him unless Leonard happens to uncover him. If he does, he probably won't say a word. Why did you bury him, anyway?"

"Bad as he was, his lights were out, and I couldn't stand the thought of coyotes or buzzards at the body, even for one night. I planned on waiting till tomorrow to confess. But I won't deny what happened. Go ahead and dig him up. He's buried just deep enough to keep the critters away."

FORTY-EIGHT

ANGELINO SALINAS DID NOT RETURN TO
Riverby in a red Camaro, but in a black hearse. The hearse
was second in a parade led by Sheriff Toke Albright, who
couldn't wait to tell his wife and son the man who attacked
them was no more. The hearse was followed by the county
coroner, the justice of the peace, Blaze in his patrol car, Tee
and Jubal with Rivers and Flo, a dingy, dented Dodge pickup
that nobody recognized, and more than a dozen other trucks
with beds and cabs full of curiosity-seekers. People wanted a
glimpse of the demon called Angel.

The district attorney and Joe Henry Leathers were there
to insure chain of custody until an autopsy could be completed. The hearse stopped in front of Doc Pierce's clinic.

Abraham parked his Dodge in front of the clinic and
walked over to Toke. "Can I see his face?"

Toke recognized him from Parker's stables. "Why?"

301

"To be sure he is dead."

Toke looked around, motioned for the funeral attendants to stop the gurney, and unzipped the shroud just enough to show Angelino's face. "Pretty messed up. Is that your man?"

Abraham nodded. "*Si*. My mission is complete. I owe you a debt."

"How did you know he had been shot?"

"I used the barn phone like you said. Overheard where Parker was to meet him."

"So why didn't you call me?"

Abraham shrugged. "I was not sure I could trust you to kill him."

"So you were out there? Did you see who shot him?"

"I see the bullet take him, but not who fired it."

Clayton Dupree was parked by the abandoned livery and watched the hearse from the seat of his pickup. He overhead people on the street talking about what happened to the Mexican. He tried to make eye contact with Tee when he parked on the square. When he couldn't get his attention, Clayton got his shyness under control enough to drive beside Tee.

Tee was surprised to see him. "Hey, Clayton. What's in the garbage bags?"

"My life. You need to tell the sheriff I got something to tell him."

Tee watched as they rolled the shroud-wrapped body into the clinic. He had seen the muddy, bloody mess when Toke dug him up. "He's pretty busy right now, Clayton. Can it wait?"

Clayton looked at his boots. "He won't like it if he waits."

"Maybe I could get Blaze to come instead."

Clayton shook his head. "Not Blaze. Has to be Toke."

"Why don't we walk over there together?"

"Can't leave my things out here on the square for some fool to stick his nose in."

Tee could tell Clayton was disturbed and serious, so he trotted over in time to catch Toke before he followed the body into the examination room. He told him what Clayton said.

Toke motioned for Blaze to approach. "Keep Abraham here from leaving until we can get a complete interview." Blaze took Abraham's arm and cuffed it to the steering wheel of his Dodge.

Toke turned to Tee. "I can't leave now. DA says I have to be here until we nail this down. And I need to keep Blaze from incriminating himself when they interview him."

Tee motioned for Clayton to drive closer to the clinic and Toke trotted out to his pickup. "Make it quick, Clayton. I got to get back in there."

Clayton looked in the floorboard. "I know who shot that man."

Toke pointed toward Abraham. "Was it him?"

"No."

"Was it Blaze?"

"No. It was the bank president, Cooper Newman."

Toke's face darkened. "Cooper Newman? What makes you say that?"

"I saw him."

"You been drinking? Blaze's gun was fired and he don't deny it."

"See if the bullet you get out of him didn't come from a long gun. Won't be from a handgun."

Clayton turned the key and started his Ford. "Your killer is out at Jory Shelton's barn right now. Probably still passed out, but he won't be for long. Best go get him. The man is a thief as well as a killer."

Toke turned to Tee. "Why would Cooper Newman shoot the Mexican?"

"Not sure, but if Clayton says he did, well, I believe him. There's more to Cooper Newman than meets the eye. I'm not saying he did the killing, but you need to bring him in for questioning. I can tell you a few things about his dealings you may not know. There's a safe over in my office that has a lot of information that may involve Cooper Newman, Jack Prince, and Wheeler Parker. Sheriff Bell knew about it."

Toke looked toward the clinic. "Well, I have my suspicions about Parker, but not the others. I need to get back in there before Blaze gets himself into real trouble. Obviously can't send him out to get Newman."

Tee put his hands on his hips. "Well, you need to send somebody. Cooper may be on his way to the airport right now."

Toke removed his badge and pinned it to Tee's shirt. "Consider yourself sworn in. I know you can handle a gun. Did you bring yours?"

Tee put up both palms in a defensive gesture. "Gun's in my pickup, but I can't go out there. I got Jubal with me and a dog that's been shot. Plus a cat. And I sure ain't no lawman. I can shoot, but never even pointed a gun at a human."

They paused as Joe Henry Leathers approached.

Toke explained the situation to him. "Think you could go out to get Newman with Tee? You're an officer of the court."

Joe Henry laughed. "Why not? Let me go over to my pickup and get myself armed. Come on, Tee, you can be Wyatt Earp and I'll be your Doc Holliday."

Tee shook his head. "Not funny."

"Toke, you go on in. If Tee won't go, then I'll be the Lone Ranger."

Joe Henry trotted to his truck. When he returned, he wore a gun belt and holster snuggled around a pistol with an ivory grip. Joe Henry's tall lean frame, bow-legged gait, handlebar mustache, black wide-brimmed hat, and manure encrusted, deep scalloped boots that reached almost to his knees made him look more like Wyatt Earp than the lawyer he was. He squatted to remove his spurs.

Tee laughed. "Why are you taking off your spurs?"

"Might have to sneak up on him."

"Why bother? Those red-topped boots will flash like a neon sign, anyway."

Joe Henry smirked as he finished unbuckling his spurs, but did not look up. He bent to pull his jeans out of his boot tops and cover the red. "Satisfied now?"

Tee smiled. "Guess we might as well go."

Harmony O'Hara walked away from the crowd of people standing by the clinic toward the new deputies. "Be still my heart. I've always known you two were a couple of throwbacks to the days of the Wild West, but never saw you packing heat. Where's your hardware, Tee?"

"You think you could look after Jubal and his pets while me and Joe Henry run a little errand? We were going to take Rivers to the vet. He's been scraped by a bullet."

Harmony smiled. "I can do that and look after all three. How long will you be?"

"No more than an hour, I hope."

"If we're not on the square when you get back, we'll be at my house or the vet's. Then I expect to be filled in on what's going on."

Joe Henry put his hand just above the driver's window of Clayton's pickup. Clayton flinched and scooted over. "Think you could lead us out there, Clayton? I haven't been down that old road in a long time and Cooper may be hiding."

"It's on the way home. Suppose I could."

Cooper Newman was against the barn door crying when they arrived. Clayton stepped out of his pickup, kept one hand on the door as he pointed toward his banker. "Behold. Narcissus. Now I must depart before the rain comes." He got back into this pickup and drove away.

Cooper Newman had a dislocated shoulder from his fall off the ladder and a cough from swallowing so much pool water. The words spilled out of him in a gurgling slur. "Is he dead?"

Joe Henry put a hand on Tee's arm to shut him up so he could conduct a legal interview. "Is who dead?"

"The Mexican. Way I figure it; I hit what I was aiming at." He continued with a drunken, barely coherent confession as they helped him to Joe Henry's truck. As Tee helped him into the pickup seat, the first big drops of rain forecast by thunder and lightning for two days pelted the hood and cab. Newman sat between them on the way back, his usual scent of aftershave and cologne replaced with the smell of alcohol, sweat, mildewed hay and cow manure.

Tee watched the busy windshield wipers as he asked the question that had bothered him since he heard what Clayton

306

Dupree said. "Why did you shoot the Mexican?" He wanted to ask why he had not let Blaze kill him.

Joe Henry took his eyes off the road. "Don't ask him questions till we get him in front of witnesses and his own lawyer."

Cooper answered anyway. "Figured Blaze was threatening him with the gun, running a bluff, trying to get him to confess. Couldn't let him run his mouth. Besides, I was locked and loaded and I'm an expert hunter. I bag what I hunt."

As if a dam opened inside Cooper at the same time the storm clouds released a torrent of rain, he continued a disjointed, besotted, tearful confession and apology for what he did, claiming he had been victimized by the two most powerful men in Northeast Texas; that he joined the consortium without knowing its criminal nature; that Parker and Prince forced him to do their dirty work when things fell apart.

By the time they got back to the courthouse, he was sober enough to talk and frightened enough to spill more beans on the consortium in front of Toke. Joe Henry agreed to represent him, and he told everything they needed to know. Joe Henry assured him the district attorney would be more interested in Wheeler Parker and Jack Prince and putting a stop to their illegal smuggling of drugs and humans than he would be in Cooper Newman. After all, the man Cooper shot was a cold-blooded killer. Nothing was mentioned about the fraudulent transactions at the bank.

FORTY-NINE

ALL THE PEWS WERE FILLED AT BY THE RIVER
Church for Morgan Bell's funeral and many stood outside, listening through the open windows and doors to Enoch Essary's
too-long sermon and Blaze Blaisdell's moving eulogy. Most
were surprised to see Melvin Cobb sitting with Peggy Bell and
her daughter. He sobbed during the entire service. Morgan
had said he would give the boy his name when he earned it,
but felt he never had. Peggy figured it was time.

The churches filled the next Sunday morning as towns-
people tried to come to grips with the killing of Morgan Bell
and the senseless maiming of Lydia and Freddy Albright.
Many seemed relieved the violent crimes were committed by
an outsider, someone not really an American. But as the details emerged about three prominent locals involved, they re-
acted with shock, dismay and fear.

The Highway Patrol captured Wheeler Parker on his way

to Mexico, and Toke Albright took great pleasure in taking custody of his old boss when they returned him to Riverby. Toke and Blaze found Jack Prince lying on his gin lot office floor, sobbing and pleading, protesting he was an innocent victim, had never seen or touched the drugs or wetbacks.

Tee watched Riverby change again in the days following the killings. Many withdrew their money from Farmers and Merchants Bank. Bank examiners arrived and the bank's board hired an independent auditing firm to determine the extent of Cooper Newman's larceny. Cooper was still holding the cash from his safe deposit box when Tee and Joe Henry took him into custody. In a deposition, he said the money belonged to Clayton Dupree. The bank agreed to reimburse Clayton for his losses immediately and wait for the courts to return their money after trials were over. They also agreed to lifetime free rental of twelve safe deposit drawers and six boxes. Clayton returned his possessions to the bank's safe deposit vault.

Jack Prince's auto dealership was closed for a period of time while General Motors looked for a new dealer. Wheeler Parker's Wheelhouse Bar and liquor store were closed as well as his horse stables. Prince's and Parker's properties were offered for sale with the proceeds to be used as restitution for victims of their crimes.

Toke took possession of the contents of the safe in Tee's office. They found more cash in Prince's safes at the dealership and his gin lot office. Even more was found in Wheeler Parker's safes at the bar and at his stables. As multiple grand juries were formed and many lawsuits discussed, Blaze called a meeting of the Hurt Circle.

The Circle members sat at their usual spots inside Prigmore's. At Blaze's request, Morgan Bell's seat was occupied by Peggy Bell. Lydia Albright sat beside Toke. Tee and Joe Henry were last to arrive. Tee almost expected the group to be suspended if not dissolved, but soon realized the death of one of their own was a reason to meet, not a reason to disband.

Tee and Joe Henry sat, looked reluctantly into all the faces. Toke and Blaze seemed the most downcast. There was an uncomfortable silence until Enoch spoke. "You boys just missed the prayer for the Bell and Albright families and Blaze, of course. We prayed for a swift recovery for Lydia and Freddy and peace for Peggy and Blaze."

Toke drummed his fingers on the tabletop. "Won't be any recovery from death, a lost eye, or a crippled son." Lydia stared at the tabletop with her good eye. Peggy nodded.

Enoch bowed his head. He seemed chastened. "No, I guess there won't. But Lydia, Freddy and Peggy are a blessing to us all. Their faith is strong. They have many years of a good life ahead of them and their strength will help them make the best of them."

Toke's bloodshot eyes scanned the big table, looking into every eye. "Y'all know Lydia never as much as hurt a fly. That son-of-a-bitch paid for what he did to her and Freddy...and Sheriff Bell, of course."

Enoch flinched, but kept his eyes down. "The Lord said, *Vengeance is mine, I will repay.*"

Abel's expression revealed nothing, and Harmony stared at her white eel boots.

Toke looked at Enoch. "How do you know he didn't use Blaze or Cooper Newman to repay?"

Blaze half-rose from his seat to get their attention. "I called this meeting because I needed to explain my actions to all of you. Not to make excuses, but to seek forgiveness."

"Though I did not kill the prisoner, I did intend to. And I put his life in danger and his body in the sights of the man who did shoot him. I take responsibility for that."

Toke Albright put both hands on the table. "I have been assured no charges will be leveled against Blaze. Even if a grand jury is convened, he will be no-billed. It's a slam dunk. Besides, he saved the county the expense of a long trial."

Joe Henry lifted his cup to Blaze. "A trial and all the appeals and complications of a man who spent most of his life in Mexico and who had a rich father could have torn this community apart for years. Thanks to Blaze, we can start healing."

Harmony tried to ease the tension. "Blaze, care to tell us how a deputy on his first day on the job went out and found the killer? And I want to hear about the angels."

Blaze looked at Toke and Tee as if asking for permission to tell the story they had heard parts of. "Well, in the first place, I didn't find him. Tee here did."

Tee shook his head. "Nope, my boy Jubal and his dog Rivers did."

Blaze clinched his jaws. "As you all know, I don't know the first thing about being a lawman. I just went out to the places where this man did his crimes. When I was out at Lydia's at the spot where she was attacked...excuse me, Lydia."

Lydia smiled. "Go on and tell your story."

"You're the only people I can tell this story, and I need to get it off my chest. Maybe you all can help me understand it."

"Go on." Everyone seemed to say it.

312

"Well, I had this feeling come over me out in Lydia's yard, a feeling I can't describe. It was death and life all at the same time—a cold chill. Then there was this funereal smell. I don't mean to be disrespectful, but you all know I worked for the funeral home occasionally. That's how I know that word, funereal. Anyway, the smell is sweet and rotten at the same time, like a decaying dead animal combined with a bed of roses or a basket of lilies. Sort of makes you queasy."

"I felt the need to offer up a prayer for God to lead me to this killer before he hurt anybody else. A bolt of lightning sort of came out of nowhere. It looked like it was right over the spot where Sheriff Bell was killed and Freddy injured. I drove there, got out, and smelled that sick smell again. I found some tracks and I found some spots that looked like the killer's car might be leaking. We know Morgan got off one shot. This message in my head said the Mexican was still around. I could almost feel him."

"Well, I drove right over the trestle where he hid his car. Because his engine locked up, I imagine. Not sure about that yet. He may have decided to wait there to collect what Wheeler Parker owed him. Anyway, I didn't see the car. I went over to Zeke's and showed him the wanted poster. He recognized it right away. Said the killer walked toward the trestle when he left the night before."

Blaze paused to take a sip of coffee. "Then I saw this queer bolt of lightning that seemed to point toward the trestle, sort of like I saw when I was at Toke and Lydia's house. I know you think it was my imagination, but I tell you, Toke, I did see it. Then this dust devil blew across the field by Zeke's, headed straight toward the trestle. It seemed to stop right on the tracks. Never saw anything like it. I know you won't believe this either, but I heard the wind whisper, *For they have sown the wind and they shall reap the whirlwind.* You know that verse from Hosea?"

Both Abel and Enoch nodded sympathetically as Blaze started to finish his story. But Harmony would not let him. "So what about the angels?"

"Well, I know folks are laughing at me, but I know what I saw. The dust devil sort of turned into a dark cloud with two faces. It hovered a few yards beyond the trestle, right where Jubal rode Sweetness away from the killer. It was like they was protecting him. You know?"

Toke's expression showed the worry he felt about his friend's sanity. "Whose faces?"

Tee was uncomfortable, but his look seemed to give permission for Blaze to answer.

"It was Jubal's grandpa and grandma. The people I killed."

Toke bumped his fist on the table. "You ain't ever gonna let that go, are you?"

Blaze looked to Harmony for rescue. "You believe in angels?"

She didn't answer so he went on. "Why would it be so strange that Jubal's grandparents might be looking out for him? They might be trapped here on earth because of what they did."

He looked around the Circle. Only Enoch seemed supportive. "Let's not be so quick to judge our friend. Isaiah says, *My thoughts are not your thoughts, neither are your ways My ways.*"

"You ever kill anybody, Toke?"

"How many times I got to tell you? You didn't kill Tee's parents, Blaze. They killed themselves. Ain't that right, Tee?"

Tee nodded. "Pretty much, but I have come to understand the guilt Blaze feels. I feel guilty, myself."

Blaze went on. "Until you've killed two people, no matter they wanted to die, you can't know how it feels."

Toke kept his eyes on his boots. "Go on with the story."

"You know how I used to fear the tracks, but I walked on those rails, looked into the ditch under that trestle and that's when a big crow flew off with a few branches in its claws. Just enough to see red paint. I noticed that powerful smell again as the crow flew over. I figured the killer was close by. Then I saw the dust devil go up the trail to Hurt Hill. That's where Tee had him all trussed up and giving him what-for. I think I may have saved Tee from killing the man."

Tee's face darkened as he looked at the faces around the table. Toke's expression and his hand over his mouth showed his deep concern for what he was going to hear next. "Then what?"

"Let me stop right here and ask what you would have done."

Toke bowed his head and moved it side to side. "I done told you more than once what I aimed to do if I caught him."

"For what he done to Lydia and Freddy, right? Then I got to thinking about those other people he crippled and the lives he ruined, about how he might get away and do it again and again. About how you might lose your job or even go to jail if you found him first and killed him. Even if I'd brought him in and locked him up, you might have strung him up in his cell or taken him out on the square and executed him right there."

Lydia looked at Toke. "And that would have been the end of you."

Harmony's voice was near breaking. "So you took him down in the bottoms to execute him yourself?"

"A box full of Morgan Bell's gimme caps was sitting in the back seat and I didn't know it. The killer sat right down on 'em. Did it on purpose. You know how Morgan was about those caps. Wore a different one every day so he could show support for the local businesses. Guess that was the tipping point."

Harmony whispered, "So, why didn't you do it?"

Tears began to roll down Blaze's ruddy cheeks. "I was never a good shot with a handgun. Could be I heard the rifle retort and it made me jerk, but Clayton says he only heard one shot, so we must have fired at the exact same time. I think God moved my hand and made me miss."

A long silence followed. Blaze put both palms down on the table as he stood. "Don't expect you or anybody else to understand, but them two faces up there above Jubal spoke to me." He patted his chest, looking for the pocket in bib overalls that was not there. He found his shirt pocket and pulled a slip of paper from it.

He unfolded the crumpled paper and read slowly. "I see Your Presence in the flight of every bird, in the eyes of people I love, in every cloud that passes. I hear Your Voice in every roll of thunder, bird's song, or loved one's voice. I feel Your Touch in the soft embrace of a gentle breeze, the kiss of a raindrop or snowflake, a hug from a loved one, the warmth of the sun."

Blaze refolded the paper, placed it on the table, rapped it with a knuckle. He looked toward the ceiling to keep from making eye contact with anyone at the table. "Someone told me those words once, and I took 'em to heart. Wrote 'em down, been carrying them with me ever since. Say what you will, I believe every word." He stood.

Tee glanced at Abel for his reaction, saw the hint of a smile. Nobody said anything. Their coffee was cold. Each patted Blaze on the shoulder as they left.

Harmony caught Tee at the front door. She turned him to face her and gave him an unexpected hug. He turned a little red. "Well, what did I do to deserve that?"

"I know tension when I see it. I saw you balling your fists and drumming your fingers when Blaze told his story. I heard you nearly did the job Cooper Newman finished. A hug's always good for that."

Tee smiled. "Well, a hug never hurts."

"Someday, when you feel like it, you can tell me what else is eating at your gut."

He wanted to tell her about Ford Donovan, the man who as much as murdered his wife and tried to kidnap his son, how he wanted to finish the job, but could not.

As he walked back to the office, he could still smell Harmony's body and feel her touch. He realized how long since he had been embraced by anyone other than his son. The hug helped.

FIFTY

TEE WAS RETURNING LOW-IMPORTANCE CALLS when he saw Abel talking to Wilda. Her voice carried well enough for him to hear her above his phone conversation. "I'm sure he'll want to visit with you about this, Mr. Gunter. He likes to interview all his clients, especially the first time. He might see you right now if that works for you."

Tee smiled as he hung up the phone. *Abel Gunter finally trusts me.*

Their reversed roles were uncomfortable at first, but Tee soon relaxed. This was his turf, after all. There was the usual farm and ranch data to enter and Tee answered Abel's few questions quickly about the return. He had the impression that Abel could easily have done it all himself.

When Tee read the documents on brokerage transactions, Abel had to explain to him how one could sell shares of stock before he actually purchased them. Using prior year returns,

Abel explained how the transactions were reported. Tee knew he would have to spend several nights studying puts and calls, futures contracts, and options trading. Abel withheld actual statements from brokers and bank statements, so Tee could not tell precisely just how well-off he was. But the rancher who lived frugally and simply held many sophisticated investments.

"So how did you learn about futures trading?"

"Back when I was a high-flying sales trainer, I thought I could sell anything. My head got so big, cars seemed beneath me, so I studied to be a stockbroker. Passed the tests, but six months in, I knew it wasn't for me."

Although Abel asked for anonymity and confidentiality when he donated, Tee knew from other clients that his contributions to needy families and local causes were generous. Many assumed tax benefits were part of his motivation. Tee now knew that was not true. Abel had not itemized his deductions on prior returns and declined to do so again this year. When the return was finished and readied for mailing along with a copy of the extension he had already filed, Abel handed Tee a folder.

"This is a story I wrote. Read it during your quiet time, then come out to the ranch and we'll discuss it."

Tee watched Abel walk to his car with Dawson close behind. When they drove away, Tee grabbed his hat. "I need to run a few errands. If I'm not back by closing time, lock up. Jubal is going home with Freddy. Thanks."

On his porch at home, he opened the typewritten pages.

THE STORY OF CLIVE, CLAUDIA, AND TRUDY

As Billy Dawson went on and on about consorting with
whores while working for oil companies somewhere in the
Middle East, Clive wondered what to make of this man
his daughter was living with. He never gave specifics about
exactly which oil companies and which countries, but
he relished going into great detail about the whores, even
doing imitations of their accents and their butchering of
English names for various parts of human anatomy. It was
barroom talk coarse enough to embarrass most grown men,
yet he told the stories in front of Trudy and her parents.

Clive tried to get his mind off what his daughter's new
roommate was saying by studying the tattoos on his arms,
but the man loved to talk with his hands, so Clive had
trouble reading the words or making out the images. What
bothered him more than the tattoos or the ribald stories
was the way his daughter sat in rapt attention, seeming to
enjoy the performance. He stared at Trudy intently, hoping
to get her to at least glance in his direction, to see the
question in his expression, the astonishment, but she knew
better than to look at her father. Clive's wife Claudia tried
to feign rapt attention, her face fixed in a painful smile that
tried to show tolerance.

Clive and Claudia winced when Trudy told them
she dropped out of college to help support them until
Dawson could find work stateside. Clive cleared his
throat. "You were less than a month away from finals."

Trudy's smile vanished. "I know that, Dad, but a
month is a long time for us to go without money. We had
to pay a month's rent in advance, stock up on groceries."

321

Clive visualized thousands of dollars he spent for a semester at Southern Methodist University. "So you have moved out of campus housing?" Another vision of money going down the drain.

Her tone and expression were condescending. "Dad, you know they wouldn't let Billy live there with me." Clive tried to smile. "No, I suppose not." He never understood why she insisted on living in campus housing when they lived less than ten blocks from the campus. Now he understood.

It seemed the new couple was there, then gone, leaving a foul smell in Clive's nostrils, a sharp brittleness to air in the room. He and Claudia sat in silence for the better part of an hour, staring at the floor, before she spoke. "Well, that just about beats all."

He silently tried to retrace the father-daughter journey he so seriously misjudged. He saw their relationship as loving and trusting; himself as her anchor and protector. Where had he gone wrong? He had dreaded the flight the next morning for a conference. Now he looked forward to it. He needed to get away.

When he returned, Claudia had worked herself into a snit. Trudy refused to take her calls and snubbed her offers of reconciliation and invitations to visit. Claudia's anger seemed less than Clive's when they first met Trudy's new boyfriend, but now she was more resolute, more determined not to give in to their daughter's folly. Clive realized he relied on Claudia to eventually bridge the gap, to display conciliatory behavior he was not prepared to engage in himself. "Let's don't give up

322

completely. *Give her a few more days. Surely she'll come to her senses."*

But Claudia remained resolute in her efforts to seal out the hurt, to close Trudy's chapter in her life and to move on. She repeatedly stated she refused to let her selfish, immature daughter steal her happiness and haunt her life for the remainder of her days.

Clive could not sleep that night and only fitfully for several nights. He replayed his role as a father to Trudy, tried to determine where he made some terrible mistake. When he could not identify a particular event that might have made his daughter become so resentful and foolish, he looked for other reasons. Maybe it was the elitist neighborhood where Trudy grew up, or the schools she attended filled with children of wealthy parents. Clive never felt he belonged in the community; had come by his house when a client of his lost everything and made a desperate offer to sell the house at a fraction of its market value. Clive made a good living, but grew up poor. He and Claudia never really tried to fit into the neighborhood. Maybe Trudy was rejected by her classmates and resentment and rebellion boiled inside until it spilled over and resulted in Billy Dawson, the tattooed thug she now lived with. Maybe they missed all the signs.

Their upscale community existed like an island in the middle of a storm-filled sea. The fashionable and expensive neighborhood where they lived was surrounded by crime-and-poverty-ridden areas. When he began driving by their small rented house on his way to work, he was shocked at the hovel his daughter lived in. He passed by slowly the first time, parked down the street, hoping to catch a glimpse of Trudy. But there was never a sign of life. There was no driveway, no cars parked in the street. The '60 Thunderbird he bought Trudy when she graduated high school was never there. He wondered if she had to sell it.

A friend of Claudia's told her she had seen Trudy working as a cashier at a neighborhood grocery. Clive began driving by. He stopped and stared, wondered what her hours were, tried to get up the courage to go in, but couldn't. A few weeks into his ritual searching, he saw Dawson standing outside an auto repair shop, leaning against an aging and beat-up black '54 Ford, smoking a cigarette. Clive cruised by, stared, but never got a glance from Billy Dawson. He made the repair shop part of his regular route to work.

A week later, the Ford was not parked at the garage. When it did not appear for three more days, Clive stopped to find out if Dawson still worked there. He pretended to be having brake problems and scanned the shop while he quizzed the mechanic.

"You got a fellow working here by the name of Billy Dawson?"

"You a friend of his?"

"Not exactly."

"What's he done?"

"Nothing I know of. Does he work here or not?"

"Had to let him go. He was overcharging customers, sticking the extra in his pocket. Came to work more than once with a snoot full, too."

Clive drove to the grocery, walked inside, saw Trudy at one of the two cash registers. He picked up a large sack of potato chips and walked to her counter. She looked at him and sneered. "You and Mom just can't stay out of my business, can you?"

He noticed bruises on her arm when she put the potato chips in a sack. "Heard your boyfriend lost his job."

"Why is that any of your business?"

He pointed at her arm. "Where'd you get the bruises?"

"I fell, as if that's any of your business either."

Clive looked around to be sure nobody was listening or watching. "Listen, Trudy. If he's hitting you, please tell me. I'll come and get you in a heartbeat."

"I don't want your help."

"At least tell me what your mother and I did to deserve this treatment from you."

"I just want to be left alone. I am grown and I want to live my own life. You treat me like a child."

"That's because you act like one." He pitched the sack to her. "Here, take that home in case you get hungry."

The next morning, the Ford was parked in the yard of the rent house. That meant Billy Dawson was lying in bed while Trudy worked.

The house and grocery store became part of Clive's regular route to work and home again. Occasionally, he would catch a glimpse of Dawson under the hood of his Ford. One morning, he watched as Dawson pulled the throttle to full speed. The car had no muffler and the noise was enough to bring a neighbor out to his porch. A yelling match ensued. The neighbor went inside, returned with a shotgun. Clive sat up in his seat, surprised at himself for enjoying the spectacle. Dawson laughed at his neighbor, but released the throttle.

A few days later, Dawson came out and jumped into the car with some urgency, sped down the street, working the shift lever and racking back on the straight tailpipe as it backfired. He repeated the process through the three gears. Anyone on the street asleep was now awake.

Claudia's friend called a month later. "I hesitate to say this, but I saw Trudy at the store again today. Her face is all bruised up and it looks like she might be missing a tooth."

Clive went to her house but found nobody home. The next morning, he went into the grocery store to see for himself. Trudy looked away as he approached her checkout counter. "Let me see your face."

She turned to face him. One side of her face was blue, one eye swollen shut, and one tooth was missing. Clive felt as if his insides might give way. "Trudy, honey. What has he done to you? I'll kill the son-of-a-bitch."

"Really? You're twenty-five years older and soft. He's forty pounds heavier and in good shape. You'll only make things worse for me. He apologized. Leave us alone to work things out."

He looked around the store helplessly, thought about throwing her over his shoulder and carrying her out. He knew he could still do it. She had to be down to less than a hundred pounds. "Trudy, haven't I always looked out for you? Come to your rescue? That's what a father does. Let me help you. I guarantee he will never hurt you again."

"Dad, please. Just let me alone. This is my problem and it's been handled."

Their talk and Trudy's tears caused stares from the store manager. Clive drove home, called in sick and discussed the problem with Claudia. She broke into sobs, then made herself recover. "She made her bed; she has to lie in it. She won't even talk to me."

Clive was incredulous, but almost understood the barrier Claudia was trying to build. He tried to build one himself, but failed. He drove over to their house in mid-afternoon, parked and watched. When a neighbor came in from work, he approached him, told him who he was. "You ever hear them fighting?"

"Two, three times a week. Lots of yelling and screaming."

Clive handed him a business card with his office and home phone on it. "If you call me next time you hear a commotion, I'll make it worth your while."

"What would make it worthwhile for me is to get that lowlife out of the neighborhood."

"I'll try to make that happen."

Clive went home, took down a framed baseball bat with a bronze plaque that said "Heavy Hitter". He won it for being top salesman ten years before.

Claudia watched him remove it. "Why are you taking that down? Thought it was one of your favorite awards."

Clive felt the heft of the bat. He was a better than average baseball player back in the day. "It is."

"So why?"

He took it to his car without answering, laid it under the seat where he kept his .22 revolver. She didn't repeat

327

the question when he returned. Their communication had been reduced to as few words as possible since Billy Dawson entered their lives. Claudia seemed to have withdrawn from life altogether.

Three nights later, the neighbor called. Clive left immediately. He dressed for the occasion every night when he came home, always ready for battle. He stopped in front of the house, put the revolver in his back waistband, and raced to the door with the bat. He heard Trudy screaming, Dawson cursing. The door was locked. He used the bat to break the window in the door, reached inside and unlocked the knob. The living room looked like the roof had been torn off and a tornado had come through the opening, as if Dawson used his daughter's body like a club or crowbar. The yelling stopped when he walked in and Dawson started for him. He pointed the bat.

Dawson paused. "Old man, I'll take that away from you and shove it up your ass."

Clive pulled the revolver. "What about this? You think you're quick enough to take this?"

Dawson put up his hands. "Now listen. I done promised Trudy I won't ever hit her again. But she started raising hell the minute she come home. But I'm done. We're done." He turned to Trudy. "Ain't that right, Honey?"

She nodded while looking at her father. "I already told you, Daddy. Stay out of this. We'll work it out."

Clive shook his head in dismay and confusion. Who was this girl? Was she on drugs? He spoke without taking his eyes off Billy. "*Little girl, that time has come and gone. Now go get in my car. I'm taking you home.*"

"*No, I'm not, Daddy. Now, you go on before I call the police.*" *She picked up the kitchen receiver.*

Clive kept the gun pointed at Billy's chest. "Turn around." He walked beside Billy, keeping the gun trained on the back of his head. With his free hand, he swung the bat against the front of Billy's right knee. It buckled; he screamed and dropped to the other knee. Trudy screamed.

Clive put the gun back in his waistband, used both hands to swing the bat against Dawson's protruding left elbow. When he screamed and reached for it, Clive landed another crushing blow to his rib cage and broke his right arm. Trudy dialed as Dawson wadded himself into a ball on the floor. Clive pulled out Dawson's right arm, placed his foot on it to hold it, and crushed all his fingers. "Don't guess you'll be hitting any women anytime soon." He considered a blow to the head, but knew it might kill him. Billy Dawson would not be beating up any women for a long time. He took a deep breath, sat on the floor and waited for the police to arrive.

Tee stared at the last line. *I am Clive* was written at the bottom in the same handwriting as Abel Gunter's signature under it.

FIFTY-ONE

TEE TOOK SEVERAL DEEP BREATHS AS HE READ Abel's story. He took several more and rubbed his chin as he laid the letter on his lap. He called Lydia to see if Jubal could stay through supper. When she said yes, he went to the Crimson River Ranch.

Tee carried the folder containing the letter as he followed Abel into his den. They sat at the round table. Dawson plopped beside his master's feet. Tee pointed at the folder. "That's a pretty amazing tale. I see why you qualified for the Hurt Circle, but what's the rest of the story? Did your daughter really call the police? "

Abel studied Tee for a few seconds. "She did. I was arrested, cuffed and hauled away while my daughter watched. Paramedics carried Billy Dawson to the hospital. He had several broken bones."

"So what did they do to you? Did they know he beat your daughter?"

"She refused to testify for me or against him, but a neighbor and one of her coworkers did. And, of course, her injuries sort of spoke for themselves."

"So they let you go?"

"No. If I had not had the gun and used the bat, I might have gotten off with a fine, but as it was, my lawyer and I reached a plea bargain. I paid a ten-thousand-dollar fine and spent three years in prison."

Tee leaned back. "Three years. Wow. I heard the rumors about a criminal past, but figured they were idle gossip. Did Joe Henry and Morgan Bell know?"

"Yes. I decided to confide in the local law before I settled anywhere. Morgan Bell looked up my story and was welcoming and understanding and included Joe Henry in our meeting. Joe Henry volunteered to represent me so attorney-client privilege came into the relationship. He helped me find this little ranch and get the title transferred without a lot of local gossip."

"Why here?"

"I've always felt a need to get back to country living, especially when I lived in an urban jungle. Always had an affinity for livestock because I grew up in the country. Plus I have family ties here. Met my wife in the old cemetery by the church. We were both tracing our ancestry. We each have a set of great-grandparents buried there."

"You met your wife in a cemetery?"

"Edmund Burke said a man who does not look backward to his ancestors will not look forward to posterity. I've always had an abiding interest in my ancestry... and my posterity."

Tee pointed to the shelves. "You find that quote in one of those books?"

"Among other things, yes."

"What happened to Claudia? Is that her real name? "

"Yes, I only changed *my* name in the story. Can't explain why exactly, but I needed to write it in third person like I was a spectator instead of a participant. I wrote it a few years ago. I needed to confess, even if only to myself. It helped a little. As to Claudia, she never visited me in prison. We speak, but she said our life together was over. Said I bring back too many bad memories."

"What about Trudy?"

Abel walked to the window and looked out. He spoke without turning, his voice cracking. "I don't know. Claudia says she disappeared right after I beat up Billy. I hired a private investigator after prison and he found an address for her in Fort Worth. I write her at that address regularly, but she never writes back. Don't know for sure if she's even there. I guess I'm afraid to go find out."

He turned to face Tee. "Do you realize how blessed you are to have Jubal?"

Tee tried to imagine his agony. "How about Billy Dawson?"

"Ironically, Billy Dawson was in the same prison I was the last year I was there. Broke into the old house where we lived. Guess he cased the joint during his visit. The owner came home and caught him in the act. Billy tried to run, but, of course, he's crippled, so the owner caught him and held him until the cops arrived."

"So did you bump into him in the prison?"

"I saw him a few times. He's the one who told me how he got caught. You would have thought we were old friends. Carried on a conversation like we had no history."

"Bet he hasn't beat up on any more girls, though." Tee tried to see a hint of satisfaction in Abel's eyes, but there was none.

"So, why did you share this with me?"

"When I heard you seemed ready to kill the Mexican for attacking Jubal, I felt you could possibly be helped by my story. Maybe learn from it."

"Learn what? I don't see you had any choice. The man had to be stopped. A father protects his children."

"That's true, and I admit I don't know the answer to such a dilemma even now. But I did have choices and the one I made turned out badly." Abel went to the kitchen and returned with two cups of coffee. "When you told me what happened to your brother, your parents, and your wife, I wondered what I would have done. Did you blame God, for example?"

Tee stared into his coffee. "Yes. Did you?"

"Yes. Living in a cell gives a man a lot of time to brood and think. I was angry, felt justified in what I did and told myself I would do it again. After a few months of shaking my fist at God, I had lost about thirty pounds and aged ten years. Then I went to a prison ministry meeting prepared to challenge the minister."

"How'd that work out?"

"He listened politely to my tirade and gave a response that made me madder. An old man who helped the preacher with his handouts came to my cell afterward. He was a prisoner, too. Had been locked up for more than twenty years for killing his daughter's husband because he was beating her. The similarity of our situations got his attention."

"He brought me a handful of little magazines not much bigger than my fist called *Plus* put out by Norman Vincent Peale's organization. He took me to the prison library and showed me a collection of books by C. S. Lewis, G. K. Chesterton, Oswald Chambers and a few others that someone donated. They looked untouched."

Tee pointed toward the shelves. "Think I saw those."

"The old man told me these men had spoken to him. He quoted an old adage that says when the student is ready, the teacher will appear. Said that different authors and preachers speak to different people and these spoke to him."

"So they spoke to you?"

Abel smiled and nodded. "You're welcome to borrow a copy of any of my books. Maybe one of them will speak to you."

"What will they likely tell me about why God allowed my whole family to be taken away?"

"You'll have to read them to find out. Maybe they will speak to you, maybe not. Want to hear my short thoughts on your question?"

Tee leaned back, unsure if he did. "Go ahead."

"Let's distinguish between the Will of God and the will of man. If we're going to blame God for the wreck that killed your brother, we have to assume God put that train and your trailer in that spot at that time. Did he? Or did your Daddy's choice to slow his responses and thinking by taking a few drinks of whiskey cause it?"

"Fair enough. And I can maybe see how my parents chose

to do what they did. What I don't understand is why God didn't stop either one from happening. And what about what happened to my wife right under my nose?"

"As for your parents, we are all given free will. They made that choice, not God. As for the man who haunts you, under pressure, for reasons you can't explain, you saved an evil man's life. Now you're punishing yourself for it. I beat a man unmercifully and crippled him for life. I saw no other way, but there were other ways. I could have found a better way to protect my daughter. What did my actions gain me—a prison record and loss of both my wife and my daughter."

"Father Bob said I had to find a way to forgive, but I haven't yet. Have you?"

Abel leaned back and stared at the ceiling for a minute or more. "It's a question I have asked myself many times. When I saw the man who abused my daughter in prison, walking with a limp, I realized the poisonous anger I consumed daily for years had left my body. I realized that poison served only to harm me, not him. I gained nothing and lost much from hating him, just as I gained nothing from harming him."

"You stopped him from hurting your daughter."

"Think about that. I was taken to jail while he remained a free man. He could still shoot a gun. He might have killed her."

"So you're saying I should forgive Ford Donovan. I don't see how I can do that."

Abel leaned and scratched between Dawson's ears. "This fellow was a stray that showed up on my doorstep one day. He helped me to heal and continues to help me every day. That's why I named him Dawson. Every time he shows his love and loyalty and entices me to love him back, I forgive Billy Dawson a little more."

"Can't imagine naming something I love after the man who caused my wife's death. I will never forgive him."

"You will have to one day. Think about it this way. In seminary, I learned if the world was a perfect place and we were perfect people, there would be no reason for God to exist and no reason for us to exist. We would have no consciences, no morals, no beliefs because there would be no need for such things. If there were no adversity, there would be no joy."

"You were in seminary? You're a preacher?"

"After prison, I spent three years in seminary."

"Ever preach in a church?"

"I did prison ministry, but got claustrophobic every time I entered the gates. I filled in for absent preachers at churches a lot, but was never comfortable behind the pulpit. Besides, not too many churches want a felon as their pastor. I felt called to come here. Not sure yet why other than it was where I met my wife. Maybe I think we'll meet here again one day."

Abel leaned across the table. "Think about it this way. If you had never been struck down, you would never know how good it feels to get up. I have always found it strange that it's only after things go bad that people realize how good things were."

"This is all sort of making sense, but I need to get my head around it better."

"We will never fully understand how things work. Oswald Chambers said we have to live a life of faith, not of understanding and reason."

"So you think there was no reason for all these things happening? Father Bob seemed to think there was a reason why I survived and why this happened to my family."

Abel laughed. "We're both right. You admit you don't know exactly what brought you here. Maybe you're here to help Blaze. Maybe I am, too. I spent a lot of time with Morgan Bell before he was killed. I hope I helped him. As for you, how many clients have you helped this year?"

Tee seemed perplexed by the question, so Abel continued. "Fact is you're helping me right now. Maybe everything that happened to both of us put us right where we are in this moment in time. I like to think you're helping me fulfill my purpose. But we may never know. That's why we have to have faith no matter how many messes we make, God will help us to turn the negatives into positives for His purposes. God will use this for good. He already has."

After a long, comfortable silence, Abel stood and patted Tee's shoulder. "I'm a lot older than you, but it always helps me to reflect back on my past, good and bad. From the time I accepted Jesus, The Holy Spirit became my constant companion. I had a hard time understanding that, especially when I reflect back on the terrible life I led even after my salvation. But then I began to imagine Him following me all those years, watching me veer off the path He chose. I sinned, hurt and betrayed the ones I loved and who loved me. He whispered to me, nudged me, tried to get my attention, but I would not listen. He followed me all the way into prison. Now, He walks in front and I follow. I even have a name for Him. Do you see the difference between following Him and being followed by Him?"

"I think I do. Makes sense. Care to tell me the name you use?"

"I think not, but I consider it respectful and loving. You'll find one of your own."

Tee stood and stretched. "I'm grateful for everything you've taught me, Abel. I want you to know that. I've overstayed my welcome and it's past time for me to pick up Jubal. He's at Freddy's."

"And how were Freddy and Lydia when you saw them?"

"She's regained partial vision. Freddy may never be the great athlete he seemed destined to be, but he's a good kid. Like you said, God may turn the bad into good. Jubal still admires Freddy. It's heartening to see how their roles reversed for a while."

Abel handed him a book. "Read this. See if he speaks to you. I had to seek wisdom outside the Bible in order to understand the greater wisdom inside Scripture."

As Tee left the room, he noticed Abel looking longingly at the book in his hand, *Mere Christianity* by C. S. Lewis, as if it were the last time he would see it. Tee offered it back. "Are you sure about this?"

"I am. By the way, C. S. stands for Clyde Staples. He liked to be called Jack. He was an atheist until G. K. Chesterton's writing and J. R. R. Tolkien converted him. He said that he believed in Christianity just as he believed the sun has risen; not only because he saw it, but because by it he saw everything else. That tidbit might make the book more interesting."

"It will. And I *will* return it."

"Another thing. That old man in prison walked with me to the prison gate the day I left. He carried his Bible. At the gate, he thumped The Good Book without opening it and gave me another piece of advice. 'Proverbs 20:22 goes something like this, *Do not say I will repay the man who does you evil. Wait for the Lord and He will avenge you.*'"

"He embraced me then and whispered these last words, 'Remember, God loves you when nobody else does.' When I look back on my life and see how I veered from His chosen path, I realized how true that is. The old man died two weeks after I left."

FIFTY-TWO

THERE WAS NO PARTY ON JUBAL'S TENTH birthday. He and Tee drove across the river and ate fried cat-fish. Tee knew the incident with Salinas had caused Jubal to wonder about his father's stability, but something else seemed to be bothering his son. They were on the way home when it came out. "What's Cutt's real name?"

It was the first mention of Jubal's grandfather, Sarah's fa-ther, in more than a year. "You forget it's Ledbetter?"

"No, I mean his real first name."

"It's Cuttsell. That was his mother's maiden name."

"She still alive?"

"No. Both his parents are dead."

"What happened to Cutt's wife?"

"Maggie was always kind of sickly and her heart just stopped beating one night." He didn't want to tell him Sarah

341

said her mother died from a broken heart. Tee found out later it was after years of abuse from Ford Donovan.

"Yours and Mama's parents and grandparents are all dead except for Cutt, right?"

"Yes. Where's this going?"

"Will I ever see Cutt or the Blind River again?"

"He doesn't work on the Blind River anymore, but I expect you will see Cutt. I thought you called him Pa or Grandpa."

"Nope. Mama said I should call him Grandpa, but he said to call him Cutt. I'd like to see him again someday."

Tee never told Jubal about Cutt hanging Ford Donovan, owner of the Blind River, upside down from a gnarled oak they called The Sentinel on Rattler Ridge, the highest mesa on the ranch. He was about to kill Ford for raping his wife and his daughter when Tee arrived. Tee saved Ford, but was too late to save Sarah. He still could not face the irony, the cruelty of that.

"When would you like to go?"

"Before school starts back."

Tee nodded, but said nothing. He had invited Cutt to visit once, but never repeated the invitation. And he knew the invitation sounded halfhearted, because it was. Cutt had been like a father to him, but he still carried the baggage of what happened and Tee had spent several years trying to get rid of that baggage. He still had dreams of killing Ford Donovan in all sorts of painful ways. Cutt probably shared those dreams. Tee feared their combined anger might get worse if they were to talk about it together. But the boy had a right to see his grandfather.

They wanted to show up at the feedlot where Cutt worked before quitting time, but Tee took too many detours through small towns trying to give Jubal a sense of the country where he was raised. It was well past quitting time when they arrived in Dalhart. They stopped at a small cafe and asked if anyone knew Cutt. The waitress smiled and said, "Sure do. Two blocks west, number 515."

Tee still wanted to drive around, to get a feel for the area again before he went to the house. He had played ball here in high school and roped in a few rodeos. The town home of the XIT Ranch was filled with cowboys who reminded him of his father and brother and himself as a young man. He drove out toward the old high school to see if it was still there, but two streets over, a sign got Jubal's attention.

Jubal pointed at the street sign. "There it is, Ledbetter Street. Guess Cutt has his own street."

Sure enough, it was two blocks west of the cafe where they stopped. Tee smiled and wondered at the coincidence. "I guess we're about to find out."

The house was modest, but solid. A small front yard, a single-car empty carport. Tee parked next to the curb, killed the engine and stared at the street and the house. It was half the size of the one he had grown up in on the ranch—the one Cutt and Maggie moved in when John T and Winona died. And it was in town. Dalhart was a small town, but still, a street was not exactly like the wide open spaces they enjoyed at Blind River. He tried not to imagine Cutt trapped inside.

Jubal fidgeted. "We going in?"

"Remember now, it's gonna be a surprise." Tee had not told Cutt they were coming and now wished he had. And he didn't know why he hadn't. His rationale was he didn't want Cutt to go to a lot of trouble or worry preparing for their visit. And Tee wanted to keep his options open about the trip until the last minute in case something came up at work. So that was how they left home—on the spur of the moment.

Tee knew he was at the right house when he recognized the cedar bench on the tiny front porch as one John T had made. He stepped back and let Jubal knock on the screen door. No answer. "Let's drive around town and maybe get something to eat at that little cafe, then come back. Maybe we can find somebody there who knows where he might be."

Halfway back to the pickup, they heard the door open. Cutt looked through the screen; put a hand over his eyes to shield them from the setting sun. Tee was not sure it was Cutt at first. He had gained weight, was totally gray and had aged a decade. He looked confused. Tee smiled. "Don't recognize your own grandson?"

Cutt kicked the screen door back against the wall, barreled out and bear-hugged Jubal. "Why, it is you, boy. Nearly as tall as your daddy." He kept one arm around Jubal and reached the other to shake hands with Tee. "You can sure tell this boy is your brother's namesake. He's Jubal's spittin' image."

"Yep. I could see that when he was a few minutes into this world."

"Well, you boys come on in the house, such as it is."

"Sorry to drop in on you unannounced, but it was sort of a quick decision. I found a day or two I could take off and we jumped in the truck and headed this way."

"Any kind of visit from my only grandson and son-in-law is better than no visit at all." He ushered them inside. "It ain't like the house at the ranch, but it suits pretty good. Come on in."

"How many plans are we interrupting?"

"You're not interrupting a damn thing."

Tee was taken aback when he entered the small den. Blind River memorabilia filled the walls and room. Photos, spurs, saddles, chaps and other ranch gear substituted for furniture. Even he had forgotten some of the deep history and fame of the ranch. It had been featured in many major magazines and John T and Cutt had been the subject of many articles in western and ranch magazines.

"This all takes me back."

"It's more a monument to John T and Winona than the damn ranch or anything I ever did."

Tee was about to respond when the front door opened and a woman walked in.

Cutt was a little shamefaced when Ruth walked in, but he held out one arm and encircled her waist. "Honey, I'd like you to meet my grandson Jubal and his dad, Tee Jessup. Boys, this is my wife Ruth."

Tee's mouth didn't open, but he felt like it did. He awkwardly extended his hand. "Pleasure to meet you, Ruth. And we apologize for dropping in this way." He couldn't keep from comparing her to the quiet, reserved and fragile Maggie.

But Ruth appeared to be Maggie's opposite with her smiling features and happy, open countenance. She had laugh lines around her mouth and eyes and soft auburn hair cut short. "Well, no apology necessary. I've heard a lot from Cutt about both of you and I've been trying to get him to take me to meet you. Course, when he told me you lived in Northeast Texas, I told him there ain't no place in Texas that's north or east."

She moved over and put her arm gently across Jubal's shoulder before Tee could respond. "And Jubal is as handsome as Cutt said. Did your grandpa offer y'all anything to drink or eat?"

Tee could see Jubal was adjusting to this new woman in his life faster than he was. Jubal looked at Tee but spoke to Ruth. "We just got here."

She led them into the small kitchen and dining area. A table and chairs of hard rock maple popular a decade earlier filled the small area. "You all sit right down at this table and I'll put on a pot of coffee." She poked Jubal in the stomach. "And there's Dr Peppers or iced tea for you, big boy. Unless you already drink coffee."

Ruth served Cutt and Tee coffee and Jubal a Dr Pepper, then started to slip into the bedroom. "I'll leave you men to talk over old times and new."

Tee wanted her to stay. The woman was engaging, but she also added needed balance to a conversation that could easily turn dark. "No need for that. Stay and listen to old times, if you care to. Besides, I want to get the straight scoop on what's been happening all this time and I can't trust Cutt to tell the whole unvarnished truth."

Cutt took Ruth's hand as she sat at the table. "I know I should have told you two about us, but well, things were pretty rough for a while. I didn't want to do anything that might upset the apple cart when I met this lovely lady. It was my decision, not hers, to wait. I planned on bringing her up there to introduce her in person."

Tee could feel the happiness aura hovering between them. "So how did you two meet?"

Cutt laughed. "Over one of the best barbecue sandwiches I ever had. Ruth owns a little cafe a few blocks from here. You probably passed it. It's called *The Lariat*. I was so low I was under the table and she pulled me out and up."

Ruth patted his hand. "Well, he wasn't under the table, but he was low. You know the history at the ranch, of course. A man born to the land, moving to town…and the loss of Maggie and Sarah." Tee wondered if he had told her about the role Ford Donovan played in their deaths.

Cutt looked out the kitchen window. "I was basically homeless. Lucky enough to find a job, but you know, I pretty much had the clothes on my back and that was it when I left the ranch. Tee, you're one of the few people who understands what it's like to be a ranch manager. Everything is provided—most of your food, housing, transportation, even some work clothes. My horse and cattle herds had dwindled before I left, so I sold what few there were, bought myself a pickup and tried to hang on."

Ruth leaned toward Tee with her hands clasped on the table. "My cousin owned a little shack on the edge of town and rented it to him. A tiny little thing, but it kept him warm and dry."

"I took most of my meals in her restaurant, cried on her shoulder almost every day. Then one day she invited me home for a meal. Six months later, we pooled our money and bought this house. Had us a church wedding."

Ruth looked at Cutt and spoke to Tee. "Tee, you know better than that. Cutt's not the type to cry on anybody's shoulder. But from what I've learned about this man's former life, he was having a tough time adjusting from being manager of a huge ranch to being a worker in a feedlot. And, of course, being alone."

Tee shook his head. "Must have been terrible. But I believed if anybody could handle it, that somebody would be Cutt."

Jubal jumped in during a pause. "So, did they name the street after you moved on it or before?"

They all laughed. Cutt reached out his hands across the table and covered Jubal's. "Son, that's a good story." He paused and looked at Ruth as if for approval. She nodded. "Your daddy knows I was never one to talk about religion or church, things like that. Let's just say I never got down on my knees. Well, when I lost my job at the ranch, I felt a pair of big hands pushing me to my knees." He pointed up with one finger.

"So I got on my knees every day for months. Then I met this wonderful woman and we found this house we could afford. It needed a little fixing up, but we did it ourselves. It'll be paid for pretty soon. I felt like my prayers were answered."

Jubal wasn't satisfied. "So why did they name the street Ledbetter?"

Ruth smiled. "You see, Jubal, that's the funny thing. This is a small town and I've lived here all my life. I never knew there was a street named Ledbetter. I was just looking for a place for us to live. The street is just one block. Didn't even notice the street name till we made an offer. Nobody in town knows the history of the name, either. Other people on the street say it never had a name until a few days before we moved in. Said their addresses were for the street at the end of this one. We like to think God's hand put up that sign. If He didn't, that's okay, too."

Cutt smiled. "See what I mean about getting on your knees?"

Everyone looked down as if considering dropping to their knees. Tee broke the long silence. "So how's the feedlot job working out?"

"When I first started, they put me in the office. You can imagine what that did to me. I asked to work the lots horseback. I liked that better. But one day, Tee, I just fell off my horse. Can't really say I was thrown, I fell off right in the middle of the herd."

Ruth held up a palm. Tee noticed the plain gold band. "It's more complicated than that. They think he passed out."

Cutt interrupted. "Remember that time I got thrown? They think that old concussion may have somehow caused me to black out all these years later."

"I can recall your getting pitched more than once, but only once when you landed on your head."

Ruth waited to see if Cutt would tell the rest. He did not, so she did. "Anyway, the fall did some back damage. He had surgery and was in and out of the hospital for weeks."

Tee shook his head. "My fault I didn't know any of that. Should have called to check."

Cutt fended off the apology with both hands. "All worked out for the better. Now, I drive a big tractor with a cab. The seats are even heated in winter and cooled in summer. I'm embarrassed at how easy my job is."

Ruth stood and rubbed her hands together. "Well, I have neglected my duties as hostess. It's suppertime. Jubal, do you like barbecue sandwiches?"

"Yes, ma'am."

"How about apple pie?"

His eyes widened as he nodded.

"Then let's you and me go down to *The Lariat* and get us some of both. You two men keep your seats. We'll be back soon."

Tee feebly offered to take everyone out to eat, but was ignored.

FIFTY-THREE

CUTT POURED MORE COFFEE AND LISTENED for the car to leave the carport. "Come on out back. I'll show you around this big spread."

Tee thought he noticed a wince of pain when Cutt rose from his chair. They had built a large wooden deck with a metal cover that spanned the back of the house. There was a new wooden privacy fence and Cutt's old pickup sat in front of a closed gate. Metal welded sculptures of brands, longhorns, and horses were nailed to the sides and back of the fence. Tee noticed a branding iron from the Blind River. The memory of using that brand filled his senses. "Surprised you got that iron hanging on your fence."

He chuckled. "You know I own that brand now."

"You own it?"

"It has to be re-registered every few years. I knew it was about to expire and Ford or his new manager wouldn't have sense enough to renew it. Your daddy or I always did that. So I registered it in my name."

"Why?"

"A little revenge, I guess."

"Are they still using it?"

Cutt winked. "I still got a couple of friends who work there. One morning at the cafe, I mentioned they were using my brand without my permission. Word got back to Ford. A rumor got started I was gonna take 'em to court. Ford's lawyer contacted me. Offered me five thousand to give back the rights. Said my claim wouldn't hold up in court."

"Think it will?"

"As long as they have been using that brand, I ain't got a prayer."

"So what do you aim to do with it?"

"I told the lawyer I would accept ten thousand. Haven't heard back. Doubt I do."

They sat quietly on the covered porch absorbed in their thoughts. Tee looked in the direction of the ranch. "You ever see Ford?"

"Once or twice from a distance. I was in my tractor cab when he came to the feedlot once. Tried to coerce the owner into firing me if I didn't turn over the brand. My boss held his ground. Ford don't have the stroke his daddy had."

"He's never contacted you personally? I worried he might bring charges against you for roping and dragging him to the hanging tree."

Cutt smiled. "A picture of him hanging by his ankles from Old Sentinel with blood running into his eyes comes into my mind's eye occasionally. Can't summon up much guilt for that."

Tee couldn't keep from laughing. "Heck, the only way I found you two that night was by following the trail of his blood. Still amazes me the sumbitch didn't die. Getting shot in the arm with a shotgun, roped and drug nearly a mile, and hung from a tree limb in freezing weather should've killed him."

They sat quietly for a few seconds before Cutt's mirth released in gales of laughter. "Might not have killed him, but it sure went a long way toward cutting him down to size."

The laughter was infectious, but it surprised Tee.

Cutt wiped his eyes with a bandanna. "I know it seems cruel to laugh at such a terrible tragedy, but I've found it's a way to cope."

"He's never filed a complaint? You've never been visited by the law?"

Cutt held up a finger. "Don't forget his wife, Hope. She shot him before I drug him off. She still has his signed confession to raping Sarah when she was twelve and molesting her till she drank herself to death."

Cutt hung his head and moved it back and forth. "My little girl died from the pain and guilt. And he forced himself on Maggie all those years. A copy of that confession is in my safe deposit box and another one is in a law office here in Dalhart."

"They told us it wouldn't stand up in court because Hope made him sign it at gunpoint. And after she had already shot him."

"Might not hold up, but don't forget Maggie's diary. It tells it all. Lawyer says the pitiful written words of a woman who died of a broken heart will be powerful. Even if we lost, the publicity would make Ford's life miserable for the rest of his days. Course, I don't want it to get out because of Sarah and Maggie. And Ruth, of course. And you and Jubal might suffer, too."

"Whatever happened to Hope?"

"She moved off somewhere. Heard she got married again and was doing okay."

Tee turned. "You know he wanted to claim Jubal was his son. But Hope told me they both got tested when she didn't get pregnant. Found out he was shooting blanks, but he would never accept it. Blamed her for his sterility. Said Jubal was proof he was right. Hope warned me that he wanted a son bad enough to kidnap Jubal and take him to another country. Said he needed to prove he could be a better father than Earl was to him."

Cutt's expression changed from laughter to pain and anger. "He is a sick, perverted human being. Even if he hadn't been sterile, anybody can see that boy is a Jessup."

Tee stroked the finger where his wedding band used to be. "Aside from those visions of him dangling from that tree, have you put it mostly behind you?"

"I guess getting the brand was the last little bit of hurt I could put on Ford Donovan. I still get a little chuckle out of that ever once in a while. When a man can laugh about something, it's behind him, I guess. How about you?"

"When I keep busy, I forget it, but I still have dreams about that night. I have a lot of guilt about not protecting Sarah, not catching on sooner to what was happening."

"Imagine how I feel. I lived with it under my nose for almost two decades and didn't catch on."

"Heck, I still dream about the two train wrecks."

"I apologize for going on about my hard times. You've been through more than I have. Both of us lost most of our families, but at least we still have Jubal."

"I think I may lean on him too much for my own needs. It's good to know you have Ruth now."

"She's been a Godsend."

"None of my business, but can you share her history?"

"Married to a rawboned cowboy day-worker for thirty years till he got killed in a horse wreck. Like most of us cowboys, he didn't have much. Left her in a bind."

"Any kids?"

"They couldn't have any. It's one of the great regrets of her life. Better watch out. I can see she's already adopted you and Jubal as her own. She's a loving, giving woman. How about you? Any women in your life?"

Tee shook his head. "Wish I would run across somebody like Ruth. Guess I'm looking for a mother for Jubal more than a companion for myself. Not many available women in Riverby. And I'm not looking because I don't know what that would do to Jubal. Plus I been told I'm too damaged to be a good husband."

"I don't think I ever told you how much I owe you for keeping me from killing Ford that night. Likely saved me from spending the rest of my days behind bars."

Tee stood and looked in the direction of Blind River. "You don't owe me anything. I talked you out of it, but after I found Sarah dead, I wanted to kill him myself. If his hirelings hadn't hauled him away when they did, I might have."

Tee turned and faced Cutt. "You think we let Sarah and

Maggie down by letting him get away with it? It bothers me he's walking around a free man while they're in their graves."

Cutt rubbed his hands together as if washing. "You asked if I had put it all behind me. Guess it will never completely go away. But Ruth told me holding a grudge is akin to drinking poison and expecting the other person to die."

Tee laughed. "I heard it's like letting your worst enemy live inside your head without paying rent."

They both chuckled. "But remember what I said about getting on my knees. It helps. You should try it if you haven't."

"You remember Father Bob. He tried to work through things with me. He couldn't explain why it all happened, but he gave me some ideas on how to deal with it. But, you know what it's like when you're a kid. I did ask for answers, but didn't hear any. My faith was tested and I failed."

"I been around a quarter century longer than you have and I'm just now finding out how things work. I never could muster the faith or understanding till Ruth showed me how. She goes into her little sewing room every morning, closes the door and gets on her knees. Told me a man is never as tall as when he is on his knees."

"Where do you go?"

"Used to come out here on the deck, but there are too many distractions and the weather doesn't always cooperate. I need complete dark and complete quiet, so I go into the closet in the room where you'll be sleeping tonight."

"So do you hear Him? Does He talk to you?"

"Not in the way you might think, but during the day or the next, or the next, I sometimes look back and see that He was involved in how things turned out one way or the other.

Thoughts come into my mind about how to work things. I think that's His way of talking to me. And it's sometimes not how I figured things would work out. Thing is, I still forget to say thank you."

Tee walked toward the fence as if leaving. "I'll try that quiet and dark thing."

He pointed toward the ranch. "But I feel like I need to go out there once more—to stand where it all happened, to get on my knees on those places, bad and good."

"I can see that, I guess."

"Cutt, one of the things I hate most is that some of the best memories of my life were destroyed by Ford Donovan. I loved that ranch and the memories of Jubal and me growing up there. Remember how we used to ride to the crossing and place pennies on the rails? Now, it all seems dark and evil. I need to recapture those good memories so maybe they can crowd out the bad."

"You're serious about going out there?"

"Think that's crazy?"

"You might be shot for trespassing, but I'll go with you. I still know two or three of the hands. I can call Cecil Blasingame to see if he might escort us around and keep us away from Ford if he's there."

"Old Cecil is still there?"

"Yep." A phone sat on the shelf of the windowed pass-through from the kitchen to the deck. Cutt dialed but didn't get an answer.

"Not at home."

"Thanks, but now that I think about it, I have to do this alone. Man can't really get on his knees in front of a crowd. I need to soak things up all by myself. Do you know if Ford is there now?"

"I don't. He's still selling the ranch off a piece at a time and buying places where he can try to hide from himself. Imagine living with yourself after what he's done. He's probably out chasing his race horses."

"Ever get married again?"

"Hands tell me they don't know for sure. He almost always brings a woman when he comes, but doesn't bother to introduce her. Rumor is he did marry again and it lasted till he got rough with her the first time."

"Yeah, Hope said he could only get things to work when he attacked her."

Tee heard the car pull under the carport. "If I go out there tomorrow, I can't risk taking Jubal, much as I'd like to. Any chance you or Ruth could maybe take him to work with you for an hour or two?"

"Tomorrow's Sunday, Tee. We'll be happy to keep him. Got a few things to show him."

The smell of barbecue and hot apple pie wafted through the pass-through.

FIFTY-FOUR

TEE TOSSED AND TURNED ALL NIGHT IN THE small bedroom at the Ledbetter house on Ledbetter Street as if a battle raged between the dark forces of his past and the unknown forces of his future. One particularly violent flailing threw his lower body off the small bed and onto the floor. When the hard blow to his knees awakened him, he found himself on his knees with his elbows on the bed. He stayed there, wondering how much noise he had made, expecting a knock on the door from Jubal, Cutt or Ruth to see if he was all right. When none came, he put his face on the mattress and took deep breaths. Cutt's advice about getting on your knees echoed in his ears.

He silently mouthed the words to a repetitive prayer he memorized years before. He realized he was going through the motions, feeling no emotion, no connection. He knew better than to ask for what he seemed to want—revenge and a big ranch of his own. He decided to ask for what God might provide: relief from the nightmares; separation from the anger and fear of the past; answers to why he was left on earth when the rest of his family was taken; how to be a better father to Jubal; how to become worthwhile enough to attract a new woman into his life; forgiveness for his lack of faith.

⊹⥽⥼⊹

Unless old habits changed, he knew he would find Cutt awake and in the kitchen at dawn. He was. Tee came out unshaven and disheveled, like he had slept in his clothes.

Cutt poured him a cup of coffee. "You look like hell."

"Looks are not deceiving."

"Heard you tossing and turning last night. More bad dreams?"

"Let's just say I didn't get much sleep. Hope I didn't keep you all from sleeping."

"Still planning on going out to the ranch? Can't say I didn't toss and turn about that last night myself. Ruth's afraid you'll run into Ford and one thing could lead to another."

"I don't think I'm looking for trouble. I just want to replace all those bad memories with the good ones from before. If I can, as you say, get on my knees at one or two of the places on that ranch sacred to me, maybe I can replace the bad with the good."

"Pisses you off a pervert owns all the property where your childhood memories are housed, don't it?"

"I guess you could say that. But I can't change it, can I."

"Never meant to tell you this, didn't want to interfere, but I went back out once right after I met Ruth. This was during the months I spent a good deal of time on my knees, trying to stop feeling sorry for myself."

360

"Did it do any good?"

"Don't want my experience to influence yours one way or the other. Best you find out for yourself."

"Think I should wait till dark?"

"No. Go when it's light. If trouble happens, you can at least see it coming."

A little over a half hour later, he stopped at the entrance to the Blind River. He pulled over to watch any comings and goings, to get his bearings. When a cowboy in a new white GMC pickup slowed and looked in his direction as if seeing a ghost, he realized he was in his father's truck, a truck that had been a fixture on the ranch for many years. He also wore a hat shaped like the ones his father wore. Hopes of arriving unnoticed diminished.

He stopped at the rail crossing where his brother lost his life, kneeled where he had lain unconscious beside his brother's lifeless body. He walked to the spot where rope horse Concho lost his life. Bad memories.

He drove onto ranch property, stopped when the front of ranch headquarters came into view. He stared at the Donovan's rock mansion and the brick and stone house where he grew up, imagined being inside. He could not see the guest house that sat behind the owner's home, the house where Earl Donovan hosted prominent politicians and oil barons. He wanted to visit the bunkhouse and horse stalls before leaving, but decided to make headquarters a last stop.

He skirted around the headquarters buildings and headed north toward Chinook, the largest of the sub-ranches on the Blind River where Cutt, Maggie, and Sarah lived when Sarah was growing up. He got out of the pickup in front of Chinook and touched the ground where he found Sarah's frozen, emaciated body that night. As he felt a drop of sweat run down his back, he figured the temperature difference between that below zero night and now had to be at least a hundred degrees. He dropped to his knees and asked forgiveness from Sarah and God.

Driving in gully washes to stay off regular ranch roads, it took the better part of an hour to reach Rooster Hill, the western sub-ranch. The sub-ranch was known simply as the west ranch until Jubal and Tee named it after Chance Mabry, the young ranch hand who lived in the small cabin that served as headquarters with his wife and daughter. Because Chance strutted like a cock of the walk, he was called Rooster. Like all the ranch houses on Blind River, a catch pen and corral sat close to a windmill in the side yard. There was no way to hide his truck, but Tee parked it behind the house and walked over to the corral.

When he settled onto the top rail, a gust of wind brushed his face. He imagined it was Jubal saying hello. Away from the watchful eyes of John T and Winona, the brothers learned to break horses in this corral under Rooster's tutelage. John T wanted them to concentrate on roping, not broncs, and Winona wanted them to only ride broncs at headquarters where she could stand ready in case of emergency. But Rooster had been a rodeo saddle-bronc rider, was close to their ages, and he allowed them an occasional can of beer.

Rooster's wife Anna was also hospitable, fun, a good cook, and not bad to look at. They had seen her serve breakfasts with good humor every spring and fall to upwards of fifty cowboys from Blind River and neighboring ranches during roundups. She frowned on the beer and Tee smiled as he thought about that. Good memories. He reminisced there long enough for the cowboys to have their lunch at the main headquarters cook-shack.

It had to be close to a hundred as he returned to the Chevy's scorching seats. He had never been a heavy sweater, but his shirt stuck to the back of the seat as he headed back to headquarters. He passed one pickup and trailer. The cowboys inside stared again at the vintage pickup more than himself. He recognized none of them. A mile from headquarters, he stopped at Rattler Ridge, the highest spot on the ranch, came into view. The old scrub oak they called Sentinel still hung on. Tee recalled the image of Ford's upside-down body hanging by Cutt's rope from one of its limbs.

He got out and walked toward the ridge, but stopped when he recalled how it got its name. Rattlers would be easily irritated in this heat. The sun bore down. He dropped to one knee in his father's old pose, studied the ridge and all that happened there. It was a favorite spot for Cutt and John T to meet at sunrise, build a fire and have coffee. It symbolized something for them Tee never understood until now. The old tree seemed to have sprouted out of solid rock and had survived with no discernible nourishment. John T and Cutt saw themselves as rock solid and survivors, too. The memory of those meetings seemed to partially erase the vision of the hanging.

As he walked back to his pickup, he paused and listened to the constant whisper of wind that seemed to be drying his sweat, murmuring a song without words, but one he seemed to understand. He walked as if a comforting presence walked beside him, behind him, and in front of him, even inside him.

A quarter mile west of headquarters, he pulled into a small dry creek bed that fed into the Canadian River during rainy season. He sat on the stone that marked the spot where Cutt and John T buried Concho. He could almost hear the horse's nicker; the whoosh of a swinging loop; feel the grass rope sliding through his hand; see the beauty of Concho sliding on his back legs to stop the calf and hold the slack while Tee or Jubal tied the calf. He petted the stone as if petting Concho, said a little prayer over the grave, and walked back toward headquarters. It was dry-hot, but he still felt lighter, cleaner, somehow. His surroundings seemed protective, friendlier, the way he felt as a boy here.

The horse stalls were empty except for one sway-backed mare. She had been locked inside the untended stall long enough to cut deep trails in the straw and muck—too long. Tee turned her out, patted her on the neck, walked her through the corral gate so she could run free. He ran his fingers along the board rails of the stalls, inhaled the sweet, familiar aroma of Panhandle dust.

He noticed a faded sign hanging over the tack room door that belonged to John T. He took it down and put it under his arm as he walked and saw the faces and soulful glances of the many horses he had groomed and saddled here in the heat of summer days and frozen winter nights. He walked the board fences of the corral where the original horse named Judson taught him and Jubal to ride. He wondered where the other horses were.

The bunkhouse was empty, so he strolled through, recalling the names of the come-and-go cowboys of his youth and the few who lived here year round. Outside, he stood behind a propane tank and studied the mesquite tree in the bare yard. Sarah had surprised him with a marriage proposal under that tree.

Bewildered there was no sign of life around the ranch manager's house, he walked over to the mesquite, wished for a chance to explore the house, to walk into the room where he married Sarah and the room he shared with brother Jubal. He tried to summon a vivid image of his family sitting at the long kitchen table where Winona served so many meals for the family and ranch hands. Good memories.

He heard himself snicker as he walked back across the yard, recalling the times he rode colts under their first sad-dle to the front gate of their house to impress Winona, his first bicycle ride in the yard, the night he and Jubal headed and heeled a runaway bull that escaped when they left a gate open. Good memories. He got on his knees behind the pro-pane tank where he had a good view of the open prairie and tried to connect the past with this present and get a sense of the future.

He lurched forward when he felt a hand on his shoulder, jumped up for a confrontation, looked into the kind face of Cecil Blasingame. "Cecil. Well I'll be."

"Tee? Cutt said you might be coming by. Said to watch out for you and keep you out of trouble."

Tee extended a hand for a shake. "Good to see you again after all these years, Cecil."

"You growed up, didn't you?"

"I did. Where are the horses and people, Cecil? I didn't expect to see many folks during work hours, but I did expect to find some horses in the stalls."

"It ain't the same ranch it was when you was a boy. We got

about half the cattle and a tenth of the horses. Ford spends his money on breeding thoroughbreds, not cow horses. Our foundation quarter horse stallions all died."

"Used to be about 170,000 acres here. How much is left?"

"A little over half, I expect. I ain't kept informed about such things. We still run cattle over most of it, but I'm told we're leasing part of it from new owners. Not even sure they're our cows."

"Who's in the house where we used to live?"

"A young fella and his wife just moved in. Didn't catch the name yet. Young Donovan runs through ranch managers like sausage through a grinder. Expect Earl Donovan is spinning in his grave."

"Is Ford here now or gone?"

"He ain't in the house as far as I know, but he likes to show up and surprise us. Says he likes to catch us loafin'."

"Well, I was reminiscing when you caught me, Cecil. Don't want to cause you any trouble. I was just about to leave."

"No trouble at all. Been nice seeing you, Tee. Guess you been told you're the spittin' image of your daddy."

Cecil appeared as a ghostly shadow as he ambled off into the sun and disappeared behind the bunkhouse. The old cowboy's departure seemed to symbolize his family's departure from ranch life. If he had not seen Cecil, he would have imagined the ranch abandoned, closed due to man's inhumanity to man.

He felt sweat form under his hatband as it seemed to get hotter and more humid on the way to his pickup. The day was about spent, so he decided to boldly take the shortest route back to the highway, the route through the front yard, the route that would take him a few yards away from Ford Donovan's house.

He drove through the yard by the manager's house, drove over the blood trail he followed that night, stopped beside the Donovan house. He stepped outside and tried to recreate the scene with Ford standing in the yard dressed in Earl Donovan's Wild West getup, complete with six shooter, tall boots, chaps, and hat.

He recalled Hope aiming the shotgun, trying to protect Jubal inside. He walked a few steps toward the house so he could see inside the front yard where Ford had stood. He imagined Cutt's rope going over Ford's shoulders and dropping to his ankles; Cutt pulling his slack, dallying and loping away with Ford's bleeding body; dragging him through the yards, all the way to Rattler Ridge. Tee felt a blast of hot, moist air and was surprised it could get any hotter. Sweat eased out of his hatband, trailed across his eyelashes and down his nose. Hot air was common here, but not this type of humidity.

He turned to walk back toward the pickup when he heard a familiar rattle. The front yard fence had stopped two tumbleweeds that appeared to have remained there for a long time. Tumbleweeds against fences provided favorite nests for rattlers. He thought of the pistol in his pickup, but decided to leave the rattler for Ford to find. Or maybe the rattler would find Ford.

The heat was even more oppressive as he walked back to his truck. The hot, clammy air came in waves. He had one foot inside his truck when he saw a new Ford pickup coming down the road he had to travel. Ford Donovan always drove Fords.

FIFTY-FIVE

THE WIND WAS RIGHT, AND THE TRUCK HAD a hard time leaving the dust behind, so the truck and dust looked like a fast moving cloud. The Ford slowed as it approached, passed close enough to Tee for him to recognize the driver, stopped in the driveway of the Donovan house. Ford Donovan stayed inside the truck, staring at what must have seemed an apparition—John T Jessup standing at the door of his '57 Chevy pickup—a scene Ford had witnessed in the same spot hundreds of time.

Tee seemed unable to move, unwilling to flee but unready to face his demons. When Ford stepped out, Tee stood on the truck's running board and put both elbows on the top of the cab, stared into Ford Donovan's eyes. Though he knew it was not possible, Rattler Ridge and The Sentinel appeared on the southern horizon behind Ford like a mirage. Tee felt the urge to rope him and drag him back there again, finish the job

369

Cutt started. But he had no horse, no rope, only the shortened baseball bat John T made years ago and a small .22 single-action revolver styled like an Old West forty-five. He had carried both in the truck for a very long time.

Ford was dressed like a French aristocrat in a black silk shirt, black slacks and black shiny loafers barely adequate to cover his toes. He had always bragged about buying most of his clothes in Las Vegas. Both arms hung loosely. One hand held a forty-five. Tee walked to the side of his truck and leaned against the passenger door to see Donovan better. He recognized the gun as the one Earl Donovan used to wear when he dressed up in his cowboy outfit and put on fast draw demonstrations for the royalty of Texas oil when they were guests at the ranch. Ford wore the gun the night Hope shot him.

Tee turned to be sure that his pistol and bat were on the seat. Ford didn't approach. Tee folded his arms and waited, keeping a lock on Ford's eyes. It was easy, because he felt energized. He imagined he could see an undulating stream of power transferring from Ford to him. The two men remained frozen until shadows began to creep across headquarters and a cooler breeze began to dry their sweat.

As it grew almost dark, Ford waved the gun back and forth and waggled it in Tee's direction. The motions made Tee think of a young girl holding a big weapon. Ford said nothing, but motioned with the weapon and both arms for Tee to leave. Tee stayed, so Ford began to walk hesitantly toward him. When he was close enough to hear, Tee reached inside the truck, pulled out the pistol and held it by his side. Ford stopped. Tee could see his lips quivering.

"What are you doing on my property?"

"I used to live here, remember? Spent the first eighteen years of my life on this ranch. Wadn't for my daddy, the place would be a barren prairie."

"That was in the past. You're not welcome anymore."

"Why not?"

Ford seemed flustered by the question. "I can't just let people come and go as they please. We got valuable property. You got no business here."

"Just trying to reconnect to my past, good and bad. You're part of the bad."

"I'll call the sheriff."

"You run on in the house and do just that."

"I have a gun."

"I can see that. I got one, too."

"What do you want? You Jessups intend to haunt me the rest of my life?"

"The Jessups and the Ledbetters. And the answer is yes."

Ford waved the gun again. "I can't allow it. I haven't laid eyes on any of you for years, now you show up." His voice broke then. "This whole ranch is a hellhole for me, too, you know. Wish I could get rid of the whole thing. I see her in my dreams every time I sleep here."

"Good."

"If you're aiming to kill me, you should know I've won shooting contests with rifles and handguns."

Tee tossed the gun back inside the pickup, picked up the baseball bat, and walked toward him. Ford cowered, whimpered like a lost puppy. Tee put the end of the bat against Ford's chest and pushed. Ford stepped back, put the forty-five against his own temple. "I'll do it." Tee felt a cold chill envelop his body.

He laid the bat on Ford's shoulder, rolled it to the crook of his arm, levered the bat against his arm until the gun came away from his head. Ford allowed it, seemed to be hypnotized by Tee's stare. Tee took the gun from his hand. "You're too big a coward to do that." Tee felt a warm glow replace the cold chill.

Ford hunched his shoulders forward, began to sob, dropped to his knees and pressed his wet face into the dirt like he wanted to be swallowed up. Tee tapped the back of Ford's head lightly with the bat, watched his shoulders heave for a few seconds, turned and walked back to his truck. He tossed the bat and Ford's forty-five inside, and drove away.

FIFTY-SIX

TEE FOUND CUTT, RUTH AND JUBAL WAITING for him in chairs on the covered deck. Cutt had a steak going over hot coals. "Just in time. Waited for you to come to supper, but can't let our boy go hungry, so we went ahead. Still like your steaks well-done?"

"Some things never change. Reminds me of the cookouts you used to have on the Chinook. Daddy was never much for outdoor cooking. Always joked that a man has to be good at something, so Cutt is a great cook."

Cutt laughed. "How many times have I heard John T say that."

Jubal walked out to play with Joe, Ruth's blue heeler. Ruth's expression was half smile, half concern. Cutt's face brimmed with questions. "So, how did it go?"

Tee accepted the iced tea Ruth offered with gratitude. "About as well as could be expected, I guess."

Cutt turned the steak. "I can see a change in you. Something happened out there."

"A pretty interesting day. I did see Cecil Blasingame." Tee was anxious to tell the story, but could see his steak was about ready. Ruth went into the kitchen to bring out the condiments and refill the glasses. He wanted her to hear. "It's a long story, and I don't want to rush it. We'll need to wait till Jubal goes to bed."

Tee forced the bedtime issue with Jubal at ten. Ruth cleared away everything but the glasses and the coals were burning embers when he returned from Jubal's bedroom. Cutt proffered a glass of amber-colored liquid and a bottle of Jim Beam. Tee was reminded of John T as he shook off both. Cutt seemed amused. "You mind if I imbibe? I don't drink too often, but from the smug look on your face, I got a feeling we got something to celebrate."

"No, go ahead."

Cutt lifted the bottle of Jim Beam. "I worried you might crawl into one of these after all that happened. I almost did. Glad to see you didn't."

"Came close. I tried to hide there a few times, but it doesn't work for me. Makes me sick."

Ruth brushed back a curl from her red hair and re-snapped a snap on a shirt that looked like one Tee owned. "I believe that was God's way of protecting you and Jubal."

"Been told that before."

Cutt was impatient. "Okay. Let's hear about your trip."

Tee stood. "Let me get something to show you first."

He returned with the forty-five. Cutt recognized it. "That's Earl's old pistol. Had those grips special made. I remember when he did. I wanted a pistol with bone grips like that so bad my teeth hurt." He paused. "You didn't do anything out there we need to worry about, did you?"

Tee smiled. "Let me tell it from the beginning." He took them through every stop on the ranch, what he felt, leaving out nothing including dropping to his knees.

Ruth seemed extremely pleased. "I am so happy for you, Tee. Remember what I said..."

Tee interrupted. "Yeah, I know. A man is never so tall as when he is on his knees. Took that right to heart. Have to admit I was embarrassed every time I did it, even when I knew nobody was watching. Cecil caught me once. He acted like it was as normal as the sun coming up."

Cutt laughed. "That's because it is normal for Cecil. When I told him what Ruth showed me, he said he wondered when I would catch on."

They listened to the night sounds on the high plains, the soft whistle of persistent wind, until Tee broke the silence. "Thing is, I don't know how to do it. How to talk to God."

Cutt leaned forward. "Are you kidding me? He heard you. Who do you think sent Ford's power over to you? Who brought that breeze, the sudden cooling and the warm glow when you were confronting Ford? Shoot, you're a regular prayer warrior."

Tee did not notice Ruth was gone until she returned holding a well-used book. She put it down in front of him, put his hand on it. "You say you don't know how to pray. Crack this book every day and you'll find out."

"I know that, I guess. Had a child's Bible when I was a kid. I read it all. But I can understand the tax code about as well as I can understand the adult versions." He held up his hands in a defensive gesture. "It's not because I don't ever read. Seems like I have to read every day just to keep up now that I'm in the tax business."

Ruth smiled as if she had uncovered a secret. "So how did you get to know a lot about the tax code and all those rules?"

Tee chuckled. "Okay. I get it. I did it by reading it."

"And was it pleasant or easy?"

"Nope."

"So how did you get better?"

Tee shook his head as if he didn't understand the question.

Ruth put her palm over the Bible. "I'll just bet you understand the tax code and all those regulations better now and read them faster than you could before. Am I right?"

"Well, sure. I guess with practice I go faster and understand quicker."

Ruth patted him hard on his shoulder. "I knew I could get you to say the key word. Practice, practice, practice. How did you get better at roping calves? Practice."

"Okay, I get it. I want you to know I have read some on the subject of religion. I read about people hearing the voice of God, but I don't. We have a preacher in Riverby says God talks to him every day."

Cutt moved his chair closer to Ruth. "Show him what you showed me."

She turned to the Book of Acts and read,

You know of Jesus of Nazareth, how God anointed Him with the Holy Spirit and with power, and how He went about doing good and healing all who were oppressed by the devil, for God was with Him. In the same way, the Spirit helps us in our weakness.

376

She turned to Romans.

We do not know what we ought to pray for, but the
Spirit himself intercedes for us through wordless groans.

"You hear that? Wordless groans."

Then to John.

If you love Me, you will keep My commandments.
I will ask the Father, and He will give you another
Helper, that He may be with you forever.

Cutt pointed toward the Bible. "I never understood until I accepted Christ that He put the Holy Spirit inside all us believers. Ruth showed me He is called the Helper in some versions of the Bible, the Comforter in others. I like to think of Him as a comforter. I imagine myself talking to Him. We're best friends now."

"Yes, but does He talk back?"

Ruth flipped through the pages. "You remember the verse in Romans where he said wordless groans."

Cutt stood so he could express himself with his hands. "Let me ask you this, Tee. Does your conscience talk to you when you are tempted by greed, anger, or maybe lust to do something you know is wrong?"

"Never thought of it like that, but I guess I do sort of hear a voice on some level saying 'Don't do it. You know it's wrong.'"

Cutt laughed. "Well, who do you think that is?"

It was nearing midnight when they finished talking. Cutt stood. "As much as I'm enjoying this, tomorrow's a work day and I need to get these old bones to bed."

Tee looked at his watch. He stood in front of them as if

preparing for a speech. "I am so sorry. I didn't realize it was so late. I'll be leaving in the morning. I want to say here and now how much I appreciate your hospitality and especially, this conversation. It will change my life."

Ruth hugged him warmly and whispered into his ear. "Thank you for coming yourself and bringing Cutt's grandson to see him. He yearned for the day when you would."

Cutt put his arm around Tee's shoulders. "You recall I told you when you were thinking of marrying Sarah I wanted to be your father and you to be my son?"

"I have not been a good son, but I promise to change that."

Cutt picked up the forty-five and studied it. "What about this? It would be like Ford to claim you stole it and send the law after you."

Tee took it from him. "I don't know if this works with the Bible and all, but I have the deep feeling that as long as I have the gun in my possession, I have a degree of control over Ford Donovan. I have a good friend in Riverby who named his dog after his worst enemy. He says it helped him to heal. Maybe the gun will help me. It's sort of a symbol of my release of hatred for the man. The gun helps me to remember how he looked on his knees, shaking."

"What if he sends the law?"

Tee felt a warm feeling as he thought of Riverby and friends like attorney Joe Henry Leathers, Sheriff Toke Albright, and Blaze. "If he comes, he'll be coming to my turf."

Ruth put her hand on Tee's arm and they waited for Cutt to go inside. "Learning how to talk to God and understand His word doesn't usually come in giant leaps. We hear a lot about epiphanies and revelations for folks, but, in my case, understanding came in tiny steps I was sometimes not aware I was even taking. Sometimes, I didn't realize how He worked in my life until days or months later. And the way He accomplishes things is often a surprise."

"You and Cutt have opened a lot of doors for me, Ruth. I can't thank you enough."

"Just remember to get rid of all that other clutter and make room for Him."

"I will." Tee was ready to go home.

FIFTY-SEVEN

TEE AND JUBAL STOPPED BY THE CEMETERY to visit the graves of Sarah and Maggie. Jubal remembered enough about that terrible night when his mother died to avoid asking more questions. They thought he was asleep in the Donovan's house, protected by Hope, Ford's wife, but the gunshot awakened him and he saw his grandfather rope and drag Ford Donovan away. He knew his mother was found dead on the frozen tundra of the ranch. He knew she drank too much. He was not ready to know more than that. They walked a few yards to visit the graves of his uncle Jubal, and grandparents John T and Winona. The boy listened quietly as Tee told him stories about each, but did not respond. But as they walked away, he turned and ran back to the graves. He kneeled beside each grave and patted each headstone.

In Amarillo, Tee laughed as he spotted his '68 black Cougar sitting on a trailer under the church parking lot light. The light was reliably on in the rectory and Tee knocked. He was surprised when a young priest answered. Tee stood silent for a few seconds. "Sorry to bother you. I'm Tee Jessup and this is my son Jubal. We're looking for Father Bob Messenger."

The young priest's kind eyes conveyed a message Tee did not want to hear. "Come inside."

As they sat in chairs in front of Father Bob's old desk, Tee recalled his first angry visit there. A look around the room told him that Father Bob no longer used the office. The priest brought them glasses of water. "Sorry I can't offer more."

He handed Tee an unsealed envelope with his name printed in a scrawl he recognized. Inside was a typewritten note.

> Dear Tee and Jubal,
> I fear my handwriting has been reduced to an illegible scrawl, so please forgive the impersonal nature of this note. God tells me you have found a church and friends and mentors to help you heal from the tribulations of your life. As I told you, He always keeps His promises.
> I hope you are pleased with what I have done with the Cougar. It gave me many hours of pleasure and good service and I know it will serve you again as well. God used it all for good. May you and your son be blessed.
> Father Bob

Tee looked away from them both as he cleared his throat. He handed the letter to Jubal to read. Jubal's eyes were full when he handed it back to his father. The priest put his hands together on the old desk. "Father Bob was very fond of you both. In his last hours, he told me you would drop by one of these days for the car you left here. Said he never changed the title, just the address so he could keep it registered. All the paperwork is in the glove compartment."

"How long has he been gone?"

"Not long. He died on April 16."

"A lot of things happened that day." Tee stood and Jubal followed his lead. "We'll find some way to bring the trailer back."

"No, Father Bob was clear. The trailer goes with the Cougar."

The young priest cleared his throat and handed Tee a sealed envelope with Tee Jessup scrawled in cursive on its front. "He also left this. Said you might want to wait until you are in a quiet time and place to open this. He said you would know when that time came."

FIFTY-EIGHT

TEE REMINISCED AS THEY PASSED THROUGH
the West Texas towns where he roped and played ball during
his high school years on the same route he and Jubal took
during their lonely, aimless journey almost two years earlier. It
felt good to have a destination, and Jubal seemed to be anxious to get home to Rivers, Flo, Blaze, Lydia, and Freddy. Tee
was ready, too. He felt rejuvenated and cleansed.

As they arrived on Hurt Hill, a flock of blackbirds swarmed
in the trees around the house. They moved in perfect synchro-
nization from tree to ground and back, making mesmerizing
murmurs as they did. Tee once considered the bird invasions
a slightly irritating cacophony of sounds, now it sounded like
a symphony. He and Jubal sat in the pickup and watched and
listened to what seemed a miracle of nature.

He drove the Cougar to town the next morning. His inbox was full, but the piled-up desk did not deter Harmony

O'Hara and Blaze. Uninvited, they sat and smiled at Tee. Harmony went first. "Didn't think you were back yet. Where's your pickup?"

"I drove that old Cougar outside. I owned it a long time ago. Brought it back from the Panhandle. Pickup's at home."

Harmony gave a disinterested nod. "We decided while you were gone that this town needs to be pulled out of the doldrums."

Tee smiled. "Couldn't agree more. Something tells me you two know how to do that."

Blaze seemed reborn. "Music soothes hurts, calms the soul. We plan on a little get-together on the square a week from Saturday night in honor of Morgan Bell, Lydia and Freddy. We'll do a little pickin' and grinnin'."

"I think that's a very good idea. What can I do to help?"

Harmony winked. "Show up…and let us use your office as headquarters and Wilda to help us get the word out. We already got posters printed and we need Jubal to spread 'em around town. By the way, I'm out of a job now that my boss is locked up, but I've got a few family portraits to paint because of the one I did for you. And I'm working on a song I think has potential."

"That's great."

Blaze stood. "You and Jubal need to be there early to help us set up chairs we borrowed from the churches. Prigmore's will be providing barbecue sandwiches and we could use a donation to help pay for that and drinks."

Tee wrote them a check and smiled as he watched them head into the beauty shop to solicit money from Verda. He surprised himself by putting aside the unreturned call slips and leaving the inbox untouched. He told Wilda he would be gone a few hours and drove out to Crimson River. Abel was on the porch as if he expected him.

They finished a pot of coffee and cold biscuits for the noon meal before Tee finished telling him what happened. "What Ruth and Cutt told me and the letter from Father Bob reaffirmed what you said. Made me wonder how I could have been so dense for so long."

"You're not alone. It takes some longer than others. Some never make it."

Tee made a waving motion toward the books on the shelves. "It seems so overwhelming."

"I've learned to take it in small steps. Occasionally, you'll feel like taking a leap. Remember how you felt when you started your first day of college? How about when you saw the books you had to read to prepare for the CPA exam? You have the rest of your life to fulfill your purpose. And God will guide you if you will surrender."

Tee was hesitant as he picked up a pad and pen from Abel's desk. "I get confused by this surrender thing. I'm programmed to take the bull by the horns, so to speak. To get things done on my own. How do you surrender?"

"Surrender might be a one-time, permanent thing for some, but for me it's an everyday thing. I ask for the strength to surrender each day and if my faith is strong, I get it."

"Cutt and Ruth told me how they pray. How do you?"

Abel went to his shelves and opened a book. "Oswald Chambers said, *It is not so true that prayer changes things as that prayer changes me and I change things.*"

Tee removed a small spiral notepad from his shirt pocket and clicked a ballpoint pen. "And what does Abel Gunter say?"

Abel put the book back in its place. "Find your quiet place. Choose your best submissive position. Kneeling works for me. Speak aloud to God when you can, even if it has to be a whisper. Don't always only imagine the words. Speak with love, like you speak to Jubal.

"Begin with gratitude. Give thanks for all your blessings. Commit them to pen and paper if you tend to take them for granted or forget them. Don't forget the small good things that we should be grateful for. We don't appreciate our blessings until they are taken away.

"Second, ask for forgiveness. You can list your sins, too. It will show you how many you repeat.

"Third, ask for healing and blessings for those you know who need it most.

"Finally, you can ask for more blessings for yourself. Ask for love, peace, patience, kindness, gentleness, faithfulness, goodness, and self-control. Whatever you feel you need most in your life. I like to live life one day at a time and so I pray to do good for just one day."

"One day?"

Abel nodded. "Then make your pledges to God."

"Pledges?"

"Promises. Say your prayers as positive affirmations, like, *I surrender. I heed your warnings and obey your instructions. I listen when you speak.*

Tee looked up from his notepad. "Anything else?"

"Then it's time to be still and listen for the voice of the Holy Spirit. For people like you and me, surrender is the hardest lesson to learn. Just remember He resides within you to protect you and love you, walks beside you for support, behind you for protection, and in front of you to lead the way. Recite Psalm 46 often. *Be still and know that I am God.*"

"Do you ever stumble over the words?"

"Sure. At first, I wrote the best prayer I could and memorized it. Tried to make it just right. I have changed it over the years, but when I knew it by heart, I could better say it with feeling and love. That's the most important thing to get right."

Tee smiled. "What about the singing you and Blaze do?"

"That's my way of keeping constantly in touch with The Holy Spirit. Your special place is paramount for prayer, but it shouldn't be the only place. For me, *Amazing Grace* has words like an affirmative prayer. I sing *Farther Along* when I have questions about why life doesn't work out and I don't understand why. I think God loves music and wants to hear our voices."

"Speaking of voices, guess you heard about the singing Saturday week."

"I'll be there."

FIFTY-NINE

ON THE SQUARE SATURDAY AFTERNOON A week later, Tee's euphoria increased as he made himself useful by hauling and setting up chairs. Watching Jubal help lifted him higher. He felt at home again. This was now his town, his people. Sadness came but did not overcome his good spirits when he saw Peggy Bell, Lydia and Freddy Albright take their places of honor on the stage. Morgan Bell had been his favorite performer, and he knew he would miss his Jimmie Rodgers songs. A fiddle sat on a small stand by an empty chair to honor Morgan. As they tuned guitars and a ukulele, blew on mouth harps, and limbered vocal chords, anticipation grew in Tee's chest. He scanned the crowd and could see he was not alone in eagerness. Jubal sat on the gazebo steps with a few of his friends.

When Abel Gunter approached, Tee felt even better. They took two seats near the back row.

Abel looked at the stage. "Been wanting to ask you since our last conversation. Did the dreams stop after you confronted your personal demons on the ranch?"

Tee smiled and held up crossed fingers. "Haven't had a single one since I got back."

Enoch Essary quietly took a seat on the other side of Tee. They all contemplated the empty chair. Enoch's voice was softer than usual. "Morgan Bell left a gaping hole in our circle. And the circle must be unbroken."

Before Tee could reply, Harmony took the microphone and introduced Peggy, Lydia, and Freddy as honored guests. "Nobody can ever replace Morgan Bell as a musician . . . or, with the possible exception of Toke Albright, as a sheriff. But you will be pleased to know that a gentleman a few of you may know has reluctantly agreed to help us out in our time of need. He made it clear he is not an adequate substitute for Morgan. And he has asked not to be formally introduced, but I know you will welcome him."

The crowd searched the stage and other faces with puzzled expressions as they saw only the usual small group sans Morgan. When the group broke into their theme song of *You Are My Sunshine* Tee was shocked to see Clayton Dupree standing beside Morgan Bell's empty chair. Clayton kept his eyes focused on his guitar, but added his voice to the choruses. Tee found his voice to be so much like Morgan Bell's that chills ran down his spine.

They played without a break for three hours, going through a litany of the old time songs Morgan loved. Tee would learn later that Clayton had asked them not to take a break for fear he might have to mingle with spectators and answer questions. As the clock on the bank inched toward midnight, Harmony and Blaze stepped back and Clayton began singing and playing without any introduction.

The crowd froze as he began a song he had written about the tragedies that occurred and the heroes involved. From the back of the stage the sound of a fiddle joined Clayton's crying voice and filled the night air. Tee crossed his arms as if to keep his heart inside his chest as he saw his son step forward playing the fiddle that had been by Morgan's chair. Jubal kept his eyes on Clayton and they exchanged visual clues as Clayton sang and played the guitar. Clayton's words were dark and bespoke tragedy and violence, but there was heroism and hope in the chorus and the final stanza. "We are heavy laden, struck down, but not destroyed. We will rise and meet again." Peggy Bell, Lydia Albright, Blaze, and most of the audience had tears streaming down their cheeks.

When the song was over, Jubal looked toward his father. Tee kept his arms folded as if he wanted to capture the moment and hold it forever. The smile of gratitude seemed fixed on his face, but he managed to place one hand over his heart and doff his hat. The boy knew what that meant. Tee took the gazebo steps two at a time and hugged Jubal, then held him at arms' length. "I thought you were getting guitar lessons from Clayton, not fiddle lessons."

"I started out that way, but I wasn't any good, so Clayton taught me the fiddle. I like it better."

"Why didn't you tell me you were coming along so well? I would have enjoyed hearing you."

"You know how Clayton is. He wanted to keep it a secret, wanted to see if I could be any good before we told anybody.

Seems like we practiced that song forever, then he changed the words when the terrible things happened. Can't play much else."

"Well, your playing was wonderful. You made your daddy proud." Tee turned to find Clayton to offer his gratitude, but Clayton was gone.

SIXTY

IT WAS WELL PAST ONE IN THE MORNING
when Jubal quieted enough to go to bed. Tee was not sleepy.
He sat on the porch holding Father Bob's envelope and a lantern as he replayed all the inspirational times of that night
and the events of the weeks before in his mind. He wanted to
capture the joy of those times and hold them forever. For the
first time in over a decade, he was filled with bliss and peace.
He didn't want it to end. He had read the letter before, but
knew it was the right time to read it again.

> *Dear Tee,*
> *This is a letter I have been writing for several years. Or at*
> *least, this is the final version of said letter. I know it is final*
> *because I write it during the waning days (possibly hours)*
> *of my life and I fear I have left some things unsaid. My*
> *excuse is that I felt you were not ready to hear them. The*
> *Voice I depend upon says you are now prepared.*

First, a confession. When I found out your parents were gone, I felt ill will toward your mother for the burden she placed on me. This was during a time when I feared losing my own faith because of other things in my life. Yes, men of God do have doubts. The burden increased my level of anxiety to the point where I was deeply ashamed. I asked God to relieve me of a burden I neither cared to bear nor understood how to bear. Your resistance to my entreaties made it worse.

As time passed, I grew very fond of you and began to think of you as a son I might have had—that God brought you to me. I realized my anger at the situation came from my own lack of faith, not yours. I was highly frustrated when I could not explain to you why such things happen. I now believe that such tribulation can have many reasons—clashes between the forces of evil, our own ignorance or sin, poor decisions. Sometimes, God may bring us trials, but he never brings hardship without a purpose. You'll see that purpose at some point if you have not already.

As you progressed and visibly softened to my requests, my faith strengthened. My pride was that of a real father when you graduated college. I began to see, once again, God was using what happened to you to strengthen both of us. And I am now content he will use it to likewise strengthen you so you can help others.

I write to caution you to look for miracles, but don't expect them. Don't necessarily expect momentous accomplishments or great epiphanies to come into your life, but be grateful if they do. The routine of life is actually God's way of saving us between our times of great inspiration which come from Him.

Stay grateful. Gratitude prepares you for reverence and reverence helps you to appreciate every blessing in your life, big or small. I pray you will experience epiphanies and life-changing moments of awe (I certainly have), but life is usually a series of small steps. Learn patience. God will give you thrilling moments, but learn to live in those common times of the drudgery of life by the power of God. Learn to watch for signs, no matter how subtle. Perhaps someone you respect recommends a book or a book falls off a shelf at your feet (that has happened to me several times), a stranger comes into your life, or you have a meaningful conversation with an old friend.

Recite Psalm 46 often: "Be still and know that I am God." The Voice I depend upon says you have a purpose. Seek it, but do not demand it. Yours may not be a momentous purpose. You may not pull people from a burning building, but it is almost certain you will help many.

When you read works by the great Christian writers (and I hope you will) you won't find stories of many accountants performing great works (however, Matthew was a tax collector). But I am confident your life will be filled with blessings for yourself as well as others. Just remember to pray incessantly and take life one step at a time, knowing He is in charge. Rely on your faith.

God bless you and keep you,
Father Bob Messenger

Tee folded the letter and placed it in his shirt pocket. He walked to the tabernacle with his lantern and went inside the corn crib. He had equipped it with a new saddle blanket for his knees and a saddle pad to use as a pillow. On his knees, he offered up gratitude, asked for forgiveness, then blessings. From the Tennessee Volunteer Chest he never returned to Wheeler Parker, he removed John T's sign he recovered from the stables at Blind River. He hung the sign on a nail above the door, and read it aloud. "I want to become the man my horse thinks I am."

When he opened the crib door, Tee smiled as he felt a rub against his leg and saw Flo. Rivers looked eagerly into his eyes from the hall of the tabernacle barn. "And I want to be the man these two think I am."

He kneeled on the blanket and whispered, "I am not the man I long to be, but I'm no longer the man I was."

Thanks for reading. If you enjoyed the book or have
questions or comments, I would love to hear from you
at jim@jimainsworth.com. Visit my website
www.jimainsworth.com for more information
for other ways to contact me. I hope you will take
a look at my other books. I would also appreciate
a short review on Amazon and/or Barnes and Noble and
maybe a mention on social media if you are so inclined.

Thanks again.

THANK YOU ...

...To Jan for her ideas and inspiration on the manuscript and cover design and for always being there when I need her.

And thanks...

...To the hundreds of clients and friends who came to our little firm for guidance. You helped me understand basic human nature, how to live and how not to live. My apologies for being a slow learner.

...To Vivian Freeman of *Yellow Rose Typesetting* (vivian. freeman@yellowrosetype.com) for making this book something you can hold in your hand or read on screen.

...To Macrogirl and Angel Laughlin for making www.jimainsworth.com hum and for answering my dumb questions cheerfully.

For every minute you are angry,
you lose sixty-seconds of happiness.
—Ralph Waldo Emerson

About the Author

Jim H. Ainsworth is the author of fourteen books. He formed and ran several small businesses, primarily in financial services, but also a retail western wear and tack store. After writing four books about finance, he left it all behind to pursue other dreams. Retracing his ancestors' trip across Texas by covered wagon and horseback inspired a memoir which led to eight novels and a story collection. Jim writes from life experiences and still lives in rural Northeast Texas. Contact him at www.jimainsworth.com or jim@jimainsworth.com.

Made in the USA
Charleston, SC
16 February 2017